reach for the dream

Anne McCullagh Rennie has written six novels, including *Reach for the Dream*, *Song of the Bellbirds* and *When the Snow Gums Dance*, all of which were bestsellers in Europe. Born in England, Anne studied music in London and Vienna and was concert manager with the Royal Philharmonic Orchestra, London, and BBC Training Orchestra, Bristol, before marrying and moving to Sydney, Australia where she now lives with her Australian husband and two daughters.

For more information visit annemccullaghrennie.com

Anne McCullagh

Rennie

reach for the dream

MICHAEL JOSEPH
an imprint of
PENGUIN BOOKS

MICHAEL JOSEPH

Published by the Penguin Group
Penguin Group (Australia)
707 Collins Street, Melbourne, Victoria 3008, Australia
(a division of Penguin Australia Pty Ltd)
Penguin Group (USA) Inc.
375 Hudson Street, New York, New York 10014, USA
Penguin Group (Canada)
90 Eglinton Avenue East, Suite 700, Toronto, Canada ON M4P 2Y3
(a division of Penguin Canada Books Inc.)
Penguin Books Ltd
80 Strand, London WC2R 0RL England
Penguin Ireland
25 St Stephen's Green, Dublin 2, Ireland
(a division of Penguin Books Ltd)
Penguin Books India Pvt Ltd
11 Community Centre, Panchsheel Park, New Delhi – 110 017, India
Penguin Group (NZ)
67 Apollo Drive, Rosedale, Auckland 0632, New Zealand
(a division of Penguin New Zealand Pty Ltd)
Penguin Books (South Africa) (Pty) Ltd
Rosebank Office Park, Block D, 181 Jan Smuts Avenue, Parktown North,
Johannesburg, 2196, South Africa
Penguin (Beijing) Ltd
7F, Tower B, Jiaming Center, 27 East Third Ring Road North, Chaoyang District,
Beijing 100020, China

Penguin Books Ltd, Registered Offices: 80 Strand, London WC2R 0RL, England

First published by Random House, 1996
This edition published by Penguin Group (Australia), 2013

1 3 5 7 9 10 8 6 4 2

Text copyright © Anne Rennie 1996
The moral right of the author has been asserted

All rights reserved. Without limiting the rights under copyright reserved above, no part of this publication may be reproduced, stored in or introduced into a retrieval system, or transmitted, in any form or by any means (electronic, mechanical, photocopying, recording or otherwise), without the prior written permission of both the copyright owner and the above publisher of this book.

Cover design by Marley Berger © Penguin Group (Australia)
Text design by Samantha Jayaweera © Penguin Group (Australia)
Cover images: woman by Ty Milford/Getty Images, landscape by Ruchos/OzStock
Typeset in Simoncini Garamond 11pt/17pt by Penguin Group (Australia)
Printed and bound in Australia by McPherson's Printing Group, Maryborough, Victoria

National Library of Australia
Cataloguing-in-Publication data:

McCullagh Rennie, Anne, author.
Reach for the dream / Anne McCullagh Rennie.
9781921901942 (paperback)

A823.3

penguin.com.au

To Jim who gave me the courage to reach for my dream and to Selwa who helped me make it happen.

Be bold. Dare to dream.
For today's dreams are tomorrow's reality.

part one

Chapter One

ALICE FERGUSON NEVER wanted today to end. February 23rd, 1952 was the best day in her entire eight years of life. As she stepped off the school bus her heart was brimming over with happiness. Her knuckles showed white against the brown paper package she clasped to her chest. Today her dream had come true. Today she possessed everything she had ever wanted in her entire life. She could not wait to see the look of joy on her mother's face. For a moment she paused to allow her five-year-old brother Ben to catch up before setting off along the rutted dirt road that would bring them to the tiny property in Victoria's prime farming country that was their home.

Despite the heat, Alice began the long walk home quickly, her brilliant blue eyes enormous in her fragile heart-shaped face, their size accentuated by her creamy Irish complexion. Unable to contain her happiness an instant longer she held her precious package up at arm's length and shouted against the wind.

'Thank you, Mum, thank you, thank you, thank you.' Then she whirled around and planted a kiss on the wrapping. Alice's happiness was a book; not just any book but the first book she had ever possessed in her whole life, presented to her today for being runner-up in the coveted regional Bush Children's Quest for Knowledge competition.

Her mother had understood how badly she wanted this book and what it represented. It was the first book Alice had ever owned—all others she had borrowed from the travelling library—and it was from her mother that she had gained the determination and courage to beat the odds of both her age and the taunts of the older, less able children.

'Think big,' her mother always said. 'Knowledge is the gateway to fortune and happiness and you have as much a right to that knowledge as the next child, but sometimes you have to fight for it.'

The temperature was still climbing even at three-thirty in the afternoon and the hot dry westerlies that had begun at dawn showed no sign of abating. It would be hard work pushing their way home against the continuous buffeting of the wind but Alice was too happy to be bothered by the weather. The familiar smell of hot wood filled her nostrils as she trudged happily along, lost in her own world, occasionally remembering to glance back at Ben dawdling behind. On either side of her the scorched brown grass bent against the wind's will. Sheep and cattle huddled in what little shade they could find. There had been virtually no rain for over four months and everything was tinder dry. In the distant haze a dense patch of bush shimmered in the heat and beyond that lay their property.

For the next twenty minutes the two children walked together in silence, squinting against the flurries of dust and getting hotter by the minute. Suddenly Ben shouted, 'Race you to the bush' and charged past Alice, flicking one of her thick raven plaits as he ran.

Alice dodged too late and pushed away the pink ribbon that had come untied and fallen across her mouth. Dear Dad. He was due home today. He would give her more ribbons but he wouldn't really approve of her prize or ever understand what it meant to her. Women were for cooking and caring for their menfolk and raising children. Even in her father's most outlandish dreams, women never featured as independent individuals.

Alice smiled benevolently at Ben. Today he could win. Today nothing in the whole world was going to bother her. At the last minute she decided to take up the chase and together they arrived red-faced and panting at the edge of the dense bush.

It was only marginally cooler in the bush despite its peaceful canopy of grey gum trees, but at least the wind had dropped and it was quieter. Here, too, the undergrowth was brown and tinder dry, the ground ready to explode with the heat. The normally friendly smell of eucalyptus was overpowering. As they walked along the final part of their journey the world seemed to crackle around them. It gave Alice the creeps and she quickened her step, encouraging Ben all the way.

'I'm thirsty,' cried Ben.

'So am I,' said Alice, already regretting her sudden outburst of energy. She shifted her school satchel more comfortably against her slim shoulders and then stopped suddenly and listened. The bush had grown silent.

'The birds have stopped singing, Ben.' Her voice sounded overloud in the unearthly hush. Not a leaf stirred. The sky glowed with an eerie yellow light through the trees. The dry air was prickly with electricity.

'We have to get home,' Alice urged, moving quickly forward. She glanced behind once more and her eyes opened wide in alarm. Ben felt her fear and followed her gaze to the tiny thread of smoke above the distant trees. As they watched, the smoke column thickened.

There was no need for Alice to say anything. Bush children are taught from birth what to do in an emergency and bushfires were a part of their lives. Only last week she, Ben and her two-year-old brother Timmy had gone through the fire-safety drill her mother insisted they practise every three months.

'I want to be certain that you will be safe because there may come a day when a bushfire starts and I am not here,' she had said and Alice's heart had constricted at the thought.

So they had practised as though it were real. They had raced round the house shutting all the doors and windows and stuffing wet towels in the gaps beneath them, filling buckets of water and carrying them to their station point. How they had laughed when little Timmy has appeared in the kitchen doorway like a white ghost, an enormous wet towel draped over his tiny form, the water dripping across the slate floor. Her mother had swept his tiny figure in her arms, her face delighted smiles, her voice loving but firm as she reminded them that this was a 'real' emergency.

Together they had followed her into the cool bathroom and giggled as they huddled close under two big towels in the old galvanised iron bath, surrounded by buckets of water. Little Timmy was perched on his mother's knee, his eyes wide with surprise, his little hands pushing at the towel over his head, while Ben wriggled on Alice's lap. Alice had played with her mother's thick black hair, so like her own, and watched her blue eyes brimming with love. They had listened as she had gone over every minute detail of what to do in a bushfire and Alice felt as though her mother's words were burned across her brain. 'Remember, get back inside the house. The house is the last to burn in a bushfire and it is the safest place. Only if the house catches fire do you then get out and cross back onto the burned-out ground.'

Then they had practised it all again. Finally they had run out into the sunshine and eaten bread and wild honey and drunk delicious homemade lemonade.

Despite Alice's knowledge and ability, she felt her confidence ebb. She quickened her step. Glancing across at Ben hurrying along beside her, Alice hoped fervently that her mother would have returned from the doctor by the time they got home. This was Timmy's third bout of tonsillitis and her mother had warned they might be late.

Suddenly a hot gust of wind caught Ben's cap and whirled it off into the undergrowth. Without thinking, he ran after it. At the same instant a terrifying crash rent the air and the two children jumped with fright. A short distance from where Ben stood a tiny flame burst out from the dry undergrowth. There was another puff and then another that quickly died.

But it was enough to terrify them both. Hand in hand they ran as fast as they could towards the end of the tunnel of trees that would lead them out into the open fields above their property. Now the wind was back stronger than before, fanning the dying flames and whipping up small clouds of smoke that eddied around, increasing as they ran. Alice's eyes, big with alarm, darted from left to right and she could feel her heart pounding in her chest as they fled down the track.

'Keep low! Don't panic!' Her mother's words kept hammering in her frightened mind. 'A fire takes time to build and there is more danger from the smoke at first.' As long as the wind kept blowing in this direction they would be reasonably safe. The fire would run in parallel with them, gaining momentum as it went. But Alice was aware that at any moment the wind could change direction and swing the fire across the track. All around they could hear the crackle of burning leaves as the wind increased and the fire took a hold. The bush to the right of them was still clear but visibility was decreasing with every step and their eyes were already stinging from the smoke. Ben started coughing.

'Your shirt!' Alice coughed as smoke invaded her lungs. Still clutching her precious book, she lifted her skirt and held it against her face.

'I'm scared,' whimpered Ben between coughs.

Alice stopped. Quickly she stuffed the book in her satchel and swung the bag back over her shoulder. Her hands shook as she dragged Ben's shirt out of his shorts and pulled it over his panic-stricken face, covering his nose and mouth. Ben started to cry.

'It's all right, Ben! We'll soon be home with Mum and Timmy,' Alice encouraged through her skirt. She forced herself to laugh as they stumbled and nearly fell. Ben's white face relaxed slightly. Together they hurried on down the track. New flames appeared at their side, the wicked orange tongues eagerly grasping the dry bush. Alice gasped at each spurt and her eyes searched in vain for a suitable clearing amongst the trees, her mother's advice echoing in her ears. Bushfires could race out of control with incredible speed. The knowledge made her heart race afresh.

As they plunged headlong down the narrow track through the swirling smoke they were forced to dodge the flying sparks. Soon their bodies were covered with falling ash and tears from the smoke made sooty rivulets down their cheeks. With relief Alice saw the white glow through the gloom that heralded the end of the bush. By the time they reached the gully the undergrowth close by was alight and the heat was biting into their skin. The flames raced up the tall gum trees with terrifying speed and in moments the tree tops were ablaze.

Alice raced down the gully with Ben and up the other side to the safety of the paddock, the image of her mother's welcoming arms and Timmy's excited cries spurring her on. Shaking with exertion and fear, they gulped in great lungfuls of fresh air, Ben hiccupping through his tears.

'Mum says it never jumps the gully,' gasped the white-faced Alice reassuringly, but her pace hardly slowed as they headed across the wide paddock towards the house.

As Alice searched the empty yard for the car her heart sank. Her mother and Timmy had not yet returned. Behind she could hear the crash of falling trees which sent great showers of ash and sparks into the air. The fire jumped from tree to tree with sickening speed and within seconds it had spread sideways. Only the existence of the gully kept it from sweeping down the hillside towards the house.

Alice took the wooden verandah steps two at a time, sobbing with exertion. When she reached the top she turned to Ben, her heart lighter just for being home. 'We'll be all right now, Ben,' she panted, 'Dad's built a firebreak around the house.'

She put her arm around her young brother and gave him a quick hug while her stinging eyes anxiously scanned the burning bush. How long would the gully stop the fire?

'We have to play the drill game now, Ben,' she said urgently, her mind racing. She steered Ben past the fly-screens through the front door and into the empty house. Throwing her satchel on the floor she raced towards the open window.

'Mum!' Ben called anxiously. He dropped his satchel next to hers and disappeared into the kitchen.

'She'll be home soon. Help me shut up the house, Ben,' Alice called, rapidly pulling the window shut. She could see the fire was still contained on the other side of the gully, but she didn't feel as confident as she sounded. This was not how it was supposed to be. Her mother's words rang in her ears. 'Some day I may not be here . . .'

'Please make her hurry,' Alice said to herself. She could feel the panic starting to return. Pulling herself together she turned and moved towards the kitchen and nearly collided with Ben. He was carrying her black puppy Matty, given to her by her mother. Matty yapped excitedly, his whole body wagging in delight.

'Oh poor Matty!' cried Alice diverted for a moment from her own fears. She stroked the tiny wriggling form, allowing the warmth of his soft body to provide momentary comfort.

'We're going to be all right now aren't we, Alice?' asked Ben wide-eyed, clutching Matty tightly.

'Sure,' said Alice. She raced back to the window and peered out, willing her mother to appear. A group of fearful kangaroos bounded across the paddock. The dirt road was empty. Then to her relief she saw the family car hurtling through the flaming trees towards the house.

'She's here!' Alice screamed, releasing all the fear pent up inside her, and rushed out of the house towards the car with Ben, clutching Matty, hard on her heels. She could see her mother frantically gripping the steering wheel and could just make out Timmy's tiny figure behind her. Now they would be safe.

Alice looked up in horror as a great burning limb broke off from a gum tree and toppled towards the moving car. She reacted instantly. Mouth wide in a screech of primeval terror she flew towards the car, arms outstretched pointing at the blazing branch, oblivious to the shower of sparks and burning cinders. Alice screamed again as her mother frantically swung the car away. But it was too late. They were travelling too fast. The back of the car slewed around and the burning log landed with all its force across the bonnet. The wave of heat hit Alice stopping her dead in her tracks. As she tried to reach the car door she could see her mother's wildly gesticulating arms through the smoke and flames and could hear her shriek.

'Get back! Alice, get back!'

Alice's screams were lost in the roar of the fire. She watched in helpless disbelief as her mother struggled with the car door, pulling Timmy close to her in a desperate attempt to shield his tiny body with her clothes. But a branch had jammed against the door and it was stuck fast and Alice could not get near for the searing heat.

Then, as Alice saw her mother crouch down over the little boy, the fire took a hold. Alice could only watch in frozen horror as car, mother and baby brother were engulfed by a wall of flame.

Ben, still clutching tiny Matty, catapulted past Alice towards the burning car. His hysterical screams jolted her back to reality. Ben was in danger of being burned alive. Summoning all her strength she hurled herself towards her brother, grabbing his arm, his hair, anything that would stop him. She succeeded in toppling the flailing boy and pup perilously close to the burning car. They fell together in a struggling heap and she covered his body with hers, pressing him to the ground until his struggles ceased. Then she lifted the sobbing terrified boy up and cradled him in her arms as great wrenching sobs shook them both.

The heat and smoke were intense and now they were both in danger of being burned alive. Alice dragged Ben to his feet realising their safety now depended on her. Dismayed, she saw that the burning limb had acted as a blazing bridge across the gully, igniting the grass and sweeping the fire across the paddock towards the house. The fire had been-burning long enough to have reached the peak of its terrible heat, engulfing everything within its reach. Flames shot along the tinder-dry grass and up the trunks to the nearby trees leaping from tree top to tree top, charging towards the firebreak, threatening to cut off their path.

'Get back in the house! We have to get back in the house!' Crouching as low as she could, Matty clutched in her arms, Alice pushed Ben towards the house. Sparks and cinders sprayed around them as they ran, singeing the hairs on their legs and shooting past them along the ground and disappearing under the house.

Alice pushed the trembling boy inside and slammed the door, leaning against its sturdy thickness. She was wheezing with exertion and as she tried to steady her shaking limbs, her mind was racing wondering what she should do first. She let Matty go and, wiping her hand across her dirt-smudged face, stepped forwards. But she had forgotten the front door catch had been faulty for years. A sudden rush of wind forced it open and she was confronted by a thick haze of smoke and ash which swirled angrily around and threatened to invade the house.

'Ben! Help!' Alice shrieked. Together they fought the door, forcing it back and slamming it shut. Then she dragged an armchair across and jammed it under the door knob. It was temporary but all she could do.

'You have to remember Mum's drill,' Alice ordered Ben. 'Go and fill the buckets!' Ben started to cry again. Alice's heart sank and tears pricked the backs of her eyes.

'You have to help, Ben,' she implored, pushing him towards the laundry.

For the next few minutes Alice rushed around, frantically trying to seal the house. In the ensuing scurry Alice was able to block out the blackness of the last half hour from her mind. Between instructing Ben and avoiding Matty who bounded around yapping and getting in the way, it was as if her mother were there guiding her.

When they went into the bathroom Alice felt hysterical laughter bubble up within her. Without thinking she cried out, 'See, Mum, I did listen, I do remember.' But then she remembered and the light in her eyes died and her mind shut down against the horror.

'Are we going to die like Mummy and Timmy?' Ben asked from his forlorn place crouched under the sink.

'Of course we're not, silly,' she yelled, barely able to hear her voice above the roar of the bushfire. She could not afford to think about her mother and Timmy now. Instead she prayed that her dad's firebreak would hold—if it did they would be safe. But there was no guarantee.

Despite the wet towels jammed against the doors, it was impossible to stop smoke from seeping through the cracks, but here at least with the concrete floor and the one small tightly-closed window, they would be safest, at least for the moment.

'We have to get in the bath, Ben,' Alice said, holding out her hand as she spoke. Ben crept out from beneath the sink and she helped him over the side of the old bath. Then she lifted the whimpering Matty in as well. Finally she got in herself and sat down in the bath, automatically pulling Ben on her knee. Ben started to cry again.

'I want Mummy,' he wailed.

Alice held him close. Her throat constricted at his words and a lone tear spilled down her cheek. She brushed it away. This was the reality Alice had dreaded. This time there would be no bread and wild honey in the sunshine.

Chapter Two

THE FIRE WAS ALREADY raging through the bush as Thomas Ferguson, returning home from three months shearing, leaped off the train from Innamincka almost before it had stopped. The world had turned orange. The town was threatened and everyone was being evacuated. There were people everywhere, some still hosing down their properties, others rushing to their vehicles carrying what precious articles they could salvage before the fire finally reached the town. Men from the volunteer fire brigade shouted orders against the roar of the flames as they dragged the big heavy hoses to the most immediately affected areas.

Panic clutched at Thomas' throat as he saw the smoke and flames down the road that led to his property. Focusing only on the safety of his wife and children, he tore across to one of his mates in the firetruck. He wrenched open the door, dragging at the heavy-set man, trying to pull him from the driver's seat.

'Hey! What the heck—' the man shouted in surprise.

'I've got to get to Mary Ellen and the kids!' screamed Tom.

'You can't get through there, mate. You'll be burned alive.'

'I've got to get to them.' Thomas choked back his hysteria. He grabbed at the man again. There was a tussle and the other man won. Thomas fell back coughing.

'Don't be a fool, mate. What good are you to them dead?' the man shouted as Thomas, desperate, came back for more. Quickly he fished in his pocket and tossed him a bunch of keys. 'Here, mate, take my truck if you really want to kill yourself. It's over by the store.'

Ignoring the warning, Thomas raced over to the ute. Leaping in, he roared away, disappearing into the smoke and haze. Within seconds he realised there was no way he could get through. Burning tree limbs crashed around him. His eyes were streaming so badly from the smoke he could hardly see and in no time he was coughing so hard he thought his chest would burst. He had no choice but to turn back.

Filled with despair he helped with the evacuation, escaping with the others as the fire raged through the tiny town leaving a path of destruction in its wake. Only late in the afternoon after the fire had passed did Thomas, now totally exhausted, attempt the journey to his property ten miles out of town. Large raindrops splattered on his windscreen as he drove along.

In all the years that Thomas had farmed this land he had never seen such devastation. His stomach churned with fear as he jolted the ute across the blackened countryside, passing the pathetic carcasses of sheep along the road, their charred bodies huddled together in death. The acrid stench and cruel sounds of suffering filtered through the truck window. What hope had Mary Ellen and the kids against a raging inferno like this? Then the heavens opened.

As the rain eased, Thomas pulled up sharply in front of the burned-out remains of his home. Leaping out of the ute, he searched for some sign of life, hoping that by some miracle his family had survived. The smouldering ground was still steaming from the sudden violent downpour. The only part of the house still standing was the brick chimney. He had lovingly built this place with his own hands—it was the one promise he had kept to his wife Mary Ellen. It was the only dream of hers he had ever fulfilled. He could see where the bricks had exploded in the intense heat and the metal run like water. He stared in shock at the surreal blackened shapes of what had once been sturdy outhouses and tall regal trees.

His heart stopped as he caught sight of the blackened shell of the car, a burned branch crushing the bonnet. As if in slow motion he ran towards the car. One glance told him the grisly truth. His beloved Mary Ellen, almost unrecognisable in death, lay slumped across the body of their youngest son. In total disbelief he stared at the bodies of his wife and child, his mind unable to comprehend the horror of what he was witnessing. Slowly one fact penetrated his fog of despair. Alice and Ben had not been in the car. There was still a chance they were alive. With a rush of hope Thomas raced back to the truck, turned the key in the ignition, pushed the truck into forward gear and stopped. Which way to drive?

Alice could tell the fire had passed through by the sudden drop in noise. The terrible roaring and buffeting had died, leaving only the sounds of burning trees crashing outside in the bush. But Alice was still uneasy. Carefully she pulled back the towel and sniffed. The air was relatively clean in the tiny bathroom. Extracting herself from the dozing Ben, she picked up Matty and stepped out of the bath onto the concrete floor. She put Matty down and cautiously pulled one end of the wet towel away from the door. When no smoke appeared she opened the door a crack, and then a little further, until finally it was wide enough for her to slip out into the corridor. Matty padded out behind her. With relief she found she could still breathe easily but then she looked down at the floor and saw their ordeal was not yet over. The cinders that had blown under the house had caught alight and smoke was seeping up through the floorboards.

'Ben, quick, we have to get out!' Alice was back in the bathroom, shaking her brother awake. His eyes opened with a start and Alice pulled him out of the bath.

Alice hurried Ben out of the front door and across the smoking verandah. Although the fire had gone through, Alice knew they were still in danger. She could see the path the fire had taken with brutal clarity but there was still plenty left to burn. At any moment the wind could veer around and rekindle the surrounding bush, and it only needed a little encouragement for the cinders to ignite the dry boards and for the house to go up. In front of them in the swirling smoke stood stark blackened trunks still burning, ready to crash down without warning. Others that had already fallen lay surrounded by glowing embers. Beyond lay the grim reminder of the burned-out car. Once more it was the memory of her mother's words that guided Alice away from the very place that had saved their lives and back onto the burned out land.

Alice could feel the heat burning through the thin soles of her shoes as they picked their way across the smouldering paddock and up the other side of the gully. At the top of the paddock Alice turned with Ben to see the house now ablaze. Resolutely she fought back her tears. Then she turned her back on her home where she had known so much joy and, holding Matty tight, led Ben away.

From the relative safety of a blackened log high on the hillside, the two watched as their home was reduced to a pile of rubble and ash. Hot tears of hopelessness tumbled down Alice's cheeks and onto her brother's head as they huddled together. Matty licked the salt tears from their faces in turn. Then, as if in sympathy, the rains came; at first single pattering spots almost mistaken for insects playing in the air; then great tearing drops that beat down on their heads and soaked them through their grubby school clothes to their skin. There was little to protect them from its onslaught. Alice crouched to the ground pulling the shivering Ben to her, trying to warm him with her body. Matty squeezed in close. For a full thirty minutes it beat down on them from the heavens, quenching the glowing embers that hissed out clouds of steam in the fading light.

Gradually the rain ceased and Alice lifted her head and peered into the gloom. Then Matty pricked up his ears. Suddenly he shot out from under Alice's body and vanished down the hillside, yapping and wagging his tail excitedly. In a flash Alice was on her feet, her pulse racing. She too had heard the truck. Her eyes scanned the landscape and relief flooded over her. There was no mistaking the figure of a man moving amongst the ruins of the house.

'It's Daddy! It's Daddy!' Alice cried, clapping her hands together. She and Ben ran down the hillside as fast as their legs would carry them, shouting and waving until their lungs hurt. But the gloom was too deep and their cries were lost in the wind. No matter what they did they could not attract his attention. In desperation they watched as their father turned and walked back to the truck. Behind him the sky had turned blinding orange, the sunset a defiance of the havoc wreaked. Desolation filled Alice's heart as she heard the roar of the ignition and watched the truck move slowly forward. In that instant she learned the meaning of hopelessness.

Suddenly Alice saw Matty and she laughed through her tears. Grabbing Ben, she started to run. The tiny dog had streaked across the paddock and was yapping and leaping about. As Alice watched, her father opened the truck door and Matty shot into his arms. Then Thomas stepped out of the truck and lifted his head, searching across the paddock. Alice was now close enough to make out his features and to see his expression of sheer disbelief.

'Daddy! Daddy!' Alice cried.

Thomas had seen them and had started to run. In a few bounds he reached them. Suddenly his big strong arms were around Alice and Ben and they were hugging and crying with joy and grief and relief. Between sobs Alice told her father of the terrible events that had shattered their lives in a few short hours. Then they just held one another close, the tiny remnants of a family united in their tears.

After the fire the local community rallied round, offering support to those families who had lost everything, providing them with food and accommodation. Alice, Ben and their father had been billeted out to a home in the neighbouring town and now, a week later, they sat on the verandah of the Adams' house watching the sun go down. Mr and Mrs Adams were no strangers to loss—their only son had died in a tragic accident—and they had given generously of their love and understanding. They knew the importance of privacy in times of grief and so had left Thomas and his children alone after the evening meal.

The events of the past week seemed a blur to Alice. In the beginning there had been so much fuss about eating and sleeping and accounting for missing persons that there had been little time for her to think. Even her mother and Timmy's funeral, held three days after the fire, seemed hazy and unreal. Alice had spent her days in silent shock.

But now, as she sat on a stranger's verandah in the stifling summer heat, the awful truth of what had happened hit her with blinding force. Her mother and Timmy were gone. There would be no more bread and wild honey in the sunshine. She would never be able to stroke her mother's jet black hair again or listen to her lilting voice. Never be able to hold little Timmy in her arms or see the laughter light up the love in her mother's eyes. She would never be able to tell her about the prize or to share those secrets about knowledge. Her eyes were haggard in her young face as she looked across at her father.

'Why Daddy? Why did they have to die?' Alice asked, her eyes glistening with unshed tears.

'I don't know, Princess,' Thomas replied heavily, his own eyes filled with sorrow.

Alice could not know the terrible sense of failure he felt as he gazed at his young daughter who so closely resembled the wife he had adored, but she could see her own misery mirrored in his face. The grief in her heart coupled with her father's anguish was too much for Alice to bear. She went to him and he put his arms round her and she sobbed as though her heart would break. Ben followed, clinging to his father, bewildered and lost.

Thomas held his two children to him and they drew comfort from one another, locked in their own private thoughts. Thomas stroked Alice's silky hair and shut his eyes, wondered how he could bear the pain of such great loss. For a moment he could see the green grass of spring and Mary Ellen's blue eyes so like Alice's shining from her joyous face. That was how she had always greeted him on his return and that was how he would always remember her. She had such a zest for life. The last time he had returned young Timmy had been just eighteen months old. He had only seen him for three months of his short life. Now he too was gone. Thomas did not know how he was going to cope. When they had lost half their flock in the floods two years ago Mary Ellen had been there to support him. She had not complained when he returned from his shearing with only ribbons and promises. She would not condemn him for failure.

'We'll start again,' she would say and it was through her strength he had always found the courage to start again. She had always been willing to listen to his dreams, however silly or far fetched, no matter how often they never eventuated. Now she was gone and there was no one to dream with. This time, he thought bravely, he would not let her down. This time he would find the strength to build again. But when he opened his eyes his courage deserted him and he knew that he could never rebuild their home, not here in the place that every day would remind him of what he had lost, not when the one person he held most dear was dead.

'What are we going to do, Daddy?' Alice's forlorn voice interrupted his tortured thoughts.

Thomas realised that she was looking at him and expecting an answer. He was now wholly responsible for these two precious children. They were the legacy of his love for Mary Ellen; but in that very instant he realised that the burden was too great. He felt utterly lost. Then as he looked at their two small trusting faces smudged with tiredness, their eyes red rimmed from crying, he suddenly knew what he would do.

'I'll tell you,' he said, drawing them both close. As Thomas began to speak his throat was tight, his voice the only sound in the still evening.

'I love you both very much and I loved Mummy and Timmy very much, but now they have gone to a better place, a place where they are safe and happy and can never be hurt ever again.' He stopped to allow the wave of emotion to pass, hardly daring to glance at their upturned faces. 'And I am going to take you to a safe place too.' He raised his eyes and looked out over their heads into the distance and his eyes grew hazy with remembrance.

'When I was a little boy I used to ride out with my big sister Bea across the black soil plains. The winds would come roaring across in our faces, whipping up the horses' manes and making them frisky. More often than not it would blow so hard even the birds would struggle in the sky. I used to wonder how they managed. Bea used to wonder too. My old nan told me it was magic. "Tommy, my boy," she used to say, "look around you. Be glad you're alive. This is a special place." Then she would lean forward very seriously and say: "It is the only place in the world I know where the crows fly backwards."'

Alice's eyes grew big in wonderment in her heart shaped face at the picture her father painted. He had always enchanted her with his promise-filled tales, not least now when she needed it so much.

'I've seen a crow fly backwards,' vouchsafed Ben.

Thomas laughed and a faint flicker of hope crept into his heart.

'Are we ever coming back here, Dad?' Alice asked after a while, unable to keep the wistfulness from her voice.

Thomas stroked her wan tired face gently with his fingertip, his expression again sombre. 'There's nothing here for us any more, Princess,' he whispered. For a second he faltered. When he continued he could feel his confidence returning. 'We're going to find that magic, Alice, and I am going to build you a palace in the black soil plains. It will be the best place on earth filled with laughter and sunshine and happiness and you will see the crows fly backwards.'

He could see it all before him. Bea would help. She would know what to do. If there were any dreams left then that was where they would be. Thomas looked lovingly at his children and his eyes were misty as he announced, 'We'll start again. We'll build a new life.'

Steadfastly Alice pushed away the tiny disbelieving murmur that niggled at the edge of her consciousness.

Chapter Three

AUNTY BEA WAS MARRIED to Raymond Downing and they lived with four of their six children in the tiny town of Billabrin in northern New South Wales. Ten years Bea's senior, Uncle Ray was an uncommunicative mixture of Scots and Irish who demanded order and restraint in all things. A gruff disciplinarian, he rarely showed his gentler side to anyone except to his wife. Aunty Bea, on the other hand, was a warm, open, soft spoken woman of Irish descent whose smile could light up a room and who was adept at getting around her difficult husband.

The four children still living at home were Nicholas, a slightly simple ten-year-old whom everyone called Buddy; Katie, three months younger than Alice, and six-year-old twins Don and Dan. The two elder boys, Billy, aged fifteen, and Paddy, aged thirteen, lived and worked one hundred and fifty miles away on the vast sheep stud and wool producing property Wangianna, affectionately known as 'Up the Top', a literal translation of its name.

Aunt Bea had an abundance of energy. Given the choice she would have kept breeding forever, but Uncle Ray was not of like mind, so when the family shrank to four, Bea turned her energy to helping the smaller members of the community. This meant the house invariably became a temporary home for invalid animals and neighbours' children, some living hundreds of miles away. However, her generous nature frequently created arguments between Ray and herself, so she was surprised how little resistance she faced when she once more raised the topic of Thomas and his two children coming to live with them.

'Those poor little mites, Alice and Ben. How will they ever get over losing their mother and brother like that? It doesn't bear thinking about.'

Bea shook her head. 'I never really knew Mary Ellen but she made Tommy happy. It's the least we can do to offer them a home until Tommy gets back on his feet.' She squeezed Ray's hand. 'We'll just be going back to the same size family we had before the boys moved Up the Top.'

Uncle Ray looked away and cleared his throat. He too had been horrified when he had heard of the disaster. Suddenly his own family had become terribly precious. However, he was still wary. In the past, in his opinion, Thomas had leaned too heavily on Bea. But Ray found it almost impossible to go against Bea when her heart was set on something.

To hide his emotion he growled, 'As long as your brother pays his way and doesn't bloody let his gambling get out of hand.'

So it was settled. Thomas, Alice and Ben would come to live with them, and Aunty Bea turned her mind to the details of their arrival.

At four-thirty on a bright March afternoon, at the end of a week-long journey, Thomas wearily turned the truck into the main street of Bill-abrin. Alice peered out of the window, chattering to Ben, encouraging him to search for her uncle's store. The loss of her mother had devastated Alice, far more than she let the outside world know. Seeing the change in her father she had buried her own misery, quickly taking on the role of mother with Ben. Since that terrible day her normally cheeky brother had become silent and withdrawn. Throughout the entire journey from Victoria to New South Wales he had hardly uttered more than five words. Now she tried to jolly him along. Natural curiosity helped. Neither of the children had ever met their aunt and uncle, although their father had talked affectionately of Bea many times and warned them to stay on the right side of their uncle. As the car slowed down, both Alice and Ben's faces were pressed against the car window.

'Well I reckon this must be it!' said Thomas as he brought the car to a crunching halt outside a small dilapidated weatherboard building which bore the words R K Downing and Sons 1892 in large faded letters beneath its red tin roof.

'I saw it first, I saw it first!' cried Ben.

Thomas pulled on the handbrake and they all got out. Alice clasped Ben's hand as she stared up at the battered wooden sign with its peeling paint, wondering what her new life with her cousins would be like.

'We're here!' she exclaimed, nudging Ben excitedly. 'Do they have horses we can ride here too, Daddy?' Alice had learned to ride the neighbour's horse when she was four and Thomas had promised one day that she would have a horse of her own.

'I don't know, Princess.'

'I'm hungry,' complained Ben.

'It's too exciting to be hungry,' laughed Alice, forgetting her misery for a little in the newness of the surroundings. Ben reacted to her enthusiasm and the two children skipped up the tiny pathway that ran along the side of the store and through the gate.

The Downing hardware store adjoined a small two-bedroom house at the back, to one side of which ran a partially screened-in verandah.

Beyond the tiny but surprisingly well tended garden lay three large paddocks, the nearest of which housed two goat pens, one empty and one containing kids, a pig pen and several tumbledown corrugated tin shacks. Alice squealed with delight when she saw the adult goats waiting patiently outside the kids' pen.

'Do you think Aunty Bea'll let me help look after them?' she asked breathlessly, remembering with a pang little Matty whom they had had to give away to a kindly neighbour.

'We'll soon find out,' declared her father as the front door opened revealing the ample figure of Aunty Bea, her arms stretched out in welcome, her face wreathed in smiles.

'Thomas!' Aunt Bea wrapped her arms around her brother's neck and gave him a kiss. Then she looked down affectionately at the two eager faces.

'Well! You must be Alice and this must be Ben.' Suddenly the children were enveloped in an enormous hug. Alice responded by wrapping her arms shyly around her aunt's ample waist and gazing up into her face. At thirty-six Aunty Bea was still a very attractive woman. Her hazel brown eyes shone out of a sunburned face etched with laughter lines and surrounded by chestnut brown hair without a hint of grey. It was her smile that amazed Alice. It seemed to radiate far beyond the extent of her generous lips and glowing cheeks.

'How good to see you!' Her aunt's eyes rested tenderly on each one of them in turn. Quickly she slid an arm around each child and ushered them inside to where the whole family was waiting politely to greet their new cousins, their faces scrubbed clean, all turned out in their Sunday best.

Aunty Bea's kitchen smelt of fresh herbs. Alice smiled shyly as she was introduced to the rather lumpy Buddy and the irrepressibly cheeky twins Don and Dan whose ears stuck out at right angles to their heads under fair hair cut short with military precision. Alice's smile died on her lips when she raised her eyes to her cousin Katie's face. Expecting a friendly greeting from the pretty eight-year-old whose long fair plaits matched her own in length and thickness, she was shocked instead to see the look of hatred in her cousin's yellow-green catlike eyes above the dutiful smile.

'You'll be sleeping on the verandah with Katie,' announced Aunty Bea cheerfully. 'It's a bit of a squash but you'll get more privacy and Ben'll go in the double bed with the boys.'

Alice's heart sank. Finally she was introduced to Uncle Ray who was standing directly behind Katie. She looked up into his weather-beaten face and saw the cold hardness of his watery blue eyes. Uncle Ray removed the empty pipe from his lips and gave her and Ben a bleak smile. Resting one hand on Katie's shoulder he reached over with the other and shook Thomas' hand.

'G'day, mate. Welcome aboard,' he drawled, but his mouth scarcely moved and he didn't sound as if he meant it.

Alice looked back at Aunty Bea who was bustling around getting the afternoon tea, and realised she was starving. There was a large chocolate cake sitting beside a plate heaped high with homemade biscuits in the middle of the freshly scrubbed pine table, chipped and scraped through years of family use. Aunty Bea handed Ray and Thomas each a glass of beer.

'You'll soon learn to fit into our funny family,' Bea encouraged. 'It's all a bit new at first but it won't take long, will it, Ray dear?'

Uncle Ray grunted noncommittally and glared coldly at Alice and then Ben. Alice shivered involuntarily, the optimism that she had felt earlier evaporating altogether.

After a few awkward moments Uncle Ray quickly downed the last of his beer and placed the empty glass on the table. 'Well, mate, I'd best be getting back to work.'

Thomas stepped forward and clasped his brother-in-law by the shoulders looking squarely into his unsmiling craggy features, his own eyes filled with gratitude. 'I'll never be able to thank you enough, Ray.'

'Just pay your board and that'll do me,' growled Ray. His empty pipe rattled angrily against his teeth as he stuck it back in his mouth and then disappeared through to the shop.

Thomas looked slightly embarrassed, but with Ray gone the atmosphere immediately lightened. The children crowded around Alice and Ben and everyone started talking at once. Even the maliciousness in Katie's eyes appeared to have vanished.

Thomas wiped the corner of his eye surreptitiously and turned back to his sister. 'Still the same generous old Bea, aren't you?' he exclaimed.

Aunty Bea smiled and drew Alice and Ben to her. She stroked Alice's silky black hair admiringly. 'It's good to have you here,' she said tenderly, 'and they are beautiful children.' She patted Ben in a motherly way then smoothed back a lock of her thick chestnut hair. 'Well, come on, sit down and have something to eat. You must be starving after your long trip.' Quickly she removed the empty glasses and replaced them with a big pot of tea as they all sat down noisily. Alice watched with interest as her aunt bent and checked inside the large oven before returning to the table and reaching for the cake. Alice caught a glimpse of two tiny furry kittens buried in an old towel.

'Born last night. Their mother left them on the doorstep,' explained Bea with a smile as she saw Alice's blue eyes open wide in amazement. She sank the large sharp knife deep into the moist thick chocolate icing.

'There's lots of fun things for you to do around here. You can help me feed them later and tomorrow morning I'll get you to help Katie milk the goats before we take you to your new school. And after afternoon tea your cousins can show you around and you can all start getting to know one another.' Alice's face lit up at the picture she painted. She put her arm protectively around the silent Ben and her mouth quivered in a brief smile. Katie smiled at Alice and offered her a biscuit. Alice took one gratefully. Maybe it was going to turn out all right here after all, maybe the malice she had seen in her cousin's eyes was simply a figment of her tired imagination.

The relief of finally being in the safe, caring company of his sister suddenly overwhelmed Thomas. He slumped down into a chair and covered his face with his hands. Distractedly Aunty Bea shooed the children outside with an extra piece of cake each and instructions not to ruin their best clothes, and went back inside to attend to her brother.

Alice shepherded Ben outside, torn between staying with her grieving father and wanting to join in with the wild unconcerned games of childhood. Once outside her original enthusiasm returned as Katie and the three boys showed them around the property.

'You'll sleep on that side,' Katie said abruptly. She pointed to the far edge of the narrow bed on the tiny verandah which was closed in on three sides by thick wooden lattice covered with battered flyscreens.

'Sleep,' said Buddy, accidentally knocking Alice and alarming her as he fell heavily in a mock dead faint on the bed. The springs complained loudly and Katie laughed and pulled him playfully to his feet, whereupon the twins jumped on the bed scattering dirt on the thin blanket.

Katie's laughter changed to rage as she took a swipe at them, shouting, 'I'll get you if you don't get off,' and they laughed and scampered away.

'Can we see the goats?' asked Alice impetuously, reassured that it wasn't just her who annoyed her cousin.

Katie wrinkled her nose and pulled a face. 'Stupid dumb things.' Her eyes narrowed as she saw her father crossing the paddock. 'My dad says he can't afford to have you and Ben living with us. He says there's enough mouths to feed without adding extra visitors.' Katie pulled her thick plaits out of their rubber bands and shook her golden hair free. She shot a triumphant look at Alice. 'But I'm sure we'll manage somehow, Mum always does,' she added lightly.

Alice swallowed the misery that welled up inside her. Her cousin's words made her feel like a trespasser, her mention of her mother sharply reminding Alice of her own loss. A tiny gnawing pain developed just below her ribs.

In the end there wasn't time to see the goats, but Alice started to feel a little better when Aunty Bea allowed her to hold the tiny orphaned kittens and talked cheerfully about the friends she and Ben would make at their new school. By the time they all went to bed Alice was once more looking forward to tomorrow.

Alice's first night in her new home was far from the exciting new experience she had hoped it would be. While the verandah was cool, the night noises were foreign and Katie tossed around kicking viciously. But whenever Alice looked over at her, her eyes were closed tightly and her breathing even. Alice woke up the next morning aching and bruised from the night's battle. But her optimism once more surfaced as, under her aunt's instructions, she followed Katie excitedly into the kitchen to collect the buckets used in milking the goats.

'They don't like strangers,' whispered Katie spitefully as they stepped out into the early morning sunshine.

When her bucket grazed Alice's shin as they squeezed through the gate that divided the garden from the paddock, Alice chose to believe it was an accident. She tossed back her long black plaits and blinked hard to dispel the tears that sprang to her eyes, determined to allow nothing to spoil her morning. Fortunately the whole family had got up especially early to accompany their new cousins so there was no further opportunity for Katie to be unpleasant. In fact, while Aunty Bea was present Katie was smiling and helpful, showing Alice how to secure the goats in the bail—a fixed wooden contraption built by Uncle Ray that pinned their heads between two slats while they were being milked— and explaining how to tie the leg rope around the goat's near back leg so it wouldn't kick and spill the milk.

Aunty Bea looked on affectionately while her daughter demonstrated her milking technique, only stepping in when the leg rope came untied and the goat kicked and struggled. Alice laughed with delight as the other three shaggy coated animals nibbled at her skirt searching for food scraps. She ran her hand gently across their rough backs and immediately fell in love with the smallest shaggiest goat who stared at her with big soulful brown eyes and butted her playfully.

When it came time for Alice to try her hand at milking, the goat waited calmly to be secured in the bale, her only movement to flick the flies from her funny crooked ear, which brought the meanness back in Katie's eyes.

'You're a natural,' exclaimed Aunty Bea. Alice grinned back, her face flushed pink with pleasure, and her blue eyes flashed towards Katie hoping her cousin's irritation would fade. How she wished she could rush home and tell her mother. Then they turned the goats loose and Aunty Bea quickly shooed Buddy, Ben and the twins out of the kids' pen.

'We won't have time for breakfast if we don't hurry,' she exclaimed, glancing anxiously at her watch.

The twins tore past Ben, arms flying, and Don's hand caught Ben accidentally on the back of the head. When he started to cry, they shouted 'Cry baby' so that Aunty Bea scolded them roundly as they hurried back across the paddock.

Alice put her arm anxiously around Ben. 'Don't worry about them, they don't mean to be rough,' she whispered. Ben looked up at his sister gratefully and she brushed away his tears. Then they followed the others up to the house.

Breakfast over, Aunty Bea bundled everyone into the battered old car and set off to the tiny one-class school at the other end of town. Alice's heart fluttered nervously as she walked beside Aunty Bea across the small playground made up of hard-packed dirt scattered with clumps of dry grass and sparsely shaded by gum trees. Ben's fingers clasped her sweating hand in a grip that hurt her fingers yet which she found reassuring. The school bell clanged and Katie, who had reluctantly stayed at a reasonable distance, grabbed Buddy and ran off towards the other children disappearing into the open classroom door. The twins had long since vanished. By the time Alice and Ben had covered the remaining distance the teacher had appeared in the doorway and with a quick kiss and a reassuring pat Aunty Bea was gone.

The crowded room smelt familiarly of sweat and old shoes. Alice's apprehension grew. Inside, twenty or so children ranging in age from five to twelve were crammed together. Katie was already sitting down at the other side of the room, her head turned away from Alice, while Buddy was sitting cross-legged on the floor with the twins, their heads bowed as they whispered together. The teacher introduced Alice and Ben to the class and Alice shifted uncomfortably in her shoes as everyone except Katie turned their eyes on the newcomers. Involuntarily her grip on Ben's hand tightened as she felt their hostile stares and she pulled him closer. As she stared back at the maze of faces, wishing at least one of her cousins could have been more friendly, one pupil stood out from the rest. The boy was a head taller than the others, deeply tanned with big brawny shoulders that threatened to break out of his threadbare shirt. It was his tiny piggy eyes almost swallowed up in his fat sweaty cheeks that caught her attention. They were like red-hot pinpricks and when she slid towards her seat she could feel them burning into her back. She and Ben were squashed in between two children close to her own age and the lesson began. But the expression in the boy's eyes haunted her and at the first opportunity she asked the little girl squashed next to her his name.

'Grunt,' she whispered back, 'can't you tell.' The little girl cupped her hand over her mouth and dissolved into silent giggles.

Later at lunch recess when Alice tried to find out more, the girl's eyes filled with caution and she ran off. Her cousins had disappeared and no one else came to talk to her and Ben in the playground. They sat quietly and ate their sandwiches alone and Alice tried to will away the day.

It was with relief that she crossed the playground at the end of the day and hurried along the main street of Billabrin suppressing her frustration at Katie who had miraculously appeared and spent the whole thirty-minute walk home chatting amiably. Once more in the safety of Aunty

Bea's kitchen Alice watched the tiny kittens lap up their milk and bathed in the warmth of her aunt's smile. As she listened to Aunty Bea chatting with her father, she could almost believe that her discomfort was imagined, but then Uncle Ray walked in. Even though they had only been there for two days Alice suddenly wanted to rush and tell her father about her terrible day and plead with him to move into their own place, but she couldn't because she was holding the kitten and her aunt was smiling and it would sound so rude and ungrateful.

Alice awoke the third day determined to believe life with her new family would work. Resolutely she ignored the apprehension she felt towards her new school, remembering her mother's advice about new situations becoming easier as they became more familiar. But then her father mentioned casually at breakfast that he was thinking of leaving soon to look for work. His words felt like a physical blow to Alice. She was still struggling with the death of her mother and now, out of the blue, her father was talking of abandoning them as well. Alice stared at him open-mouthed.

'Don't look so surprised, Princess. When your mum was alive I went away. We can't just live off your aunt forever.'

'But Daddy, you promised. You can't leave us, not here, not now.' Alice's face crumpled. Her whole world seemed to be disintegrating around her. Weeping, she rushed into his arms and buried her head in his shirt. All the emotion she had suppressed in her attempt to play the mother poured out as her whole body shook with terrible wrenching sobs. Ben promptly burst into tears and followed his sister.

'Come on, Princess, now you've set Ben off too,' said Thomas, an edge of irritation in his voice. 'I'll be back in a few months. Where are my brave little soldiers?' Thomas held his two children to him looking helplessly at Bea over Alice's quivering shoulders.

Controlling herself with a great effort Alice sat up, blew her nose and slipped from his knee.

Aunty Bea's heart went out to the little girl. 'Come on let's wash your faces and get you both ready for school,' she said cheerfully, clasping a small hand in both of hers.

Alice glanced up at her aunt and then back at her father. 'We'll be okay, Dad,' Alice said tonelessly but the pain beneath Alice's ribs had returned. All she could see in front of her was a vast yawning void.

A solemn, tear-streaked Alice set off down the main street of Billabrin with Ben and her cousins. To add to her misery she remembered far too clearly the hostile reception she had seen given to new pupils at her old school. Being a newcomer was bad, but she had underestimated quite how bad. The little girl who had whispered to her the day before finally revealed in hushed tones outside the toilet door that all newcomers were supposed to carry a terrible disease that would make your hair fall out if you touched them before they had been in the school for one month. There was no easy way to deal with such a situation so Alice stuck her chin in the air determined to bury herself in her studies. Ben on the other hand promptly dissolved into tears and it took Alice several minutes to calm him, by which time the teacher had sent someone looking for them. Alice crept into the classroom behind Ben, not daring to raise her head.

The situation did not improve over the next few days. Alice learned that the 'disease' could only be banished by being officially accepted and there was only one person who could pronounce you officially accepted. That person was Grunt. His full name was Damien Grant and he was the oldest boy in the school. His size alone terrified Alice. His nickname, which referred to his noisy breathing and had been earned when he was a newcomer himself, was now spoken in reverence rather than scorn. He had promoted himself Official Acceptor of Newcomers when he realised he could physically overpower the other children and no one was game enough to challenge him. Like all bullies he had his own special following from whom he had chosen two boys to be his henchmen. They were Duncan Mitchell, nicknamed Dunk, who was much the same build as Grunt although slightly shorter, and Andrew Phillips, a younger, thinner boy who had once played a fairy in the school pantomime which had earned him the unenviable name of Flos.

The following Tuesday Alice did something very foolish. She was sitting under a gum tree quietly eating her lunch with Ben, watching a big bull ant crawl along a stick in the sunlight and thinking of her father's promise to take them all on a picnic. Close by Don and Dan were arguing amiably over football cards while Buddy looked on. Earlier Dan had given Ben one of his precious cards which he had promptly hidden in the bottom of his lunchbox.

'Life is improving,' Alice was thinking when the ant was suddenly plunged into shadow. She looked up sharply to see Damien Grant towering over her cousins, his arms crossed, thick legs spread wide apart.

'Your cousin's a cry baby,' boomed Grunt. Alice froze. She cowered down as she saw him jerk his head in their direction and her arm shot around Ben. Mesmerised she watched the little flap of leather bobbing up and down on Grunt's wornout shoe as he tapped his foot impatiently in the dirt, and shuffled his own meagre handful of cards. Don's eyes flew open in terror. Buddy ran and hid.

'You can have that one if you like, sir,' said Don, trying to look very brave.

'And this one, too,' gasped Dan. Hurriedly he pulled his best card from the pile and shoved it under the bully's nose. Alice felt her anger mount as Grunt leered triumphantly and snatched away the card, spilling the others in the dirt.

'You don't talk to cry babies,' he spat, his face too close to Don's. 'Here.' He tossed the smudged and crumpled remains of an old card towards the quaking Don and it landed in the dust with the others. Then he lifted his foot poised to trample them all, a thin self-satisfied smirk on his face.

Alice's rage boiled over. Forgetting her terror she rushed forward. 'You don't have to be so mean!' she cried indignantly. Pushing his ugly foot away she stooped down and retrieved the precious cards.

She heard the twins gasp and saw Don's fleeting look of admiration as she handed the cards back to her cousin. Grunt stopped as if he had been struck, his foot hovering close to Alice's head, and she stared at the filthy toe with its broken nail poking through the jagged hole. Dunk and Flos standing close by quickly suppressed their snickering, their eyes wide in anticipation. Like cat and mouse, Grunt and Alice eyed one another in the tense silence. Then, very slowly, Alice stood up. She started violently as Grunt's foot crashed to the ground and his body blocked her path. His snuffles turned to snorts of rage and he glared at her, hand poised to strike, his eyes mere slits in his greasy fat face. Alice started to tremble. Not knowing what else to do, she glared back, her heart beating frantically in her chest. She had forgotten that he daren't risk touching her for fear of the other kids' derision. Instead he wiped his nose with the back of his hand and jeered, 'Scaredy-cat.' Then he turned on his heel and walked off.

Alice's legs crumpled underneath her and she wanted to cry with relief. Shakily she picked herself up after she had made certain Grunt was completely out of sight.

'We won,' she whispered to Ben as they walked home.

Later that afternoon, Alice accidentally walked into an argument between Uncle Ray and Aunty Bea. Quickly she retreated into the backyard, startled by the anger in her uncle's voice.

'Why don't you just admit your brother's a compulsive gambler?' Ray shouted.

'What do you mean?' Despite her aunt's gentle reply, Alice felt her cheeks flush hot at his biting words.

'I mean he's all bloody talk. He's been here two weeks and we haven't seen a brass razoo. I reckon we'll be lucky to get any board out of the mongrel this side of bloody Christmas.'

'Oh, Ray,' Bea sighed. 'Give him time. You have your weaknesses too. I'm sure he'll find the money.' Alice's heart started to thump as she heard a new note of anxiety in her aunt's voice.

'Never mind my weaknesses, he's been down the pub every day since he got here, closeted with the SP bookie.' Alice heard the angry clack of her uncle's pipe against his teeth. 'And this afternoon he tried to borrow twenty pounds off me. So much for promises.'

Alice slipped away towards the goats, hot tears blinding her path. The following day Thomas announced he was leaving to find work.

'Look after your brother, Alice,' he said brightly, chucking her under the chin. 'And I'll be back before your birthday.'

Alice's blue eyes filled with misery. The day she had been dreading had finally arrived. She clung to her father and Ben, hugging them close, trying to ignore her growing emptiness. 'I promise I'll ring and I'll send you lots of postcards and when I get back we'll start planning your palace.' Thomas kissed the top of her head. Alice's face lit up momentarily at his words and she blocked out the worrying whisper at the back of her mind.

As Alice waved goodbye until her father's truck had disappeared into the distance, the pain beneath her ribs became a solid lead lump. Four months was a lifetime and there was still the unfinished business of Grunt and the Official Acceptance. Yet her dad had promised he'd be back for her birthday in August. Firmly Alice shut her ears to all else save the fact that her father would return.

Chapter Four

AFTER THOMAS' DEPARTURE life settled down to a gentle routine. Katie continued her meanness but in contrast the twins were less aggressive, although they continued their practical jokes and games. Alice no longer expected friendship from her cousin so when Katie engineered her way out of milking the goats, Alice was relieved rather than disappointed. She had soon learned that Katie not only hated milking the goats but was extremely bad at it, and the goats responded by butting nervously and running away when she approached. Without Aunty Bea's assistance to secure them they kicked viciously at the milk bucket so that every day was a struggle to milk them. Katie complained bitterly, blaming Alice's presence. To keep the peace Aunty Bea who was growing fond of the slim, big-eyed girl and had been amazed at the goats' immediate response to her gentle touch, suggested that Katie get the breakfast ready while Alice and Ben did the milking.

Alice gave all the goats names and poured her love and affection on them, bringing them fresh food scraps each day so that they soon came running whenever she called. Her favourite was the smallest, shaggiest goat with the crooked ear and funny stumps for horns, who had captured her heart the first morning and whom she named Silly because of the soppy way she looked at her.

Each afternoon after school she hurried across to the paddock in search of the goats, her pockets stuffed with potato peelings and apple cores, eager to share her day's activities with her four-legged friends. Silly was always waiting in the same spot close to the levee bank that surrounded the town. When Alice called she would turn her soulful brown eyes towards the sound and bleat mournfully. Then, lowering her head, she would charge towards Alice in anticipation of the treats that bulged from her skirt. Alice would fling her arms around the goat's neck and rub her cheek against her hard rough coat and reach across to stroke her funny deformed ear.

'I'm sure there will be a postcard in the next mail,' Alice whispered to Silly hopefully one afternoon two weeks after her father's departure. And when the long-awaited card did arrive filled with promises scrawled in small black writing, she displayed it excitedly to Silly who bleated dolefully and tried to eat it. Alice snatched it away from her eager mouth just in time, laughing with happiness.

Life at school gradually became smoother although always at the back of Alice's mind was the knowledge that a showdown with Grunt was inevitable, so when she discovered on the very day she and Ben were officially out of quarantine from their 'disease' that Grunt had been struck down with a mysterious illness which promised to last several weeks, she could hardly contain her glee. Her optimism soared when no one else showed any inclination to conduct the Official Acceptance ceremony. She became braver in class, gaining praise from the teacher and admiration from some of the other pupils, and she allowed her insatiable need to learn to surface once more.

In June the twins turned seven and Aunty Bea announced they were all going on a picnic, complete with chocolate birthday cake. The day would have been a success except that just as they were about to leave Aunty Bea had to rush off to an emergency over a friend's dog who was having problems giving birth. Uncle Ray vanished in the store with Buddy, pleading too much work, and Katie disappeared across the road to a friend's house leaving Alice with Ben and the already grossly overexcited twins.

For the next half hour Don and Dan chased one another around the yard, slamming the gates between the paddocks and the garden and jumping across the plants in imitation of the latest racing cars. Finally Aunty Bea returned and a relieved Alice helped pile the picnic basket and the renegade children into the back of the truck. After a minor hiccup when

Dan suddenly dashed from the truck to retrieve his cap, Aunty Bea and the six children headed off down to the creek. It was when they returned at the end of the day that they realised disaster had struck in the form of Silly. Buddy saw the goat first. He stopped just outside the gate pointing and laughing. Alice gasped in horror and pushed past him.

'Oh, Silly, no!' she cried in anguish.

Silly looked dolefully up at her from the middle of Aunty Bea's lovingly tended flowerbed, the sleeve of Uncle Ray's best Sunday shirt hanging from the corner of her mouth. At that moment Uncle Ray emerged from the back of the house and saw the damage. His face registered shock, then rage, then icy cold control. He gave Alice no chance to explain her innocence.

'Can't you shut a gate, girl?' he shouted. 'I'll shoot that bloody goat.'

Alice's legs began to tremble. She knew it was useless to explain that she had shut the gate securely and checked it twice before they got into the truck. As she returned headbent to the house, she remembered Dan's last-minute dash before they left for the picnic. She hadn't paid much attention at the time as she was busy getting comfortable jammed between Buddy and Katie with Ben on her knee. Suddenly she was smitten with a terrible loneliness and longing for her mother and father and her home as it had been, and when Ben slid his hand silently into hers Alice felt the tears pricking the backs of her eyes.

'He won't really shoot Silly, will he?' whispered Ben.

Alice swallowed hard and shook her head bravely, but in her heart she wondered. From then on her times with Silly became even more precious and she longed even harder for her father's return.

The mail came twice a week and each time Alice waited eagerly for another postcard, but weeks turned to months and still there was nothing. With her usual resilience Alice pushed her disappointment away and looked for other things to occupy her mind. Her eagerness to learn about Aunty Bea's activities grew, which delighted Bea and diminished her own disappointment in Katie's lack of interest.

One afternoon, two weeks before Alice's birthday in August, Aunty Bea invited her to accompany her out to the Evans' property a good two hours drive across dirt roads from Billabrin to attend a friend's youngest child who had broken out in a strange rash. Bea and Ray, both staunch Catholics and regular churchgoers, were well-respected members of the community. While Bea was not a trained nurse she was skilled in the healing power of herbs, a knowledge gleaned from her own mother, and she was often called upon to help with minor ailments. When her second son Patrick came into the world earlier than expected Bea, with only a neighbour to assist her, gave directions from the bed between contractions and cut and tied the umbilical cord using sewing scissors and a ball of string from the dresser. Father O'Reilly the parish priest, who arrived shortly after the birth to bless mother and child and share a drop of whisky with the proud father, spread the tale of Patrick's arrival through the district. When, three weeks later, Bea assisted a friend in the birth of her baby, the two incidents cemented her role as unofficial midwife of the district. Often called upon to help, her loving care also extended to animals and their offspring.

'I'll need you to help and it'll be a good chance for you to learn,' said Aunty Bea glancing quickly at the overcast sky.

'And I can tell Dad when he gets back for my birthday,' Alice exclaimed, climbing into the battered old truck next to the supplies. When they arrived at the Evans' house Alice followed Aunty Bea's instructions carefully, handing her what she needed from her bag, and spent the rest of the time helping to amuse the other younger children while Bea talked to the sick child's mother. Mr Evans showed his gratitude by presenting them with a newly slaughtered lamb—a rare treat in place of goat's meat—neatly arranged in two shallow boxes and covered with gauze against the flies. After much persuasion Aunty Bea gratefully accepted the gift and entrusted Alice with the job of putting it in the icebox on their return home.

The adventure started to turn sour when it began to rain on the way home and by the time they were back onto the black soil the road had turned to dark sticky mud. The truck got bogged down three times and on each occasion Aunty Bea and Alice were forced to get out and push the truck free. By the time they got home it was pitch black and they were both exhausted. Alice staggered in under the boxes of meat, grateful to be back safely, and after depositing them carefully in the icebox and closing the door tightly, she collapsed into bed and slept, despite the furtive giggles from the boys' room.

A few hours later she woke with a start at the sound of Uncle Ray roaring her name. Dragged bleary-eyed into the kitchen, Alice stared puzzled into his chilly blue eyes and winced at the sting of his tone.

'That was in my icebox, girl,' he growled. Alice followed the movement of his thick index finger as he jabbed at a large dead blowfly lying on the side of the box. 'You've ruined the meat. Didn't your mother teach you anything?' As he walked away he muttered, 'God save me from the stupidity of sheilas,' and Alice thought she would die of misery. But that was not the end.

The twins, once more up to their tricks, seized the opportunity to put a great hairy huntsman spider on her pillow and she shrieked in fear as it ran away, and even when the boys were roared at by Uncle Ray the hollow emptiness inside her stayed. Just as sleep had her once more secured in its cradle, Aunty Bea shook her back to reality.

'It's your dad on the phone,' she said excitedly. Suddenly Alice was awake and the world was wonderful. She rushed to the phone ignoring Katie's sleepy grumbles, but when she listened the line went dead.

'He said he had to go, Mrs Downing,' the operator explained.

Alice hung onto the receiver, overwhelmed with disappointment. Her eyes circled with tiredness seemed to fill her whole face and the hopelessness in their depths wrenched at Aunty Bea's heart.

'I know you are exhausted, possum, but I wanted him to tell you himself,' she explained gently her eyes grave, drawing Alice to her. 'Because he really loves you. It's just that he's had to take this shearing run further up north. It's a really good run for your dad, but it means he won't get home till Christmas.'

Alice's mind went numb. With her mum gone, it had only been the knowledge that her father would be home in time for her birthday that had sustained her and now even that had been taken from her. Not even Aunty Bea's gentle rocking hug could soothe her pain. She crept back to the cramped verandah. Curled up in a tight ball on her side of the tiny bed, not daring to cry for fear of disturbing Katie or of waking the four boys crowded together in the now silent adjacent room, Alice stared out into the darkness as the tears trickled silently down her cheeks. Her dad had promised. She could have borne anything just knowing he was coming back to get them. Now it would be another five long months. And there was no mention of his missing her birthday. Nothing. He hadn't even waited to speak to her on the telephone.

Chapter Five

ALICE WOKE UP with a jolt while it was still pitch black, and with the strong conviction that something really dreadful was about to happen. Then she remembered that it had already happened. Today her father had been due home. It was also her birthday. Mum and Dad had always made her feel so special on her birthday. This time neither parent would be there. Ignoring the ache in her heart she slid her feet on to the cold wooden floor. It was nearly September and the mornings had lost the biting cold of the winter months but she still shivered as she dressed. In a few hours the sharp morning frost would be replaced by a brilliant clear sunny day.

Vigorously she brushed her long wild black hair in an effort to warm herself, making it cling crackling to the brush and sending tiny sparks out in the dark. With fingers that fumbled against the cold she captured her flying waves on the top of her head with two white satin ribbons. They were a replacement for the pink ribbons that had been lost in the fire. Their tails floated down her back mingling with her glorious unruly locks that flowed around her shoulders. Normally she was only permitted to wear her hair loose on Sundays but today she decided to take the risk and leave it free. Aunty Bea, she was sure, would understand her need to look extra specially pretty today. Quickly she crept into the boys' room, reached across Buddy's sleeping bulk and shook Ben by the shoulder.

'Come on, Ben, it's time to go and milk the goats,' she whispered, anxiously peering at the twins, but they did not stir. Aunty Bea had been right in insisting that Ben help with the goats. Once on their own, his nervousness had quickly disappeared and Alice had been pleased to see some of his old cheekiness return. He had proudly insisted on having his own particular job of cleaning out and refilling the water trough each day. Alice loved their daily trek in the ghostly early mornings and it had strengthened the bond between the two of them.

Ben opened one sleepy eye and then rolled back under the covers. Before Alice had time to shake him again he suddenly sat up, instantly awake. He opened his mouth to say something and then changed his mind. Quickly he stumbled out of bed and pulled on his clothes. Together they tiptoed into the kitchen to collect the milking buckets and then out across the frost-covered ground to the pens, the crisp fresh air bringing a glow to their cheeks.

The goats caught their scent as the children approached and looked up from their patient grazing, their bodies thin shadows in the dim grey light. Alice opened the new stiff catch on the goats' pen and called them softly by name, delighting in their response as they ambled towards her searching for titbits. She was glad she had got up so early and had plenty of time. Today she did not want to hurry. Today she wanted to savour every moment of her morning ritual. She talked quietly to the animals as they jostled against her for the food scraps and laughed as she was butted from behind.

'Silly!' she exclaimed in mock anger. She threw her arms around the goat's neck willing away her lingering feeling of concern. Today was going to be a glorious day. For an instant Alice had a strong sensation that her mother was watching and the feeling filled her with joy. She smiled across at Ben who was weaving about, his outstretched arms hidden in the flapping sleeves of his flannel shirt.

'Ben! What are you doing?' she exclaimed.

'Being one of Uncle Ray's shirts,' replied Ben, his eyes sparkling with mischief. Alice giggled. 'I thought Milly or Billy might be feeling hungry.' He waved a sleeve under an imaginary goat's face and made chewing faces. Alice could not resist the temptation to join in and for the next few minutes they both cavorted about the pen before collapsing in a helpless giggling heap. Tears of laughter streamed down Alice's face and she wiped them away with her sleeve while the goats looked on unmoved. Catching her breath she picked herself up. Ben skipped off to refill the water trough and play with the kids while Alice peacefully tended the goats. Away from prying eyes she could forget her differences with her cousins and escape her uncle's disapproving stares.

'It's my birthday today, Ben,' announced Alice wistfully once the milking was over and the goats were turned free with their kids to wander for the day. As Alice picked up the bucket of fresh warm milk and started back towards the house, Ben fumbled around in his pocket. Alice waited, curious.

'You thought I'd forgot,' he said sheepishly, holding out a tiny oblong package wrapped in crumpled newspaper. Alice's face lit up as she accepted the bundle and carefully pulled away the paper wrapping displaying a clumsy wood carving.

'I made it myself,' Ben added bursting with pride.

'Oh Ben,' Alice's eyes filled with tears at the admiration she saw in his eyes. She threw her arms around Ben's neck.

'I'm going to make today the best day ever for everyone,' she announced, her chin set firm. 'We'll have to wrap your present up and pretend I don't know so you can give it to me with the others after tea tonight,' she added, suddenly maternal. Carefully she replaced the wrapping around the precious gift.

'Do cousins get presents?' asked Ben.

'I don't know,' said Alice soberly, then she brightened. 'Perhaps they don't. But I've got this.' She patted the gift happily and turned as she felt a tugging at her knee.

'Are you back to wish me a happy birthday, Silly?' she laughed, rescuing her skirt. Suddenly Silly leaped and frisked around her, and the other three goats, as though sensing the importance of the day and fearing they might be missing out, barged back across the paddock towards her butting each other with their horns in an effort to reach her. All Alice's earlier apprehensions vanished in her delight at the goats and her happiness at Ben's present. Now it didn't matter what happened for the rest of the day. This was a lovely birthday celebration.

'I still think Silly's a dumb name for a goat,' remarked Ben swinging himself around and bowling an imaginary ball as they hurried back to the house. Aunty Bea greeted them at the door, a beaming smile on her face.

'Did the birthday girl get the milk today? If you'd asked I might have let you off just this once,' she said and for a few seconds her attention was wholly on Alice.

Alice beamed back and showed her the bucket of milk. With Ben's help she quickly strained the milk through the prepared muslin into a clean bucket and poured it into a jug ready for breakfast. Then she followed her aunt inside and swore inwardly when she saw everyone else sitting around the scrubbed pine kitchen table, their chores for the morning completed. She hadn't realised she and Ben had been so slow. Hoping Uncle Ray would not notice their lateness she shoved Ben along to his seat and slid silently into her place beside him. Uncle Ray did not look up from his large breakfast of three chops, two eggs and several thick pieces of toast. Beside his plate stood a big mug of black steaming tea.

'Took your time this morning, young lady,' he announced tilting his mug. The silence thickened while he continued to eat. Alice's mouth went dry. Then Uncle Ray raised his head and his thick black eyebrows shot up in astonishment and knit together like a looming storm across his craggy sunburned forehead.

'What's with the hair?' he asked, glaring at Alice.

Alice jumped as his fork clattered on his plate. All eyes turned on her. It seemed to Alice as if the room had grown darker and she glanced briefly past her uncle out of the window to check if the sun had disappeared behind a cloud.

'Aren't you going to wish your niece a happy birthday?' interrupted Aunty Bea cheerfully. 'Alice, give your uncle some milk for his tea.'

Alice's face cleared and she smiled gratefully up at her aunt. Her blue eyes sparkled once more in the early morning light as she poured the milk into Uncle Ray's cup and then tucked into her breakfast. But Uncle Ray was not easily deterred.

'Well, girl?' he growled, ignoring Aunty Bea's question. 'And no badgering your aunt.' Alice looked entreatingly across at Bea. The words were out of her mouth before she could stop herself.

'You said I could wear it like this for my birthday, Aunty Bea.'

'I said no such thing,' Aunty Bea retorted quickly then relented. 'But if your uncle agrees then I won't argue.' The morning was getting late and she had a busy day in front of her and the last thing she wanted was a long argument with Ray about something that was so minor. Alice misinterpreted her briskness for annoyance and her heart sank.

'I do not agree,' Uncle Ray snapped.

'But Uncle Ray—' Alice was not sure what made her quite so brave that morning. Perhaps it was the earlier strong sensation that her mother was near, or the reassurance she had felt from Aunty Bea when she had entered the kitchen. Perhaps it was because she was nine years old, or simply that a birthday was the one day in the whole year that you could do what you wanted without question. She regretted it instantly. Uncle Ray stood up pushing his empty plate away from him, the chair scraping noisily against the kitchen tile floor.

'Birthday or no birthday, my girl, no child from this family is going to school with their hair flying around like some young hoodlum. You will ask your aunt to do it for you properly.'

Alice's eyes blazed with indignation.

'Now eat up and we'll fix your hair, together,' interjected Aunty Bea quickly. 'By the time you've all finished gabbing you'll be late for school then we'll both be cross. You don't mind the ribbons do you?' she asked looking over at her husband. Uncle Ray grunted.

'Silly damned things,' he muttered as he walked out.

'You can have it loose for your birthday tea, tonight,' Aunty Bea whispered conspiratorially as she untied the ribbons from Alice's unruly locks and started to brush her hair, having shooed the other children out to clean their teeth.

'Am I having a birthday tea?' exclaimed Alice in astonishment.

'Of course,' Aunty Bea nodded. 'Now keep still.' Ignoring her aunt's last command Alice threw her arms around Aunty Bea's thick waist and pulled her arms tight. The apron tickled her chin as she spoke.

'I love you Aunty Bea, thank you,' she said.

'Now don't go squeezing all the breath out of me while I'm trying to fix your crowning glory,' joked Aunty Bea gently, renewing her brushing. Swiftly Aunty Bea gathered the wild dark hair back off her face and twisted it into two thick silken plaits then she retied the ribbons at the ends into two plump bows and stood back to view her handiwork.

'There you are, my girl. That's a compromise both your dad and your Uncle Ray would approve of.'

A brief look of longing crossed Alice's face at the mention of her father to be replaced by a beaming smile as Alice pulled a plait forwards and stroked the shiny ribbon lovingly with her finger.

'I knew you'd understand,' she said softly. 'Can I really wear my hair loose when I get home tonight?'

Aunty Bea bent and kissed her lightly on the top of her head and pushed her gently towards the door as the twins burst in fighting and Katie and Buddy jostled to be first outside down the path. 'Of course you can, sweetie. Now go and have the best day ever at school.'

Alice winked at Ben who had reappeared. Everything was going to be all right. The joy she had felt when she had hugged Silly returned. Birthdays with cousins could work. She skipped out of the house and down the verandah after the others.

As Alice entered the school gates her happiness evaporated. Damien Grant stood staring straight at her. On one side stood Dunk, and on the other, Flos.

Events quickly escalated out of Alice's control. Determined that Grunt's presence would not spoil her birthday, she joined in with school as though he were still absent. Yet she could feel his eyes boring into her as she waited her turn to jump rope in the playground and the hairs on the back of her neck tingled in the classroom as she took the active part she had developed since his departure. Steadfastly she ignored the inner voice that warned her to fade once more into the background. Defiantly she answered the questions, her hand up more often than not, her own actions gaining her courage until Damien was asked a question he could not answer.

'Well, Alice, tell him the answer.' All eyes focused on Alice. Without thinking Alice replied and suddenly realised her terrible error.

'You should have known the answers, Damien,' scolded the teacher. 'We went over this several times at the end of last year so you cannot make excuses this time that you were absent. And here's little Alice, who wasn't even here, getting it all correct. Not very good, Damien.'

Alice's eyes flew in horror to the teacher's face, unable to believe she could have been so insensitive. Surely she must know whom she was dealing with. But the red-faced Damien and the sudden hush that followed told its own story. After the class was over Alice dawdled behind, not wanting to risk a confrontation, wondering if the word 'newcomer' was only hammering round and round in her head or if she really had heard it whispered. The strange looks she had been given by some of the other kids as they went outside had set her heart racing and now as she fumbled for her recess biscuits she decided she could last until lunch before she went to the toilet.

Lunch recess dragged on interminably as she hovered close to the other children, surreptitiously glancing over her shoulder to keep an eye on Grunt. Her worst fears were realised just before the afternoon class started when Flos sidled up to her and whispered the words 'Official Ceremony' close to her ear. Alice jerked her head away as though she had been struck. Flos patted the side of his nose.

'You aren't really dumb enough to think it had been forgot?' he sniped, trying to look tough.

Alice blanched as he winked slowly. Her legs were like jelly as she walked back into the classroom. Grunt was already seated, arms folded. He glared over at her and nodded. Everything seemed to Alice to be moving in slow motion. Her head started buzzing and she prayed fervently that he would be struck down with another bout of his unpronouncable sickness.

The final bell for the end of school jangled across the school yard, but for once Alice didn't join in the rush as the other children crowded out into the fresh air. Instead she stared vacantly down at the initials scraped across the old school desk in the sudden silence, wishing she could jerk herself back in time and run into her waiting mother's arms at the school gate. Finally she was pulled out of her reverie by Ben gently jogging at her elbow.

'Can we go home now?' Alice's eyes were dark pools as she stared up at her brother. The knot in her stomach tightened. Not wanting to alarm Ben she nodded quickly, a brave smile hovering around her tight lips. Collecting her books together she slung her bag on her back and nudged Ben cautiously outside, silently grateful for his company. Halfway across the deserted playground Alice froze as Grunt's voice boomed out into the silence.

'Hey, new girl, Alice Ferguson!'

Alice's stomach lurched and her hands went clammy. She waited, one foot still poised in midair, wishing she could disappear into the ground.

'We've all been looking forward to your Official Acceptance Ceremony,' he said sternly to Alice's back. 'Isn't that right, fellas?' Alice turned slowly, the blood starting to pound in her head. Her eyes dilated at the sight of Grunt standing arms crossed, legs akimbo, a short distance away. Behind him stood his six grinning flunkies.

'Yeah, mate,' chorused the group.

'I was really sorry to have missed our last date so we'll make it a really special ceremony for you.' He sniggered loudly, moving towards Alice and at the same time signalling for his group to follow. 'We wouldn't want to disappoint them would we, fellas?'

'Nah, mate,' they chorused obeying his signal. Flos' voice was loudest.

'Shut up, Flos, you don't have to yell like a girl,' commanded Grunt. Alice reached shakily for Ben. 'Dunk, tell Alice we want to welcome her.' Obediently Dunk stepped towards Alice.

'We want to welcome you,' he said.

Alice braced herself and then relaxed when nothing happened. She smiled hesitantly.

'Thank you,' she murmured. Her grasp on Ben's hand tightened and she started walking towards the road. Immediately Grunt pushed roughly past Dunk and blocked her path. Ben cowered behind her.

'Going somewhere?' demanded Grunt arrogantly, arms folded once more, thick legs spread wide as he swayed back and forth, the jagged edges of his worn out boots mocking his swaggering stance. A whiff of stale sweat hit Alice as she gaped blankly at Grunt's fat toes wriggling out through the front of his shoes. Slowly she plucked up courage and her eyes travelled across his dirty frame until they locked with his. As she squinted into his mean little eyes her knees turned to water. She backed away colliding into Ben. The two toppled to the ground and Ben started crying. Grunt straddled their bodies.

'Try looking where you're going next time,' he sneered. The group sniggered. Grunt hovered over Alice relishing her discomfort. Slowly he leaned down and picked up one fat silky plait between his finger and thumb and pulled. Alice had no alternative but to rise to her feet. Once upright he let go of her hair and grabbed the front of her uniform pulling her face so close that his pudgy nose nearly touched hers and she could smell his stale breath.

'There are a few lessons you have to get right, Alice Ferguson, to be officially accepted. One is newcomers pay, the other is you don't try to outsmart me if I decide not to help the teacher.' He gave Alice a shove and she jerked backwards.

'I never meant to show you up,' Alice blurted out almost losing her balance and realising her attempted apology had only made matters worse. Her heart slammed against the sides of her chest as Grunt's face turned dark red and his thick neck muscles bulged momentarily before he laughed rudely in her face.

'That's just the point, dumb girl. You couldn't 'cos I'm the best, aren't I, fellas?' He held his arms wide for expected adoration.

'Sure, mate,' they chorused again. Dunk's head was going like a yoyo. Alice felt the disgust rise in her gorge.

'My dad says you don't need to be mean to people,' she retorted, immediately regretting her words. The bully was back towering over her again. 'Oh he does, does he, Miss Clever Clogs? So who's being mean?'

Ben picked himself off the ground and wiped away a tear from his cheek.

'My dad's going to build us a palace,' he said shakily, pressing himself against Alice. Alice held him protectively to her wishing he hadn't spoken.

Grunt sniggered. 'And I suppose the cry baby'll be the frog prince. Don't tell me. He's going to build you a place like Buck House and we'll all have to dance around you and bow.' He waltzed around the two frightened children holding up pretend skirts and curtsying as he knocked them around in a circle.

Ben looked up at Alice his eyes filled with fear. Sick with rage and misery and not knowing what else to do Alice cast caution to the wind. 'I have to take my brother home,' she declared, jutting her chin out in defiance.

'I have to take my brother home,' Grunt mimicked. 'Alice from the palace has to take her brother home.' The group broke up in raucous laughter. The bully had both her plaits in his hand again. 'Alice from the palace, that's nice.'

The group took up the chant. Alice's dizziness increased. Suddenly Grunt put up his hand for silence. He surveyed the group.

'The time has come for the newcomers to pay,' he announced grandly. The chant changed.

'Alice must pay! Alice must pay!'

Grunt leaned towards Ben and glared at him. Ben gaped back, a mouse hypnotised by a snake.

'Boo!' Ben leapt in the air his eyes rolling with fright. Grunt laughed harshly. In one easy movement he pulled out his pocket knife and held it up to his mates. The colour drained from Alice's cheeks and she gasped involuntarily. The group went silent.

Dunk wriggled uncomfortably. 'Hey, mate, you can get done for having one of them.'

'So?' Grunt glared back at Dunk still clutching the unhappy Ben.

'You know, expelled.'

'I know, idiot.' A sly expression crept into Grunt's face. 'And who's going to tell, huh?' He flashed the knife point up close to Dunk's nose and Dunk took a step backwards.

'Course not, mate,' exclaimed Dunk.

'Well then?'

'Doesn't matter,' Dunk said quietly but Alice could see the fire had gone out of his eyes. She wasn't ready for Grunt's next move. Swooping down on Ben he grabbed a handful of hair and twisted, yanking Ben's head sideways. Ben yelped with pain.

'It's not good to have sisters who think they're too smart,' Grunt snarled, the knife gleaming next to Ben's ashen cheek. The others looked on in gleeful horror.

Alice's terror was replaced by blinding rage. The memory of her promise to her father to protect Ben rang in her ears, and not any person alive, not the meanest school bully, not God himself, was going to make her break it. Turning on Grunt in pure fury she tore at him screaming, 'Don't you touch him!'

For a second Grunt was taken aback by the sheer ferocity of her attack. Her teeth bit into his wrist and he dropped the knife before he had time to realise what was happening, cursing with pain as her teeth dug into his flesh. Ben shot out from between them and tore outside the school yard and hid behind a tree. The next few moments were pandemonium. Quickly recovering from his shock, Grunt turned his vengeance on his attacker.

Suddenly Alice was lying on her face in the mud and blows were raining painfully down. Funnily enough only one boot did any real damage, the others chopped around in the air before they finally clipped her ineffectually, but there was no mistaking Grunt's boot. Shielding her face with her arms Alice moaned with pain as she tried to dodge the fraying leather packed hard with dirt. Its jagged edge scratched along her skin time and again, scoring harsh red marks and peeling white grazes across her legs and forearms. She tried to grab it as it flew across her face and cried out in agony as it jabbed her in the chest. At one point she succeeded in holding onto it for a second as she dug her teeth deep in to Grunt's pasty skin and was rewarded by his stream of invectives. Then the kicks redoubled in force.

With every blow Alice kept thinking this must surely be the last and the teacher would hear and come running to stop them, but no one came to save her. In a detached sort of way she wondered where Ben had escaped to and how he would cope when she was dead. Suddenly she felt herself borne aloft and she realised this must be the way to heaven, until the sharp stabbing pain in her head brought her back to the reality that she was being lifted up by one plait. She felt dizzy and sick but as she reached her hand to her hair suddenly all the tension ceased and she fell back onto the ground. She was hardly aware as the triumphant Grunt stepped over her pitiful muddied form and let out a jubilant cry, holding his prize aloft. Then suddenly she was left, bruised and quaking, in the deserted playground.

It took a few moments for Alice to realise her attackers were gone. Gingerly she sat up. Her mouth quivered as she peered cautiously around her into the empty silence. Her whole body started shaking uncontrollably. After the paroxysm had passed she raised her hand and carefully felt her throbbing head. Her trembling fingers slid through her unruly hair, now matted with dirt, until she felt something warm. She pulled her hand away and gasped in horror at the bright red blood, her heart once more hammering in her chest. Now she was going to bleed to death. Her pulse slowed to an easier pace when, on re-examination, she discovered the bleeding had stopped. Her hand flew back to her head searching for her ribbons and with growing horror she felt her hair.

Despair threatened to swamp her as she realised the enormity of Grunt's deed. Squeezing her eyes tight shut in a futile effort to stop the tears, she wondered what she had done that had turned her life into one long and continuous stream of punishment. Worse still, how she could ever face her one ally, Aunty Bea, in this state? She opened her eyes and stared choking with misery at the blood-spattered remnants of the ribbon Aunt Bea had so lovingly tied that morning. Suddenly she remembered Ben.

Panic dried up her tears as she stumbled to her feet. Frantically she scanned the horizon but he had vanished. With a great sigh of relief she spied him behind the tree. Clutching the ribbon in one tight fist, she raced across to Ben, but as she saw the fear still visible in his tear-streaked face she knew even there she had failed.

'Oh Ben,' she mumbled hugging him to her, her voice charged with emotion, and slumping down beside him. Then from nowhere the twins came running towards her.

'What happened to your hair?' exclaimed Don in stunned disbelief. It was too much for Alice. Why did her mum have to die and her dad leave her and all this happen? Unable to hold back her tears one moment longer, Alice put her head on her knees and sobbed until she could sob no more.

Don and Dan ran helter-skelter down the path, up across the verandah and straight into the kitchen where Aunty Bea was preparing tea. Their school bags careered noisily along the floor before them as they entered screeching at the tops of their voices.

'They cut off her hair! They cut off her hair!'

'What on earth are you making all this noise about and why are you all so late home from school?' demanded Aunty Bea irritably. It had been a long tiring day and Uncle Ray had just stumped off out of the house after a futile argument about nothing. Katie and Buddy put their heads round the door at the rumpus.

'They cut off her hair, Mum,' repeated Dan.

'Cut off whose hair and where are Alice and Ben?' A dishevelled Ben slid quietly in through the door as she spoke. The room suddenly fell silent. Aunty Bea's expression changed. Quickly she walked out to the verandah. The sight that met her was pitiful. Alice was limping slowly and painfully towards the house. Despite the mild weather she had wrapped her school jumper around her head and knotted it under her chin. The hem of her muddied school dress was coming down and one sleeve was torn. Even at this distance Aunty Bea could see her face, like Ben's, was grubby and tear-stained and there was a large bruise just below her left eye. Panic-stricken Aunty Bea rushed forwards. Alice kept walking, her eyes dull, her expression empty.

'Oh, my poor girl! Whatever happened?' exclaimed Aunty Bea, trying to draw the little girl into her arms. Alice resisted, fear flitting across her face, her hand tightening on the jumper sleeve knotted around her chin.

'I'm really sorry about my school dress, Aunty Bea, I really am. I'll mend it tonight, I promise,' Alice offered urgently. 'Please don't tell Uncle Ray,' she added almost inaudibly. Her shoulders started to shake.

'Oh Alice, you silly. The dress doesn't matter. We'll fix it up together, you and me. Tell me what happened.'

'They were going to cut off his hair.' Her voice was barely audible.

'What are you talking about, sweetheart?' Aunty Bea asked gently. 'And why have you got your good jumper knotted around your head?' She attempted to undo the offending garment. Alice stepped back in sudden alarm and some of the fire returned to her eyes.

'Ben. They didn't do it, Aunty Bea. I didn't let them. I kept my promise to look after Ben like Daddy said, I really did,' she said in a rush. The fear returned to her eyes. 'I couldn't stop them,' she trailed off.

'Sweetheart, nothing is ever that bad,' said Aunty Bea matter of factly, 'and I still don't know what you are talking about.' Despite Alice's resistance she pulled the jumper from her head. One hand flew to her mouth and she gasped at the sight. Alice's right plait had been cut clean off just below her ear leaving her looking like a bedraggled animal.

Alice held her breath, not daring to move under Aunty Bea's stare. Then her aunt's eyes suddenly filled with tears and she opened her arms. Alice's face crumpled with relief and she walked into Aunty Bea's embrace.

Uncle Ray's reaction to Alice's predicament took everyone by surprise. Normally cold and controlled, he roared into the house like an injured rhinoceros. Alice was setting the table for the evening birthday dinner, her long hair now cropped in a jagged boyish style reaching just below her ears. She looked up in alarm as her uncle stormed through the door and flung his hat on the peg, his face dark with rage.

'Alice Ferguson! Where are you?' he bellowed.

Alice cowered behind the table clutching the knives and forks in her trembling fingers. Hearing the commotion Aunty Bea came running inside.

'Ray! Thank goodness you're home. Alice has had a terrible day today.'

'So have I!' thundered Uncle Ray. 'Where is the girl?' A fork clattered to the floor. Ray swung round and advanced menacingly on Alice, swaying slightly on his feet. 'Stand up straight, girl, and explain what you mean by biting another child.'

Alice shrank back against the chair, not daring to look at her aunt, wondering miserably if it was possible to make a dash for the back door before her legs buckled under her. She coughed at the strong smell of rum and cigarettes. Her mouth moved but no words came out.

'Well girl, have you nothing to say for yourself?'

'If she did he deserved it,' intervened Bea quickly, aware Ray had been drinking. 'I think we'd better leave this till later, Ray. The poor girl's had a shocking time.' Bea's words only inflamed Ray's anger. He rounded on his wife.

'Don't you tell me what to do, woman!'

'For goodness sakes, Ray,' Aunty Bea exclaimed exasperated, 'haven't you noticed the state of your niece?' Alice waited fearful. It was the first time she had ever seen Ray and Bea openly arguing. Uncle Ray leaned his hands on the back of the nearest chair, ignoring Alice for the moment, his rage transferred to Bea.

'Now you listen to me! My mate Bill told me he was up helping Sid Grant fix his tractor over at his place today when Mrs Grant comes flying into the shed dragging young Damien behind. He saw the teeth marks on the boy's leg.' He drew himself up to his full height, oblivious of the grim set of Aunty Bea's mouth. 'What were you thinking of, doing such a disgraceful thing?' he shot back at Alice. 'How dare you bring such disgrace on this family. If you wish to live under this roof you will behave decently towards others.' He stabbed his finger viciously towards Alice who backed away terrified.

'No, Ray, you listen to me,' retorted Aunty Bea, struggling to stay calm. 'Damien Grant attacked Alice after he threatened to cut off Ben's hair, and of course Alice rushed to Ben's defence. So instead he cut off one of her plaits, but first the cowardly little beast and a couple of his horrible little friends kicked and punched her. If I ever get my hands on them . . . I assure you if there's any talk about disgrace it won't be against our niece. Come here, Alice, poor love.' She held out her hand to Alice, who crept cautiously towards her aunt, choking back her misery.

'Look at these, Ray.' Bea pointed out the bruising around the sticking plaster on Alice's forehead and the grazes and red and purple marks on her arms and legs. 'All that lovely hair,' she murmured soothingly, fingering the spiky black locks. She drew the trembling little girl into her arms and suddenly all the puff went out of Ray. Shocked he stared at Alice, the colour draining from his face as he finally comprehended.

The twins and Ben burst into the room and stopped dead at the sombre scene. The door banged shut behind them only to reopen as Katie came tearing in, her long fair plaits flying out behind her, followed by Buddy, dusty and dishevelled.

'I think it's time we had Alice's birthday tea, don't you Ray,' said Aunty Bea firmly.

Ray looked at his wife and back at Alice, ashamed of his own blundering blindness. 'Righto. I'll just go and wash up,' he muttered. 'We'll talk about that other business later, love,' he added gruffly in a rare show of affection to his wife.

'Fine dear,' replied Aunty Bea smiling determinedly.

Ray turned to his children with forced cheerfulness. 'Hello, boys. Katie. All cleaned up and ready for tea then?' He ruffled the anxious Ben's hair. At the door he turned back to Alice. 'Not much of a day, eh?' Alice's bottom lip trembled. 'New hair style's more practical,' he added more gently as Alice's hands crept up around her short cropped hair and she smiled feebly struggling to control the silent tears that oozed from the corners of her eyes.

'Nothing like a change for a birthday girl,' said Aunty Bea briskly picking up the plates and handing them to Alice. 'Now run along everyone and get cleaned up while Alice and I get tea on the table.'

Whatever else Aunty Bea said out of Alice's hearing, no further reference was made to the incident. In the weeks that followed Alice could almost believe Ray's attitude towards her had changed.

At school, now that Alice had officially undergone her acceptance ceremony, Damien was no longer an immediate threat, but she still trod warily. Few of the other children knew the truth behind Alice's suddenly short cropped hair, so Damien's display of the scars on his leg, which he claimed were Alice's teeth marks, far from causing Alice further problems actually elevated her in the eyes of her peers. Before long her nickname 'Alice from the Palace' was chanted in quite a different tone.

Yet the core of loneliness would not leave Alice. She longed to have a friend in one of her cousins and as she trundled off to milk the goats each morning she realised that even her brother had changed. He had started to copy the more rowdy behaviour of Don and Dan, deciding that safety in numbers was better than risking a further bullying incident at school, and Aunty Bea had said he could look after the pigs with his cousins instead of helping with milking each morning. This he joined in with great gusto squealing with delight and getting filthy when the four boys cleaned out the pig pen and dropped hints to Alice that now he was big she didn't need to worry about him. Alice was happy to see her brother return to being a normal healthy young rascal but she missed his easy companionship. Silly's warm friendliness became even more precious.

'I still have you, don't I, Silly?' Alice sighed, lovingly fondling the goat's funny crooked ear. 'And like Mum always said, no one can steal your dreams.' Silly bleated mournfully and butted her gently. Alice laughed and felt better. She was not entirely alone in the world.

Chapter Six

THE WEEK SHE met Billy and Paddy would be etched forever in Alice's memory. It was the September school break. The main shearing was over at Wangianna, the sheep stud property where the two boys worked, and they were allowed a few days break before the next big rush preparing the stud rams for the October sales.

Alice was feeling unusually happy. She had just learned that Grunt would not be returning to school the next term as he was to start work on a property two hundred and fifty miles from Billabrin. It was also only three months before her dad would be home for Christmas. Life was improving. She had even been allowed to assist in minor ways in her uncle's hardware store. And that's where she was, checking some of the stock, when Billy and Paddy jumped out from the mail truck and strode up to the store. Billy's cheerful laughter interrupted her counting. She looked up at the two young men blocking the sunlight in the doorway, big bushman's hats framing their faces. The taller of the two boys stepped forward out of the glare.

'So this must be my new little cousin Alice!' he exclaimed, his voice surprisingly deep. At fifteen Billy had just broken into manhood. He was a good head taller than his father, good looking, strong muscled, with a stubborn chin, his body tanned golden brown from his work outdoors. His thick brown hair threatened to turn into curls around his ears and his smile held the same radiant warmth as his mother's. There was an air of suppressed energy about Billy and Alice was immediately drawn to him. Thirteen-year-old Paddy was also good looking but his strong resemblance to his father made Alice wary.

'I'm your big cousin Billy and this is your other big cousin Paddy,' Billy explained cheerfully, slapping his brother on the shoulder, his eyes creased in smiles. Paddy grinned at Alice and she relaxed.

Suddenly Billy swept Alice up in a great bear hug and swung her around in the air. He planted a big kiss on either cheek and placed her breathless and laughing back on the ground.

'They were right about you being a beauty, but whatever happened to your hair?' he exclaimed, his brown eyes shining in admiration. Their expression was reciprocated in Alice's own blue depths, but a deeper unspoken emotion told Alice she could trust Billy. She replied candidly, catching her breath.

'One of the boys at school cut it off and then Aunty Bea finished the job.' She pulled at the short strands of hair that remained from her long lavish locks and wrinkled her nose. 'It'll grow again,' she said philosophically. Billy shoved one hand in the pocket of his baggy shorts, tilted back his big bushman's hat and listened. It took Alice only a few moments to realise that she adored her eldest cousin, by which time she had told him everything that had happened since her arrival at Billabrin.

'Well, with me and Paddy around nothing like that'll happen again,' announced Billy grimly after Alice had finished telling the last gruesome details of her battle with Grunt. 'Righto, now let's go and find Mum,' Billy said, his tone brightening. Catching Alice off guard Billy whirled her into the air again and dumped her squealing and squirming with delight on his shoulders.

'She's a wriggler this one,' added Paddy. Laughing together the three of them went in search of Aunty Bea.

Aunty Bea was ecstatic at the boys' unexpected homecoming and her happiness was reflected in the rest of the family, all except Ray who seemed more taciturn than usual and Katie who once more struggled to be the centre of attention.

'What's got up Katie's nose?' inquired Billy loudly.

'Ssh! Now don't go stirring up trouble the minute you enter the house,' remonstrated Aunty Bea with a knowing glance. 'She's just a bit put out, probably growing pains.'

During the rest of the day, despite their age difference, Alice discovered that Billy was the easiest person in the world to talk to. Billy, returning her affection, teased her unmercifully. When she introduced Silly to Billy they laughed at the rhyme and then she confided her love for her goat and how she had drawn such comfort from the animal's friendship when everything else appeared so black. Billy was immediately serious and he nodded in understanding, his reaction endearing her to him even further. Yet Billy could never ignore the opportunity for a good laugh and so without malice Silly became the butt of the family jokes and everyone laughed because the boys were home and Alice enjoyed having such a cheerful good humoured cousin to adore. Before Billy was in the house two days he was chafing for something to do.

'Let's go and find some of me old mates and stir up a bit of action in the town,' he said wickedly to Paddy across the table, watching his mother out of the corner of his eye.

'You'll do no such thing Billy Downing and don't you go stirring up the McIain boys or Mr McIain'll be looking for a couple of new rouseabouts!'

'Would I do anything like that, Ma?' Billy retorted in wide-eyed innocence while Alice listened with mounting curiosity.

'I know you, Billy, and yes you would. Just let them be, you know what they're like. They'll be gone back to their posh city school in a week's time.'

'Aw, come on, Ma, what's the harm in stirring up a bit of action? Old George wouldn't know what was going on anyways—he's too busy playing cards and betting on the horses. Actually I'd forgotten the brats'd be back home. They're the ones who usually start it.' Billy was purposely winding his mother up.

'Elizabeth would know. Nothing misses their mother's eagle eye,' replied Aunty Bea sternly. 'And I'll thank you to show some respect for your employer.' Bea stopped abruptly and glanced at Alice. 'Please, Billy, you'll make me say things I'll regret. We've had enough fuss already in this family and you know you'll only irritate your father further.' A glance passed between mother and son and Alice felt the sudden rise in tension.

'It's okay, Mum, I won't.' Billy put his arm around his mother and gave her a squeeze. She relaxed. Then he planted a big kiss on her cheek and disappeared into the back room, re-emerging with a conspicuously new .22 rifle tucked under his arm.

'Where did you get that?' Aunty Bea asked sharply.

'A present,' Billy replied evasively. He beckoned to his brother, the twinkle returning to his eye. 'Come on, Paddy, let's see if we can knock off a couple of pigs.'

'Don't you go near those wild pigs, they're wicked beasts,' cried Aunty Bea in alarm as Billy and Paddy headed towards the door.

Billy turned briefly and said, 'Don't worry, Ma,' then both the boys were gone.

Billy and Paddy walked across the wide flat scrubland above the town, searching the ground for rabbit droppings.

'I wish we could've borrowed the truck,' complained Paddy, waving away a persistent bushfly. He shifted the two dead rabbits slung over his shoulder. 'I'm sure if you'd have let me ask, Dad would've let us use it.'

Billy frowned and kicked at a bit of dirt. 'I told you I wouldn't want him to put himself out. Anyway, when's he ever bothered to listen to you since we started Up the Top?'

Paddy sighed. 'Why d'you always have to fight him? I still reckon we could've given it a go.'

'And start a third world war?'

Suddenly a battered, fawn roofless car roared up past them, bumping over the uneven ground, stirring up a dry ochre dust cloud.

'Going somewhere, fellas?' yelled out a voice.

'Kev old mate! Nick!' Billy shouted back in surprise at the sight of his old school friends, his face splitting into an enormous grin. He started to run. The truck slowed down levelling with them. Two boys much the same age as Billy and Paddy beamed back from the vehicle.

'Come to stir up trouble then, have ya?' cried the driver, Kev.

'Still the same old heap of junk, eh?' retorted Billy.

Kev pulled a face as Nick swung the rear door open and he and Paddy tumbled into the car laughing and shouting. Then Kev pressed his foot to the floor and the car roared away across the property.

'Had more luck than us,' stated Nick twisting round in the front seat and nodding at the rabbits.

'More fun going for a quick burn up,' replied Billy. 'Good to see ya, Nick.' He slapped Nick's shoulder. 'Hey, it looks like we're not the only ones out having a bit of fun today.' He pointed to a small black dot in front of a patch of dust weaving across the paddock in the distance.

Kev swung the car onto the uneven dirt track and for the next ten minutes the boys chatted amiably together as they dodged rocks and bumped over dried potholes and crevices. Kev misjudged a cattle grid and the car shot across too fast and bounced over a large stone. There was a loud thump and Kev stopped the car with a jolt.

'Bugger,' cursed Kev, slamming his fists on the steering wheel. Quickly he got out of the car and peered underneath. His face was serious as he straightened up. 'Looks like it's the oil sump. I don't know whether I can fix it,' he said, disappearing under the car again.

'Hang on, maybe these blokes'll give us a hand,' said Billy as the patch of dust turned into a battered ute lurching from side to side along the invisible track. Then his face creased in annoyance as the ute drew closer and he recognised the vehicle and its occupants. The driver had a brilliant red head and wasn't more than twelve years of age. His dark-haired companion, closer to fifteen, was leaning half out of the cabin waving a rifle and shouting inarticulately.

'Help us? You've got to be kidding, mate!' exclaimed Nick. 'That's Snake O'Seanessy and his pint-sized cousin, Bluey McIain. Back for the hols from the big smoke,' he said, putting on a posh accent.

'I know,' said Billy grimly.

'Looks like Snake's been into his dad's grog again too,' pointed out Paddy.

'That'd be right. He's already nearly wiped himself out a couple of times when he was half tanked,' said Billy rubbing a small scar over his right eye as Bluey stopped the ute just short of him. Billy couldn't help noticing the empty beer bottles on the ute floor.

'G'day, Billy. Just doing a spot of rabbit shooting,' said the red-haired lad, grinning sheepishly up at Billy, then reddening as he saw the older boy's disgust at his cousin's condition.'

'You been into the grog, too, you young idiot?' challenged Billy.

Bluey's grin disappeared and his blush deepened.

'What's it to you?' retorted Bluey. He'd had a couple of sips of whisky to please Snake and had then spent the next half hour persuading Snake to let him drive as they lurched across the countryside, finally convincing him when Snake nosedived the ute into a large pothole. The bruise on Bluey's cheekbone where he had been thrown against the side of the car door still throbbed. Any criticism from outsiders was the last thing he needed.

Billy shrugged. 'Don't blame me if you kill yourselves before the day's out.'

Bluey scowled. Before he could reply Snake half-lurched half-fell out of the truck, bottle in one hand, rifle in the other.

'Well hello. If it isn't Uncle George's chief bloody rouseabout telling us all how to live,' Snake laughed drunkenly. 'Let you out for a few days, has he?' He lurched towards the car still waving his rifle around and caught sight of the rabbits. 'Out catching rabbits too. Helluva sport. I'm a good shot too, you know.' He peered down the barrel of his rifle and then hurriedly let his arm fall. 'But I've gotta have a pee first.'

'Time to go, fellas,' insisted Billy. He could feel his temper rising. 'Any hope with the car, Kev?'

Snake steadied himself. 'Can't go yet. Gotta shoot rabbits,' he pronounced. He took a final swig from the bottle, tossed it away and belched.

'You're so drunk you couldn't hit a four-ton truck,' goaded Billy in disgust.

'C'mon, coz, let's go,' urged Bluey from the ute, but Snake was too caught up in needling Billy.

'You reckon, wanna bet?' he slurred, ignoring Bluey. Unsteadily he raised the rifle to his shoulder. Squinting down the barrel he aimed just past Billy's right ear, his finger poised above the trigger, the gun sight dancing small circles in the air.

'Crikey! Don't be an idiot, Snake!' shouted Bluey leaping out of the ute towards his cousin, convinced he was drunk enough to shoot. Snake swung round and shot into the scrub.

'Don't be a girl, Bluey, wouldn't waste me bullets on him.' He grinned stupidly, peering down the barrel again. 'I'll knock off that branch there, then I'll have a pee.' Suddenly a goat shot out from the scrub.

'Don't shoot!' screamed Billy just as Snake squeezed the trigger. The goat dropped to the ground. Billy rushed across and stared down at the motionless animal, hoping against hope that he was wrong. But his worst fears were confirmed. The funny crooked ear he had watched Alice fondle so lovingly was unmistakable. Tears of rage sprang to his eyes.

'Jeeze, mate, I'm sorry. Whose goat is it?' asked a tentative voice behind him.

Blinded by fury at his own failure to protect Alice from this misery, Billy whirled around. 'You creep!' he spat and landed a fist square on the red-head's chin. The astonished Bluey lurched backwards and toppled to the ground, his eyes watering with pain. Angrily he got to his feet and rushed at Billy, fists held high.

'It's only a flamin' goat,' he sputtered but Billy wasn't listening. Brushing the flailing Bluey aside he ran at Snake.

'I'll get you for this!' he roared, striking Snake a glancing blow across the temple. Snake tried to retaliate, missed, tripped over his own feet and fell. Bluey rushed forwards, fists still raised to fight, and then quickly changed his mind as he caught sight of the madness in Billy's eyes.

'Come on, let's get away from these flamin' maniacs,' Bluey urged, dragging his dazed cousin quickly to his feet and pushing him protesting towards the ute. His whole jaw was throbbing where Billy's first swipe had landed.

'You promised Ma,' whispered Paddy hoarsely in Billy's ear as the truck roared to life and the two boys disappeared. 'What the hell d'you do that for? Now we're in real trouble.'

'D'you think I care?' choked Billy. Then he saw the goat was still alive. 'Quick, if we get it back to Mum she might still be able to save it. Kev, you've got to get that flamin' heap of junk going. Now!'

From her perch on the old galvanised steel windmill beyond the levee surrounding Billabrin, Alice basked in the improvement in her life. Gazing across the miles of flat dry scrubland she decided she would have a bet with herself to see who she could see first, Billy and Paddy or Silly. A flock of galahs flashed brilliant pink and grey overhead, their cries filling the air, and Alice wondered for the hundredth time where the crows were and if she would ever see one fly backwards. If she did she would tell Billy. She fingered the apple core stuffed deep into her dress pocket which she had saved for Silly, and sighed contentedly. It felt good to be alive. She drifted into a daydream. After a while her foot went to sleep and she realised she had been up on her perch for far too long and the light was starting to fade. Her eager glances turned to anxious searching. Then she saw the approaching car. She watched as it vanished behind a tree and didn't reappear. Then she heard the thin sound of frustrated cries and caught sight of two figures hurrying across the paddock towards her.

'Billy!' she cried happily. She scampered down the steel ladder and raced towards her cousins.

Billy's face was red and his chest was heaving from the exertion of running with Silly's dead weight. Paddy came panting up behind.

'Did you catch a pig?' Alice asked eagerly, gazing inquisitively at the bundle. Her words died on her lips as she recognised the limp white body in Billy's arms.

'No, no, you didn't,' she cried out, her eyes suddenly enormous. She froze where she stood, blocking Billy's path.

'It was an accident,' Billy panted, trying to push past without knocking her over. 'We've got to get her to Ma.'

Alice reached out slowly and touched Silly's crooked ear, and for one brief instant Silly's eyes flickered open and Alice saw the soppy expression that had captured her heart. Then with a shudder Silly gave up her hold on life. Alice let out a little cry and Billy saw the raw pain in her eyes. He stopped and, glancing down, saw the goat was dead.

'She's gone, little Alice,' he whispered unable to hold back his tears. He nodded to Paddy who slipped away quietly.

'But you promised.' Alice felt as though all the air had been crushed out of her. She sank to her knees. Without a word Billy laid the dead goat in her arms. Alice stared down at Silly in disbelief, and the tears spilled down her face. Cradling Silly's head against her cheek, the rest of the world was blotted out as her harsh sobs filled the afternoon sky. Billy let her cry. When Alice's sobs finally ceased he very gently took the goat once more into his own arms.

'I'll help you bury her, little Alice,' he said and his eyes too were red. 'We'll bury her next to my old dog.' They walked home in silence.

'I loved her, Billy, and she loved me,' whispered Alice as Billy collected the shovel, and he nodded in understanding. Then, like some precious gift, he lifted the lifeless Silly in his arms and carried her down the hill and buried her. Alice stroked the fresh mound with her hands and wet the dark earth with her tears while Billy waited patiently. When all her grief was spent she placed a little sprig of gum leaves on the top of the grave and stood up. Her eyes were dry now but in their depths a new layer of grief was carved in deep brilliance. Billy clasped Alice's hands tightly in his own, wishing he could wipe out the pain.

'I'll never forgive those creeps for what they did to you. Never,' he whispered and Alice knew he meant it.

Chapter Seven

AFTER SILLY'S DEATH something happened inside Alice. It was not that she became harder it was just that she knew nothing could ever affect her in the same way again. On the days when the pain was not too unbearable, in some strange way she rejoiced in her newfound feeling of freedom. Once you had known such unadulterated pain, everything else seemed paltry by comparison. Uncle Ray's stern discipline was almost welcomed by her and in return his attitude softened. Even Katie's petty jealous niggles were reduced to insignificance.

Only Bea recognised this fundamental change in Alice. Even though, as the days went by, Alice's natural exuberance gradually reappeared, as did her unruly thick black hair that insisted on growing at such a great pace that it was soon jutting out at all angles above her shoulders like some wild, exotic bush, Bea still worried about the child. So it was with great relief that she heard, two days before Christmas, that Thomas was coming home.

'It's the best thing that could have happened to the kids. What a lovely Christmas present,' Aunty Bea said happily to Ray. 'Alice is like an overstretched wire at the moment. Her father coming home should get her to relax a bit.' Her face clouded and she looked up at Ray. 'Tommy worries me sometimes. I wonder if he realises just how much hope Alice is pinning on his return.'

Uncle Ray frowned. 'At least she's stopped moping around the place after that damned goat. Dunno as I'd call her father's return a present though. I'm off to get some parts.' He tilted his wide-brimmed hat with one finger and strode towards the door.

'Could you take Alice with you when you fetch him from Walgett?'

Ray stopped dead and then turned, frowning. 'Fetch him! What's wrong with his truck?'

'Didn't I tell you? He sold it,' Bea replied, adding quickly, 'for a really good deal, so I was assured. I didn't actually talk to him.' Ray snorted in disapproval. 'Don't make it difficult for Alice, please, dear,' Bea pleaded.

'I'm not making anything difficult for anyone,' Ray answered sharply. Then, seeing the concern in his wife's face, he added, 'I'll fetch the mongrel.'

Bea's expression relaxed. 'Don't be late, dear, and don't call him a mongrel in front of the children. He's trying to be a loving father. I'll go and tell Alice the good news.' And she disappeared cheerfully out the back before he could reply.

Alice was overjoyed at the news of her father's return and became even more excited when she learned she would be allowed to go and meet him at the station.

'We'll keep it a surprise for Ben until you get back because there isn't enough room for all four of you in the truck. That way Ben won't be disappointed at not going with you,' Bea explained.

'For Christmas! I can't believe it, Aunty Bea.' Alice hugged Aunty Bea excitedly, her blue eyes sparkling.

'That'll be Uncle Ray back now,' said Bea delighted as a truck turned into the street. 'Just don't chatter too much on the way. Your uncle's had a busy morning. There's a good girl.'

'I won't, I promise. Oh Aunty Bea. I'm so happy!'

Alice bounded towards the road, a grin stretched across her face, and pulled at the door almost before the truck had stopped. Uncle Ray frowned as he pulled on the handbrake and a breathless Alice tumbled into the seat.

'What's made you so happy all of a sudden then?' he growled. He pushed his hat off his forehead and slapped his hands back onto the steering wheel. Alice stared boldly up at her uncle and was surprised to see a twinkle hidden in the depths of his stern eyes.

'We'll get back when we get back. May take a while,' Ray called over Alice's head. Aunty Bea nodded and the vehicle jerked forward. Halfway down the main street Ray slowed down as Father O'Reilly, his black cassock hitched around his knees, wobbled towards them on his bicycle.

'Morning, Father,' Ray called out.

'Morning, Father,' cried Alice, waving excitedly.

'And isn't it a very splendid one at that, little Alice,' beamed Father O'Reilly pulling sharply on his brakes and coming to a stop by the driver's window. 'And where would you be taking your uncle today?'

'We're off to get my dad,' Alice bubbled. She glanced quickly across at Ray. 'We don't have to keep it a secret from Father do we, Uncle Ray?'

'Your dad. Is that so? And it's a secret too! Well then, I mustn't be keeping you chatting all day,' replied Father O'Reilly quickly, pulling his bike clear of the truck, his ruddy cheeks crinkling above his wide smile. 'Bless you both. Take care of the little one,' he nodded to Ray.

'Thank you, Father. I'll do that,' replied Ray moving off. Alice waved happily until the priest was a mere speck in the distance.

'So your aunt's told you what we're up to, has she?' Uncle Ray said gruffly once they were well clear of the town.

Alice smiled up at her uncle. 'Sort of, but I'd like you to tell me too,' she replied tactfully, struggling to contain her exuberance. Lips pursed, she stared firmly out at the bumpy dirt track ahead. Uncle Ray glanced at her out of the corner of his eye and his mouth twitched. He pulled his hat brim straight.

'I'm glad to see you've at least learned to curb your behaviour, young lady.' He paused. 'I don't know that I'm all that keen on all this to-ing and fro-ing but anyhow, that's what your aunt wanted, so I said I'd go along with it.'

Alice twisted her fingers around the bottom of her blouse. 'You're a good man, Uncle Ray,' she announced, the picture of innocence, her face puckering with laughter.

'What's this "good man" stuff, my girl? You've been listening to your aunt too much. You're getting too cheeky by half!' His grimace was almost a grin.

Alice wriggled in her seat. Finally, unable to keep silent any longer she burst out, 'I'm so excited!'

'I'm sure you are, my girl. He is your dad.'

For the next ten minutes Alice chattered away excitedly until Ray told her she had talked enough. Then she gazed out of the window her mind in a whirl, the silence comfortable as they travelled towards the little town of Walgett. After two hours Ray turned off the main track and drew up near the small country railway station.

'We'll wait here.' He nodded unsmiling towards the unfenced track. Now that Thomas' arrival was imminent even Alice's excitement couldn't sustain Ray's light-heartedness. 'The train won't be too long now.' Sure enough within half an hour the long red goods train appeared as a spot in the distance and in no time at all it was in front of them and sliding noisily to a stop. Impatiently Alice scanned the trucks packed with animals and freight for any sign of her father. Then at the far end she spied a neatly dressed man of medium height stepping down from the train leading a spirited horse. Alice's composure burst.

'There he is! That's him! Daddy! Daddy!' She hurtled out of the truck and down towards her father. He saw her coming and opened his arms wide to greet her.

'Daddy! Daddy! You're home! You're home!' Alice hurled herself into his arms.

'Princess!' shouted Thomas catching her and twirling her in his embrace. 'Where's Ben?' Alice hugged him tight wrinkling her nose as he placed her feet back on the ground.

'There wasn't room for him in the truck so Aunty Bea said it was best to keep it a surprise for him. You smell new,' she exclaimed in one breath.

She buried her face in his chest enjoying the rough feel of his stiff new shirt and the smell of his aftershave. As they hugged, the horse pressed her long nose between them and blew warm air into Alice's ear. Alice drew back startled and turned her head. Tentatively she reached up to stroke the long silky brown nose and her heart missed a beat. Here again were deep brown eyes that gazed at her inquiringly from out of a soft, gentle face. The horse nuzzled at her, lifting her lip affectionately, searching Alice's arm for hidden sugarlumps. Laughter bubbled up inside Alice and frothed over into sound.

'I'm sorry, I don't have anything for you!'

'Whoo, get back there!' ordered Thomas. He pushed the horse backwards and adjusted the reins that had been lying loosely around his arm. 'Just watch her, she can be a bit skittish.' His eyes rested tenderly on his daughter. 'You look more like your mother every day,' he said, his expression suddenly serious. Alice's stomach lurched at his words and she saw the memory of her own pain echoed momentarily in his brown eyes.

'I love you, Daddy,' said Alice. Thomas reach over and patted the horse's neck.

'And I love you,' he replied soberly.

Wanting quickly to re-establish the light mood, Alice asked eagerly, 'Is she your new horse, Daddy?' Thomas' smile returned. He shook his head.

'Let me introduce you to Sheherazade. I think the two of you are going to get on just fine.'

'You mean—' gasped Alice, not daring to voice her thoughts.

'That's right, Princess, she's yours. I bought her for you just like I promised when you first learned to ride. I'm sure you'll quickly learn to manage her,' Thomas grinned.

Alice couldn't believe her ears. She jumped up and down not knowing who to hug first, her grin even bigger than before. In her excitement she tried to hug both horse and father and failed, making Sheherazade step back nervously. Impetuously Alice reached her hands up to the horse's wide neck and stroked her, whispering softly. The horse responded by flicking her tail and blowing more hot air down Alice's blouse.

'Is she really mine?' she exclaimed in awe. Thomas nodded happily, watching her amazement turn to joy. 'Mine?' she asked again clapping her hands, still wanting to make sure she had heard correctly. 'Mine?' Her happiness was infectious.

'You'll have to look after her, mind you,' Thomas said squeezing Alice affectionately. 'Feed and water her, brush her down after rides, muck out the stable.'

'Of course! Oh Daddy, she's so beautiful!' Alice cried, running her hands once more down Sheherazade's sleek golden-brown flanks. 'Where did you find her?' Then her face fell and she looked quickly up at her father in concern. 'What about Uncle Ray?' She lowered her voice and glanced over her shoulder. 'He'll never let me keep her. Can you talk to him, Daddy, please, please?'

'Of course he will, Princess,' replied Thomas nonchalantly. As he spoke, her uncle's footsteps crunched behind and his shadow fell across her face. Beseechingly she looked up into his crusty unsmiling face. His eyes were hard and there was no sign of the twinkle she had glimpsed earlier. Ray ignored her and looked across at Thomas.

'G'day, Thomas. Whose is the horse?' He pulled his pipe from his pocket and began tapping the bowl in the palm of his hand. 'Set someone back a few pence, I dare say. She's not just your average filly.' He stuck his pipe in his mouth.

'G'day, Ray. How ya going?' greeted Thomas smoothly. Ray waited.

'Mine,' Thomas continued, breaking the awkward silence. 'Made a few extra bob on my last job, you know.' He tapped his nose knowingly, his eyes full of secrecy. 'I got her for Princess. She's worth it.' He winked at Alice.

'Oh yes,' said Ray ominously. 'For Alice, did you say?' Alice cringed at the irritation in his tone.

'Yep! For my girl,' beamed Thomas.

'Not if I have anything to say about it, it isn't,' Ray replied sharply, removing his pipe. 'I don't need any flamin' horses mucking up my yard.' He stuck his pipe back between his teeth and glared at the horse. Alice held her breath.

'Come on, Ray, give the girl a go,' implored Thomas agitated.

The crease between Uncle Ray's brows deepened. 'Reckon I've seen that horse before,' he announced.

'You can't have,' Thomas burst out. 'I won it in a bet fair and square.'

Uncle Ray raised his eyebrows. 'Sure you did too, but what's that got to do with anything and what are you planning to do with it now?'

'Like I said, it's a present for Alice.' Both men looked at Alice. Ray opened his mouth to speak and took in Alice's crestfallen expression. Changing his mind he caught his pipe and shoved it in his pocket.

'Dunno about you, Thomas Ferguson. There's some blokes whenever they come here they always bring trouble,' Ray sighed loudly. 'Right now we'll have to borrow a blinkin' horse float to get the damn thing back home. We can't just leave it here in town.' He turned to go.

'Does that mean yes, Uncle Ray?' exclaimed Alice dancing up and down.

'Not yes, just maybe,' he replied reluctantly. 'We'll have to talk to your aunt. Something very familiar.' He scratched his ear. 'Are you sure you got her in a square deal?'

'Couldn't have been squarer,' laughed Thomas giving Alice a nudge. 'There, I told you there'd be no problem keeping Sheherazade.' He looked across her to Ray. 'Alice here was getting skittish.'

'Sheherazade! Now what sort of a name's that?' Ray shook his head.

'I could call her Sherry, it's easier,' interjected Alice hopefully. 'I promise I'll look after her, Uncle Ray.'

Ray looked down at her eager face. 'You've got an answer for everything, haven't you, girl,' he replied, but his tone was more friendly. 'Right now we'd best go down to Elders and see if we can hire this float.' The pipe was back in his mouth. 'Something still worries me about that horse,' he muttered.

An ecstatic Alice trotted next to Thomas and Uncle Ray as they returned to the truck. Alice watched wide eyed, as her father and Uncle Ray manoeuvred the horse into the float they had borrowed and hitched it onto the back of the vehicle, still unable to believe that all this was real. Then the three squeezed into the cabin with Alice in the middle and drove slowly down the road back home.

*

Aunty Bea gave her brother a big sisterly hug.

'You look great Tommy,' she announced, her face all smiles. 'And smart,' she added, stepping back. 'Have you come into some money or something?'

'Maybe,' teased Thomas.

'Well, whatever it was, all that fresh air and hard work has done you the world of good. You look like a different man.' But Aunty Bea suspected it was more than just fresh air and hard work that was making her little brother look so well.

Without warning Ben hurtled into the room and stopped dead unable to believe his eyes. 'Dad!' He flew across the room and hung like a chimpanzee around his father's neck.

'My, this is a changed young man,' exclaimed his father at his son's greeting. 'Living with your cousins seems to be doing you a lot of good.'

'It is, it is,' encouraged Aunty Bea. 'They've both been fine.'

Alice could contain her excitement no longer. 'Come and see what Daddy's got me, Aunty Bea!' She grabbed her by the hand.

'What have you been up to now, Thomas?' Aunty Bea demanded with mock severity as Alice tugged insistently.

'Nothing,' replied Thomas wrapping Ben in a bear hug.

'All right, Alice, I'm coming! We'll let your father have a bit of time with Ben.' It was good to see Alice so bubbling with joy and excitement and it promptly wiped out the previous unease she had felt. This Christmas would be good for everyone.

'A horse!' exclaimed Aunty Bea stopping in her tracks.

'Her real name's Sheherazade,' explained Alice stumbling over the word. 'But I'm going to call her Sherry—I can keep her, can't I?'

'Why not?'

'Uncle Ray said only maybe.'

'A maybe from your Uncle Ray! That's like gold dust!' Aunty Bea confided mischievously. 'Don't worry, I'll have a quiet word with him when all the fuss has died down. I've told you often enough he's all growls.'

Alice beamed. Her world was suddenly rich. Thomas sneaked up behind her. Lifting her high he placed her gently on the horse's silky back.

'We're going to have to get you a saddle and teach you how to ride her now, aren't we?' he announced and Alice stared down at him in adoration. Then she leaned forward and pressing her body against Sherry's strong back, stroked her sleek coat and breathed in the soft warm smell of horse.

Thomas stepped back. 'I knew you'd fix it all, sis.'

'Who is she?' inquired Bea casually.

'Who's who?' asked Thomas.

'The woman who's put the roses back into your cheeks.' Alice went very still.

'You don't miss much do you, sis,' he said sheepishly. He jerked his head towards Alice.

'Never did when you were young. Same as you've always been, head in the clouds, money burning a hole in your pocket.' She dropped her voice so that Alice had to strain to hear. 'But I only ever saw that look in your eye once before and that was the day you marched in and said you were marrying Mary Ellen.' She laughed and patted his cheek affectionately. 'She has to be special,' she continued quickly, relieved to see her brother's fleeting look of pain quickly replaced by a rueful grin.

'Actually, she's very special,' he admitted.

The clunk of metal sounded against hard packed dirt as Alice involuntarily tightened her grip on the horse's mane and the startled Sheherazade stepped backwards. Quickly Alice loosened her grip and patted the horse's neck, talking soothingly to her. Thomas patted the horse reassuringly and she settled again whisking the flies with her tail.

'As for Sheherazade,' he said looking approvingly up at Alice, unaware of her tension, 'she's the real new lady in my life. Look at the two of them, both as fidgety as each other. I knew it was the right thing to do. They're already firm friends. One day I'll buy you a top thoroughbred, Princess.'

'What about some clothes or a home?' asked Aunty Bea quickly. Then, to lighten her comment, she added, 'Well, come on, Tommy, aren't you at least going to tell me whether this new woman in your life is pretty or not?'

'I'll do better than that, I'll introduce you to her.' Grinning he put his arms up to help Alice get off.

'No,' shrieked Alice and jerked upright, startling herself with her own vehemence. No one reacted. Then she realised her cry was in her head. She smiled crookedly at her father. Lifting her leg across Sherry's back she allowed him to slide her gently back down to the ground.

It hit forty-two degrees on Christmas Day, melting the icing on Aunty Bea's delicious chocolate cake so that it ran down onto the plate in a dark sticky mass. But no one really minded because all the family was together, including Billy and Paddy, and everybody was smiling. Even Katie was happy. Aunty Bea made them each a little homemade surprise which she hung on the gum bough that substituted for a Christmas tree. Then, after attending the Christmas Day service taken by Father O'Reilly, they all squashed around the table and tucked into the hot roast lamb Billy had brought back as a gift, ate the cake with spoons, and sweltered. By the end of the day everyone was too full and too hot to bother with any more food so they nibbled on bits of cold leftovers and cake. Finally, well after sunset, the children flopped exhausted onto their beds while the adults sat out in the cool.

Ray sat relaxed and mellow on the verandah, a glass of rum at his side, puffing on his pipe while the cicadas sang in the trees. Alice's heart sang with them as she headed towards the bathroom. It had been a beautiful Christmas Day. Different but beautiful. In church she had sent a prayer to her mother to watch over them and she was sure she had heard. She stopped as Aunty Bea's voice drifted across on the still summer night jerking her back to reality.

'I'm really glad you've found yourself a new girlfriend, Tommy. I hope it works out. Dorothy sounds nice. I'm sure the kids will be excited to meet her. They need to have a woman to look after them when you all move into your own place again.'

'Dotty,' said Thomas, 'she likes to be called Dotty.'

Dotty! The name echoed in Alice's ears. She hated her already and they didn't need anyone to come and look after them, not now, not ever. Alice shut her mind to the thoughts that swamped her, refusing to allow anything to spoil Christmas Day. She finished cleaning her teeth and headed for the verandah. Perhaps this woman wouldn't be so bad, she thought, trying, to be generous as she climbed onto the bed next to Katie. She could be a friend who came to tea sometimes but no more, not special like her mother and certainly never as pretty.

Alice lay on the bed unable to sleep, flapping the sheet against the heat until Katie grumbled sleepily. Her arm flopped against her face and she caught the faint tang of horse. Today was the first time she had dared to let the horse have her head and she and Sherry had flown like wild things across the paddocks as the sun tipped over the horizon at daybreak. What better way to celebrate Christmas? She wriggled with pleasure at the memory. Finally, unable to bear lying against the hot sheets any longer, she slipped out of bed in search of a cool drink. Aunty Bea and her father were still talking. Alice stopped, not wanting to learn more yet unable to deny her curiosity, her hand tensing on the drinking water tap.

'Look, I didn't mention it before but I'm having a few problems with my girlfriend. I thought about it and I think it's better not to ask her to visit right now.' Thomas spoke rapidly. 'Dotty's only young and I can't throw the kids on her straightaway . . . The thing is, I haven't actually told her about them yet.' Alice grew suddenly cold despite the heat.

'What do you mean you haven't told her about them yet?' Aunty Bea demanded sharply.

'Now don't panic, sis. I've thought it all through. The easiest thing is if I leave them with you. The kids are happy here, they love you. You could look after them, that sort of thing. I know you're going to love her, sis.' The next sentence rooted Alice to the ground.

'So you're just going to abandon your own children, are you?' exclaimed Bea. 'Do you ever intend any of us to meet this woman?'

'Of course I'm not abandoning them, I'm just asking for a bit of time. Look, give me six months. I swear I'll tell her then. We need time to get to know one another without worrying about anyone else, that's all. I promise as soon as she gets used to the idea we'll fix something up about the kids. She'll make a great mum given half a chance, but if I tell her now I know I'll lose her.' His voice cracked. 'I don't think I could bear that.'

There was silence for a moment. Alice had to strain to hear the next bit. 'I need time too, sis. Every time I look at Alice I see Mary Ellen.' Thomas blew his nose. When he continued his voice was stronger. 'I have to have another shot at life. I can't spend the rest of my life grieving, but if I don't get a break, how will I ever cope?'

'Keep your voice down or you'll wake the children,' whispered Bea more gently.

'She's gone, Bea. She's been gone nearly a year. I have to get on with my life. Six months isn't so long. The kids'll be fine with you and that'll give Dotty a chance to get used to the idea of an instant family. I'll work something out. We might even have one of our own on the way by then.' He sounded almost cheeky. Alice felt as though someone was squeezing her insides.

'I know you're lonely, Tommy, but if you're that uncertain of her, you'd be better to let her go now,' Aunty Bea warned, irritation fighting compassion. 'And what about the kids? Do you intend telling them? Have you thought about them at all?' Irritation was winning. 'Come on, Tommy, grow up!' How could he do this to his own flesh and blood? She had never understood his selfishness, unwilling to see it for what it really was, always excusing him as her baby brother. Even now she was torn. But what would it do to Alice and Ben? Her earlier premonitions were turning into grim reality.

'Don't get cross. It's my life.' A chair scraped loudly in the night air. 'Okay, okay, I'll tell Dotty about them and I'll bring her here but I'll say she's got six months to get used to the idea. How about that? Then everyone knows and no one gets hurt.' His old bravado was returning.

Bea could feel herself giving in to him. At least if the children were with her she would know they were safe and loved.

'And you'll tell Alice and Ben yourself in the morning?' insisted Bea, still unhappy at his vagueness.

'I'll tell Alice and Ben in the morning. Look, it's just going to be a bit of a holiday.'

'And what if Dotty doesn't like the idea of stepchildren?'

'Don't gnaw it to death, sis. Let's worry about that when we need to. Anyway, you'll think of something. You always have before.' The laughter was back in his voice.

'Yes I always have,' Bea thought ruefully, 'and your selfishness has always hurt.'

'And the kids both really love you,' Thomas added kissing Bea loudly on the cheek.

There was no laughter for Alice. With a sinking heart she realised that this man was now her father in name only. Any real commitment he had towards her and Ben had vanished. They could be parcelled off whenever it suited him, at the whim of an unknown girlfriend. It was only because of her new state of mind and the freedom she had found on Sherry's back that Alice was not totally crushed. Yet she was struggling. She loved him—he was her dad—but what of his promises to build his princess her palace? What had she and Ben done that had made him want to hide the fact that they existed, even for a day? She did not understand, but as she stood in the hot night air she resolved that despite everything she would never let him see how much he had hurt her. She would learn to like his new girlfriend and she would do everything within her power to make him proud of her and Ben. She would also never expect anything from anyone or rely on anyone ever again. She crawled back to bed wishing she could obliterate the last few hours. She would remember this Christmas Day for the rest of her life. An unreal sense of calm descended upon her.

On Boxing Day Thomas explained to Alice and Ben as briefly as possible that he had a special friend and they were taking a six month holiday together. Ben was more interested in going fishing and Alice nodded politely and gave him a quick hug, revealing nothing of her inner turmoil. Thomas congratulated himself to Bea, too caught up in his own relief that neither child had created a scene to notice Alice's emotional retreat. But Bea heard the brittle note in her niece's assumed cheerfulness.

Later on that day Thomas slipped his arm around Alice and Ben and started talking excitedly about his plans. He explained how he would bring Dotty home after the holiday and that they would all get to know one another really well in good time but that they had the rest of their lives to do so. Alice nodded at her father's words, once more smiling politely, seeing all her hopes of getting back to being a little family dwindle to nothing. As they talked, Alice watched her father from under her long dark lashes, her determination to please him fighting her misery at knowing his deceit. Suddenly she felt more desperately alone than she had in her entire life. To reassure herself she put her arm around Ben. Thomas was delighted at how well the children, Alice in particular, had apparently taken the idea of a stepmother and said so to Bea out of the children's hearing. Even Aunty Bea, although concerned, was lulled into believing that this particular hurdle was surmountable.

No one, however, had bargained for the force of Alice's emotional reactions. Overnight the calm she had felt when she discovered her father's treachery vanished completely as she ricocheted from loneliness and rejection to growing anger. It was the betrayal of her mother's memory, not his lies and deceit, that hurt Alice most deeply and which was translated into silent fury. She simply could not understand how he could even contemplate anyone replacing her own beautiful mother. It was all she could do to play-act her way through the rest of the day.

When Thomas left the next day amid more smiles and promises to return, the dam finally burst. Alice seemed to have lost control of her limbs. In the space of half an hour she accidentally broke her aunt's favourite sugar bowl, knocked Uncle Ray's last tin of tobacco into a pool of water and spilled a new consignment of nuts and bolts he had been carefully sorting across the lounge room floor. Finally she stepped back onto

Katie's small cardboard box of ribbons and tiny figurines and a fight ensued. When Uncle Ray roared at her, far from being contrite she roared back at him that she didn't care about anything or anyone any more and then charged out across the paddock to where the one creature she trusted in the world was standing grazing contentedly.

Sherry lifted her head. Her ears pricked forward in pleasure and she trotted eagerly towards the running girl.

'Oh Sherry, I hate them all!' cried Alice. Leaping onto the horse's strong, sleek back she dug her bare heels into her flanks and urged her into a gallop. Streaking across the dry brown paddocks, her hands buried deep in Sherry's thick mane, her knees clinging to Sherry's sides, she let the tears course down her cheeks. Damn Uncle Ray, damn her father, damn Katie, damn everything. How could her father have given her Sherry and then behaved like that to her and Ben? Perhaps even Sherry was just temporary. She had to face the truth, no matter how much it hurt. Her father didn't want them and he was never coming back. She clung harder to Sherry, her mind whirling in miserable confusion.

As they pounded across the levee and into the open grassland beyond, her anger and anguish were replaced by a rush of energy. She was alive. She was free. She would take the world on herself, she would create her own destiny. No one would ever break a promise to her again. She would carve out her own path; she would find life's magic and when the time came to love someone she would love them so truly and so utterly that there would be no betrayal, no deceit, no false promises, only complete trust and union. Above all she would never again allow anyone to make her feel so completely abandoned.

Alice laughed exultantly, the wind rushing against her open mouth and pulling at her hair. She had never felt this wonderful in all her life. Gradually her grip on Sherry loosened and the horse slowed down to a canter and finally a walk. A great sense of peace descended on Alice as they ambled slowly towards the river.

'Whoa there, Sherry.' The horse reacted to her murmured command. Alice pulled her mane gently and Sherry lifted her head high and whinnied. Together horse and rider stood on the flat black soil plains silhouetted against the late afternoon light.

'This place is so beautiful,' Alice whispered in awe. 'I can do it, Sherry' she continued. 'I can, I know I can.'

Yet as she looked across the vast imposing emptiness so different from her old home she felt once more daunted. Like a whisper on the wind her mother's words floated into her head. 'Take courage, Alice. Remember it's deeds not words that will get you where you want to be.'

Alice sighed deeply. There was another bit that she couldn't remember. 'It's so hard, Mum. I miss you so much,' she murmured.

Words were so simple. She had never meant to get in the way of her dad. She had tried so hard to copy Aunty Bea, who was always cheerful and trying to make everyone happy. She had tried to get on with her cousins. She had thought she was succeeding in part even with Uncle Ray. Then Dotty had to come and ruin everything. But there had to be more to life than this, more than polite words and rejection and disappointment. There had to be something wonderful. The exhilaration she had felt moments ago had to have come from somewhere. Her eyes rested idly on a few peacefully grazing sheep reminding her of the animals she had healed with Aunty Bea. She sniffed the clean country air and her spirit revived. Into her head popped forgotten words and with them the most incredible idea. As her mother's advice sang in her head she could picture her smiling face and almost smell her perfume. 'Be bold, my love, and dream. Once you know your dream, reach for it with all you've got.' Tiny shivers ran down her spine as she whispered the last part aloud. ". . . For today's dreams are tomorrow's reality.' Suddenly everything was blindingly clear. She gasped at her own temerity. Yet it fitted. Her hands grew sweaty against Sherry's mane. When she spoke again her voice was strong.

'One day I'll make Dad proud of me. I'll do it, Mum. Then he'll never need to hide me and Ben, or lie to us or leave us ever again. I'll build my own palace and I'll breed sheep which will be famous all over Australia. Dad'll have to be proud of me then.' It was a wild, impossible dream, especially in such a male-dominated world as the Australian sheep farming industry, where traditional roles of men and women went deep and to cross the line into the male domain brought tight-lipped disapproval and obstruction from both sexes. But as Alice gazed out across the great expanse of land it was as though her spirit were released.

Behind horse and girl the sky turned brilliant orange and pink, its vibrant colours stretching across the celestial dome and painting the underside of the smattering of clouds. As Alice gazed up into its fiery hue a solitary dark shape flew up from the nearby clump of gum trees and hung in the air above her head. Thinking about it afterwards as she and Sherry wended their way peacefully home across the darkening land, Alice was never absolutely certain whether it was just the clouds moving slowly beyond or if in fact the bird had really been flying backwards.

Chapter Eight

RETURNING FROM HER early morning milk deliveries, Alice cantered across the fields, revelling in the rush of crisp cold air against her flushed cheeks and the pleasure of Sherry's strong body moving beneath her. Aunty Bea would be delighted with her work. She had visited everyone Bea had asked her to and had a long list of repeat milk orders, which Alice knew would help out financially.

The dew was still on the ground and clouds of steam rose from Sherry's sweating flanks and billowed from her nostrils as they cantered across the remaining distance between the levee and the home paddock. Alice gave a little sigh as they slowed down to a walk to allow Sherry to cool down. Riding with Sherry in the early mornings was the best part of her life.

Dismounting, Alice threw her arms around the horse giving her customary quick hug. 'You're my best friend,' she murmured into Sherry's strong neck. She had long ago given up hoping she and Katie would be friends. Katie had made it quite clear she only tolerated her. Determined not to let thoughts of Katie spoil the day, she slipped off the saddle. 'I'll be back after school,' she added, tossing the horse blanket across Sherry's back. Fixing the blanket securely, she gave the horse one last pat, gathered the saddle up in her arms and hurried through the gate. Locking it behind her she checked the list for Bea was safe in her pocket and ran towards the house. She had been longer than usual and could hear Ben yelling for her to hurry up.

As Alice reached the house she paused in surprise at the sight of two cars parked outside Uncle Ray's store. One she immediately recognised as belonging to the local police sergeant. The other she had never seen before. Briefly she wondered what had brought visitors at such an early hour, but telling Bea about the list was uppermost in her mind. Quickly dumping the saddle in its usual place she burst into the kitchen.

'Guess what, Aunty Bea—' she panted and stopped dead at the sudden silence.

The police sergeant looked up from his conversation with Uncle Ray and a heavy-set stranger. The man, a good ten years younger than her uncle and with a large nose, continued to stare aggressively at Ray. A red-faced Uncle Ray swayed back and forth on his heels, hands thrust deep in his pockets, avoiding Alice's gaze, while Aunty Bea appeared intent on murdering a piece of toast.

'Morning, Alice,' said the sergeant cheerfully, breaking the silence.

'Hurry up for school, Alice,' snapped Aunty Bea without looking up. 'You're far too slow this morning. The others have already left.' The toast crunched under her attack.

One glance at Uncle Ray's expression told Alice this was not the moment to start asking questions. Startled at her aunt's uncharacteristic abruptness, Alice hurried through to the verandah to collect her belongings for school. As she hunted, bits of conversation drifted through the thin walls of the house.

'She's too skittish to be a reliable racer like some of my top horses, but she comes from a good blood line so I was planning to breed from her. It was only by pure coincidence that I got wind of her whereabouts at all. I thought she'd gone for good. The only reason I'm bloody up here is because I put a new manager on my property a couple of weeks ago and I wanted to check out how he was going.'

Half listening, Alice searched for the history book she would need for class. Her uncle's sudden angry expletive brought her up sharply.

'Is there no end to your brother's stupidity?'

'Ray, please!' It was Aunty Bea's voice.

'Please nothing. I thought we'd got past all this when he left but the bloody horse—stolen! Well, if the horse is yours you'd better take her back.'

The hairs on Alice's neck stood up. Her stomach lurched. Surely they weren't referring to Sherry? Trembling she strained to listen.

'What are we going to tell Alice?' she heard Bea ask.

Panic hit Alice. Without waiting to hear more she tore back into the house, but the men had already left.

'What are they doing to Sherry?' gasped Alice, the colour draining from her face.

'Listen, Alice, sweetie,' Aunty Bea's strained tone confirmed her fears. Brushing past her, Alice raced outside after the stranger who, halter in hand, was marching purposefully across the yard towards Sherry's paddock with Uncle Ray and the police sergeant in close pursuit. Ever inquisitive, Sherry meandered towards the gate.

'Run, Sherry, run!' Alice screamed, her whole being focused on the horse, and stopped abruptly as she collided with the solid bulk of Father O'Reilly wobbling dangerously on his bicycle. Alice, bicycle and priest fell to the ground in an undignified heap.

'Well now, is that a way to greet an old friend, young lady?' Father O'Reilly's booming voice washed over the shocked girl along with the faintest reek of whisky.

'They're going to take Sherry!' Alice gulped, gesticulating wildly as she wrestled to break free from the bicycle and his dark priest's robes.

'And why would anyone be wanting to do that, might I ask?' replied Father O'Reilly once more on his feet. His blue eyes twinkled with interest as he carefully smoothed his hand down his dust spattered black robes and picked up his bicycle.

'You don't understand!' cried Alice scrambling to her feet. 'She's mine, Father. You've got to stop them!' Wide with terror her eyes never left the stranger for a second. The halter was on and the stranger was leading Sherry out of the paddock. As Alice started to run, the priest grabbed her by the arm. Unwanted tears smarted at the back of Alice's eyes as she fought to escape from his grip.

'Don't stop me, Father! Please don't stop me!'

'Well now, young Alice, 'tis best not to rush in with the angels. Life has a way of working things out for the better if we all calm down and behave in a civilised fashion.'

'No one else is being calm and civilised,' she shrieked. Wrenching her arm free she tore towards the stranger. Planting her feet firmly in front of Sherry so that she was in danger of being stepped on, she thrust her chin forwards, her heart clamouring in her chest as she tried to grab the halter.

'You can't take Sherry. I don't care what anyone says, she's mine. My dad gave her to me,' she screamed.

The man tightened his hand on the halter, jerking the horse's head, and his harsh laugh jarred in Alice's ears.

'Look, girlie, this horse is mine and I'm here to take it back to where it belongs—on my property. Now move out of my way.'

Biting her bottom lip to stop it trembling, and fighting back the tears, Alice turned imploring to the police sergeant. Sherry nuzzled at Alice.

'I'm afraid he's right, Alice,' nodded the police sergeant.

Alice's eyes seemed to sink into her face with misery.

'I'll deal with this,' barked Uncle Ray. 'Alice, get back into the house immediately, before I take a stick to you.'

'Well now, I don't know that that will be entirely necessary,' interrupted Father O'Reilly hurrying up behind. 'Good day to you, Hal Tyson. There wouldn't by any chance be anything unlawful happening here, now would there?' Alice and Ray looked startled. The irritation in Hal's face was replaced by wariness.

'Do you know this man, Father?' asked Ray.

'We have met over the odd cup of tea,' replied the priest smoothly.

'Business is what brings me here, Father,' replied Hal equally smoothly. 'Business and this horse.' He nodded his head towards Sherry.

Uncle Ray rubbed his hands together in discomfort. 'Look, Hal, as I said, if my brother-in-law's done the wrong thing then you just take the horse. Alice'll recover.' Alice wondered how long she could hold back the tears.

'So who owns the horse, Hal?' Father O'Reilly asked suddenly, all his friendliness evaporating. He put his arm around Alice. Her whole body was trembling.

'I do, Father, and I can assure you, there is nothing crooked about this one on my side,' replied Hal his smooth exterior crumbling slightly under the priest's steely glare.

'Go on.'

'Seems one of my stable hands wasn't too happy at being given his marching orders. Ended up stealing Flying Start and then offloading her in a bet. My new manager reckoned he'd seen the horse in the district. Just to be sure I called up the sergeant and he confirmed Ray was the new owner.'

'But how can you be sure that Sherry is the horse that went missing?' insisted Alice, still trembling.

Hal laughed and looked appealingly at the assembled group. 'This is getting ridiculous, fellas. I don't have to prove anything to this girl. Come on.'

'He's right. Alice. Stop making a nuisance of yourself.' But Uncle Ray's voice no longer carried his earlier conviction. Alice's shoulders slumped and the fight went out of her blue eyes. Suddenly Hal could not meet her gaze.

Scowling, he said over Alice's head, 'Look, I know this is all a horrible mix-up but as I explained before, the horse is worth good money. She'll make a good breeder. I can't just give her away.' He looked uncomfortably across at Ray. 'But I wouldn't want to break the little girl's heart. Listen, mate, make me an offer I can't refuse.'

'You know we haven't got that sort of money, Ray.'

Everyone whirled round at the sudden appearance of Aunty Bea. Her eyes were red from crying but there was a note of steel in her voice. 'Alice, sweetie, you have to let the horse go.' Aunty Bea's face mirrored Alice's misery. 'I wish I could change things but I can't. Prolonging it won't make them better, so come on, say goodbye to the horse and we'll go and do something special together.'

Alice knew then that this was the finish. Struggling to hold her composure she said, 'It's all right Aunty Bea, I'll go to school.'

'That might be best, love.'

The hopeless finality was too much for Alice. Turning her head so that the men would not see the tears she could not stop from trickling down her cheeks, Alice stepped towards Sherry. For the last time she clasped her hands around the warm golden brown coat and pressed her cheek against her neck. Always sympathetic to Alice's moods Sherry bent her head as though to a foal and nibbled at Alice's hair. It seemed to Alice that life was made up of saying goodbye to those she loved. Sherry shifted her back legs and whickered softly.

'Oh Sherry, I can't bear to let you go,' whispered Alice. Bea laid a hand on Alice's shoulder, gently pulling her away from the horse. Alice brushed her hand swiftly across her eyes. Tears blurred her vision as, head held high, face averted from the company, she walked towards the truck. Bea knew that now was not the time to offer comfort.

The day had not been a success, despite both Bea's assumed jollity on the way to school and Alice's abortive efforts to concentrate on her lessons. Even Ben's attempts to comfort her had been unable to penetrate her numbness. Now, in the afternoon when she normally rejoiced, her steps dragged as she walked up to the paddock dreading to face its emptiness, yet wanting to spill out her grief where she and Sherry had known such happiness. Her misery turned to anger at the sight of a black-robed figure leaning against the gate whistling softly. She changed direction and jumped when Father O'Reilly spoke.

'I was thinking that somehow it wasn't right to let a pretty young lady like yourself grieve all on her own.'

'I'm all right, you needn't have worried,' Alice said politely, edging away.

'Well now, 'tis very glad I am to hear that and now are you going to tell me the truth?' At his words Alice whirled round, her bright accusing eyes more brilliant in her anger. Like a wounded bird, she flew at him.

'Well what did you do about it? Why didn't you stop him? You could have stopped him and you just let him take her. My Sherry. You let him take her. She was the last present my dad ever gave me, and you let him take her.'

Her body sagged and she covered her face with her hands as great racking sobs shook her shoulders.

Gently Father O'Reilly drew her to him and enveloped her in his black robes. After the first bout of sobbing had passed Father O'Reilly was relieved to see the fury return to her reddened eyes.

'He made it all up, Father, just so he could steal her from me. He's the thief, not my dad. I hope all his horses drop dead or run off with the brumbies or refuse to work for him ever again.' At her last damnation Father O'Reilly burst into loud laughter.

''Tis good to see your fighting spirit return, my girl, but I'm sure you don't mean what you say. You wouldn't be wanting young Sherry there to suffer, now would you?'

'No, of course not, Father, but I just can't bear the thought of her not being here any longer.' She took a deep breath. There was pain in her eyes as she said, 'I would have expected it from Uncle Ray, but even Aunty Bea let him take her.' She sniffed several times and wiped her hand across her nose. Father O'Reilly handed her a crumpled handkerchief. Twisting one corner between her fingers, Alice gave the priest a long stare.

'You knew something else about that man, didn't you?'

'Maybe I did and maybe I didn't. Some questions are best not asked. All you need to know is that your aunt and uncle are good people and the horse belonged to the man. It's as simple as that. Now blow your nose.' Alice blew her nose loudly and handed him back the handkerchief.

'I'll be all right now, thank you, Father,' she said, sniffing bravely.

Resting his gaze on her tear-blotched face, Father O'Reilly could believe her. The pain was still there but the worst was over.

'Don't be giving up hope now will you, young lady. The way our Lord works is often incomprehensible. If it was meant to be it was meant to be. Be strong now and remember, 'tis always darkest before the dawn and I'm thinking your aunt might be looking for a cuddle or two.' With those platitudes he led her firmly back to the house and the care of Aunty Bea.

Uncle Ray went to bed in a very bad temper.

'It tears me apart to see Alice's misery but I really don't think we can entirely blame Tommy this time,' said Bea trying to sound reasonable.

'Don't start making bloody excuses again, woman. Trust him to get muddled up in something like this.' Bea shut up like a clam. Ray lumped down into the bed pulling the covers angrily up around him leaving Bea with hardly any. The room bristled with tension. Just as Bea was convinced Ray must have dozed off he growled from under the sheet. 'D'you think I didn't see poor little Alice's face?'

'So what can we do about it?' Bea ventured hopefully. 'You know we can't afford to buy the horse back.'

'I'm working on it, woman. I'm working on it.'

Aunty Bea relaxed. Leaning across Ray's broad back she placed a kiss on his bristly cheek.

'Sometimes you can be a real softie,' she whispered, but he was already snoring.

A few days later Alice and Katie were woken by the sound of torrential rain beating down on the tin roof like a thousand jackhammers. The wind blew the rain in through the wooden slats soaking the girls in moments and forcing them to move into the main part of the house. They quickly dragged their things into the boys' room and attempted to finish the remainder of the night crushed together in the tiny space between the beds and the door, Katie grumbling and tossing and turning.

The rain lasted for almost three weeks and it seemed to Alice as though the sky were weeping for her. It also gave her something else to think about. Going to and from school became a game as she and Ben and her cousins splashed their way through the puddles. The gravel roads were only just passable. All other roads turned to thick heavy mud that clung to the wheels of vehicles and bogged down farm equipment. Properties were cut off and the party lines ran hot with reports of local flooding and calls for assistance. Uncle Ray, being the local agent for Ford and Massey Ferguson tractors, was suddenly very much in demand. The road to Walgett was open so equipment could get into Billabrin but from then on it had either to be taken out on horseback or flown out to more isolated properties.

When more rain was predicted the people of Billabrin started to get edgy. Then a creek south of Billabrin burst its banks flooding a couple of low lying properties, and it was decided to take the precaution of reinforcing the levee bank surrounding the town. Everyone worked feverishly around the clock. While the men filled and carted sandbags, Aunty Bea with Alice and Katie helped the women make sandwiches and cups of tea which Ben and the twins helped hand out. Buddy surprised them all by working alongside his father doing a man's work for twelve hours solid without complaint. For a while everyone in Billabrin held their breath.

By the Thursday of the third week the rain eased off. The swollen rivers subsided. The danger was past and the townsfolk relaxed. However, many of the roads were still impassable and there was spot flooding on some properties.

The next night, over the evening meal, an exhausted Uncle Ray, staring straight at Buddy, announced 'Well, one good thing's come out of it all, the boy's as strong as an ox. You could have knocked me over with a feather the way he just kept doing what he was told without getting in a muddle.'

Buddy beamed at the sudden unexpected praise.

'Now I can really set you to work in the store,' he wagged a finger at Buddy who grinned back proudly. Don thumped Buddy cheerfully on the back and he wriggled to escape. 'Got a call from Hal Tyson earlier today,' went on Ray taking a large mouthful of food. 'He's back up on his property. Needs a new gearbox for his tractor. His seized up in the wet.'

'He's the one that took Alice's horse, isn't he Dad?' announced Dan. Alice tightened the grip on her fork. Aunty Bea glared at Dan and Ben kicked him under the table.

'Nice bit of lamb,' continued Ray.

'A present for that job you did the other day,' said Aunty Bea, one eye on Alice.

'Might not be the only present if I get out there and fix up his gearbox quick smart.'

'Don't expect me to eat any lamb that comes for that mean, horrible old man,' spat Alice.

'You'll eat what you're given and be thankful,' snapped back Uncle Ray. His voice was back to normal as he spoke to Aunty Bea. 'Sounded in a rare panic. Can't get to some of his stock to drop the feed. Said I'd get over right away. Joker Hilton said he'd fly me out first thing tomorrow.' He looked knowingly at Bea. 'Told you I was working on it.'

Alice shoved her plate forwards and stood up. 'I'm not hungry any more,' she muttered.

'Sit down and finish your meal,' ordered Ray.

'I said I'm not hungry,' retorted Alice defiantly.

'Do what you're told,' barked Uncle Ray.

'I'm not your daughter, I don't have to,' stormed Alice and flung out of the room. Uncle Ray's face contorted with rage as he rose from his chair.

'Leave her be, love,' Aunty Bea said quietly. 'She's still pining for that horse.' Ray's anger suddenly subsided. 'She's a wilful girl.' He gulped down his tea in one movement.

'Working on what?' asked Katie inquisitively.

'Nothing you need worry your pretty little head over, my love.' Uncle Ray smiled at his daughter. Katie looked quizzically at Bea.

'I've no idea what he's talking about,' she replied quickly returning to the topic that had prompted Alice's fury. 'The Tysons' property's out towards Mrs Harper's place, isn't it?' She suppressed a sneeze. 'I promised to drop in on her this week. The dressing was due to come off one of her cats this week. The poor old soul's arthritis is so bad she can't manage very well by herself and she won't have a bar of vets. Funny old dear. The only two she'll let near her animals are Alice and myself. Would you mind stopping over so I can fix it? It'd only take ten minutes, Ray, enough to have a cuppa and then we could go on to your other jobs.'

'Her cats again, eh?' quizzed Uncle Ray. 'No worries.' However at breakfast the next morning, after one look at Bea, Ray changed his mind.

'You won't be flying anywhere, my good woman, except straight back to bed. You look terrible. Mrs H'll have to manage on her own.'

'I'll be all right. It's only a chill. I really feel I must go,' insisted Aunty Bea. She stood up and immediately sat down again as the room swam around her. 'Perhaps you're right,' she admitted sheepishly, shivering violently.

'Of course I am. You've got the flu. It's Saturday—Alice can come instead.' Alice who had still not recovered from last night's burst of temper, looked up across the table, her eyes flashing dangerously.

'I'm not going anywhere near that revolting man until he gives me back Sherry. Why can't Katie go instead?'

Uncle Ray lost his patience. 'All this over a bloody cat's dressing! You sort her out, Bea. This is just wasting time.' And he slammed out of the house.

'Come on, Alice, don't be trying,' said Aunty Bea tiredly, hugging her cardigan to her, struck by another bout of shivering. 'You know Katie doesn't have your expertise even if Mrs Harper would let her near the cat.'

'I'd faint at the sight of blood anyway,' added Katie triumphantly. Aunty Bea started coughing.

'Please don't ask me Aunty Bea,' implored Alice. 'I loved Sherry, and he took her from me.'

'I know, dear, and I wouldn't normally insist, but it's not the cat I'm worried about, it's Mrs Harper,' Bea answered, breathless from the coughing. 'She's a proud old lady who insists on living on her own when she really can't cope. Her own family won't have anything to do with her because she refuses to leave the property. I worry that something could happen to her at any time. The cat's just my excuse to visit her. A couple of the other ladies have offered to take turns but she'd smell a rat. Mrs Harper may be old but her mind's as sharp as a tack. But if you went it would just be part of the normal routine.' Bea sank back in the chair drained by the effort of explaining. Alice was immediately contrite. Bea was looking and sounding worse by the minute.

'I'm sorry, Aunty Bea. I'm being really mean. Of course I'll go. But I'm not setting foot on that man's property, even if all his sheep are drowning.'

By the time Alice had listened carefully to Aunty Bea's instructions about helping out Mrs Harper and had sorted out the correct medicines to take for the cat, she was secretly looking forward to the trip. Not only would this be the first time Aunt Bea had trusted her to deal with a situation entirely on her own but it would also be her first flying trip.

'And please try and get on with your uncle,' finished Aunty Bea weakly, trying to summon up the energy to move. Then to Bea and Alice's surprise Katie spoke up.

'Come on, Mum, I'll help you back into bed,' she offered. 'Then Buddy and I'll clear up while Florence Nightingale here clatters around the countryside.' She pulled a face at Alice.

'D'you know where everything goes?' provoked Alice in return. She kissed her aunt on the cheek. Clutching the medicine box, she flew out of the door, her mind already whirling at the prospect of her first flying experience.

Thirty minutes later, still furious with her uncle, but undeniably excited, Alice followed as Ray, having stopped the truck on the airstrip on Joker Hilton's property, stepped out beside the hanger.

Thirty years before, Joker's American father had arrived in Australia with a wad of thousand-dollar notes in his pocket, determined to 'do' Australia. After three months he had fallen irrevocably in love with both the country and the wreck of a single engine Cessna which he had rebuilt from scratch. Quickly he added to his collection. He had passed on his obsession to his eldest son Joker, now twenty-eight, who also operated an informal flying school. Together they owned a number of completely refurbished planes, including one which was on permanent loan to the Royal Flying Doctor service, a four-seater Cessna, which Ray and Alice would be flying in today, and some smaller two-seater planes used when giving flying lessons, not to mention the other wrecks that kept being added to the family collection. Joker's ambition was to set up his own local airline but he was still fighting red tape. However, in emergencies like these, his planes proved invaluable.

Joker was busy loading up the four-seater plane as Ray and Alice approached.

'G'day Ray,' he smiled. 'Looks like the weather's on our side.'

'G'day,' replied Ray. 'You've met my niece, Alice.'

Joker nodded at Alice. 'Pleased to meet you. This your first trip?' Alice nodded eagerly. Joker patted the side of the plane. 'Fuel's topped up and she's all checked out. Just get her loaded and we're away. What've you got to go in?'

'Tractor engine and spare parts and a couple of other bits and pieces I promised to drop in on the way back.' Joker signalled to another young man and together the three men heaved the gearbox into one of the rear seats and strapped it down tightly. After two more trips they were ready for takeoff. Uncle Ray sat in the back seat next to the gearbox, with Alice in the seat next to the pilot, her precious box stowed safely away.

'Looks like you're the spare pilot today, bright eyes,' laughed Joker. 'Your uncle looks pretty settled next to his precious gearbox.' Alice grinned across at Joker.

'Should be a pleasant flight over to Hal Tyson's place,' commented Joker casually over his shoulder as he started his pre-takeoff checks. 'With a mob of over twenty thousand sheep to look after and five hundred head of cattle, I'd be worried too with all this water, not to mention those horses that Hal brings up here from time to time.'

At the mention of Tyson's name Alice's rage resurfaced. Careless of the consequences she whirled round and flashed accusingly at her uncle, 'I meant what I said. I'm staying in the plane unless he promises to return Sherry.'

Ray's face darkened with embarrassment. 'I've had enough of your bad temper, Alice Ferguson. You're coming with me because your aunt's ill and you'll do what you're told. Not another word about that damned horse; now turn round and do up your belt.'

'Is Bea not well today?' inquired Joker solicitously. 'Sorry to hear that.' He leaned across and helped Alice adjust her safety belt so it fitted securely.

Furious at having walked into a reprimand in front of Joker and unwilling to admit that some of her anger was displaced nervousness both at the thought of flying and at having to face Hal Tyson, Alice crossed her arms and stuck her chin in her chest. But in seconds curiosity got the better of her as she examined her surroundings. As with all four-seater planes of this type there were dual controls. That meant that both in front of the pilot and on Alice's side there was a control column similar to a car steering wheel and, on the floor, left and right pedal controls that were also the brakes. The plane smelled not unpleasantly of grease and stock feed. Joker thoroughly checked all the instruments in the cockpit, finally tapping the altimeter. Unable to resist asking what he was doing, Alice laughed at Joker's reply.

'I thought for a while back there the smoke'd start pouring out of the top of your pretty head. It did seem an awful waste to be angry if this is your first flying trip.'

'It was nothing really,' Alice blushed.

'Good.' Joker flashed Alice a brilliant smile. 'Here we go.'

All thoughts of Hal Tyson vanished from Alice's mind as the engine roared and the propeller whirled into action. Then they were speeding down the tiny runway. Gently Joker eased the steering column back and with a final thrust the plane tipped its nose up to the clear cobalt sky and they were airborne. Alice gazed down in amazement at the houses now appearing like miniatures, the great white gums, dolls' toys you could clasp in the palm of your hand. Alice let her breath out in a rush, delight winning over nervousness as she tried to take in all the new sights, the roar of the engine making conversation almost impossible.

After a while Ray shouted over the noise. 'There's a gravel strip to the east close to Mrs Harper's property where we can put down fairly safely.'

'Sounds good,' shouted back Joker. 'ETA is close to seven-thirty a.m. At this rate we should make Hal's place by eleven-thirty.'

Alice watched in fascination as Joker radioed through to the two dest inations to report their estimated time of arrival and stared in wonder through the tiny little window next to her seat at the world below as the plane hummed its way through the sky.

The stop-off at Mrs Harper's was quick and trouble free. It took Alice no time to change the cat's dressing and do all the jobs Bea had requested. After a quick cup of tea, some homemade cake and promises to return when the roads were again passable, they were once more airborne. Alice felt herself tense up as the prospect of facing Hal Tyson grew nearer. Should she stick to her threat and refuse to budge from the plane, thereby creating a scene and infuriating Uncle Ray, or should she swallow her pride and admit defeat to this man she loathed? Then Joker did something quite unexpected that took her mind entirely off her troubles.

'It's your first time in a plane, right, Alice?' he shouted. Alice nodded.

'Well, nothing like jumping in at the deep end. What I want you to do is hold the steering column steady while I fill in my log book.'

'Me, fly the plane! You're not serious?' she shouted wide-eyed.

'Absolutely!' grinned Joker. 'She's all yours.' Hands sweating, heart thumping with nervous excitement, Alice clasped the steering column tightly, her eyes glued to the nose of the plane. Joker flicked a switch and, with one eye on Alice, took his hands off his own steering column and calmly reached for the log book. When the plane bumped as it hit a small air pocket, Alice instinctively pulled the steering column back sending the nose of the plane shooting upwards. Immediately Joker adjusted the steering column his side so the plane was once more steady.

'Hey, easy does it. You don't want us to go into a stall and fall out of the sky!' he laughed. The colour drained from Alice's face.

'Sorry,' she mouthed tensely.

Joker calmly put away his log book with his free hand and grinned cheekily at Alice. 'If you'd let her be, the autopilot would have corrected for you.'

'Oh.' Alice looked disappointed.

'You're doing fine, kiddo. Just relax. Remember, I have control of the plane at all times so just follow my instructions, and take smaller movements.' He flicked the autopilot switch. 'Now it's just you and me!'

As Joker talked her through the movements— nose up, nose down, banking to left and right—Alice gradually relaxed and began to get the feel of the plane moving under her fingers. Her legs were just too short to reach the pedals, but it didn't stop the exhilaration, a sensation she had not felt since her rides with Sherry. But it was a different exhilaration. There she was queen of the plains. Here she was empress of the skies. Joker broke into her thoughts.

'Autopilot's back on again. We can all have a rest.' Alice breathed freely for what seemed the first time in hours.

'She's not bad for a beginner, not bad at all,' Joker shouted over his shoulder. Ray's reply was lost over the engine noise. 'How did that feel, Alice?'

'Amazing!' exclaimed Alice, glowing with pleasure. 'Would you teach me how to fly?'

'Anytime, kiddo, anytime. Come back when your feet can reach the pedals,' laughed Joker, checking out of the side window.

'She most certainly will not,' chipped in Uncle Ray from the back as Joker lined up over Hal's property for the descent. 'You stick to women's work, Alice. Cooking and washing and looking after the menfolk is all you need to be bothered with, and doing what you're told.' But not even his reprimand could dampen Alice's sense of elation.

She was still feeling light-headed from her experience as the plane rapidly dropped altitude and bumped and slid its way to a final stop on the homemade airstrip in the paddock close to the homestead. Remembering her earlier threats, Ray barked for Alice to alight before she had time to argue. But Alice's mind was working again. The flight with Joker had sparked another thought. Out here on your own property you would need to be able to fly. She wondered why she hadn't thought of something so obvious before. She surprised Ray by getting out without protest and even gracing him with a smile. For the sake of a bit of pride she had no intention of putting off her flying instructor before her first proper lesson.

Hal's sunburned face was crinkled in a worried frown as he approached the group. Alice braced herself for the inevitable meeting but his two blue cattle dogs created just the diversion she needed. Taking one look at Alice they leapt off the truck and greeted her like an old friend, fawning over her and wagging their tails. Alice fussed gratefully over them, glad for the excuse to avoid Hal's gaze. She need not have worried, however, because Hal was far too concerned about his own situation. After nodding tersely at Alice and admonishing the dogs to behave like workers, not flamin' lap dogs, he greeted the two men.

'G'day, Joker, thanks for bringing this bloke over so quickly. Am I glad to see you, Ray. Tractor's bogged down in the second paddock, but if we're careful we can get the truck up there with the gear.'

'G'day, Hal. Certainly didn't expect to see you again so soon. Where's your manager?'

'He's off checking for strays with my son. We were hoping to start mustering two weeks ago which is a bloody joke. We've managed to move most of the stock to higher ground but the worry's getting the feed up to them. If we're really desperate we can still use some of the horses, but I'd rather not if we can avoid it. It'd be so much slower.'

'Serves you right, you mean old man,' muttered Alice viciously under her breath.

'At least we got the rams down into one of the home paddocks,' continued Hal as the three men heaved the gearbox into the truck. 'But even that wasn't absolutely safe. Had to move my best one again the day before yesterday because of the risk of flooding. Stubborn bloody animal, but brings me in a lot of money.'

'We'd best get on with it then, mate, 'stead of standing around like a bunch of old women,' growled Ray. 'It'll take us the best part of the day to fix the gear, that's if the problem's what I think it is. Alice, go up to the house and make yourself useful.'

'Tell the missus we'll be looking forward to a nice hot tea on the table when we get back, if she's still there,' added Hal. With those words the men got in the truck with the dogs and drove off.

Alice pulled a face at the receding truck. Hot tea on the table. Blow that. Was that all that was waiting for her when she grew up? That and washing and sewing. Not if she had any say it wasn't. Reluctantly she walked up to the house.

But to her delight Mrs Tyson was out and the house was spotlessly clean. The note on the table, which explained that the evening meal consisting of cold meat, bread and fruitcake was in the pantry, indicated that Mrs Tyson also had independent thoughts. Alice laughed out loud. That meant she had the whole of the afternoon to herself. Enough to find Sherry if she was still on the property. Quickly Alice ran out the back to look for the tackle shed. As she opened the second shed door a voice said behind her, 'There's no one here, only me, if you're looking,' Alice wheeled round to see a young Aboriginal girl with luminous dark eyes, whom Alice guessed was about the same age as herself.

'Who are you?'

'I come up to the house to help some days.'

'I'm Alice. You wouldn't know if there was a golden brown horse with a white nose called Flying Start up here at present, would you?'

The girl shook her head. 'I only help out sometimes when the boss' wife has to go visiting.'

'Oh,' said Alice. 'Well I've got a job to do too. So see you.'

Alice headed off to the next shed praying it would reveal what she was looking for. It did. On one wall was a selection of bridles, saddles and whips. Ignoring the saddle, Alice grabbed a bridle and headed confidently towards a group of horses grazing at the far end of the paddock, only to find herself sinking up to her ankles in mud halfway across. Returning she was relieved to find the girl had vanished. Donning a pair of overlarge gum boots she headed back towards the horses. The boots slowed her up but eventually she reached the group. Being good solid work horses they did not shy away from Alice and it wasn't long before she had managed to slip a bridle over one and swing herself on its back.

It felt wonderful to be on the back of a horse again but over the next two hours she saw no sign of Sherry. Despondently she returned to the paddock. Her legs ached from urging the horse along and her heels hurt from where the boots had rubbed, but most of all her heart hurt. Well at least she'd soon be out of this place. The men had said they'd be home before dark. She allowed the horse to meander across the paddocks on the high side of the homestead, letting it feed as it wished. Just as she had decided to turn back a large grey lump caught her attention in the lower corner of the paddock. For want of anything better to do she nudged the horse into a walk. As she crossed the paddock the grey lump became a full grown ram that seemed to be butting at the wire fencing, not naturally but strangely back and forth in short, tired bursts. Alice urged the horse forwards until she was close enough to see that the animal's head had got caught in one of the small squares in the tight wire fencing. The ram's big curling horns made it impossible for the animal to free itself.

'Oh, the poor thing,' muttered Alice as she slid quickly to the ground and tied the horse's reins to the fence.

In terror at the movement behind it, the exhausted ram once more pulled back from the fence, its horns repeatedly jamming against the small wire square. Gingerly Alice approached the rapidly tiring animal. Tossing up whether to rush back to the house and search for a pair of wire cutters or attempt to free the animal herself, she chose to try the latter.

'You got to shove the mongrel beast's head forwards before you can turn it to free it, then it should just slip through—that's if you can move the bugger,' she'd once heard a mate of Uncle Ray's explain to Ben, but this was a big ram and she was just a slip of a girl. Undaunted Alice sank her fingers into the thick wool folds around the ram's shoulders and pushed. Immediately the stressed animal pulled back, its eyes wide. For ten minutes Alice struggled but the beast was far too heavy and kept pulling back, jamming its horns each time against the tough wire fencing. When the ram was too exhausted to fight any longer it seemed to hang rather than stand. But even then the sheer weight of its head was too much for Alice to manipulate.

Realising she was getting nowhere, Alice made a quick decision. Praying that the animal would still be alive by the time she returned, she leaped on the horse's back and dug her heels into its sides. Wishing it would respond like Sherry she urged it as fast as she could back to the house. Charging into the tackle room her eyes scanned the gear for fence cutters. Not a pair in sight.

Forcing herself to calm down, Alice methodically searched the shed and finally found what she was looking for. She was back up on the horse urging it towards the paddock just as Hal and Ray drove up in the truck. Ignoring the angry cries, Alice forced the horse into an unwilling gallop. The ram was hanging horribly as she leaped to the ground, its tired eyes glazed with fear. Struggling against the weight of the great head Alice forced the punishing wire into the teeth of the cutters and pressed. To her relief the wire gave way. Two more snips and the ram was freed. Realising the pressure was gone from around its neck, the ram staggered off away from Alice. To her amazement, despite its terrible ordeal, it was grazing within moments as though nothing had happened. Alice sat back and laughed with relief. Then suddenly an angry shout brought her back to reality.

'What the bloody hell d'you think you're playing at, you stupid girl?'

Triumphant, Alice looked up into the accusing faces of Hal and Uncle Ray. 'I got him free. The silly fellow got his head stuck in the wire fencing and nearly killed himself, but no one would think it now.' Alice pointed to the ram still peacefully munching. The two men looked at the hole, at the little wisps of wool hanging from the cut strands and finally at the fence cutters in Alice's lap. Hal's next words died on his lips. Slowly his expression changed to wonder. His tone was entirely different when at last he spoke.

'That was a bit of quick thinking on your part. I guess I owe you one.' He smiled crookedly at Alice. The adrenalin rush was receding in Alice. She stood up slowly, the fence cutters in her hand and stared woodenly at Hal.

'That's quite all right, Mr Tyson. Maybe you should check your animals more often.'

'I guess I deserved that, you little minx,' Hal laughed harshly. 'What with the panic of getting the mob up on high ground, we didn't have time to check him yesterday. Must have got caught during the night.' His face split into a grin. 'You're quite a girl. You know you've just saved the life of my prize ram. He won three ribbons in the last two Easter Shows and I've got enough orders to fill a book for servicing.' He pointed to the animal. 'That's next year's earnings.' He stepped forward and patted Alice vigorously on the shoulders.

Alice remained unbending but she did not miss Ray's brief nod of approval as he started back towards the truck, nor the pride in his face.

'Hey, Ray, just before we go,' said Hal stepping back, 'there's something I want to say to your young niece and I don't think she'll believe me without a witness. Alice, look at me.' Alice's eyes were expressionless as she obeyed. 'I pride myself in being fair in my business dealings and in paying my debts. This rather changes things and, well . . .' He paused, looking slightly embarrassed. Removing the fence cutters from Alice's grasp he continued, 'If I were you I'd stick around at home for a while as I've decided to give you a horse.' As Alice's expression didn't change he added, 'Used to go by the name of Flying Start, got renamed recently by some stubborn individual with a mind of her own. Got some outlandish name Shehera . . . Sherry something. As soon as the roads are dry I'll personally see she's delivered back to Billabrin.'

Alice stared at Hal. Then she started laughing and the laughter turned to tears and then she just stood not knowing what to do. Finally she held out her hand to Hal. Shakily she replied, 'I reckon that's a pretty fair deal.'

As Hal returned her handshake he could feel his own eyes prick. It wasn't just what Ray had told him earlier, there was something about this girl that made you want to do things for her.

Chapter Nine

TRUE TO HIS WORD Hal Tyson delivered Sherry back to Alice. Alice was overjoyed. Grinning from ear to ear she led Sherry out of the horse-box and back up to the paddock while Ray and Hal headed down to the Shearer's Arms. However it was not only the return of Sherry that once more brightened Alice's life. It was Uncle Ray's obvious change of attitude towards her. Gone was the gruff, terse disinterest. Instead he was friendly and encouraging and in his own way boasted about her to his mates. Then Ben and Alice finally received a postcard from their father, saying he and Dotty were both well. 'Very busy with work but promise we'll be home very soon. Love you both,' it ended. Ben hugged Alice after they had read it together and she hugged him back, enveloped in a sudden feeling of futility. It had been over a year since her father had left for his 'holiday'.

Life was improving for Ray, too, and indirectly it was Alice's doing. In a further display of gratitude over the rescue of his best ram, Hal Tyson had placed a few words in the right ears with the result that Ray got offered a big contract from the area representative for Massey Ferguson tractors in Dubbo. As well as running the local hardware store, Ray had spent most of his life tinkering with motors of one sort or another. His skills as a mechanic were legendary. The agent quickly saw that if he brought Ray in on the deal he stood to sell far more tractors than he could ever have sold on his own.

Word travels fast in the bush and suddenly for the first time in their lives Bea and Ray had money in the bank. Aunty Bea's radiant smile was permanently glued to her face, despite the fact that Ray had to travel away from home more frequently. The boys all got new clothes, and Bea took Alice and Katie on a shopping spree to Dubbo.

'I love it, Aunty Bea! It's so pretty!' exclaimed Alice in delight, twirling round in her new skirt in the main street of Dubbo. Her figure was starting to fill out and the short-sleeved top accentuated the curves of her developing breasts. Katie, unable to hide her annoyance at her cousin's happiness and fully aware that her own breasts were already bigger than Alice's, purposely brushed too close to a couple of local boys and felt a lot better when they turned round and gave her a low wolf whistle.

Aunty Bea, slipping her hand firmly through Katie's arm, drew the girl to her. 'Where would you like to go for lunch, girls?'

'Somewhere terribly expensive, Mum, so that I can make all the girls at school horribly envious,' said Katie, 'that is unless Alice has to rush home and rescue another sheep. Only joking,' she added quickly seeing her mother's brief frown of annoyance. She hooked her free arm under Alice's in a token display of friendship.

'We're going to have to separate the girls, Ray,' said Bea rubbing her tired feet that night. 'Katie is so jealous of Alice, especially with Alice accompanying you on some of your trips, even though she's no interest in flying with you herself. The two rubbed each other up the wrong way all day. And I worry about Katie and the local boys. She was openly provocative today. Do you suppose we could afford to send her away to boarding school like we always dreamed of?'

'My little Katie live in the big smoke?' Ray sounded shocked.

'I thought about it all the way home, Ray. The girls are growing up. I think sending Katie to a good Catholic boarding school is just what she needs right now. I'm sure Alice would understand.' Bea sighed. 'If only Tommy had left some money for situations like these. But he hasn't, so that's that. Anyway, Alice's heart is set on flying and that would be out of the question if she went away,' Bea rationalised, 'and she wouldn't want to be parted from Ben either. She's too conscious of the promise she made her father. And Sherry for that matter. She loves the two of them more than anyone else in the world. Don't you agree, Ray?' Bea sat back in her chair and sipped her tea, satisfied that she had thought of all angles.

Ray pulled on his empty pipe for a while.

'If that's what you want, dear,' he said eventually, 'then I'm happy. My little girl was bound to turn into a young woman one day, and she's always been more interested in being a lady than mending a fence. The discipline won't do her any harm either.' He felt unsuccessfully in his pockets for his tobacco and gave up. Finally he smiled, his teeth gripping his empty pipe.

'You know, I reckon Alice'll end up a better pilot than the lot of us. She's a smart cookie that one. She watches me like a hawk on our trips together, can't wait to get her hands on the controls. We must have done ten trips by now and I've not been able to catch her out on a single question yet. Joker's really impressed with her too. Said he'd give her a couple of lessons and take her on as a pupil if she's still as keen at fifteen. I insisted that she pay her way but he'll help her, he's like that.'

'Well that's settled then. I won't mention anything to Katie or Alice until I've got everything sorted out.' Bea was relieved. 'That verandah's so squashed for them now they are growing up. It really is time we got them a bed each. Katie looks terribly washed out and tired and I'm sure I heard one of them padding about in the middle of the night a couple of times last week.'

Bea voiced her concerns about the girls' health again one evening a few days later as they were getting ready for bed.

'I'm gone as soon as my head hits the pillow,' laughed Alice.

'And you, Katie, are you sleeping properly?' Bea asked. 'You look very tense and those dark marks under your eyes worry me.'

'I'm okay, Mum,' Katie replied quickly. She shot Alice a menacing glare and climbed into bed trying to look relaxed. 'I've just been finding school work so hard lately.' She warmed to her subject. 'There's so much to do and it takes me such ages, and then when it's hot at night it's so hard to sleep.'

'I know, darling, but it's no good studying late into the night and then not being able to cope during the day, is it? Was it you padding about at about three o'clock the other night?'

Katie slid further under the covers. 'I was getting a drink.'

Bea patted her daughter on the shoulder and gave her a goodnight kiss, straightening the sheet around her shoulders. Katie smiled feebly and lay back against the pillows her eyes half closed. As soon as Bea had left the room Katie turned on Alice, her eyes flashing with malice.

'If you even think about letting Mum know I've been going out at night I'll let that stupid horse of yours out of its paddock,' she hissed.

'You dare!' hissed back Alice. 'As if I care what you do with your life. Anyhow, you'll get caught out and I hope it's soon.' With that she heaved the heap of Katie's clothes off her side of the bed and dumped them on the floor.

'Don't you threaten me, and don't touch my clothes,' Katie voice crescendoed.

'Shut up, idiot, or you'll have Aunty Bea straight back in here,' retorted Alice. Katie quickly arranged herself in an exhausted pose and lay listening anxiously. Alice got into bed and, giving the bedclothes a tug, tucked them tightly around herself and started to read her book.

'You wouldn't really tell, would you?' whispered Katie eventually. 'You can come too if you like.'

Choosing to ignore her cousin's plea, Alice lifted her head out of her book. 'Did you know that a good ram can produce enough stuff to make over a thousand lambs?'

'Ugh, you're disgusting,' groaned Katie, and rolled over.

Alice rode home, elation from her first flying lesson with Joker making her oblivious to the heat. She had managed to persuade him to start teaching her as soon as she could pay for the lessons and she could still hear the roar of the engines as they taxied down the runway, and feel the surge of the plane and accompanying flutter of excitement in the pit of her stomach as the nose tipped upwards and they were airborne. Although she had felt those sensations many times when travelling with Uncle Ray, this time it was different. This time she was not just a passenger she was a pupil and when the plane flattened out from its ascent she had been allowed to take the controls and fly the plane herself under Joker's instruction.

Katie would be leaving to attend St Vincent's College in Sydney soon. Bea had been almost apologetic when she told the girls but Alice was secretly relieved not to be parted from Bea or Sherry and for at least part of the time to be able to escape Katie's jealousy. Besides, it meant she could carry on flying.

Thinking of the money she had saved up for three more lessons, Alice sauntered jauntily back up to the house, slowing down at the sound of Katie's shrill cries. The next minute Katie burst through the kitchen door, tears of rage streaming down her face, slamming it shut behind her so the whole house shook. Quickly Alice stepped back into the shadows wondering what had been going on and then stepped cautiously into the kitchen. Bea, who was chopping onions furiously, looked up sharply as she entered.

'Were you involved in these midnight jaunts too?' she demanded, white with anger. Alice stared at her feet.

'Well, Alice. Did you sneak out too to meet some of the local boys after Ray and I were safely asleep?'

Alice's cheeks burned with misery, torn between wanting to keep her aunt's trust and dobbing in her cousin.

'Come on, Alice, I know all about what's been going on, so tell me the truth. Next thing I know one of you girls will get yourselves into real trouble.'

'No, I didn't,' replied Alice finally, unable to lie to her aunt. 'By the end of the day I'm so tired all I want to do is sleep.' Bea wiped her face with her apron. Alice felt like a traitor.

'But you knew?' Bea persisted fanning herself in the heat.

Alice nodded reluctantly. 'Why didn't you tell me?' Bea looked at Alice closely. 'On second thoughts, don't answer that.' She shooed Alice out of the kitchen to get ready for the evening meal. Deciding it would be better to risk Bea's wrath at being late for dinner than to face a raging Katie, Alice grabbed a couple of apples and a brush and ran back up the paddock to Sherry. Happily absorbed in brushing down Sherry while she peacefully munched away, Alice jumped at her cousin's touch.

'You told her, didn't you?' spat Katie in her ear. Whirling round Alice stared into eyes dark with hatred. 'I knew I couldn't trust you to keep a secret, you mean tittle-tattle.' Sherry backed up.

'Whoa there, girl. No I did not. She found out herself,' retaliated Alice, trying to settle the horse down. 'Anyway, serves you right. I told you you'd get caught. Move over.' She gave Katie a shove and continued to rub down Sherry's gleaming flanks. 'What happened?'

'Don't shove me,' snapped Katie. 'Mum caught me and Frank kissing outside at two in the morning. Then she yelled at me. I'm grounded till I go away.' It had been more than just kissing but she wasn't about to tell Alice. Disappointment and humiliation at being caught semiclothed and the tongue-lashing her mother had given her fanned the flames of her bitterness towards Alice.

'You've ruined everything. Now going away to school will be awful,' Katie went on. 'Mum'll get into the nuns' ears and it'll be worse than being in prison. I'll be the most hated person in the school. I won't have any friends and it's all your fault.' Katie started to sob. 'I was so looking forward to going to St Vincent's and now you've spoilt it all.'

'It won't be like that, Katie,' said Alice, feeling a sudden pity for her cousin. 'This'll all blow over before you go away. Aunty Bea loves you, she's not going to make your life miserable. She was petrified one of us might get pregnant.' Katie shook her off, her mouth twisted in spite.

'So you've been sucking up to Mum again, you little sneak. Well, you may have wrecked my life at school but I'm still the eldest one here and I'm still Daddy's favourite, and don't you forget it. I may be going away but don't ever think you can take my place.'

Any pity Alice might have felt evaporated forever.

'I don't sneak, and I don't steal,' she said very quietly. The two girls faced one another, each gripped with her own fury. Katie broke the silence, her voice shaking when she spoke.

'That's what you say. As for me, this, my sweet innocent little cousin, means war.' Giving Sherry a vicious slap on the rump she spun on her heel and strode back towards the house leaving Alice trembling with suppressed anger.

Alice went back to grooming Sherry until she felt more in command of her emotions, then she returned to the house to clean up for tea. Alone in the bedroom something made Alice reach under the pillow and check the tin where she kept her precious savings. It had been hard earned and she was relieved to find it was all there. Katie had watched her count it last night, jeering at her for saving for such an unfeminine activity as learning to fly, which had precipitated yet another fight. Carefully she recounted the money then withdrew half of it and hid it in the drawer amongst her underclothes.

Bea was rather subdued at dinner that night but, to both girls' relief, she made no reference either to her fight with Katie or her conversation with Alice.

Ray, however, beamed proudly across at Alice. 'Are you going to tell us how you went on your first lesson, girl?' he demanded. 'It's like Central Station round here, what with you learning to fly and Katie off to the big smoke to learn to be a lady in a few weeks. It's all pretty exciting, don't you reckon Katie?'

White faced, Katie forced herself to smile, mumbled incoherently, then to everyone's surprise, promptly burst into tears and fled from the room leaving a stunned silence.

'Oh dear,' said Aunty Bea quietly, rising from her chair and following her out.

Katie was lying face down on her bed sobbing into the pillow.

'Are you ready to talk to me in a more civilised manner, Katie?' Katie's sobs grew louder. Aunty Bea put her hand on Katie's shoulder.

'Come on, sweetie, we have to clear all this up and you know it. Sit up and let's get it all over and done with.'

'I didn't mean to be so horrid to you, Mum,' Katie cried, sitting up and throwing herself into her mother's arms.

'I'm sure you didn't, but you know what you did was wrong, don't you?' said Bea stroking her gently. Katie nodded, her sobs muffled against Bea's shoulder. Gradually she subsided into hiccups and sat up, her blonde hair falling in a tangle around her tear-stained face. Gently Bea reached over and felt Katie's forehead.

'Come on, you'll make yourself ill if you keep this up. How about you blow your nose and we have a little chat.' Katie sniffed, unwilling to meet her mother's anxious gaze.

'I know I shouldn't have gone out, but it isn't just about Frank and getting into trouble and all that,' she mumbled.

'Oh?' asked Bea, wondering what else was to come.

'You'll just think me stupid if I say it.'

'Tell me anyway, darling. If it's making you this upset it's better out in the open.'

'It's . . . Oh, it's everything, this room, Alice, me.' Katie stopped suddenly and stared at her mother. Bea waited. Finally she blurted out, 'And now you're sending me away. Why don't you and Daddy love me any more?' She covered her face with her hands, rocking backwards and forwards in misery.

'Oh darling, what are you talking about? Of course we love you. We love you so much we want you to have the best we can give. That's why we're sending you to school in Sydney.' She pulled her daughter to her and hugged her, rocking her in her arms like a small child until Katie calmed down. 'You'll love it at St Vincent's. It's a good school. You can learn to be a lady just like you've always wanted, and you'll make new friends.'

'But Alice will have you all to herself,' Katie said in a small voice.

Bea pushed her daughter gently away from her and looked her in the eye. 'I think it's time you and I had a good long talk. Why don't I brush your hair while we're talking?'

'Oh Mum, you haven't done that to me since I was a little girl,' cried Katie, falling back into her mother's arms.

'Shall I serve up dessert, Aunty Bea?' asked Alice solicitously from the doorway.

'Would you, Alice dear?' said Bea, her arm around Katie. 'Tell Ray we'll be out shortly.' She turned back to Katie. 'Now where's your hairbrush?'

In the instant before Katie handed her mother the hairbrush, the two girls locked glances, and Alice could not deny the obvious triumph in her cousin's eyes.

'She's just got a case of the nervous nellies,' said Ray when Bea explained the problem later that evening. 'But we're doing the right thing sending her off to the nuns. Any more late night adventures and goodness knows what trouble the girl'd have got herself in. I don't like to admit it but Alice seems to have a great deal more sense than our own daughter.'

'I wish I could disagree with you,' said Bea, a note of sadness in her voice. 'You don't suppose we've caused all this by giving Ben and Alice too much attention, do you? Sometimes I think Alice and Ben are so much easier to deal with than our own. You don't suppose we are making a mistake—not that we really have a choice. I wish Tommy'd show some interest in his kids.' Bea gave a long sigh. 'I think I finally convinced Katie we're not sending her away to punish her.'

Ray continued to suck on his pipe, his expression unreadable, the clouds of blue smoke floating gently above him. Finally he took his pipe out of his mouth.

'You worry too much, luv. Katie'll be all right. She'll love playing the little lady in Sydney and we'll both feel a lot happier knowing she's out of harm's way at St Vincent's.' He relapsed once more into silence.

'I think I'll go and make another cup of tea,' said Bea, still deep in thought.

But Ray was right about Katie. Within a few days she had cheered up, and took great delight in ramming all the benefits of going away to school down Alice's throat. To Alice's confusion she also made an effort to be pleasant and apologised for her earlier reference to Alice's place in the family. Alice did not feel like being nice to her cousin at all but she was anxious not to upset Aunty Bea, who was harassed enough over Katie's imminent departure, so she swallowed her own resentment and attempted to get involved with some of Katie's activities. Rather unwillingly she agreed to lend Katie some money to make up the difference for a present for Ben and the twins on a last-minute trip into Walgett.

'Mum said I could borrow the other ten shillings out of the milk money jar as long as I replaced it, but you're not supposed to know,' Katie whispered to Alice as she asked her advice over the presents. The whole Downing household knew that you never touched the milk money jar without Aunty Bea's permission. 'I'll give you back your money before your next flying lesson. Just remind me to collect my last lot of pay from the bakery. I keep forgetting.'

The day before Katie was due to leave for her new school, Bea walked into the kitchen to find Alice replacing the lid of the milk money jar.

'What are you doing, Alice?' Bea's voice was quietly controlled. Alice jumped and turned round quickly.

'Oh, you gave me a fright,' she replied, recovering. 'Putting back the ten shillings you lent Katie for the boys' presents.' Alice laughed across at her aunt. 'I know I'm not supposed to know. It's all right, I won't start helping myself, Aunty Bea.'

'The ten shillings I lent Katie?' repeated Aunty Bea unsmiling. Alice's smile faded.

'Katie,' Alice said relieved as her cousin walked in, 'tell Aunty Bea you just asked me to return the money because you were too busy packing.'

Katie stared boldly at her cousin, her eyes wide with surprise. 'I don't know what you're talking about.'

'Don't be silly, Katie, you asked me to return it only a few moments ago.'

'Is this true, Katie?'

'That's one rule I've never tried to break, Mum,' Katie replied, looking innocently at her mother. 'Anyway, why should I want to? I got paid from the bakery and Dad gave me some going away money before we went shopping, so I had plenty.' Katie shifted her gaze back to Alice. 'You told me you needed a bit more to pay for your flying lesson last week, but you never told me you were helping yourself from Mum's milk money.'

Alice's stomach knotted as the truth slowly dawned. How could she have been so stupid as to fall for such an obvious trick? Rage boiled up inside her. She wanted to wipe the fat smirk off Katie's face.

'Alice.' The coldness in Aunty Bea's voice sent a shiver down her spine. 'You were putting the money back, weren't you?' Colour flooded Alice's face.

'I was putting it back for Katie, you know I was.' The girls glared at one another. Aunty Bea shook her head.

'Come on, Alice, this is so unlike you. Katie, are you sure you didn't borrow the money?' Katie's face crumpled and she started to cry.

'See, it's always the same. You always side with Alice. Congratulations, Alice, see what you've done. You all want me out of the way, that's why you're sending me to Sydney. You just want to forget me so that darling little Alice can have all the attention. It's always been like that ever since she and Ben came here.'

'Darling, we've been through all of this before,' Bea said quickly, filled with guilt. 'You know that is quite untrue. I realise the last few days have all been a bit of a strain for you, what with everyone rushing around trying to get organised, but I really am too tired for all this. Please, Alice, if you are that desperate for money, ask me next time. Now we have to finish your packing.' Bea turned and walked out of the room. Katie mouthed one word: 'War' before following her mother.

Suddenly the rage Alice had felt dissolved into fear. She started to shake as she raced outside towards Sherry's paddock only to halt in breathless relief at the sight of her horse peacefully grazing, the gate securely closed. Thank goodness there was only one day to go.

The departure day dawned hot and oppressive, promising storms later. After going through the motions of kissing her cousin goodbye and watching the truck leave for the station with Ray driving an excited Katie and Bea, Alice turned her eyes to the sky with a great sigh of relief and held her arms up to the overdeveloping clouds. At least for the next few weeks she could live her life in peace, and have the whole bed to herself. Somehow she would find a way to repair the damage Katie had caused between herself and Aunty Bea. Ben came up behind her.

'I know you didn't take the money, sis, I walked in as Katie was helping herself.' Alice swivelled around abruptly. 'When she saw me she just laughed and waved the note in my face.'

'Why didn't you say something?'

'And have Katie call me a liar too? Wake up, sis. We've got a home and Aunty Bea and Uncle Ray love us, but they're still not Mum and Dad.' He shoved his hands in his pockets. 'D'you think Dad's ever coming home?' he asked abruptly, taking Alice by surprise. At his words unwanted tears sprang to Alice's eyes. Carefully she wiped them away as though removing specks of dust.

'I dunno, Ben,' she said seeing the flicker of hope in Ben's eyes die. Suddenly her world felt terribly empty. 'Tell you what, howabout you and I buy him a really nice present and send it to him?' She had enough money saved to pay for her next flying lesson with a little over. After five minutes of discussion Ben wandered off looking more cheerful.

Suddenly she needed to see that money. Leaping up, she ran back to the verandah and frantically felt in her underclothes for the little bundle. It was gone. Dismayed, she reached under the mattress and pulled out the tin. It was empty except for a carefully folded scrap of paper. Tears of frustration blinded Alice as she unfolded the note. Finally she read the words: 'Thanks for the extra cash. Happy flying. K. D.' Today's date was written under Katie's initials. Scrunching the note into a tiny ball she hurled it as hard as she could across the room. Then, clasping her hands around her head she pressed her face soundlessly into the bed.

After a while her rage subsided and she raised her head. Swallowing hard, she retrieved the crumpled paper, smoothed it carefully, put it in the tin and replaced the tin under the mattress. She would just have to work a bit harder and wait a bit longer for her next flying lesson, but her dad's present would have to wait, and she hated the thought of disappointing Ben.

'Katie Downing,' she said aloud, 'neither you nor anyone else can take away my love of this place, or destroy what I already have. While you're learning to be a lady—if that's possible—I'll be reaching closer to my dream.' Her heart was once more steady as she walked slowly down the verandah steps to the rumble of distant thunder.

Chapter Ten

WITH KATIE AWAY at school the tension in the Downing household dropped dramatically. Alice's obvious happiness was enough to convince Aunty Bea that she had done the right thing keeping the girls apart. Alice took over Katie's job at the local bakery and, with the help of her other odd jobs, slowly replaced the stolen money. She managed to stretch to one flying lesson every three to four weeks and continued to learn all she could about looking after and breeding animals. When she wasn't working or at school she contentedly rode Sherry out across the plains and drank in the beauty of the land she loved. Yet part of her chafed against the memory of the men's averted eyes and shuffling feet, when, on her travels with Ray, she asked what to look for when buying good rams and breeding sheep. Aunty Bea's explanation that men felt embarrased discussing things like that in front of a woman only served to frustrate Alice further.

With Katie's return home for the holidays came the tension but only for short bursts. Far more interested in impressing everyone with her newly learned graces and spending time with her new school friends, mostly children of wealthy property owners, Katie spent most of her holidays staying on their properties. Alice hated the look of defeat that came over Aunty Bea when Katie complained their house was small and pokey compared with those of her friends, completely overlooking the struggle that Ray and Bea had had to afford to give Katie a good education. When Katie did deign to invite her friends home Alice was not in a hurry to intrude in the friendship and the two cousins, while outwardly courteous, kept their distance. During those times Alice felt Aunty Bea push her away not wanting to show too much affection for her niece for fear of resurrecting Katie's thinly disguised jealousy. Alice was always relieved when term resumed and she returned again to the close comfortable relationship she had developed with her aunt and uncle.

When Billy and Paddy returned from Wangianna, it was a different story. The three of them joked and laughed together as they had when they were kids. But then sometimes she caught Billy looking at her with an expression she could not quite read and she suddenly became shy and unusually aware of her own body. Then he would break the tension by picking her up and whirling her effortlessly around as he had when she was younger.

'See, kiddo, you're not too old that I can't still protect my little cousin.' Planting a kiss on her cheek and patting her like a young pup, he headed up to the pub with Paddy.

One hot evening at the end of the Christmas break when Alice was fifteen and a half, she and Billy escaped from Katie's teasing and strolled along the levee bank together. The frogs croaked and the crickets chirped in the dimming light. It was these moments in Alice's life that she cherished. She felt so safe and secure with Billy. Yet unaccountably her heart skipped a beat as Billy casually slipped his hand around hers. She looked up at him in surprise, pushing away the silly thoughts that raced through her head, but he simply smiled back at her the open warm smile she had always known. Common sense reminded her that he was merely indulging his baby cousin, yet tonight his proximity stirred new and disturbing emotions inside her. Together they walked on in silence towards the dry riverbed, Alice not sure whether to leave her hand where it was or withdraw it. In the shadow of the tall pylons of the big bridge Billy stopped. Gently he slipped his arm around Alice's waist and they stood surrounded by the sounds of the bush.

'When I'm feeling homesick at Wangianna I think of this place. Listen to the wind talking in the trees,' Billy murmured as he stroked her hair gently. 'Remember the day I met you when your hair was cut like a boy's? You looked such a mess.' Alice held her breath, not wanting to break the magic of the moment, convinced that he must hear the pounding of her heart. Quite naturally he pulled her to him so that she could feel the heat of his lean hard body burning against her own.

'Do you know how beautiful you've become, little Alice?' Spellbound Alice could not speak, her blue eyes enormous in her heart-shaped face. Automatically she obeyed the pressure of his finger that tilted her head upwards. A shiver ran through her as his lips lightly brushed her own, her pulse deafening in her ears.

'I like coming home when you're here, little Alice,' whispered Billy. Drawing back he stroked her cheek with one finger. 'And you have the softest skin, little coz.' Alice could not make sense of the words that tumbled from her lips still burning where his mouth had grazed them for so fleeting a moment. She pulled away, feeling uncomfortable more at her own reaction than at his unaccustomed behaviour, then suddenly Paddy's voice broke the tension.

'You coming up the pub or not?' he called, emerging from the dimness.

'I'll just see Alice back home,' replied Billy far more calmly than either of them felt. 'C'mon, kid, or Mum'll start fretting.'

With a jolt she was back to reality and safety. She was just a kid. Yet she had seen something deeper in Billy's eyes and she had felt the first awakenings of desire in herself. That night as she lay in bed running her fingers over her lips, remembering the touch of his lips against hers and the confusing emotions their softness had stirred, she went over the whole incident coldly and rationally. It had been nothing more than a cousinly kiss. If she hadn't turned her head his lips would have landed on her cheek. Yet the look she had seen in his eyes had destroyed forever the safe childish intimacy they had enjoyed for so long. When he and Paddy returned to Wangianna she experienced a confused mixture of sadness and relief.

The annual picnic races held at Come-by-Chance in July were the high point of the social calendar and country folk travelled hundreds of miles to attend. After the unrelenting year-round demands of working a property, the relaxation and fun of the races came as a welcome break. Everyone prepared for the races weeks beforehand and each year the attendance grew. This year was the highest on record. Ray always had a bet on the races and this year he was determined to win on at least one, so Bea listened diligently to the galah sessions in the weeks building up to the races to learn amongst the regular chatter who might be the favourite mounts and jockeys, passing any tips on to Ray. The day arrived to set out for the races. No one complained on the long bumpy ride across dusty tracks riddled with potholes, even when they blew a tyre, nor that their journey was further slowed down by dragging Sherry's loosebox behind the truck. When they finally arrived, all dusty and thirsty, Alice tumbled out as eagerly as the boys.

The bush racecourse was a hive of industry. Men from surrounding properties were busy marking out the racetrack and rebuilding the bough sheds for members' stand and bars; while others were erecting makeshift toilets surrounded by whitewashed hessian walls and setting up camp. Everyone was shouting greetings and some had even already got stuck into the grog. Alice hobbled Sherry and then helped Bea unload the tucker boxes at their campsite by the creek, while the boys cut fresh leafy branches and spinifex to lay across the roof of last year's bough shed. The rough frame made from thick branches appeared as sturdy as when they had erected it, the shade it provided essential for their comfort. Ray went off to help the men and Bea organised the campsite. Alice and Buddy unloaded the suitcases and the twins set up beds, then Dan got the billy going for the first of many cups of tea. In a spare moment Alice hung up Bea's new dress made specially for the ball that took place at the end of the week. Halfway through the afternoon Billy and Paddy rolled up and there were hugs all round. Katie was the only one missing—Bea and Ray had agreed that with all the handsome ringers on the loose, it was best she remain this year at school in Sydney.

At sundown Father O'Reilly held a church service and married two couples and christened four babies; then the women handed round magnificent cakes and pots of tea for supper. As Alice and Bea brought out their cake a great roar went up announcing the arrival of the booze truck. Then everyone pitched in to roll out the beer barrels. When finally laid out the line of barrels was nearly as long as the racetrack itself from truck to bough-shed bar. Everyone finally fell into bed tired but happy. The next day Alice helped Bea cook endless slabs of steak and peel miles of potatoes. She didn't care that her back was aching and her eyes were permanently smarting from the smoke from the barbecue and that she had twice burned her fingers on the billy. To Alice the races were pure magic.

On the third day of races, Alice tucked the strands of her unruly black hair firmly under the big bushman's hat with slightly unsteady hands, while Ben held Sherry's reins. She wondered if this time she had finally gone too far entering herself in the men's under-twenty-fives race. Several weeks earlier she had been bodily removed from a shearing shed, and prior to that had been caught trying to sneak into a ram sale—Uncle Ray had not been at all pleased. Determinedly she tucked the shirt Ben had scrounged from a friend into her jeans and tightened the belt around her waist, her mouth set in a determined line. A woman's place! If they didn't keep on going on about a woman's place maybe she would never have been goaded into taking on the bet. Ben, too, was having second thoughts.

'This isn't such a good idea, Alice. The blokes are all nearly twice your size and half of them have been full since they got here.'

'You can't run out on me now, Ben,' said Alice between gritted teeth. 'Anyway it's too late. Larry's put my name down. If the blokes are full maybe they'll ride in the wrong direction.' She laughed with more confidence than she felt and adjusted Sherry's girth for the third time.

'I know someone's going to recognise Sherry. Are you sure about Uncle Ray and Aunty Bea?'

'Stop panicking, Ben! You're making me even more nervous,' Alice hissed over her shoulder. 'Aunty Bea's entering the Fashion on the Field competition along with all the other mums so that'll keep her busy for most of the day and you heard Uncle Ray say he was determined to win the hay-bale pole-vaulting this year. After that he'll go down the bar tent as usual, complaining about his thirst. They won't be bothered with this race.'

'It's not going to work,' nagged Ben. 'If you win they're going to find out who you are anyhow, and then we'll both be in a heap of trouble.'

'I don't care. I just want to win to show them,' retorted Alice defiantly, hitching her foot into the stirrup and jumping smartly onto Sherry's back. Seeing the anxiety in Ben's face she added, 'We'll be right, Ben. I'll think of something when we win!' She patted Sherry's neck and glanced towards the racetrack where the contestants for the race were starting to line up. As she had hoped it was friendly pandemonium with no one really in charge and everyone shouting at one another. Sensing Alice's agitation Sherry skittered sideways.

'Steady there, old girl,' said Alice, reining Sherry in tightly. 'I'll give it a few more seconds and nip in just as they start.' Pulling her big bushman's hat more firmly over her face she tightened the string securely around her neck. 'Wish me luck, Ben.'

'Go get em, sis.' Ben shoved his hands deep into his pockets, fingers crossed, as Alice urged a nervous Sherry quickly through the throng towards the starting point.

At the last minute, head down, Alice spurred Sherry forward and got into position just as the starting gun went off. Eyeing off her nearest contestant Sherry leaped forward on Alice's command and charged down the racetrack with the others, the choking ochre dust rising around them. Quickly horse and rider left the immediate chaos of the more inebriated riders and Alice realised she was neck and neck with the first six contenders. The adrenalin surged in her blood as they thundered down the track. Her face well shielded by the big hat, her whole mind focused on the finishing line, she eased forwards into fifth place. As they hurtled past the halfway mark her nearest rival almost knocked into Sherry who swerved violently. Steadying the horse, Alice charged on amidst the deafening pounding of hooves and yells of the onlookers.

Almost horizontal across Sherry's neck, her bottom raised from the saddle, Alice urged Sherry on. Feeling the tension in her mistress, Sherry responded. As the gap between her and the winning post closed, Sherry edged past horse number four and then past number three. Damn it, but she was in second place. If Sherry could just keep the momentum she could even win. Alice's whole being was concentrated on the space between Sherry and the straining and snorting black horse in front. Gradually the gap closed. Now the two were neck and neck. By now a large crowd had formed and roared its encouragement as the two horses hurtled towards the finishing line. Standing straight in the stirrups, Alice willed Sherry to find that extra edge. A shout went up as horse and rider flew past the finish, half a head in front of the big black horse. Alice could hardly breathe with excitement. She had done it. She had won. Reining Sherry in, she collapsed across the animal's shoulders, wondering who was sweating more, she or the horse.

'That was a great race, lad,' said a voice. 'I always knew that horse was a goer. How did you persuade young Alice to let you ride her?' Suddenly sober, Alice looked down and stared into the eyes of Hal Tyson. At the same time a gust of wind caught her hat and spun it carelessly across the dirt. Too late Alice's hand flew to her head as the last bobby pin slid from her jet black hair letting it tumble freely around her shoulders. Hal's eyes opened wide in astonishment.

'Well, I'll be blowed. You're a damned good rider, you cheeky minx. You know you'll be disqualified of course?' he added as one of the judges forced his way through the crush around Alice, words of congratulations dying on his lips.

'I don't know what got into you, girl, doing a thing like that,' roared Ray at Alice as he shot the bolt home on Sherry's loosebox. 'Don't you ever learn?'

Alice listened politely, determined not to get upset as Uncle Ray pointed out the extent of her misdemeanour. While she had expected to cause a stir, she had not realised the amount of disapproval her actions would arouse nor the sting in some of the shocked rebukes she would receive from others at the races. Furious at the shame he felt Alice had brought on the family, ignoring Bea's quiet aside that he might be overreacting, Ray made the family pack up then and there so they not only missed the rest of the holiday, they missed the ball and Bea's chance to wear her new dress. For that Alice felt really bad. Only the memory of the exultation she had felt at winning kept her from dissolving into tears throughout Uncle Ray's long tirade and the frostily silent journey back to Billabrin.

She had beaten the lot of them fair and square. Even the disqualification announced over the loudhailer was in itself a sort of recognition. At least Ben had got off relatively lightly, Alice having insisted on playing his part in the idea down. Ben squeezed her hand surreptitiously and the twins kept their eyes lowered for fear of showing their admiration. Buddy lay back asleep mouth open.

It was when they pulled up at the house and Ray announced that she was indefinitely grounded from flying that her defences finally crumbled. Aunty Bea's comment was the final icing on the cake.

'Alice dear, you have to realise that there are rules that you just don't break,' she said trying to smooth things over. She was disappointed but there would be other annual picnics. The relationship between Ray and Alice concerned her more. She sighed. It felt like a physical blow to Alice. 'We have our place, Alice and the men theirs. That's the way it is. If you risk breaking the rules you must bear the consequences.'

'But it has nothing to do with flying, Uncle Ray,' Alice pleaded, her bottom lip trembling dangerously.

'You've embarrassed your aunt and got the whole district talking. Maybe this will teach you how to behave.'

It took Alice three months of solid hard work and coaxing before Ray finally relented and allowed her to fly again. For that she knew she had Joker to thank in part. Her biggest disappointment was that she had planned to do her first solo flight on her sixteenth birthday, just six weeks after the races.

Chapter Eleven

ALICE CANTERED TOWARDS Joker's property, her stomach fluttering with anticipation. Despite the unexpectedly chilly April morning she was already sweating, and her hands gripped the reins unusually tightly. The last few months had been the longest in her life. Even when she had once more been allowed to fly, so many other obstacles had got in her way, but today, finally, she was going solo.

Shifting her hip on Sherry's back she rechecked that her log book was still safely in her jeans pocket and then patted her breast pocket for the umpteenth time feeling the reassuring crinkle of the well-thumbed note. Funny old Ben. In the last two years they had once more grown closer. Ben was such a mixture. One moment he was yahooing with the twins, the next minute he was serious and thoughtful and writing poems. She could hardly believe he would be fourteen next birthday. She smiled at how surprised she had been when, on an impulse, she had shared her dream with him and instead of scoffing as she had feared, he had looked at her with quiet admiration. A few days later she had found the note on her pillow with the tiny bunch of cream straw flowers. She had laughed through her tears as she read his clumsy attempt.

Roses are Red
Violets are Blue
Don't grow up too quick, sis, 'cos
I want to be part of your palace dream too.
PS. Sorry the rhyme went a bit wrong at the end. love Ben.

The poem had become her good luck charm. Today she hoped it would prove so again. She could see the waiting Cessna gleaming in the early morning sunlight on Joker's runway, ready to take her on her first solo flight. Quickly horse and girl covered the remaining distance. Slipping down from Sherry's silky back, Alice turned her out into her usual paddock.

'Wish me luck,' she whispered. Sherry snorted in reply as Alice ran towards the hangar where her instructor was waiting, her hands busy trying to recapture her unruly black hair that had escaped from its elastic band. A lone crow hung in the air above.

'Ready to go solo?' greeted her instructor. Alice grinned broadly.

After going through the necessary ground drill and listening to her final flight instructions, Alice boarded the plane. She had expected to feel more nervous or at least excited, instead she found herself settling calmly into a routine that she had followed countless times before, effortlessly remembering all the actions, her body reacting as though she had been born in the cockpit of a small plane. The takeoff was near perfect. As she completed the circuit around the airfield she might have been having another lesson. She guessed the three other dots that had appeared near the hanger were Joker and the other three instructors. Only after the required time when she came in to land did it register what she had done; momentarily she lost concentration and the right wing tip suddenly lifted in an unexpected pocket of air. In a split second her concentration was refocused. Like a record played a thousand times in her head, she heard her instructor's voice talking her through the procedure.

The landing was not the smoothest she had ever done and as she taxied towards the hangar the sudden release of tension set her whole body quivering. Halting the plane almost at Joker's feet, she snapped off her safety harness, opened the door and leaped out onto the tarmac. She had been in the air a full six minutes. Rushing towards Joker she threw her arms around him, almost choking him with her exhilaration, and planted a big kiss on each cheek.

'I did it, I did it! I don't believe it! I was so calm. My first solo. I thought I would never get there,' Alice shouted, her eyes sparkling, her face split in an enormous grin. Joker grabbed her by the shoulders and shook her.

'I told you from the start, you're the finest pilot for your age I've ever met. If you hadn't mucked up this'd just have been another routine flight. Beats all of us hands down, doesn't she lads?' He turned to the three instructors who had also been watching Alice's flight path in the sky. 'But don't get too cocky mind, you've still got to get your licence and your uncle says you've got to pay.' He gave a big wink and patted her on the head as if she were his own child. 'Now, where's your log book?' Thrusting the log book into Joker's hand, Alice hugged each of the instructors in turn, unable to stand still, as he filled it out and returned it to her.

'Now run along to that hospital of yours, we don't want you losing your new job after this do we?'

'Thank you, thank you!' Alice exclaimed bursting with pride, her glance including all four men. 'I love you all.' Her enthusiasm was contagious. Giving Joker a final tight hug, she tossed back her jet black hair that had once more escaped its ties, whistled up Sherry, and was gone, leaving a sense of emptiness in the air.

'The next three lessons are on me,' Joker called out but she was already out of earshot. He grinned sheepishly at the other three men. 'You could fall in love with a girl like her if she stuck around long enough.' The youngest instructor blushed furiously.

'I went solo, Sherry, my first solo flight. I can't wait to tell Ben and Aunty Bea,' carolled Alice.

The adrenalin was still pumping in her veins as she urged Sherry along the rugged track. How pleased Ben would be. While her own dreams drove her to learn more and more about the land and caring for animals, she had watched with delight as Ben's fascination with motors and all things mechanical grew, creating a bond between him and Uncle Ray. Yet only he understood how much today's success meant to her. Today was a part of her dream.

'Look out Queensland, here I come!' she shouted exuberantly.

Sherry shied as a flock of pink galahs flew up across their path, bringing Alice quickly back to earth. Steadying Sherry she glanced anxiously at her watch. She was cutting things fine if she was to get back on time for her shift in the local hospital kitchens. Matron was a difficult woman and a stickler for detail. Lateness or sloppiness were attributes she abhorred and Alice had already been warned once. Two late marks and you could look elsewhere for work. Next year once she had completed her leaving certificate she was determined to take the animal husbandry course in Dubbo but for now she was thankful to have the job as kitchen hand despite matron and her stern ways. She tossed up whether to take a short cut through the scrub across the creek and decided she would. Last time it had knocked fifteen minutes off the trip. With the lack of rain over the past few months the creek should be pretty low.

She soon realised she had made the right decision. Even allowing for dismounting to coax a nervous Sherry across the creek she was making good time. Sodden to the waist she leaped back onto Sherry and urged her into a fast canter. At this pace she should easily make it back in time. Ignoring the chafing of her wet jeans against her thighs, she relived the exhilaration of her solo flight. Totally absorbed in the magic of its memory as she sped through the scrub, she failed to see the overhanging branch in enough time to duck. The force of the impact lifted her clean off Sherry's back as the horse thundered on. Reaching out to save herself she fell savagely on her right wrist. Pain shot up through her arm before she lost consciousness.

Robert McIain, heir to the famous merino station Wangianna, whistled happily as he rode through the scrub towards the creek, one hand balancing the rifle across his saddle. He had spent the last two days riding, checking the fences and searching for stray stock across the vast property that stretched hundreds of miles across the rich black soil plains of New South Wales. At twenty, Robert had grown from the scrawny McIain brat into a strong handsome young man. Intense dark brown eyes leapt out of an open and friendly face, tanned from the constant outdoor work the family property demanded. The brilliant red hair that had earned him the nickname Bluey as a child had faded to a rich copper chestnut and was now covered by a wide-brimmed hat. His blue working shirt, sleeves rolled up to the elbows to expose tanned brawny arms, was open part way down his chest and tucked casually into a pair of well-worn moleskin trousers, his brown elastic-sided working boots resting lightly in the stirrups. Robert rubbed his chest.

Heck, but it felt good to be away from the back-breaking work of stump pulling. That bloody ute. If he had to get under the bonnet once more he'd blow the bloody thing up. Still, they had made good clearance last week in the paddock and now he was allowing himself a few days' break. Checking the property to Robert, though long, was less strenuous work. God he loved Wangianna: the long wide house where he had been born surrounded by its deep verandah and carefully tended gardens, the hundred year old ghost gums that shaded the house from the ferocious heat of the sun, and the wool shed and station hands' quarters that made up the homestead. But most of all he loved the land. There was a special beauty in this land of harsh contrasts. It was a love he had inherited from his grandfather and his mother and he felt proud to be the fourth generation heir of a family who had crossed the world with nothing and built their home from a shack in virgin bush into the most famous merino stud in Australia.

Robert pushed his hat back from his face and scratched his head as he scanned the scrub for movement. This was great pig country. He'd be bound to get a good one to spit-roast tonight. His eyes lit up as he spied a razorback, the biggest of the feral pigs, half hidden in the dry sandy grass. Grinning excitedly he stopped his horse and aimed his rifle. Before he could get the animal in his sights something scared the pig and it vanished back into the scrub. Briefly irritated Robert lowered his arm. Still, that mean-eyed brute proved he was on the right track. There'd be plenty more of those. Nasty vicious creatures. Those tusks could make a fair old mess of you, but the pigs made great eating. Jamming his hat straight he nudged his horse forwards and followed the track where the pig had vanished.

Alice had no idea how long she had been unconscious or even why she was lying on the ground. All she was aware of was an intense throbbing in her head and arm and that there was no sign of Sherry, Panicking that Sherry might also be hurt she sat up too quickly and fell back, overcome with dizziness. To her relief, Sherry, who had been grazing close by, sauntered over and nudged her warm muzzle against Alice's cheek, blowing gently in her face. Alice sat up more cautiously, trying to ignore the dizziness and jarring pain in her arm.

'It's all right Sherry, old girl. Hold still.' Sherry waited patiently, aware of her mistress' distress. Waves of nausea flooded over Alice and she thought she was going to black out again. Ten thousand hammers beat inside her head and she was pretty sure her wrist was broken. If she could just reach up and pull herself onto Sherry's back she'd be fine—Sherry'd get them home. Biting her bottom lip against the pain she tried again to stand. Cradling her right arm against her body she pulled herself slowly to her knees against Sherry's solid haunches. Sherry tried to nibble her ear.

'Steady girl, steady,' Alice gasped. She was nearly up. As she put her full weight on her foot she cried out in agony. Not her ankle as well! Tears stung the backs of her eyes. Persevering she hobbled upright on one leg and leaned weakly against Sherry trying to work out the least painful way to heave herself into the saddle. Suddenly from out of the scrub burst a wild pig snorting and grunting. From her haze of dizziness Alice saw it was coming straight for them. Alice's scream drowned out the gunshot, her heart thumping wildly as the startled Sherry bolted and she toppled forward into the empty space.

'What in God's name do you think you're doing falling off your horse in pig country? Don't you know anything? If you can't bloody ride the thing stay in the home paddock.'

Excruciating pain took Alice's breath away. Twisting round she stared up into intense brown eyes in an unreasonably handsome face. Her rescuer was standing over her, a rifle in his hand, his face contorted with anger.

'Sherry! What have you done with Sherry?' she cried as she saw the rifle. Dizzily she tried to stand up and failed, fighting the churning in her stomach. The young man knelt down, his own anger melting immediately.

'Take it easy. I'm sorry, I didn't mean to sound so rude. I was just so relieved you weren't hurt.'

She tried to speak again and instead threw up. Filled with embarrassment, she reached for the proffered handkerchief, grateful for the soothing coolness of her rescuer's fingers against her throbbing temples as he held her steady.

'Sherry? Is that the name of your horse?' said her rescuer, slipping his arm around her shoulders. Alice nodded, her eyes searching frantically, the handkerchief still clutched to her mouth.

'She's right here hobbled to mine.' Alice lay back in relief in her rescuer's arms, cradling her broken arm and trying to ignore the thumping pain then suddenly remembered the pig. She lifted her head and was shocked to see the dead pig only feet away from where she had fallen.

'Yes,' continued Robert sternly. 'Those things don't look much, but they can gore you badly. D'you wonder I shouted at you?' He didn't like the colour of her face or the ugly bruise on her forehead. Alice bristled at his accusation but she felt too unwell to argue.

'You look pretty crook, kid,' Robert went on, 'and that's a beaut bump you've collected on your head. You could have concussion. We'd better get you home. D'you think you can move?' Alice winced as he tried to help her up.

'I think I've broken my arm,' she whispered, her stomach still churning. 'And my ankle hurts like hell.' The effort of talking was making her feel faint again.

'Let's have a look.'

Her face twisted in pain as Alice allowed him to take her hand in his own callused fingers.

Robert's face softened into a brief grin exposing perfect white teeth. 'I was hoping to spit-roast that porker tonight but seeing the mess you've made of yourself, reckon I'll have to change my plans.' For a moment Alice forgot her pain, mesmerised by his crooked smile.

'There's only one thing for it.' Gently he laid the white-faced girl back on the ground. 'I'm going to put that arm in a splint and then get you on my horse. D'you think you can hold on a minute?' Alice nodded. The world seemed to be disappearing in a swirling fog.

Quickly Robert walked over to the grazing horses, pulled a piece of cloth out of his saddlebag and tore it into several strips. Alice was only half aware of his movements as he made a temporary splint and tied the largest piece of cloth as a sling around her arm. Unhobbling the two horses the young man tied Sherry to his mount and led them back to where Alice was lying.

'Hold tight. This may hurt.' Alice braced herself through the thickening fog. Sweeping her up in his arms he set her on his horse, the unavoidable jolting sending shock waves of pain through her body. Once straddled across the horse he held her steady with one arm and leaped up beside her.

'I'm sorry, I couldn't avoid that. Are you okay?' His heart contracted with concern as Alice swayed in his arms, her blue eyes misted with pain. Alice nodded, unable to speak as she struggled to focus on his spinning image.

'What's your name?' She heard his question from a great distance.

'Alice. Alice Ferguson,' she managed to say before she passed out.

'Alice Ferguson,' exclaimed Robert as he steadied the swaying girl against his chest. 'Not Alice from the Come-by-Chance races? No wonder I kept thinking I knew her. She's far more stunning than her photo.' He glanced down at Alice feeling slightly foolish at having spoken aloud, amazed at the transformation from the scrawny tomboy pictured in the district newspaper to the beautiful young girl in his arms. He shook his head annoyed at his wanderings—the girl was hurt and he had to get her home as quickly and as gently as possible. Hopefully Alice would stay out to it for most of the two hours' journey home, that way she would be more comfortable. Turning his horse towards Billabrin, he set him into a fast walk. Sherry followed immediately, anxious not to be parted from her mistress.

From time to time Robert glanced down at Alice to check that she was still secure. Each time he was shocked at the effect this straggly kid turned beauty had on him. She looked so vulnerable lying in his arms, the ugly bruise on her forehead standing out against the parchment coloured skin. Her jet black hair tickled his chest where his shirt had fallen open and the soft warm perfume of her body made his pulse race. He moved her gently so she was not pressing on her broken arm and she stirred slightly. He frowned as he hurried the horses towards Billabrin. Concussion was not something to be taken lightly.

As the horses bumped across the wide paddocks Alice drifted in and out of consciousness, her head lolling against her rescuer's shoulder, his arm an iron band pinning her to him to stop her falling. She was vaguely aware of the tang of male sweat mixed with fresh washed cotton and she wondered in her dreamy state who her hero was. Then, as they reached the levee bank of Billabrin, reality intruded and she threw up down the front of his shirt. Soft damp cotton wiped her mouth and cool rough fingers pressed against her throbbing temples before she drifted back into semiconsciousness. The next time she awoke the horses had stopped and her hero was shaking her gently. She shifted in his arms and opened her eyes. They were outside her uncle's hardware store.

'This your place, Alice?' Alice nodded weakly, unable to make her mind work properly. Wincing, she tried to pull herself straight and felt the resistant strength of his arm as he held her secure.

'Don't try to move. Let's just get you inside.' Alice relaxed. Despite the returning throbbing in her head and arm, her heart missed a beat when she saw the gentle concern in his intense dark eyes as he dismounted and lifted her carefully from the horse. Alice could feel herself drifting away again.

Katie, back home for the school holidays, came sauntering towards them from behind the house.

'Robert McIain what are you doing with my cousin?' Her tone changed as she saw Alice and she ran the rest of the way. 'Alice, what happened?

'She's had a fall, Katie. She's broken her arm and she's badly concussed. You'll need to get her to a doctor.'

'I'll get Mum.'

In seconds Bea came rushing from the back of the house.

'Alice, you poor luv. Whatever happened? Bring her straight into the bedroom. Katie, go and ring Dr Ashton.'

Carefully Robert laid her on the bed and she sank gratefully against the soft pillows. The last thing Alice remembered before she lapsed back into unconsciousness was the vision of Robert taking off his hat and running his fingers through his thick chestnut hair as he stood talking to Aunty Bea.

Robert took the journey home slowly trying to make sense of his whirling emotions. How could he possibly have fallen in love with Alice? The whole idea was ludicrous. Three hours ago he had never met her, although he had heard plenty of unflattering tales about the skinny girl who liked to defy authority. Now he was telling himself that this kid who puked down his shirt had captured his heart. No, he was being idiotic. He pushed his hat firmly back on his head, forcing his thoughts away from Alice. As he was leaving the Downings' place Katie had reminded him about Caroline's party. Perhaps he would go after all, if only to shake this childish notion from his brain.

But as he guided his horse through the narrow sections of wood in search of a suitable camping ground, the vision of Alice lying against him kept intruding on his thoughts. How could someone change so much in one year? It was her eyes that had caused the damage. He had never seen such incredibly blue eyes—a man could get lost in them forever. His heart beat faster just thinking about them. He had felt so good with her lying in his arms as they rode to Billabrin. Even with her dark hair matted like a gorse bush framing her pallid, sweating face, she was still beautiful.

He shook his head in disgust. He must have gone soft, drooling over a kid who wasn't even conscious long enough to ask who he was. Robert was not a conceited young man but his mates never let up on how the sheilas all adored him, teasing him that he was the catch of the century, although he was never quite sure why and often wondered whether it was him or Wangianna girls were interested in. If any of his mates could read his mind now they'd laugh him out of the pub. Anyway, his mother had her eye on the daughter of a rich local pastoralist for the next mistress of Wangianna.

Robert cringed, thinking what his mother's inevitable reaction would be if he were to bring Alice home. He could hear her words already. Totally unsuitable, the girl is totally unsuitable, apart from being far too young. If you must marry into such a family, which I would not encourage, Katie would be marginally acceptable because she at least is being given a proper education. You must remember who you are. You have to choose someone capable not just of running Wangianna but being mistress of Wangianna, not rush off and marry the first wild scrap you feel you must rescue. Where is her education? Her breeding? His own thoughts disturbed him. Shaking his head as if to rid himself of an annoying buzz he quickened his pace and headed for one of his old campsites down by a creek.

Ten minutes later he dismounted, hobbled his horse and pulled off his swag. Rubbing his hands together in the chill evening air, he quickly lit a fire and boiled up a stew in his billy. As the sun slid beneath the horizon and the land faded into darkness Robert sat very still frowning into the fire, hands warming around his tin cup, watching the sparks fly and listening to the bush. Finally he stood up, threw another log on the dying embers, yawned and climbed into his sleeping bag. For a long while he lay on his back gazing into the dark velvet sky ablaze with diamonds, his thoughts torn between his heart and his head.

'Forget her, mate,' he said eventually, and rolled over to sleep.

Three days after Alice's accident Katie walked onto the verandah carrying a large bunch of flowers. Alice's concussion had been worse than at first was suspected but today she was beginning to show signs of improvement. Bea had given her a sponge-down earlier on and now she was dozing, propped up with pillows, having spent most of the day drifting in and out of sleep, dreaming of Robert. A cushion supported her plastered right arm now in a clean white sling.

'Present from your admirer,' sang Katie in a teasing tone. Alice opened her eyes sleepily.

'For me?' she asked, amazed. A faint pink tinged her cheeks. Holding her good hand out she accepted the flowers, drinking in their fragrance. Roses of all hues and hothouse orchids.

'He's called twice while you were still unconscious. Mum took the calls,' said Katie, watching Alice's pleasure like a cat stalking a bird.

'Did he really?' Alice fingered the velvet rose petals, her heart fluttering with excitement. 'Was he really as gorgeously handsome as I remember, or did I dream it all?' she continued unwisely. 'I don't even know his name.'

'I don't think you'd want to,' Katie offered.

'What do you mean?'

Katie paused, purposely playing with Alice, drawing out the agony.

'Your hero is Robert McIain.' Alice still looked blank. 'You've got a short memory. The McIain brat, Bluey. You know—the one that shot your goat.'

'He can't have, he was far too kind to have done anything like that,' Alice said defensively.

'Poor Alice, you're such an innocent,' said Katie, gloating at her cousin's pain. 'Billy told me. Bluey and his cousin were laughing and carrying on like nothing on earth when they shot her, as though she were some prize they had finally won after months of trying. He had to break up a fight over who'd get the skin and who'd cook it for dinner,' Katie lied. 'What'll I tell him if he calls again?' she finished casually.

Alice couldn't reply. Poor darling Silly! How could they? Tears choked her throat. She shut her eyes and lay back against the pillows, the vision of Billy carrying the dead goat clear before her. The one person in the whole world to rescue her and it had to be him. As Katie moved towards the door Alice opened her eyes, dark lines of suffering etched in her face.

'Tell him I hate him and I never want to have anything to do with him till the day I die.' Alice let the flowers slip to the floor and turned her face into the pillow overwhelmed by disappointment, misery and disgust. Gloating, Katie turned to leave and nearly bumped into Aunty Bea carrying a jug of homemade lemonade.

'How is she, Katie? asked Aunty Bea quietly, thinking Alice was asleep.

'She's fine, Mum. Just told her about the phone calls,' Katie replied triumphantly on her way out.

Bea placed the jug on the bedside table and picked up the flowers. 'Look at these, aren't they beautiful. What a thoughtful thing to do. He was very worried about you.' Alice didn't move. Aunty Bea laid the flowers on a chair and felt Alice's forehead. Relieved she had no sign of a temperature, Bea then fussed around straightening the blankets and tucking them around Alice's toes. 'What a surprisingly nice polite young man Robert McIain has grown into. He sounded so shy and embarrassed when he rang. I said maybe you'd feel up to talking to him tomorrow.' Alice opened lacklustre eyes. 'Maybe the day after. Try and get some more rest. You look terribly tired again, love.' She left the room in search of a vase for the flowers.

Chapter Twelve

A LITTLE OVER TWO weeks after the accident Alice got out of bed shortly after eleven feeling almost like her old self. Katie had returned to St Vincent's in Sydney and everyone else was out. The house felt peaceful. Alice leaned forwards and examined the bruise on her forehead in the dressing table mirror. It had faded to a mixture of yellow, purple and grey and was now only slightly tender. The colour had returned to her face and her eyes had regained their old sparkle. Her right arm was still in plaster, the sling hanging loose around her neck.

'Very tasteful,' she announced pulling her hair across her face with her left hand in an effort to hide the ugly mark and screwing her face up as she struggled to brush her jet black mane using the wrong hand. Her brush froze against a particularly stubborn knot as the telephone shrilled through the house. Alice's mouth went dry. Bea had mentioned there could be some calls for work for Uncle Ray and to make sure she answered them, but what if it was Robert again? What should she say? Aunty Bea had been very short with her when she had announced if he rang she would have nothing to do with him. She had been too miserably angry to mention Katie's revelation about Silly to Bea. Deciding she was being cowardly she hurried out of the bedroom into the main part of the house and then hesitated as the phone continued its unrelenting shrill. Her palms were sweaty as she picked up the receiver.

'This is the Downing Residence,' she said feeling silly but not wanting to admit who was speaking.

'Is that you, Bea?' Alice immediately recognised the crackling voice of Mrs Small who ran the post office.

'It's Alice, Mrs Small. How are you today?'

Mrs Small weighed over seventeen stone and did not approve of Alice. She had voiced her disapproval to several of the hospital kitchen staff. After an abrupt conversation, Alice replaced the phone with a list of contacts for Uncle Ray and some deliveries of her own. Sighing with relief, she returned to her room to finish getting dressed. The safest thing to do was to get out of the house. Bea and Ray had left earlier with the ute so her only transport was Sherry.

Confident she was now well enough to ride despite her broken arm, Alice decided to ride Sherry into town to pick up the groceries and do the few errands from the list Aunt Bea had left on the kitchen table. Slamming the door behind her, Alice headed for the paddock, wishing she could forget the look she had glimpsed in Robert's eyes just before she had passed out. One handed she clumsily mounted Sherry and headed into town, trying to sustain her rage and hatred of Robert yet unable to forget how she had felt lying in his arms.

The errands took longer than Alice had expected. Everyone she knew seemed to be in town today and they all wanted to stop for a chat and inquire how she was and hear about her adventure. By the time the last job was finally achieved the bounce was back in Alice's stride, she had fourteen new names on her plaster and laughter in her eyes. Staggering under the mountain of groceries, concentrating on balancing them precariously between her sling and her good arm, she wasn't quick enough to step aside when a tall young man shouting cheerfully to the owner bowled out of the local stock and station agent's store and straight into Alice.

'Oops sorry ma'am,' he said, trying to catch the flying packages, then stopped in amazement.

Alice stared straight into the dancing brown eyes of Robert McIain. Blushing to the roots of her hair, she grabbed at the carton of eggs as it slid towards the ground. Robert caught it just before it hit the footpath. Both of them bent down to rescue the other parcels.

'Alice!' stammered Robert, his own colour heightened, a grin of delight spreading across his face. 'How good to see you. I was so relieved when

I heard you were on the mend.' Confronted with this girl he had alternately longed to meet again and tried in vain to get out of his thoughts, his words tumbled out. 'How are you feeling now? You're looking much better.' He reached across to help her up but she avoided his hand.

For a brief moment their eyes met, the obvious admiration in his sending Alice's pulse racing. Damn it, he was even more handsome than she remembered. She cursed her reaction. If only it hadn't been him. But then her rage returned. He might be able to fool others with his winning ways and handsome face, but not her, she thought. Quickly she reached for the other parcels and stood up.

'Much better, thank you,' she replied stiffly. Still dizzy from his close proximity, she set off almost at a jog back up the main street.

'Hey, wait a minute,' cried Robert running after her still clutching the eggs. 'At least tell me you're okay. I was really worried about you.' Alice stopped and stared boldly up at him, her heart pounding.

'I'm okay. Thank you for rescuing me. I really appreciate what you did and thank you for your concern. Goodbye.' Turning on her heel she headed down the street as fast as she could. For a second Robert faltered. Then, refusing to be brushed aside, he strode after her.

'I don't want to be thanked. Look, you're going to drop the lot again if you go this fast. Where did you park your car?' Alice didn't reply, instead she strode determinedly across the road towards Sherry. 'You came shopping on your horse with a broken arm?' exclaimed Robert, his long strides easily keeping pace with Alice.

'So?' What kind of a helpless swooning female did he think she was?

'Oh nothing, you're just amazing. In fact you're the most amazing girl I've ever met. Could you slow down just for a second?' He dropped his voice, his words caressing Alice. 'At least let me run you back to your place with your shopping and we can come back for Sherry? I've got the Landrover, it'd be much easier.'

'No thanks. I can manage,' Alice replied tightly, retrieving the eggs. She started to stuff the groceries inefficiently into the saddlebag with her good hand, feeling increasingly hot and bothered. When Robert showed no sign of departing she snapped. 'Can't you take a hint? Go away.' Robert stepped back in surprise.

'I know I've upset you somehow but at least let me pack these in so they stay there till you get home,' insisted Robert unable to leave her to her stumbling efforts. Suddenly Alice felt exhausted.

'I'm not doing a wonderful job, am I?' she admitted with an embarrassed laugh. Allowing him to take over, she rested against the hitching rail, her legs trembling from the effort of walking so fast. She watched him from under her thick dark lashes, glad for the respite and convincing herself she wasn't weakening by allowing him to help her. Quickly and efficiently Robert repacked the saddlebags, his broad fingers nimbly finding space for every item, feeling Alice's eyes on him as he worked.

'There you go,' he said, shoving the last package into place, wondering why he couldn't tear himself away from this stubborn beauty who two minutes ago had dismissed him. He gave Sherry a friendly pat.

Alice slipped off the rail and removed Sherry's nosebag. Her eyes rested on Robert's second shirt button and she rebuked herself for wanting to reach out and run her fingers against his chest where her head had lain.

'Look, could you tell me what it is I've done to upset you?' demanded Robert unable to bear the suspense a second longer. Alice looked him full in the face but Robert couldn't fathom the expression in her eyes.

'It's just that I don't understand how someone who can be so kind and wonderful and thoughtful could have done such a mean thing before, and not even mentioned it,' she choked.

'Done what?' The bewilderment in his voice was too much for Alice. Her emotions, already in turmoil, threatened to spill over.

'It doesn't matter,' she muttered. Jarring her arm as she clumsily climbed onto the hitching rail, she swung her leg over Sherry before she realised she had forgotten to untie her. Before she could dismount Robert held out the reins. She tried to snatch them from him but he clasped her hand in his. Shock waves coursed through them both as their fingers met. Startled, they stared at one another. Robert was the first to recover.

'Did you know your eyes turn green when you're mad? Could you give me a clue?' Through misted eyes Alice noticed how his quirky smile lit his eyes. Perhaps she was being a damned fool making so much of something that had happened years ago. Yet she kept seeing the picture of the lifeless Silly and hearing Katie's words and remembering the pain and loss she had felt.

'Let go of my horse,' she spat fighting back the tears.

'Okay, okay.' Robert dropped her hand and she snatched up the reins, rage fighting the undeniable attraction she felt for this man.

'I hate you. You're horrid and cruel and if you don't remember what you've done then you're even worse than I thought. You, you . . . McIain brat!' Jerking Sherry round, Alice dug her heels into her flanks and charged down the main street. She would not cry. She was obviously still weak from her fall otherwise she would not have churned herself up into such a state.

The next few weeks were the longest in Robert's life, as he struggled against his growing love for Alice, knowing he was crazy to waste his time pursuing someone who had made it so obvious she despised him, yet unable to put her out of his thoughts. No matter how hard he worked, images of Alice continued to haunt his dreams and fill his waking moments. He kept rationalising to himself that there had to be a simple explanation for her show of contempt.

The weather, consistent with his mood, turned dull and miserable. Heavy thunder clouds rolled around the sky finally emptying themselves on the parched ground and quickly turning the dirt roads into impassable bogs. Robert wrote Alice three letters each of which he then tore up in disgust, instead deciding to sending her more flowers but he quickly dropped that idea realising delivery would be impossible because of the shocking roads.

'Let it go, mate' he scolded himself. 'The girl hates you.' Knowing he should just forget about her but unable to help himself he decided to ring the Downing household one last time. His hand was unsteady as he lifted the receiver and was put through by the operator. The line crackled as he spoke.

'Hello.' It was Katie. Robert nearly put the phone down. He took a deep breath.

'Hi, Katie, it's Robert McIain.'

'Hi, Robbo,' Katie said cheerfully. 'How'ya goin? I just flew up from Sydney last night. Isn't this weather revolting?'

'Not great. I was wondering if Alice was about?' said Robert casually.

Katie's mind started ticking over fast. 'She's out. Sorry. Wouldn't do you any good if she was. She's sworn never to speak to you ever again.' Her tone became conspiratorial. 'Whatever did you say to her last time you met? You're definitely not her favourite person, that's for sure.'

'Oh, really. Nothing much . . . I dunno,' said Robert, unable to keep the disappointment out of his voice.

'You've really got it bad for her, haven't you?' said Katie, fishing.

'I don't know about that. I just don't like riddles I can't solve,' said Robert defensively. Katie saw her chance.

'Look, the whole world listens in on these party lines. Are the roads good enough up your way to get through so we could meet for coffee? Maybe we can talk and I can help a bit.'

'Oh. Actually I'm flying in to Billabrin in two days' time to pick up some equipment I ordered. Why don't we make it lunch?'

'Okay. I'll meet you at the Isaacs' place at midday on Thursday,' replied Katie, controlling her elation.

Wangianna station was over one hundred and fifty miles from Billabrin and with the roads impassable from recent rain, flying was the only option. Sam and Lily Isaacs had a well-maintained house with a couple of large paddocks, one of which they had turned into a small landing strip. Katie was waiting there in the ute as Robert landed the plane and from there she drove them to Mrs Harvey's Tea Shoppe in Billabrin.

'You're a really good sport to meet me like this, Katie. I just want to know what it is I'm supposed to have done to upset Alice and to try and sort it all out,' said Robert candidly over lunch. 'Do you have any idea why she's so angry with me?'

Katie watched Robert carefully over her cup as he sat stirring his coffee despondently, one elbow resting on the table. A worried frown marred his handsome face, and he looked tired.

'The stupid bitch doesn't deserve him,' thought Katie viciously, 'and she's not getting him.' Her yellow-green eyes showed only understanding as she spoke.

'She's got you too, hasn't she?' Her long eyelashes fluttered onto her soft cheeks and her fingers tightened around her cup.

'What's that supposed to mean?' Robert frowned into his coffee, hunching his broad shoulders.

Reaching out across the table, Katie laid her hand gently over his roughened sunburned hand. 'I don't know how to say this without hurting you more. You wouldn't be here talking to me if you didn't care about her.' Robert's frown deepened.

'You might as well know the truth. Alice is in love with Billy. At least that's what we all thought at first. But then she started laying it on with Paddy as well. She's got them both dancing on a string over her.' Warming to her subject she continued. 'It's been awful. Every time I come home there are arguments and fights and Alice is in the middle of them.' Well it was partly true, it was just that Katie had shifted the emphasis of who caused the fights. 'At the moment both my brothers are fighting about who's going to partner her at the debutantes' ball in July. Mum and Dad don't like it one bit. But they can't send her home. She's got nowhere to go. So they just try to keep her as busy as possible. Deep down I know they feel really sorry for her, but Mum looks terribly tired.' She withdrew her hand, pleased with her convincing lies, and flicked back her long blonde hair, opening her eyes wide as if to stay tears. 'I've tried to help but Alice doesn't want to know.' Robert blushed crimson and shifted embarrassed in his chair.

'I had no idea. What a fool I must have looked.'

Katie leaned forwards quickly. 'No don't think that. You've been so kind and thoughtful. She catches us all like that.' She fiddled with the tablecloth.

'Look, I hope you don't think I normally go around saying horrible things about my family but I just don't want you to get hurt any more. You do understand, don't you?' Robert nodded. Her words had had just the reaction she wanted. The expression in Robert's eyes was blank. Katie sat quite still while he digested the information, then she reached over and squeezed his hand comfortingly. She drank down the cold remains of her coffee and pulled a face. 'Ugh, I shouldn't talk so much.'

'We'd better get going. I don't like the look of that sky,' said Robert flatly.

'Did you know we were both being presented in July at the Bathurst Masonic Ball?' said lía tie, purposely changing the subject as they stepped out into the fresh air. Robert brightened, grateful for her tact.

'Things get around on the grapevine. I've partnered debs for that ball for the last three years. We've got a heap of relatives living over that way so they pull me out of mothballs each year.' He laughed briefly and rubbed the stubble on his chin. 'Actually this is the first year I haven't been organised to partner anyone.' He hesitated. 'I was going to ask Alice if she had a partner but now that you've told me all this you've just saved me from making a further fool of myself.' He gave Katie a regretful smile.

'I'd love you to be my partner,' Katie said wistfully. 'That is if you felt you could, me being Alice's cousin and everything.'

'Would you want me to, knowing how I feel about Alice?'

Katie laughed softly. She had half promised Russell Heaton that he could partner her but she could fix that. 'I'd be really flattered if you would.'

'I'd be delighted to.' Katie beamed. 'Thanks for listening and being so understanding,' continued Robert. 'Why don't we make a foursome with my cousin and Sophie next time you're home? You've met Snake, haven't you?'

'I'd love to,' Katie replied, repressing her jubilation. Sophie was her best friend. The two girls frequently spent weekends with Sophie's aunt and uncle at their home in Mosman, one of Sydney's smart northern suburbs. 'Or you could come up to Sydney if you were feeling a bit down and we could do something—just as friends, of course.' Katie smiled engagingly. 'The break might do you good.' They had reached the ute. She reached into her shoulder bag and pulled out the stub of a pencil. Scribbling quickly on a scrap of paper she handed Robert a phone number.

'I might just take you up on that,' Robert said, pocketing the scrap of paper. He glanced anxiously at the sky again. 'We better get going. Those clouds are looking nastier by the minute.' Katie could hardly conceal her triumph as she drove him back to his plane. It might not be love at first sight but she'd work on him. Whatever else, if she couldn't have him, Alice certainly wasn't going to either.

Having Robbo as her partner also solved another problem. Katie had been furious when Aunty Bea had announced that the girls would be presented locally and not at Sydney Town Hall with most of her school friends. Her first reaction had been to scream at her mother, demanding who would see her and how she could ever be expected to face her friends again. Everyone knew the only place you took your debut was at the Sydney Town Hall. However, she had been somewhat placated when her mother explained that this particular Masonic Ball in Bathurst was an annual event which was very highly thought of.

'They invite the grand master of the organising lodge down from Sydney to receive the girls and many of the big property owners from around attend, including the Conways and McIains, and everyone goes to a lot of trouble.' But Katie had still only been half-persuaded. Now with Robbo as her partner none of her friends could possibly look down their noses at her. It was with great glee that Katie announced her news to the family just before leaving for Sydney at the end of the weekend.

'Who's your partner?' she then asked Alice pointedly.

'I don't have one,' said Alice quietly.

'Well I'm sure you don't have to worry, Alice,' said Aunty Bea quickly. 'Either Billy or Paddy will be your partner if you don't have anyone else you want to ask.'

That night Alice lay in bed watching the stars, unable to sleep, thoughts revolving round and round in her head. She'd always been too busy to get seriously involved with any of the local boys and although she had gone to a couple of dances no one really interested her. The whole business over her accident had put the debut completely out of her mind. She would ask Billy to be her partner and tell him to ignore Robert. Dear protective loyal Billy. As for Robert partnering Katie, she told herself firmly, there was absolutely no need to feel anything because she had no interest in a heartless bloke who didn't give twopence for the life of a defenceless creature, even if he was good looking and had enticing brown eyes. Katie was welcome to him.

But she lay awake until the stars faded into the dawn haunted by the emotions Robert had stirred in her. She wished with all her heart that she could deny their existence, but she couldn't.

Chapter Thirteen

ALICE GOT HER opportunity to ask Billy about the ball when he arrived home unexpectedly at the beginning of June. Normally a busy time with lambing, Ray and Bea were surprised when he walked in announcing he had two weeks off.

'Lambing's a bit lean this year,' was all he said.

Ray, who was overworked at the time, didn't press him further and Billy was in no hurry to tell them that Melon, the Aboriginal head stockman at Wangianna, had been forced to break up a fight between Billy and another jackaroo. It would have passed unnoticed except that George McIain had discovered Billy was drunk at the time and had told him to go home and cool his heels for a couple of weeks.

'You're lucky it was me that found out and not the missus,' George had said as his parting shot. 'She wouldn't have given you a second chance.' Billy had doffed his forelock in thanks and walked off the property cursing to himself. Bloody McIain mob. Bloody stupid sheep. He was coming to hate his job. There had to be more to life than staring up a sheep's arse.

Seeing Alice outwardly cheered Billy. Delighted, he agreed to partner her at the ball, teasing her for being his kid cousin. But his thoughts were very different. While he had not attempted to kiss her since that day under the bridge, as Alice grew into womanhood Billy had found himself falling more and more deeply in love with her. However Alice continued to treat him more like an extra brother, so for the time being he knew he had to be content to play the protective cousin. But the effort made him tense and moody.

Billy wasn't the only person who was tense and moody. Robert had tried everything he could to put Alice from his mind but as the ball date approached his temper became shorter and his moods blacker. Finally he could stand it no longer. Action, any action, was better than nothing. Picking up the telephone he dialled the number on the crumpled scrap of paper, only to discover Katie was out. Cursing, he left a message and stormed off to the paddocks.

Katie received Robert's message the following day when she and Sophie had escaped for the weekend to Mosman. Immediately she called him back.

'Hi, Katie,' Robert replied to her enthusiastic greeting. 'Look, I was wondering if I could take you up on that offer of yours. How about dinner and a movie next Friday?' The sound of Robert's voice sent the blood rushing through Katie's veins.

After making arrangements of where and when to meet, Katie put down the receiver triumphant and immediately went in search of Sophie. Sophie's aunt and uncle were only too happy to include Katie as one of the family. Unable to get down to Sydney very often, Bea and Ray were extremely grateful that they were willing to act as proxy parents to their daughter. Back at school on the day Robert was due in Sydney Katie flipped through her wardrobe wondering which of her clothes was sexy without being too blatant. Deciding nothing was suitable she borrowed a daringly short dress from another school friend and dashed off to Mosman. She was surprised to find a long faced Sophie on her own when she ran into the house.

'Some relo just died and they've had to rush off to a funeral,' Sophie explained. 'They'd start a family feud if they didn't attend. Aunt Jemma was really worried about Robert staying even though I told her we'd be fine on our own.' She pulled a face. 'It could've been great but you know what she's like. She's convinced if one of us breathes near a boy we'll fall pregnant, so Uncle Matt insisted Johnny come over and be our chaperon and we've got to be home by ten-thirty.' Johnny was Sophie's cousin, twenty-two and extremely conservative when it came to girls. Except for

Jane. He had been infatuated with Jane for the last six months and had twice almost asked her out. Katie prayed Jane would be one of the guests.

The party was in Cremorne, not far from Mosman. Robert knew he was drinking too much, but at least Katie was laughing and the dull ache that never seemed to leave him these days had been anaesthetised for the moment. Robert had also made a pact with himself not to mention Alice at all during the weekend. Close to ten-thirty someone suggested they all go down to Balmoral Beach. Katie caught Sophie in the bathroom.

'What about Johnny, will he let us go?' she whispered.

Sophie's eyes sparkled with mischief. 'Have you seen him? He's been completely soppy over Jane for months and I saw them kissing in the kitchen. He'll probably want to come too. What do you bet I can get him to stretch our curfew?' Sophie was right. Johnny, his arm around Jane's waist, agreed they could all stay until eleven o'clock. Most of the guests were around the same age as Robert and had their own transport. Noisily everyone scrambled out of the house and piled into their various cars and roared off towards the beach. Someone lit a bonfire on the sand. Once more fortified with drinks they filled the air with their off-key renderings of 'The Road to Gundagai', 'Click Go the Shears' and 'Waltzing Matilda'. Robert's voice was one of the loudest.

Despite the heat from the fire and wine, Katie was soon freezing. The dress she had borrowed, whilst warm enough indoors, was not designed to stave off the biting June night air. The wind whipped around her scantily-clad bottom, blowing stinging sand onto her bare legs. The evening had started surprisingly well. In fact up until they left for the beach she was having a great time. To her amazement, far from her having to play the ministering angel, Robert had not mentioned Alice once since he had arrived. He had complimented her on her dress several times during the evening and they had danced close, making her feel incredibly aroused. To any onlooker she might have been his latest girlfriend. Yet Katie could feel the hidden barrier that kept her at a distance. Now Robert was hopelessly drunk and she feared her plan to shift from sisterly understanding to sexy lover had gone badly awry. She stood arms folded against the wind, her miniskirt flapping against her thighs, wishing they had gone back to Sophie's aunt's place instead of coming to the beach. Robert lurched towards her. Grinning stupidly he took another swig from his bottle of beer and flung his arm around her shoulders. At his touch the throb of desire increased between her legs. Despite his intoxication he was still rivetingly handsome. Sophie was wrapped around the young man who had driven her to the beach. There was no sign of Johnny and Jane.

'You've got great legs,' Robert slurred oblivious of Katie's shivering.

'Could we go, Robby, I'm freezing?' She pressed herself to Robert trying to gain some warmth from his body. For once she wasn't going to fight her extended curfew.

'Go? The night's still young. C'mon I'll warm you up.' Robert slid his arm down to her waist, squeezed her and swung his free arm wide. The action cost him his balance and the two tumbled together in a heap on the sand. Katie's dress dragged up over her bottom exposing skimpy black panties and causing ribald comments from several of the other blokes.

'Did anyone tell you you've got great legs?' Robert repeated, half on top of Katie. His words dissolved her irritation. One of the partygoers started reciting 'The Geebung Polo Club' but was shouted down by another who insisted on giving a very drunken rendition of one of Hamlet's soliloquies. Robert groaned and sat up.

'Even I'm not drunk enough for that,' he muttered, staggering to his feet. Katie got to her feet brushing the sand from her dress and arms, laughing at Robert's futile attempts to help.

'It's time we all went home,' announced Robert loudly, hiccupping. He was having trouble focusing. Swaying he pulled out his car keys and dropped them. Buoyed up with hope, Katie snatched up the keys.

'I'll drive, it'll be quicker.'

It took ten minutes to drive to the house with Robert insisting on singing his own ribald version of 'Onward Christian Soldiers' for the entire journey. Katie parked the car and searched for the front door key in her evening bag. By the time she had found it Robert had failed three attempts to get out of the car.

'I think I'm pissed!' he declared grandly, finally staggering out of the car. 'But what a great way to be!' He started to climb a nearby lamppost. After a small scuffle Katie managed to get him inside and they wove their way along the hall and into the visitor's bedroom where Katie pushed Robert onto the bed with a sigh of relief. When Robert started singing again she firmly put her hand over his mouth. Sitting up, Robert slid his hands up her bare legs and pulled her to him.

'You've got wonderful legs,' he slurred moving his hands up and down her thighs. Katie's stomach tightened in anticipation. 'Alice has got wonderful legs too but she doesn't think I'm a decent bloke.' Tears of self-pity sprang to his eyes. Katie's heart sank at the mention of her cousin. 'You think I'm a decent bloke, don't you, Katie?' he said, wrapping his arm around her waist. Katie's pulse quickened as she allowed Robert to pull her onto his knee. 'You're my best friend, Katie. You are the best friend a man could ever have. You understand. You know I really love Alice, only she's not being a good sport. How can you love someone who's not being a good sport? She's not being a good sport. You're a good sport, aren't you?' Katie's fingers shook with excitement as she stroked his cheek.

'Yes, Robbo, I'm a good sport and you're a decent bloke.' She kissed him full on the lips. Robert's hands slid up around Katie's back and she felt the pressure of his mouth returning her kiss. Her heart started thudding madly. Everything was going to be all right.

The sun streamed into the bedroom window and two kookaburras laughed raucously in a nearby tree. Robert opened his eyes and immediately closed them against the brightness and the searing pain in his temples. How could he have been such a damned fool to drink so much last night? He had no idea how he had got to bed. The last thing he remembered was heading off to the beach. He certainly didn't remember getting undressed although he must have because he hadn't got a stitch on. God, what an uncouth lout Katie must think him. He sat up cautiously, clutching his head with one hand, and reached out, his eyes still half closed, searching for his shirt. His hand closed over soft nylon. Opening his eyes with a start he saw he was clutching a pair of skimpy black panties. At the same time Katie rolled over beside him, half pushing back the covers.

'Is it morning already?' she mumbled sleepily. With a jolt Robert was fully awake. Horrified he started at the naked girl beside him.

'What the heck—?' Then the awful truth dawned on him. Pulling the sheets back over Katie, one hand clutching the quilt to hide his own nakedness, he grabbed his briefs and shirt that were lying on the floor and pulled them on. Then he searched around for his trousers.

'Come back to bed, Robbo. There's no rush,' Katie murmured.

Robert turned crimson. 'Katie I'm really sorry. This is awful. This is all a ghastly mistake. I never meant this to happen.'

Katie sat up, her long golden hair tumbling enticingly around her firm creamy breasts. 'I'm not, Robbo.' She stared boldly at him holding out one hand.

Robert sat down hard on the bed not knowing where to start. 'Katie, look, I . . .' He stopped, unable to continue such a serious conversation half clothed. 'Where are my trousers?'

Katie's eyes teased him. 'You insisted on hiding them under the carpet,' she giggled. 'You said that way they wouldn't get crushed.' Robert felt hot with embarrassment. He stared at the floor and saw a trouser cuff peeping out from under the corner of the rug, but Katie was too quick. Kneeling on the bed she grabbed Robert and pulled him back.

'You were fantastic, Robbo. I never knew it could be as wonderful as that.'

Robert groaned. Firmly he put Katie's arms aside and rescued his trousers. Consumed with embarrassment he pulled them over his legs and zipped them up. Reluctantly he looked back at Katie still boldly naked on the bed.

'Katie,' he said, his eyes firmly on her face, 'really, I never meant for any of this to happen. I feel terrible. You show yourself willing to be my friend and I do this to you. It should never have happened. Whatever will Sophie's aunt and uncle think? What about her cousin? Oh God.' He sat down on the bed, his head in his hands.

'It's all right, Johnny's not a problem. Aunt Jemma'd kill him if she found out he'd gone off with Jane instead of checking up on us. Anyway, he need never know. We'll be up and gone before he wakes. He'll sleep like the dead,' replied Katie soothingly stroking the back of his neck. She had heard him creep in at about four and go straight to his room. 'And Sophie's not going to tell.' Her voice grew more intense. 'It was meant to happen, don't you see Robbo, darling.'

Robert drew abruptly away from Katie and tossed her dress at her.

'Put this on,' he ordered, keeping his voice low. 'Now listen here, Katie, as far as I am concerned this is all a dreadful mistake. It was never meant to happen. I never meant to take advantage of you.' Katie pouted. Tossing the dress aside she slid catlike out of bed and slowly picked up a towel and draped it around her. She was starting to panic. They were supposed to spend the whole weekend together. 'You know there's only one girl for me and that's Alice,' continued Robert. 'You've been so good and understanding about everything. I should never have got stuck into the booze. I don't know how I can ever make it up to you. I will understand if you never want to see me or talk to me again.'

Katie's eye flashed dangerously. 'I didn't think you were that sort of person,' she cried angrily. 'You just use me like I didn't matter and now you're just going to walk off, is that it?'

If Robert could have blushed deeper he would have. 'You know it's not anything like that, Katie,' he stammered, wishing he could extricate himself from this mess. 'You're a beautiful, sweet girl, I could never treat you like that. I've just made a hash of everything. Please forgive me.'

'Will you still take me to the ball?' Katie said in a small voice.

'Of course, if that's what you want,' Robert replied formally.

Katie struggled with her inner turmoil. She had lost and now there was only one safe course she could take. The consummate actress, she smiled shakily.

'You don't need to worry about me, Robbo. I don't mind, really. It's not as if it was the first time or anything. We'll forget the whole episode.' Opening her eyes wide she gave a low laugh. 'You were wonderful. I just hope you haven't given your heart to someone who simply tramples on it.' Stepping towards Robert she dragged her fingers lightly across his cheek. Then purposely she changed the mood. 'I'll go and get dressed and then let's go out and have some fun at Luna Park.'

'Under the circumstances I think it's best I go back home,' responded Robert quickly.

Katie's face fell. 'No,' she almost shrieked; then, collecting herself, she repeated, 'I don't mind if you stay, honestly.' But Robert ignored her plea. Slumping back on the bed she watched in silent dismay as he finished getting dressed, shoved his wallet in his back pocket and picked up his car keys. He looked so madly sensual yet she could see there was no way to stop him from leaving.

Finally he turned to her, his hand on the doorknob. 'Katie, I am truly sorry I misused your friendship. I promise you I will never do so again and I will never embarrass you by referring to this ever again.'

His words echoed in the stillness after he was gone.

The day of the Masonic Ball arrived at last. For the last month the whole of Bathurst had been buzzing over the coming event. Knowing that accommodation would be at a premium, Bea had long ago booked them all into a hotel near the local Catholic church. She, along with the other matrons—as the debutantes' mothers were called—had spent all day decorating the tables and arranging flowers in the hall.

By five-thirty the place looked a picture. Large floral arrangements stood in each corner of the room with a long low arrangement spreading across the front of the stage where the band would sit. Twisted streamers of apricot and white hung from the walls. Stiff white tulle had been arranged in scallops along the outer edges of tables, which were covered by starched white tablecloths, with tiny sprays of apricot baby-doll roses placed at each gather. In the middle of each table the theme of apricot and white was carried through with small bowls of flowers. Cutlery gleamed and glass sparkled. On the Downings' table Bea had splashed out and placed a single apricot rosebud next to each neatly inscribed place name. The red carpet had been rolled out in the centre of the hall ready for the presentation of the debutantes and the eleven tiny posies had been laid out to be handed to each girl. Heaving sighs of relief and congratulating each other that they had finished everything in time, the matrons hurried off to their hotels to get their girls and themselves dressed for the ball.

Alice and Katie excitedly prepared for the evening as Bea fussed round them. Katie was the first to be ready. Spraying a final dab of Femme on her wrists and behind her ears, she checked herself nervously in the mirror. She had to look irresistible for Robert. She twisted and turned admiring all angles of her reflection. Mrs Garvin had excelled herself in her dressmaking. The full white taffeta skirt with its chiffon overlay stood out like a cloud. The bodice, cut decorously low around the neck, was pulled in viciously at the waist, clinging to Katie's figure and emphasising her full breasts. A big tartan sash fell from Katie's right shoulder across her full skirt and was tied loosely at the left hip. A tiny ballerina tiara glinted in her corn-coloured hair which was piled in soft curls on her head and around her face. Around her neck she wore a tiny gold heart-shaped locket with a green stone in the middle that matched the yellow-green glow of her eyes. The necklace and the perfume were both presents from her father. A tiny matching taffeta bag dangled from one wrist. Let Alice beat that, she thought, as she rustled her way down the stairs.

Alice was totally unaware of the impact she made in her white tulle gown overlaid with lace. The closefitting bodice cut in a flattering curve at the neck, little puffed sleeves and layers of billowing skirt, made her appear like a waif from another time. Tiny mother of pearl sequins, every one lovingly sewn by Mrs Garvin, outlined each flower in the lace making the dress shimmer as she moved. Her jet-black hair was piled high on her head in much the same way as Katie's, her tartan sash making the two a pair of opposites. Pretty drop earrings matching the stones in her tiara twinkled against her olive skin. Her eyes had turned deep sapphire and her face was flushed with excitement as she followed her cousin downstairs.

Billy gaped at the vision of this Alice so different and fragile from the tomboy he knew on the horse. Even Paddy felt less sure of himself against her beauty.

'Stop gawking and get a move on or we'll all be late,' said Katie crossly, loathing how her own brothers drooled so over Alice. Robert had agreed to meet her at the hall with the other partners for convenience sake, but she was extremely nervous at how he might act with Alice in such close proximity.

The atmosphere in the tiny room off the foyer of the hall was tense with excitement as the matron in charge of the debutantes, dressed in dramatic purple and gold, ordered the flower girls, four little nine-year-olds dressed in frilly white dresses with fresh flowers in their hair, to get into line and gave them all their final instructions.

'Remember ladies,' she finished, 'this is your evening and your behaviour must be exemplary. Everyone will be watching you and everyone knows who you are. Now girls, are you ready?' She pulled the skirt of one of the little flower girls' dress straight and removed the fingers from the mouth of another who was nervously chewing her nails.

A loud fanfare from the band in the hall heralded the arrival of the dignitaries, the Mayor and Mayoress of Bathurst, the masters of all the lodges in the district and their wives, the master of the organising lodge and his wife the matron of honour who would present them with their posies, and the special guest, the grand master of the lodge. Alice's heart fluttered with excitement as she greeted her Mason escort. Despite all the turmoil and disasters in her life she was actually making her debut. Gratitude and love for Bea and Ray overwhelmed her and for a split second she longed for her dad to see her now.

The main lights had been dimmed leaving only enough to focus on the girls in their billowing white gowns and twinkling tiaras. The mood of the three hundred guests was electric as the procession moved slowly into the hall. Suddenly nervous, Alice searched for Billy's familiar face over Katie's shoulder. She was totally unprepared for her response to seeing Robert dressed immaculately in the McIain colours proffering his arm to Katie.

The dark green and blue tartan kilt, blazing white sporran and dark velvet jacket set off his tall sturdy figure, contrasting brilliantly against the white of Katie's dress and the red of the carpet. The dirk in his knee-high socks completed the effect. Somehow the whole attire made him even more manly. As he turned to lead a triumphant Katie through the arch of steel their eyes met for an instant and Alice thought she was going to faint. Hurriedly she grabbed Billy's arm, determinedly blocking out Robert and Katie and concentrating on her cousin.

'Are you okay?' whispered Billy, noting how pale she had become. Alice nodded and squeezed his arm. Then it was her turn and Billy was leading her through the arch and up to the grand master.

The presentations completed, the debutantes' posies collected and the carpet rolled up, with a roll of drums the master of ceremonies invited the grand master to open the ball. The grand master addressed the guests.

'It is indeed an honour to be invited here today and it gives me great pleasure to invite these lovely young debutantes and their partners to open this evening's proceedings by performing the debutantes' waltz. So now . . .' The grand master paused. Everyone held their breath. Raising his voice the grand master declared, 'Let the ball begin!'

Immediately the band, dashingly attired in bright apricot shirts and black trousers, struck up the opening bars of 'The Pride of Erin'. The eleven debutantes, as had been so carefully rehearsed, swept into the middle of the hall in their partners' arms while the music swelled, and within moments the empty space was a sea of frothing swirling white and black.

'Don't they look lovely?' said Aunty Bea proudly, resplendent in emerald green which set off her thick chestnut hair and added a glint of green to her hazel eyes.

Ray squeezed her arm. 'You've done well, luv.'

'Did we do okay, little Alice? I feel a right charlie in this rig,' said Billy ruefully as they circled the floor. Alice had got over her shock at seeing Robert and she smiled genuinely up at her cousin.

'You were terrific, Billy. I'm really proud you're my partner.' Billy held her tight, breathing in the soft fragrance of her hair and some of his tension left him.

After the formal part of the evening was over, the mood relaxed. The dance music changed from the more formal foxtrots and waltzes to progressive barn dances and lively Latin American styles. Refusing to allow her confusion about Robert to disturb the evening, Alice set out to thoroughly enjoy her debut. Billy was a reasonably good dancer and they had earlier agreed that they would stay away from Robert and Katie. Alice danced with great gusto and seeing Aunty Bea and Ray thoroughly relaxed added to her enjoyment. They had already had a number of dances and now several other friends had joined their table where, to Alice's fascination, Uncle Ray was regaling the others, with much laughter, of the time when he was escort to debutantes. Despite having consumed at least three-quarters of a bottle of Scotch he was still acting the perfect gentleman although his yarns got taller and taller and longer and longer. After a particularly energetic dance Alice sat down exhausted but exhilarated and accepted a glass of champagne from Billy, which she drank thirstily.

'I have to slip out for a moment, Billy,' she said putting the empty glass on the table.

Billy watched her shimmer her way to the door wondering how he was going to last the evening without kissing her. He helped himself to a small Scotch and caught Robert also staring at Alice. Turning away abruptly, Billy tossed back the drink and immediately poured himself another.

Alice stepped out into the cold night air and gasped at the beauty of the moonless sky studded with a million brilliant stars. Shivering, she hurried down the dark lane that ran beside the hall and disappeared into the ladies room. The smell of cigarette smoke and men's voices drifted through the head high open window as she checked her dress in the long mirror placed there for the evening. Inquisitively she stood on tiptoes to discover who of her friends were out stealing a quick smoke and drew back, suddenly alert at the mention of Billy's name.

'Reckon we'll get some free entertainment from Billy later on tonight,' announced one of the young men.

'What d'you mean?' Alice heard the heavy intake of breath followed by violent coughing. 'Struth, where d'you get these?'

'Off the back of a truck, where else?' The two young men laughed. 'In the pub the other night he was swearing blind if any of the McIain mob went near his precious Alice he'd punch their bleedin' lights out. He's that jealous of any other blokes going near Alice. Didn't you see his face when some of the fellas were talking to her? Me, I wouldn't risk it. Mention her name and you could find his fist in yér face.'

'Why's he got it in for the McIain mob?'

'Dunno the full story. All I know, the other night he was fighting drunk by the time we got back to Wangianna and blathering on like an idiot. Now Mrs McIain's given him his marching orders. Got caught drunk on the job, again, bloody idiot. He's had it in for the McIain mob for years. Remember all that fuss when Snake killed that bloomin' goat when we were kids?'

Alice heard no more. She gave a stifled gasp and sat down hard on the nearby chair trying to digest what she had just heard. Billy sacked? Billy in love with her? It couldn't be true. Slowly another truth sank in. Snake had killed Silly, not Robert. Katie had got it wrong. Alice's heart lifted. All the emotions that had smitten her at their first meeting poured back stronger than ever. As quickly as her happiness erupted it fizzled into shame. She'd made a complete fool of herself thinking he cared in the first place. Now it was too late. Whatever Robert had originally felt towards her he had got over pretty quickly, otherwise why had he agreed to be Katie's partner tonight? From the way they had been smiling and laughing together it was obvious to Alice she couldn't be further from his mind. She started to shiver again. Suddenly she no longer wanted to be at the ball. Taking several gulps of cool fresh water, she dabbed at her mouth with one of the neatly laid out cotton towels and tried to think straight. Well she couldn't stay here all night. For one thing she'd freeze to death. She ran quickly up the lane back into the hall and joined in with the progressive barn dance. Three partners on, the dance ended and she faced Robert McIain.

'Could you bring yourself to dance with the McIain brat?' Robert asked, his heart racing, hoping she would not turn on her heel and march off the dance floor.

'Robert, I have to explain,' stuttered Alice, blushing furiously as the music started. Delighted, Robert slipped his arm around her waist and guided her into the waltz. For a full minute Alice's senses spun as she felt his hand in the small of her back and gazed into the endless depths of his dark brown eyes.

'You were going to explain something,' murmured Robert unable to take his eyes off her. He could not believe that finally she was in his arms. Alice's blush deepened.

'I'm really sorry I've been so rotten to you.' The words tumbled out in a confused muddle. She stopped, overcome with embarrassment, missed the beat and trod on his toe. 'Oops, sorry. Oh golly. Look, you don't have to dance with me,' she blundered. It was all too hard. Robert's arm tightened around her.

'You know you're the most beautiful girl in the room, don't you?' Alice looked at the tip of his nose, her wide eyes like deep azure pools.

'I thought it was you who shot Silly,' she blurted out. Robert stopped dancing.

'Who's Silly?'

'My goat,' Alice said. 'But now I know it wasn't you and I'm really sorry, and you sent me all those flowers and phoned and everything . . .' Understanding dawned in Robert's eyes.

'Is that what this is all about? Why didn't you tell me? I never knew that goat was yours,' he said leading her back into the waltz.

'Katie said that you and . . . well . . . and then Billy found her . . .' Alice tailed off. Robert executed a perfect backward waltz turn to avoid bumping into another couple. His reply was gentle when it came.

'It was an accident. We were fooling around and the goat ran out of the bush at the wrong time. I was still really upset at Snake for shooting it, though. I hate hurting animals.' He paused, embarrassed. 'How awful. No wonder you were mad at me.'

'It's all so long ago I don't know why I got so chewed up,' replied Alice politely as they circled the floor, relieved the truth was now out. This whole exercise, she realised, was mere courtesy. In a moment he would leave her and return to Katie and that would be the end. Right now, though, this was her moment. She could feel the warmth of his body as he pulled her closer, guiding her around the other dancers. Surely he must feel the thumping of her heart.

Through the throng of ball gowns Katie watched the two dancing as though they had known each other forever, her catlike eyes mere slits above her false smile. Searching around in a frenzy she grabbed Russell who was getting a drink for his partner.

'Russell, dance with me, please,' she wheedled, turning on all her charm.

'What! Has your pretty boy deserted you for someone else?' teased Russell looking across the dance floor. He put down the glasses and whirled her around whispering in her ear. 'How can I refuse when you were so fantastic the last time we were together. Why don't you lose him altogether after the dance and we can have a repeat performance? I know a great place we could go.'

'Just shut up and dance,' hissed Katie. At their table Billy glowered across the dance floor and downed another whisky.

'Alice, I have to tell you something . . .' murmured Robert, his cheek almost touching hers, the blood drumming in his ears. Finally he could pour out the truth he had tried to deny, that he had loved her from the very first moment he had set eyes on her. For a second his cheek brushed against hers, inflaming his longing for her. Alice's legs turn to water.

'It's okay, you don't need to tell me,' she sighed, her heart flapping against her ribs. Her moment was over. She just knew he was going to confess he loved Katie. Robert's arm tightened around Alice.

'Alice, I—' tried Robert again. A big hand grabbed Robert pulling him roughly aside and Billy's voice grated harshly on her ears.

'You keep your stinking rotten hands off my girl, you little creep.' Billy, now very drunk, confronted Robert, his fists clenched menacingly by his side. Alice jumped to speak but Robert stopped her. Riled at Billy's unexpected attack and intoxicated by Alice's nearness, Robert saw no reason to make things easy for Billy. Raising his hands palms open he replied quietly.

'Listen, mate, we're all having a really nice time so why don't you just take it easy and wait your turn.'

'My turn for my girl, you stuck up bastard! In a pig's arse,' roared Billy and he hit Robert square on the jaw, sending him flying backwards into a group of dancers.

'No, Billy, no!' shrieked Alice. Robert struggled to his feet trying to remain calm and was immediately flattened again. When he finally stood up he was roaring mad.

'If that's what you want, mate,' he said peeling off his jacket. Billy already stripped to his shirt was yanking at his tie.

'This is men's stuff, Alice. Move out of the way,' rasped Billy.

'Billy, Robert, please, no! No!' Alice pleaded pulling ineffectually at Billy's shirt tails, but Billy wasn't listening. Alice lost her balance and fell sideways, breaking the heel of her shoe as the two men locked together.

'You sneaky little cow,' whispered Katie leaning over her. The debs started screaming. The band stopped playing and the entire company stared at them momentarily frozen in horror.

'Steady on Billy,' called Paddy, forcing his way through the stunned crowd only to stagger back into the arms of the gold and purple clad matron as Snake's fist caught him on the chin. The matron in turn fell against her small husband and all three landed in a heap.

Alice heard an ominous rip as she struggled to her feet tearing the precious sequined lace of her dress. From the far end of the hall Aunty Bea clapped her hands to her mouth.

'Oh my God! Billy's in a fight!' she gasped and came streaking across the hall with Ray hard on her heels.

'You must stop this at once!' cried the matron waving her gold evening bag futilely around with one hand as she dragged herself up on her husband's sleeve.

'You stay away from my girl, you flaming sheila,' shouted Billy at Robert, his chest heaving with exertion.

'It's a free country. I can bloody well dance with who I like,' yelled Robert. He lunged at Billy. By now the place was in uproar. Paddy and Snake were going at one another hammer and tongs and a few more had joined in for good measure.

Billy charged at Robert knocking him down again, somehow miraculously managing to stay upright himself. As Robert sat up groggily, one hand clutching his bleeding nose, several burly masons descended on the fighters. Snake and Paddy were quickly subdued but it took two men to hold Billy down.

'You mongrel, bastard,' roared Billy struggling. 'You and your whole bloody McIain mob just stay away from my Alice.'

'How could you Billy! You've ruined everything,' shrilled Katie rushing towards Robert. 'Russell, give me your hankie.' Grabbing the proffered handkerchief she knelt down and held it against Robert's gushing nose.

'You keep out of this, Katie.' Billy was too drunk and too furious to care who he hurt. Ray was at Billy's elbow.

'That's enough, son.'

'I'll kill him,' snarled Katie between gritted teeth. Robert looked across at Alice. Katie, still clutching the handkerchief to his face, saw the longing in his eyes. Billy saw the look too and suddenly all the fight went out of him.

'This is inexcusable,' roared the master of the lodge.

Ray's voice was rock steady as he fixed his watery blue eyes first on the master and then on Billy. 'It's time we were leaving, son,' he said quietly. He nodded to the two burly men holding Billy and they released their grip. Bowed with shame, Billy shambled towards the door. Aunty Bea rushed up. 'Oh, Billy how could you behave like this?'

'Come on Mother,' Ray ordered. 'Enough's been said. Alice, Katie, you too, back to the hotel. Bob here'll make sure the McIain lad's attended to.' Bob, one of the men who had restrained Billy, nodded in acquiescence.

'I'll collect the rest of the family,' said Aunty Bea, unnaturally calm. Suddenly none of this touched Alice any longer. Ignoring the horrified stares of the guests she gathered up her ripped skirts and battered shoes and tripped out of the hall behind Ray and her cousins. Even the gimlet eyes of the matrons boring into her back as the door closed behind them could not affect her. She had seen the longing in Robert's eyes in that final glance and that was enough to rekindle hope. As the family trooped away the band started playing the cha-cha.

Once outside, the cold air and the walk back to the hotel helped to sober Billy up. 'You love him, don't you?' he said to Alice outside the hotel.

'I didn't know how much until just now,' Alice whispered. 'Don't take it badly, Billy.' Her blue eyes were solemn as she stared up at her tall handsome cousin. Billy smiled brokenly at Alice.

'And I let you down,' he said in a cracked voice. 'He doesn't know what a lucky bloke he is.' Then he turned away to hide his own misery.

Chapter Fourteen

ALICE CANTERED ACROSS the paddocks towards Joker's air strip, the early August sunshine lifting her spirits. It was impossible to feel morbid on such a day with the soft wind against her cheeks and the feel of Sherry's sturdy strides beneath her. Today was the sort of day her mother would have said you can reach out and touch the sky. The two saddlebags slung across Sherry's haunches bulged with various items of mail and machine parts she was delivering today. Mrs Small had called her up late last night to say the mail man had another crisis with his family and could she take the deliveries to the outlying properties. As she travelled she mulled over the last couple of months. It had taken over three weeks for Ray to calm down after the Masonic Brawl, as the debutantes' dance had been dubbed, and he forbade the name of McIain to be mentioned under his roof. He had also grounded Alice from flying but finally had been persuaded by Bea to relent as it was not Alice who had started the fight.

Katie had returned to Sydney, which always made Alice feel better; Billy had headed up north in search of a new job, which had made Bea both sad and relieved; and Paddy had returned to Wangianna talking about quitting and joining Billy. But what was in the forefront of Alice's mind and had been since the night of the disaster was the intense look of longing she had seen in Robert's eyes as he had sat slouched on the dance floor cradling his bleeding nose. She would never forget the wave of happiness that had swamped her as his eyes had burned into hers. Yet in the cold light of the following morning as she had stared at her tattered and muddied dress doubts had crept into her mind. Now, two months later, she wondered if she had simply imagined the whole incident.

The only solution, she thought as she reined Sherry in and slid from the saddle at her usual paddock on Joker's property, was to put all thoughts of him out of her mind. With only a few more months of school left she was planning to do a course in animal husbandry next year and these trips and her other job at the hospital would help pay her costs. Anyhow even if the look had really held all that promise, Alice said to herself as she heaved off the heavy saddle bags, why hadn't Robert contacted her?

'The relationship could never work,' she muttered as she staggered towards the hangar. And from all accounts Robert was practically engaged to some rich girl whom his mother had picked out. 'Good luck to him. Who cares,' she lied blowing at a strand of wild black hair that had escaped from under her Akubra and hurrying towards Joker who had appeared from the hangar, dressed in grease-covered overalls, rubbing at an engine part with an oily rag.

'G'day, Alice,' he greeted cheerfully. 'Got a bit of a hitch!'

'Oh yes?' said Alice unperturbed, striding towards the plane to load the gear. Joker often had hitches. She had purposely got up early to leave plenty of time for all hitches and hold-ups.

'Don't bother to load up in that one,' continued Joker. 'Motor's stuffed. I've had to pull the whole thing out.'

Alice turned, a look of concern on her face. 'How long will it take to fix?'

'Won't know till I've got the parts,' replied Joker. 'But you don't need to worry. Young Bluey here showed up this morning. I'm sure he wouldn't mind running you over to the stations.' Alice nearly dropped the saddlebags in amazement as Robert appeared from the shadows of the hangar. Her legs started to tremble. He looked so incredibly handsome in his white moleskins and open-neck shirt, his Akubra half shading his deeply tanned face. All traces of bruising from Billy's fists had disappeared.

'G'day, Alice,' he said looking slightly awkward.

'You wouldn't mind taking this young lass for a turn in your plane, would you young fella? But no beating one another up, mind!'

'No worries,' replied Robert. Alice gave a wry grin, blushing furiously. The whole district had heard about the Masonic Brawl. 'Is this it?' asked Robert relieving Alice of her burden. 'Where are we headed?' He sounded far calmer than he felt.

Alice told him. 'It shouldn't take long, but a couple of the spare parts are fairly urgent,' she explained. 'If we get going straightaway we should be back here by lunchtime.'

'Righto, let's go.' Robert's face split in a wide grin displaying dazzling white teeth. 'My girl's parked out by the petrol pump.'

'Watch the weather, kids, and behave yourselves,' called Joker as Alice followed Robert's long strides back out into the sunshine.

As Alice had predicted the deliveries were straightforward and by midday they were all completed. As they sauntered back to the plane after the final delivery Alice felt a sadness descend on her at the thought of heading home. Occasionally as they walked Robert's fingers accidentally brushed the back of Alice's hand sending small electric shivers up her arm. Then, without warning, he slipped her hand in his. Alice looked steadfastly ahead, her heart racing as they crossed the remaining distance to the Cessna.

'It's been a great day,' Alice said at last, too shy to look into Robert's eyes.

'Thank you for letting me help you,' returned Robert correctly. As she attempted to withdraw her hand to board the plane he covered it with his other hand gently forcing her to turn to him. 'Mum got Cook to throw in some food for me before she left for town today. Would you feel like joining me for lunch?' He too sounded breathless. Alice's heart leapt.

'I'd love too. Here?' she replied quickly. He still had hold of her hand.

'I thought over at Wangianna. I'm supposed to be checking out the windmill up in the paddy paddock. I know a lovely spot near there.'

'Where you take all your girlfriends,' Alice retorted lightly and immediately wished she could bite out her tongue.

'I'm not like that, Alice. Anyway, there's only one girl for me since I met you,' he said huskily.

'Oh yes?' Alice's heart started beating against her ribs.

'I meant what I said at the ball. You are the most beautiful girl I have ever met and . . .' he paused.

'And?' whispered Alice almost inaudibly.

'And I don't ever want to lose you.' His eyes were filled with yearning. Alice thought she would burst with happiness. Her fingers, enveloped by his rough callused hands, quivered uncontrollably. Slowly Robert leaned over and brushed his lips against hers. Alice held her breath. 'I've wanted to do that since the first moment I met you,' murmured Robert. Aware that they were on someone else's airstrip he stepped back. Trying to sound normal although the racing of his heart was making speech difficult he said, 'Come on, let's go and see what this windmill's doing; anyway, I want to show you some of Wangianna.'

Twenty minutes later they landed smoothly on the airstrip near the homestead and taxied the plane close to the hangar. As Robert disappeared into the darkness reappearing with a motorbike, the thought flashed across Alice's mind that she was glad Mrs McIain was safely in town.

'Ever ridden one of these?' asked Robert. Alice laughed and shook her head. 'One rule. Hang on tight,' explained Robert flashing Alice a dazzling smile. 'Pete knows.' He gave a whistle and a black and brown cattle dog came hurtling out of nowhere and leaped onto the back of the bike. Tongue lolling, ears pricked, he stared adoringly at Robert, ready for action. 'Down, Pete, and wait your turn,' ordered Robert.

The dog obeyed, ears down, and then leaped up at Alice who in turn petted him, the two striking up an immediate friendship. Robert looked at Alice with renewed respect. 'He doesn't usually act like that with strangers—you must smell good. That's enough Pete.' Swinging one leg over the saddle he waited while Alice climbed gingerly on behind before stamping on the pedal. The motor roared into life. Securing her hat more firmly on her head, Alice shyly slid her arms around Robert's strong muscular frame, shifting her body closer to make room for Pete on the tiny space behind.

'Hang on!' shouted Robert as he tested the throttle. The heat of Robert's body burned into her own as they raced across the bumpy tracks and up towards the paddy paddock. Halfway across one of the fields kept for the famous Wangianna rams, Robert stopped and half-turned to her.

'I wanted to show you some of this,' he said helping her off the bike, his pride visible. As Pete rushed off to inspect a rabbit hole Robert pointed to twenty or so fat merino rams, their wrinkled coats an emblem of their quality. 'See those, they're some of the top rams in the world. And this,' he swept his arm around indicating the land, 'one day this will all be mine and with the right woman by my side, what more could a man want?' Alice stared in awe across the vast flat plains. There was a magic about this land that touched the very core of her being. The colour, the ancient grandeur, the peace, the way land and sky melted into one at the edges of sight. Robert felt the intensity of her feelings. Turning to her he fingered a strand of her wild black hair.

'Isn't it glorious, Alice?' he sighed trying and failing to disguise his intensity. Without warning he removed her hat so her hair tumbled free, and kissed her gently on her soft laughing mouth. Alice gave a sigh of pleasure and returned his kiss. But what started as a casual caress turned into a passionate embrace that overtook them both, sending fire blazing through their veins. Neither of them wanted to draw apart and when they finally did they were both breathless.

'What was that?' gasped Alice, her heart still racing.

'That was the beginning of how much I love you, my Alice,' replied Robert huskily. 'I adore you. I've adored you from the moment I first laid eyes on you.'

'Your Alice?' Alice's laughter was cut short as he drew her into his arms and kissed her again, this time more tenderly yet in a way that was almost timid as if he were afraid that in kissing her too hard she might shatter in his arms. Inexperienced though she was, Alice could sense the undercurrent of suppressed passion and longed to burst its dam. She responded in the only way she knew. Eyes closed she returned his kiss with as much fervour as he, allowing him to gently prise apart her lips so she felt the tip of his tongue in her mouth. Shuddering with a newly discovered ecstasy she pulled away, afraid she might drown in the delight.

'Didn't we have a dam or something to check out?' she ventured shakily, gazing up at him through her long thick lashes, fingering his shirt, half afraid to meet his gaze.

'The windmill.' Robert managed to keep his voice steady while his heart thumped madly in his chest. He longed to cover her lashes, her cheeks, her neck, her luscious red lips, with millions of kisses. Yet fearful his unbridled passion might scare her, instead he kissed her lightly on the hair. 'You always smell like spring. How do you manage it?'

Whistling up Pete they remounted the motorbike and sped towards the paddock. The paddy paddock had earned its name because of the quantities of paddy melons that grew there each year, bitter green melons the size of a man's fist that children learned to split and squirt as a game. As Robert dodged between the melons twisting and bumping, Alice pressed her body close to his, one hand clutching her hat which refused to stay on, her long black mane escaping its band and flowing out behind with the yellow dust, her whole being still throbbing from his kiss.

The day was becoming unseasonably hot so after Robert had inspected the windmill, which appeared to be in good working order, they spread out the small rug Robert produced from his bike bag and sat down in the shade of a great gum tree near the dam and drank the homemade ginger beer. Then together they enjoyed the delicious cold pies, salad and homemade cakes supplied by Cook. When they had eaten their fill they relaxed in comfortable silence listening to the birds and sounds of the bush around them under a deep blue canopy. Alice wanted this exquisite moment to last forever. After licking them both, Pete lolloped off and lay panting in the shade. Robert rolled lazily over on one elbow and reached for Alice's hand.

'You have no idea how happy I feel now that you have finally come back into my life,' he murmured, gently tracing each fingertip in turn.

'I feel as though I have found the other half of myself,' Alice whispered reaching out and stroking his cheek. 'I think my heart might burst with happiness.'

'I never realised until today how much I love you,' said Robert gently drawing Alice into his arms. He kissed her on the lips, softly at first and then more passionately, pressing her gently backwards until she was lying on the ground. Alice's pulse quickened as she returned his kiss. This time she thought she was ready for his embrace but she was not expecting the delicious tumult it created within her. When Robert released her she waited still caught up in the intensity of his love, incapable of movement or coherent thought. Robert stared down at her beauty and the open expression of love in her face and his whole body ached with longing.

'Alice am I, have you . . .?'

'There's never been anyone else,' Alice said, her eyes wide with arousal.

Robert kissed her again, long and hard, the tip of his tongue caressing her lips and gently forcing them apart, his tongue exploring her mouth and setting her body on fire. Alice sighed as he lifted his mouth from hers. She quivered at his touch as he ran a finger down her cheek, outlining the soft contours of her neck and shoulders, responding to the restrained urgency in his love and held her breath as almost tentatively he outlined her firm breasts with his fingers, seeing the nipples already straining through the thin cotton of her blouse. Robert's fingers hovered over one button.

'You can undo it if you like,' Alice whispered almost inaudibly.

'Alice, I love you so much.' Robert undid the button with trembling fingers, his voice, husky with desire. 'I feel so lucky. I've never felt like this about anyone else.' Alice gazed at him her whole body quivering in anticipation. 'You're beautiful. You don't know what you do to me, how much I want you. Every day I wake up thinking of you, imagining your smile and your wonderful body close to mine and I wonder if I can bear the longing. But it's not enough. I want to make sure I wake up being able to reach out and touch you and hold you for the rest of my life.' Alice suddenly became aware she had been holding her breath. Fumbling, Robert did up the button. 'I love you and I want to cherish you always, but I don't want to ask anything more of you until we're married.' Alice sat up in shock, her breath coming out in a rush. 'You will marry me, won't you?'

'You're joking?' she replied abruptly.

'Is this a joke?' Carefully he pulled out of his pocket a small gold friendship ring with two entwined gold hearts and laid it in the palm of her hand. 'I got it engraved.' It said *Alice from Robert*. 'We'll choose a proper engagement ring together.' Alice's eyes glistened with tears of joy as he slid the ring on her wedding finger. Then she reached up her arms around his strong sunburned neck and hugged away the anxiety still hovering behind the love in his dark brown eyes.

'Oh Robert, I love you so much, but what about your mother?' Robert pulled away sharply.

'What about my mother?'

'Aren't you supposed to be engaged to—?'

'My mother may think she knows who I should marry, but I choose my wife,' said Robert firmly. 'Now was that a yes?' Alice nodded, laughing through tears of joy.

'Oh Robert, I don't believe this is happening.'

'Just say yes!'

'Yes! Yes! Yes!'

She almost jumped out of her skin as abruptly he let her go so she almost fell backwards and leaped to his feet.

'There's only one thing for it,' he yelled. Pulling his shirt over his head he tossed it on the ground and raced over to the dam. Still wearing his moleskins he jumped into the water and swam ferociously out into the middle where he did a series of movements that reminded Alice of a war dance. Alice sat laughing at his antics.

'Are you quite mad?' she cried.

'Yes, but it was my only alternative. Come and join me.' Joyously Alice sprang to her feet. Throwing off her jeans and blouse she jumped in after him and swam to greet him. For the next few minutes they swam around releasing some of the pent-up energy their proximity had produced. Then, standing waist-deep in the water, Robert, feeling more in control, took Alice once more in his arms where she clung to him, her long slender legs twined around his waist, her black hair streaming down her back.

'Alternative to what?' teased Alice still thoroughly aroused, outlining his lips with one fingertip.

'You know very well.' As they kissed again he felt his desire build and he wondered how long he dare hold her before his willpower gave out. Firmly he carried her back to the bank.

'Get dressed before you start causing me trouble again,' he laughed slapping her playfully on the rump and tossing his shirt to her. 'Use that to dry yourself.' Then he sat down several paces away with his back to her concentrating on watching the sun dry out his moleskins.

'You know, I haven't been able to get rid of this strange feeling that fate has been drawing us together,' said Alice when they were both once more fully clothed. 'There's something I want to tell you.' She hesitated just a moment but Robert was listening intently. 'I have this dream. It's like . . . well, it's like a furnace burning deep inside me . . .' There was a new energy about her as she explained how she had felt when her father had deserted her and the promise she had made to herself to build the biggest sheep stud farm in Australia.

Robert didn't say a word after she had finished. Instead he became brusquely efficient packing up the remnants of the picnic and the rug and shoving it all in the bike bag. Whistling Pete, he swung his leg over the bike and stamped it into life. Alice looked at him in concern and her heart went cold.

'What's the matter? Did I say something wrong?' she shouted in alarm. 'You don't think I'm just after . . .?' But her words were lost over the roar of the engine.

'Get on. There's something I've just remembered,' Robert shouted back, jerking his head and avoiding her gaze. Revving up the bike they roared back across the paddy paddock with Alice clinging on tight, through three more fields until he reached the place where the prize Wangianna ewes were grazing with their lambs. His speed trickled almost to a walk as his eyes searched the paddock. Despite her confusion at Robert's unexpected mood change, Alice watched the lambs in delight, some frolicking in the grass, others lying down or suckling their thick-woolled merino mothers. Most of them were now eight and nine weeks old and already marked, their floppy tails removed, their coats starting to take on the distinctive merino curl.

Unable to find what he was looking for Robert took off once more across the paddocks and stopped outside one of the sheds near the jackaroos' quarters where an Aborigine in his early forties was standing twisting a piece of wire with a pair of pliers. Dismounting Robert grabbed Alice's hand and walked over to the man.

'Melon, you know Alice,' said Robert.

'Certainly do, Miss Alice. The young boss here never stops talking about you.' Melon's dark face split into an enormous grin and he touched his hand to his big bushman's hat jammed over a thick mop of black curls. The colour in Alice's already flushed cheeks deepened. 'Come to check me out have ya, young fella?' laughed the black man.

'That's right, Melon. No, I wanted to find out how those two little latecomers you told me about are going.'

'Come and see for yourself.' Melon turned and walked round the side of the shed to where a makeshift pen had been erected. Alice watched enchanted as twin lambs, their curly white coats still damp from having been washed, the umbilical cord still hanging from their underbellies, staggered towards them on very wobbly legs, bleating imperiously.

'Listen to the noisy blighters, you'd think they were starving to death and I only finished feeding them an hour ago,' said Melon. He finished twisting the wire and fixed it as an extra hinge onto the gate of the pen.

'No luck with the mother, then?' asked Robert.

''Fraid not. She was too far gone when I found her. She was a good breeder too. I tried the poor little buggers with three other ewes but they were all too mean to share.'

'Poor old tart. You always were a soft touch, Melon. I knew I could count on you.' Robert and the stocky weather-beaten man grinned at each other. Alice could see there was a very close bond between them. Still bursting with happiness at Robert's proposal she couldn't keep the grin off her face either.

'But they're tough 'uns, that's for sure.' Melon winked at Robert and jerked his head at Alice. 'What you two young things been up to, then 'eh? You look like you both swallowed a jug of cream.'

'I just asked Alice to marry me, Melon, and she said "yes",' replied Robert beaming.

'You done him a big favour, Miss Alice,' said Melon, his white toothy smile reaching his ears as he nodded to Alice. Robert lifted the catch to the pen gate and beckoned to Alice to follow.

'Reckon from now on these two've got every chance of growing into good strong breeders like their mother, don't you think, Melon?' Robert picked up one of the lambs and gave it to Alice. Her eyes opened wide with delight as she took the wriggling, bleating animal in her arms. It smelt of warm slightly sour milk and seemed to be all legs. The lamb looked up at Alice, its cries getting louder.

'I know,' murmured Alice enchanted. 'It's a wicked world. No one feeds you enough, do they?' Alice noticed a small black mark on the tip of its little nose. Robert inspected the other lamb which was pure white all over.

'These are the start of your dream,' said Robert. Alice's mouth dropped open in amazement.

'But I can't take two of your top lambs,' she gasped gently placing the lamb on the ground. It nuzzled up to her hand searching for milk.

'If you don't they'll die,' replied Robert. 'And anyway I'll get them back again as soon as we're married!' Alice laughed and blushed. 'You heard what Melon said. Often we have to let orphaned lambs like these die if they can't pirate onto another ewe, because it's just such a lot of work to rear them by the bottle. These two obviously weren't pushy enough, so you'd be doing them a favour. Also to be strictly businesslike that black mark on the nose could mean it might cast a throwback.' Alice looked puzzled. 'Have a black sheep as its first lamb, so there are two points against it. Although this one's as clean as a whistle. Not a spot of black.' He stopped, watching the pleasure on Alice's face.

'Oh Robert, I don't know what to say.' She had been absolutely sure that Robert disapproved of her dreams, but now joy bubbled up inside her. One lamb was trying to suckle onto one of her fingers, while the other tried to push it out of the way. She turned to Melon. 'Can I give them some more milk?' Melon nodded and disappeared, reappearing with two bottles each half full of milk. Alice knelt down as the two lambs jostled to be first.

'I'd like to think this made up for Silly,' Robert said quietly, taking one of the bottles.

'You don't have to make up for anything,' she replied, her eyes full of love. 'Oh, goodness, there's so much I want to learn about.'

Robert grinned like a small boy. 'Well, you're their mum now by the look of things.' The lambs were straining the last drops from the bottles. Finding there was no more food they lost interest and Alice stood up. Her face was radiant as she looked at Robert, trying to assemble a disapproving expression.

'You're not to do that again.'

'What?'

'Suddenly turn all efficient and businesslike like that. You scared me half to death. You could at least have looked at me.'

'I'm no good at secrets. My eyes always give me away. You'd have guessed I was up to something. D'you think your folks'll mind?' Alice shook her head.

'Aunty Bea'll help,' she decided. Her eyes were brilliant sapphire. 'Thank you,' she said suddenly shy.

The mention of Bea made them both aware of the time. Alice glanced at her watch. It was far later in the afternoon than she realised. Reluctantly she suggested they head back to Billabrin. Melon went in search of a box to transport the two lambs. Robert ran his fingers through Alice's hair tracing the curve of her high cheekbones down to her soft smile. Tilting her chin he kissed her hesitantly on the mouth. Aware Melon would reappear at any moment, Alice drew back embarrassed, her cheeks crimson. Suddenly Robert's eyes lit up.

'What am I thinking of? I'm not flying you anywhere. Mum should be back from town by now. Let's go and break the news to everyone now.' Grabbing Alice's hand he ran back to the bike. 'We'll be back later,' he shouted to Melon as they both hopped on. This time Pete raced on ahead as they drove back to the main house and parked on the hard-packed dirt of the driveway.

Melon watched them for the distance and shook his head. Robert's roughened fingers closed protectively once more around Alice's hand as, despite the heat, they raced up the steps two at a time onto the wide verandah.

'Anyone home?' yelled Robert excitedly. Almost immediately Elizabeth appeared through the fly-screen door. She stopped in her tracks, a look of surprised disapproval on her face as she caught sight of Alice.

'Hello, Alice. This is unexpected.' Elizabeth's steely gaze hovered over her fleetingly before they came to rest on Robert's face. 'Robby dear, you have a visitor.' Alice gave an involuntary shiver.

'Oh' said Robert surprised. 'Who?'

'Katie Downing. She arrived here just after two in a very agitated state. We've had a long talk. I tried to raise you on the Cessna radio but you'd obviously switched it off.' She looked pointedly at Alice. 'Robby, I think you have a few things to sort out.'

'Katie?' Robert exclaimed. As he spoke Katie appeared at the door looking white and drawn. Alice stepped towards her cousin.

'Katie, what's the matter—nothing dreadful's happened has it?'

Katie gave a short laugh. 'It depends how you look at it. Robbo, I have to talk to you.'

'Sure, Katie, what's up?'

'In private.'

'There's nothing that can't be said in front of Alice,' Robert said, suddenly defensive.

'I think it would be better if we were alone for a few moments.'

'I think it would be a good idea, dear,' interrupted Elizabeth firmly.

Alice blushed uncomfortably and shrugged her shoulders. 'It's okay, Robert,' she said. Robert and Katie disappeared inside.

Unsmiling Elizabeth turned to Alice. 'Why don't you wait out here in the breeze, Alice. I'll organise us both a cool drink.' With that she vanished inside.

Alice sank down into one of the wide wicker armchairs on the verandah and stared across at the brilliant sunset, chewing at her fingernails, a horrible gnawing feeling in her stomach. Elizabeth returned with fruit juice and for the next half hour Alice struggled with polite conversation, the gnawing sensation increasing. Whatever Robert and Katie were discussing had to be something major and Elizabeth knew what it was. Why else this artificial attempt at friendliness towards her? The minutes dragged on until finally Robert reappeared on his own looking very pale. Elizabeth slipped silently into the house.

'Robert, what is it?' said Alice fearfully. Robert walked Alice to one end of the verandah and stood fingering the railing. Finally he turned to face her, his own face in shadow against the dying sun.

'I don't know how to tell you, Alice, except straight.' The gnawing turned to churning. 'Katie's pregnant and she says I'm the father.' Alice thought her legs were going to buckle under her. She opened her mouth to speak but nothing came out. When she finally spoke it was as though someone else were talking.

'It can't be true.'

Robert was still standing by the verandah's edge his fists clenched so the knuckles showed white.

'Alice . . .' he choked on the words unable to continue.

Suddenly Alice's numbness turned to fury.

'You slept with Katie?' she spat. 'You slept with Katie and then you came on to me with all that love and cherish stuff?' Tears of rage pricked her eyes but she would not cry. 'Did you mean anything you said or was I just another of your conquests to brag about? Did you ever have any intention of marrying me?' Robert blanched at her attack.

'Alice, I love you and I would do anything in the world to make this all go away.' The pain was visible in his eyes.

'Too right you would. So now you're going to dump Katie too. When did you do it?' she screamed. 'When? Where? After the ball? Before the ball? Was that all a lie too?' She was beside herself now, wanting to say anything to hurt him the way he was hurting her.

'I don't know.'

'What d'you mean you don't know?'

'I don't remember a thing about it.' Alice stared at Robert. For a moment a flicker of hope showed through the terrible blackness.

'You mean perhaps you're not the father?'

Robert shook his head. 'Sit down, please, and I'll try and explain.'

'I don't want to sit down, I want to stand,' Alice cried. Something registered in her brain. She cleared her throat and said more quietly, 'I want to stand while you tell me everything.' Robert shuffled uncomfortably.

'All right. Look, I got really depressed when you refused to have anything to do with me and Katie offered me a shoulder to cry on. Then after the long weekend everything got really bad and I met Katie in Sydney.' To Alice every word was like a death knell to their love. 'Again just as friends, she never meant anything more to me, truly Alice. She took me to a party and I . . . I got drunk and that's all I remember until . . .' His unfinished sentence hung between them in the silence. He looked imploringly at Alice. Her eyes were brilliant blue and hard as crystals.

'Until?'

'I woke up the next day and she told me we'd made love.' The pain in Alice was unbearable. There was a ringing in her ears and she could hardly breathe.

'How can you be sure the baby's yours, Robert?'

'Would I lie about the father of my own child?' Alice whirled round and stared into Katie's glittering catlike eyes.

'Well you've lied about just about everything else in your life, why stop now?'

'Alice, please . . .' Robert exclaimed. Alice looked up at Robert and her composure snapped.

'I'm sorry. I really thought—' The words choked in her throat and tears shimmered on the edges of her thick black lashes. The pain in her eyes pierced Robert's heart as he watched her misery, helpless to do anything. Very slowly Alice slipped the friendship ring off her finger and laid it on the table. She dared not look at Robert again. When she finally looked up Katie was standing beside Robert, her fair hair a halo softening her features in the fading light. Alice thought she had never seen her cousin look more glowingly beautiful. For an instant they stared at one another and Alice blanched at the unmistakable look of triumph in Katie's eyes. It was enough to change Alice's misery to black icy rage.

'Game set and match, Katie. Congratulations,' said Alice her voice like granite. She held out her hand.

'Do you think I meant for this to happen?' cried Katie.

'Who knows? The keys please. I take it you drove over,' Alice demanded frostily. Katie put the ute keys in Alice's upturned palm. Robert jerked forwards at her words.

'But you can't leave now,' he spluttered. 'It'll take you hours to get home. What about the kangaroos— it's far too dangerous.'

'I'd rather die than spend one more second in your company. Have a wonderful life.' Alice turned swiftly on her heel. Without another backward glance she strode down the verandah steps, climbed into the ute and drove out of Wangianna station.

Chapter Fifteen

'YOU HAVE TO GET over it,' said Ben. 'You can't let one lousy drongo ruin your life.'

'I love him, Ben, I really love him,' sobbed Alice. 'What have I done to Katie that she hates me so much? How can I ever be happy again?' Alice buried her face in her pillow to hush the sobs that racked her body.

'I'm upset for you too, sis, but he's marrying Katie and we'd better get used to it. How many times have you told me it's a waste of time and energy getting upset about things you can't change? He's a bastard but you're being a wimp, Princess.' Ben's words jerked Alice's head upwards, no one had called her Princess since her father left. Rather than adding to her misery it made her feel more protected. She stopped crying, sat up and blew her nose.

'I am not a wimp,' she said sulkily. 'Don't be so horrid.'

'Well don't act like one then,' persisted Ben.

Alice gulped. He was right, she was totally ignoring her own advice. She was also ignoring the devastation Katie's revelation had caused Bea and Ray.

'Okay, so what do you suggest?'

'I dunno—. Do something outrageous.'

'Like what?' Alice said flatly. She could feel her morale crumbling again.

'Come on Alice, what about your dream, our dream? No one can ever steal that from you, whatever else they may try to do.' Alice looked with new eyes at her brother.

'When did you suddenly grow up?' she said amazed.

Relieved to see that he had finally got Alice listening, Ben continued quickly. 'What's the next step in our dream?'

Crossing her legs on the bed Alice hugged her knees to her chin, thinking. 'Well, we've got the livestock—all two of them.' She laughed half-heartedly. Her eyes blazed suddenly. 'Which I'm keeping and I'll make damned sure they're far more than just the start of our dream.' A healthy anger had replaced her misery. 'What we need is—'

'—land' interrupted Ben impatiently. 'And to buy land we need money. How much have you got?'

Alice thought. 'About six pounds.'

'With my four that makes ten. At one pound an acre, if Hungry Spirit comes in at thirty to one on the Wednesday races tomorrow, that's three hundred acres of good grazing land.'

'Hungry Spirit—what d'you know about him?'

'Nothing, but with a name like that how could we lose?'

'You're asking me to throw my money away on some horse we know nothing about because you like his name? You're crazy!' exclaimed Alice.

'I know!' replied Ben grinning triumphantly. He had got her smiling for the first time in three days.

Occasionally in life, when everything else goes wrong, strange things happen. Hungry Spirit came in at seventeen to one and Ben, grinning from ear to ear, collected their winnings from his mate and went to find Alice.

'Why don't you ask Hal Tyson if he knows of any land around his place,' suggested Ben fanning Alice happily with the notes. 'I did a bit of asking around and it's good grazing land there. Never know, he might even sell you some of his.'

'You're full of surprises, Ben,' laughed Alice.

'Better than moping around.' He cuffed his sister playfully.

Alice thought about his words as she was returning from a special delivery for Mrs Small the following Friday. Her heart still ached with misery over Robert and she refused to speak to Katie, but Ben had shaken her out of her despair and she was back fighting. She made a mental note for her and Ben to visit the stock and station agents the next day to see what property was available.

She was flying the four-seater Cessna Skylane 182, its call sign XDX standing out clearly on the body of the aircraft. The small back passenger seat and the one next to the pilot had both been removed to hold the mail and large deliveries. Other packages could be stuffed into the fuselage behind her. It had been a bit of a squash on the way there but once relieved of its load the plane was easier to handle. Alice mouthed the call sign 'Xray Delta Xray', glad of the excuse to escape the atmosphere of the house. Having announced she was pregnant, Katie had dropped out of school. She had been getting bad morning sickness for the last two weeks but now with her pregnancy no longer a secret she played on her mother's emotions, alternately acting contrite and repentant and then fussing over her wedding plans, always bringing the conversation around to her needs and those of the expected baby. The wedding was planned for the beginning of October and Aunty Bea, who had maintained a strained cheerfulness, was torn between looking after her own daughter and trying to reach Alice who had withdrawn into an impenetrable shell.

After the first terrible wave of misery on the Saturday evening when she had arrived home from Wangianna, Alice had not shed a tear in front of the rest of the family and instead had smiled and laughed with the others. Only her laughter was hollow and her smile far too brittle. She had immediately tripled her efforts at her studies, working late into the night until she fell into an exhausted sleep, although never forgetting to tend to Sherry or the two orphaned lambs Robert had insisted Alice keep, who bleated insistently whenever they saw her approach.

Alice altered course for home mulling over the best land to buy with the money from her amazing win. She had checked the weather forecast before takeoff. A storm front moving up from the south was expected over the western plains area between three and five that afternoon. Now Alice could see heavy overdeveloped cumulonimbus clouds south of Bilabrin and moving north at high speed.

When she had taken off the air had been hot and close, typical of the prelude to a big storm. For the last half-hour she had been battling strong headwinds which had been gobbling up the fuel. Checking her map she estimated she should be flying over the Johnsons' property very shortly, then it was only another twenty minutes and she would be home. Her eyes flicked briefly across her petrol gauge and she decided she had just enough in the tank to get her home safely. Scanning the grey-green scrubland below for the familiar row of trees that hid the creek beside the Johnsons' property, she realised something was badly wrong. The creek was too far west and the dam, her other point of reference, was the wrong shape. In fact she didn't recognise any of the landmarks that should have been around the Johnsons' property. She rubbed her eyes and looked again. Then she saw the comforting glint of sunshine on the galvanised tin roof of the house. Heaving a sigh of relief she flew towards the building until she could make out the large black lettering standing out clearly on the homestead rooftop. It read 'Bowen'.

'Bowen?' she swore over the roar of the engine. She must have muddled up one of the tiny towns on the way back. This meant she still had a good hour's flying left. She definitely couldn't risk flying further without refuelling. Luckily the Bowens were used to her dropping in unexpectedly. She reached for the radio.

'Bowen Station, Bowen Station, this is Xray Delta Xray, do you read, over?' There was no reply. After the third attempt the reply came crackling over the transmission.

'Xray Delta Xray this is Bowen Station. Fraser here. Is that you, Alice?'

'Hi, Fraser! Yes, it's Alice Ferguson here again. Just looked at my petrol gauge and I'm going below my safety reserve. Can I come down and have a top-up from your pump?' Alice liked Fraser. The big blond twenty-three-year-old was always teasing her about her tomboyish approach to life, claiming they never should have given women the vote and that he wanted his women 'barefoot, penniless and pregnant in the kitchen'. Alice quickly learned he in fact felt the exact opposite, admiring the independence and spirit of women in the outback.

'No problem, Alice. Bit blowy down here. Where are you?'

'I'm about fifteen miles from your property coming in from the north-west. Should be able to see your landing strip shortly.'

'Righto! There's no one at the house at present. I'm down at the bottom paddock struggling with bloody tree stumps. Help yourself, but the pump's a bit temperamental. I've got a mate of yours here. I'll send him up to give you a hand. You don't want to hang around too long though, I just heard over the radio they're expecting bad electric storms later today.' The radio crackled noisily, making it hard for Alice to hear.

'Thanks Fraser. I heard the weather forecast too but I should be right. It's just the wind that's hard work. I can see your landing strip now.' She altered course and fifteen minutes later neatly landed her aircraft, taxied over to the fuel pump and stepped out into the gusty wind.

Shielding her eyes from the dust she watched as a battered ute drove up and a brown and black cattle dog leapt off the back. Alice's gut twisted as she recognised first the dog and then Robert. Furious at Robert's lack of sensitivity and miserable at having to confront him, Alice almost jumped back into the plane and took off again without refuelling. Then she pulled herself together realising what a damn stupid thing to do that would be. Stony-faced she marched up to the pump. The cattle dog rushed over to Alice, jumping up and wagging his tail furiously, whining with pleasure. Alice patted him, tears blurring her vision.

'Hello, Pete, you silly old thing.'

'Hi, Alice,' greeted Robert embarrassed. 'Fraser doesn't know—'

'Hi,' interrupted Alice grim-faced. She pushed Pete gently down and tried to pick up the fuel pump but her fingers were shaking so much she couldn't get the lever out.

'Here, let me.'

'No, thanks.' But the stubborn thing was still stuck. Alice had no choice but to stand back and let Robert help her.

'We've been down clearing the bottom paddock,' said Robert by way of conversation.

'Oh,' said Alice. She then ignored him until the plane was refuelled. As Robert replaced the pump Alice reached into the cockpit and called up on the radio. 'I'll leave the money for the fuel up at the house.'

'Don't be a dill, Alice. You don't owe me a thing.'

'Don't argue with me, Fraser.' Alice gave a metallic laugh. 'Enjoy your stump pulling. See ya!' She' returned the radio to its pocket.

'I'll take the money to the house if you like,' offered Robert. Ignoring him, Alice quickly deposited some money under a brick on the porch and checked the outside of the aircraft. Satisfied, she got in, clipped on her seat belt and started the engine. Filled with misery Robert stood with his hands in his pockets watching Alice take off.

'There goes my one chance at real happiness, Pete,' he said, fondling the dog's ears. 'Struth, how could I have been such a fool as to get myself into this mess and not even be able to remember bloody doing it.' Pete whined and wagged his tail in sympathy. Disconsolately Robert filled the ute's tank with petrol and headed back to help Fraser.

'This has got to be the last bloody stump I'm pulling today, mate, I'm buggered,' he called over the radio as he jolted over the wheel ruts.

Five minutes after takeoff, with the wind behind her, Alice set course for home, her mind in turmoil. It would have been easier if he had shouted at her or refused to help her but he had to be utterly nice. Utterly hatefully loathsomely nice and vilely handsome. She shouldn't let someone so revoltingly handsome cause her so much misery. And casual, like there had never ever been anything between them. She couldn't bear the pain. Alice ground her teeth in miserable frustration. Why had he needed to pretend he loved her in the first place? If only she could hate him more. If only she could stop feeling. The plane gave a sudden lurch jerking her mind back to flying. She realised she could not afford to think about Robert or she wouldn't make it home at all.

At least she wasn't heading directly into wind any longer, but the wind strength was building, thumping and buffeting the plane and it took all her skill to keep on course. The glaring white of the clouds had darkened to a menacing grey and the storm front was now fast approaching Billabrin. When the storm hit she guessed she'd be in for a pretty rough time. She glanced anxiously at her watch. 3.40 pm. Just under three hours of daylight left, but even with this wind and the darkening skies she knew the way from here so well that she should be home and safe well before dark. A flash of lightning split the sky in the distance as Alice wriggled to get more comfortable in her seat. She flew on, brushing away the hot silent tears that rolled down her cheeks. Another lightning flash jagged its way across the sky. The radio crackled into life startling Alice and she listened as Robert and Fraser discussed the course of action for pulling out the tree stump.

'What you doin' up there, Bluey, having a picnic? Put your foot on the gas, and let's get this bloody thing out of the ground and call it quits.'

'I'm doing my best, mate. Some of these ruts are bloody awful. Don't be such an impatient bastard.'

'Too right I'm impatient. Me tongue's hanging out for a drink. This wind isn't helping any, either.' Alice turned the radio off, unable to bear the pain of Robert's voice stabbing at her like a thousand daggers. 'Bluey, I never called him that,' she thought miserably. Two seconds later she switched it back on again. Better to fly with the radio switched on in this weather. She had to calm down and start behaving responsibly instead of letting her emotions dictate to her like this.

The two were still chattering on. 'She's a bloody big stump, Bluey, but I reckon we can do it in a couple of goes without pulling the guts out of the tractor. I might just give it a good hard yank for starters.'

'Don't be a bloody idiot, mate, trying to do it on your own. I'll be there in forty seconds.'

'D'you think I'm that bloody stupid, Bluey? You'll be the one driving the tractor.' Alice laughed at Fraser's dry wit. She guessed the radio silence was while the two men sorted out who was doing what. Fraser was talking again.

'Okay, Bluey, easy does it. Hold it there, mate, hold it there!' Suddenly Alice's hair stood up on the back of her neck as the screech of a racing motor filled the airwaves.

'Jesus mate the whole bloody thing's coming down on top of me!' screamed Robert. 'Back off, Fraser. For God's sake, back off!' The radio went dead.

Alice jerked from her misery, the adrenalin suddenly pumping through her veins. Grabbing the radio she called, 'Bowen Property this is Xray Delta Xray. Fraser I'm returning to the strip.' Her heart in her mouth, Alice banked the plane steeply, thrust the throttle forward and charged back towards the airstrip. With every second that passed she visualised Robert crushed beyond recognition under the tractor. Willing the little plane to fly faster she fought against the desperate fear that when she reached the two men she might be too late to help. Precious time was eaten up battling against the wind before she finally slithered the plane to a halt.

Fraser leapt out of the ute and rushed over to Robert. The tractor had flipped backwards over on itself throwing Robert only partially clear so he was lying on his back, his right leg pinned under the bonnet. The culprit, a huge tree stump, its ugly grey mound standing like some malicious sentinel, its great roots bared to the sky where the two men had cleared around it, had not budged an inch. Robert was grey with pain.

'Jesus, mate, you'll never get me out of here now.'

'We'll get you out of here, mate, don't you worry,' rasped Fraser. Not daring to go too close to Robert he quickly summed up the situation. If he didn't move the tractor Robert would die. With the tractor lying the way it was there was little hope of him jacking it up off his crushed leg on his own. Even if he had the physical strength to jack it high enough the risks of toppling it and Robert being crushed to death were too great. Whichever way he looked at it, the risks were intolerable but he couldn't just leave him there. Robert moaned.

'Hold on, mate!' cried Fraser and raced back to the ute and grabbed the radio. His hand shook as he pressed the speak button. 'Xray Delta Xray, Alice can you hear me?'

'Xray Delta Xray receiving you Bowen Property. I have landed. What do you want me to do, Fraser?' Alice was at her most efficient. Fraser had no idea of the turmoil within her. At his next words her heart went cold.

'Robert's trapped under the tractor. I daren't try moving it on my own. I need you to bring the other tractor up here with extra chain to pull him free. It's in the shed to the right of the house away from the petrol pump. The chain is in the far corner of the same shed.'

'Got that, Fraser. I'm on my way,' replied Alice.

'And don't drive the tractor too fast or you'll flip that one too.' Wiping the sweat out of his eyes Fraser leaped out of the ute, grabbed the first-aid box and ran over to his friend. Robert was still semiconscious. Blood poured from a large gash on his forehead millimetres from his right eye and he was lying at a very awkward angle. There was no telling what internal injuries he had suffered, but at least he was still alive. Tying his handkerchief tightly around Robert's head to staunch the bleeding as best he could, Fraser then wrapped his jacket around him.

'Listen, mate, you're going to have to hang in there a bit longer till we can pull this thing off you and get you out of here and onto the plane. Alice heard us and turned back, thank God. She's on her way in the other tractor now. How's your back?' Robert stretched his white lips in a caricature of a smile.

'Pretty crook, mate.'

'Can you feel your toes?'

'I dunno,' Robert croaked.

'We only need to lift the tractor a few inches and we'll be able to drag you free. It's going to hurt like hell, mate, but there's no alternative.' Fraser fished out his hip flask 'Here take a slug of this.' He poured some rum down Robert's throat. Robert sputtered and gasped but managed to swallow quite a lot.

'Reckon that stuff'd clean out the insides of a carburettor,' said Fraser trying to jolly Robert along. 'Have some more.' He gave Robert another good swig of rum.

Twenty minutes later Alice arrived on the second tractor. Quickly and efficiently under Fraser's directions she backed the tractor into position and they fixed the extra chain over and across the fallen tractor and back onto the second tractor chassis, taking every precaution they could think of to minimise the danger of crushing Robert if something went wrong when they started to pull.

'When I tell you drive forward but if you hear the engine start to wind up stop immediately. You ready?' ordered Fraser once he was satisfied the chains were as secure as possible. Alice nodded, biting her bottom lip.

'Here goes, mate,' muttered Fraser under his breath, praying he wouldn't do more damage to Robert when he dragged him free.

On Fraser's command Alice inched the tractor forward, listening intently to the engine noise, feeling the tug as the chains tightened lifting the tractor just a fraction off Robert's leg. It was enough for Fraser to drag him clear. Robert promptly passed out but Alice was at his side in a flash. Quickly she bandaged Robert's leg with old rags from the ute and carefully placed makeshift splints from tree branches around his leg, securing them while Fraser made a temporary stretcher out of sturdy young saplings and rope. By the time they had finished the first drops of rain had started to fall.

'Just as well he's passed out. He's not going to be comfortable in the ute. You ready to lift him in?' Alice nodded, her face as ashen as Robert's as she finished covering him with a groundsheet. Robert's eyes fluttered open.

'You decided to wake up, did you, mate?' said Fraser giving him another swig of rum. 'You've got yourself a beaut sheila there. She's going to fly you to Walgett Hospital, lucky bastard,' said Fraser trying to sound cheerful. Alice busied herself checking the stretcher. Robert moved his eyes to Alice.

'How's it going, mate? Are you ready?' asked Fraser.

'She's right,' slurred Robert. Fraser could see the rum was taking effect but still it was not going to deaden all the pain of moving him again. He handed his friend the end of a thick piece of rope.

'Here, bite on this.' Fraser and Alice lifted together. The rope fell from Robert's hand as he passed out again almost immediately they started to lift him onto the stretcher.

The journey back to the plane was an agonising thirty-five minutes. Alice sat up with Robert in the back of the ute sharing the groundsheet, sick with fear that they might not make the hospital in time, her head bent against the driving rain. Checking and rechecking Robert's pulse, she watched the shallow rise and fall of his chest to ensure he was still breathing. With each jolt her eyes flicked back to Robert's grey face as she prayed silently that he would not feel too much pain, too distraught to worry about her recent anger and hurt, fighting off her terrible feeling of helplessness. The evening was closing in fast due to the bad weather. The track was becoming increasingly slippery and boggy. Finally the interminable trek back to the plane came to an end.

'How much room in the plane?' asked Fraser as they reached the strip.

'Enough for the stretcher and me. We'll have to poke the stretcher up and across where the mail bags go. Doubt if there's enough room for you as well.' Alice kept the groundsheet covering Robert but both she and Fraser were soaked through by the time he was strapped in and she was ready for takeoff.

'Are you going to be able to manage, Alice?' shouted Fraser against the rain and wind.

'I'll have to.'

'Here, give him some more of this if he comes to.' He handed Alice his rum flask. Her hands were shaking and her teeth chattering. 'You could do with a swig yourself.'

Alice put the flask in the cabin door pocket. 'After we've landed.'

Fraser took a last look at Robert lying ashen and still in the tiny plane. 'Listen, mate, you bloody well hang in there, d'you hear?'

'I'll do my best,' mumbled Robert his eyelids fluttering open for a moment.

'I'll radio Walgett Hospital you're coming,' yelled Fraser to Alice. 'Keep in radio contact while you're flying.' He leaned over and gave her a quick kiss on the cheek. 'You're a beaut sheila. He's a lucky bloke.' Alice had a lump in her throat as she did her pre-takeoff checks and taxied the plane down the strip. The rain was still bucketing down and the track was turning to sticky mud. The takeoff was the worst Alice had ever done. Over and over once they were airborne she kept silently repeating, 'Let him live. Please God, let him live.' On the ground Fraser tried to radio the hospital but couldn't get a response.

The winds were now much stronger and slewing across the plane. As they climbed rain pounded horizontally against the windscreen and visibility was almost nil forcing Alice to fly by her instruments. Reception on the radio was getting worse and after ten minutes all she could hear when she tried to raise Fraser was loud crackling. Glancing from time to time at Robert she could see the blood had soaked through the bandage on his leg and forehead. His breathing was still shallow and uneven and he looked terrible. Mad thoughts raced through her mind. Because she had turned back to save him perhaps everything would somehow suddenly be right again. Perhaps the baby wasn't his, perhaps they could adopt it. What if after this Katie suddenly refused to marry Robert? What if he refused to marry her? Maybe the whole thing was a pack of lies and he'd never slept with Katie in the first place. By twenty past five she estimated they were one hour from Walgett. She would just make it before dark as long as she kept her mind on flying. To do so she had to stop these wild imaginings and think of Robert as an emergency patient. Right now she had to block out her own suffering. The adrenalin surged in her veins as the engine started to splutter. She tried the radio again but all she got was static.

Ben was lying under Uncle Ray's ute trying to fix the exhaust, wishing he could try out the new radio transmitter he had just finished building. Last night he'd picked up Perth radio as the level of the ionosphere dropped. But the deal was: fix the exhaust, deliver the spare part and then play with the radio. His arm was getting tired and bits of dirt kept falling into his eyes.

'Nearly there,' muttered Uncle Ray from the other side of the car thumping the exhaust pipe with a hammer. Surreptitiously Ben glanced at his watch. Twenty past four. He'd still have time to give it a test. He'd call Phil up as soon as he had finished here and then beat it out to the scrub. Uncle Ray gave a final jarring bang with the hammer and the piece slipped into place.

'That should fix the bastard,' said Ray.

Ben scrabbled out on his back rubbing his greasy hands on his overalls. 'Can I take her for a run now, Uncle Ray?'

'Why can't you try out your radio contraption here, son?'

'I'm testing it for reception and transmission and I need to be away from the house. Phil and I are testing it together.'

'You're pretty handy with those homemade radios of yours,' Ray said admiringly. 'All right, you can take the old girl for a drive after you've delivered the spare parts. But take it easy d'you hear. I don't want your aunt arriving home from Walgett to find she's got no transport for tomorrow.'

'Thanks Uncle Ray.'

'That's enough now,' Ray said gruffly. He'd become fond of Ben and his passion for anything electrical. 'And be back in time for tea at Mrs Bloomfield's or we'll both be in deep trouble.'

'Yes, sir.' Pulling off the overalls he had been wearing over his jeans and shirt, Ben slid into the driver's seat. By quarter past five he had dropped off the delivery and, after a bit of fiddling around with the radio, got through to Phil.

'It actually works. Isn't that amazing!' Ben said excitedly. 'What's the reception like your end, Phil?' There was a lot of static interference but he could just make out Phil's reply. 'Okay Phil, I'll give it another go, just let me fix something.' A sudden crash made him jump. He lifted his head and saw a fork of lightning split the clouds in the distance. He suddenly noticed how dark it had become. 'That storm's not helping any.' This time he got no reply.

'Drat, now I've lost him completely,' said Ben. Bloody unpredictable weather. It was as close as all Hades. Flying ants—a sure sign of a coming storm— were everywhere. The storm was doing its usual game of circling Billabrin before it came roaring in with all its fury. He fiddled with a couple of connections and heard Phil's voice quite loudly. Two large raindrops splattered onto the car windscreen. The hot wind started gusting whipping up the dust. 'Listen, Phil, it's going to start pouring with rain any minute. I'd better get back home.'

'Okay, mate.' Just as he was about to cease transmission he heard another faint voice struggling against the interference. The message kept fading and increasing against the static, but Ben kept listening.

Alice was becoming increasingly alarmed. The engine was still refusing to give full power and they were experiencing considerable turbulence. Robert, now in increasing pain, moaned every time the plane bucketed against the wind. Visibility was very poor and the light was fading rapidly. Forty miles from Walgett Alice still had not made contact with either the hospital or Walgett airport, despite repeated calls. Surely Walgett Tower should have been able to pick up her signal by now. She reached once more for the handset.

'Walgett Base, Walgett Base, this is Xray Delta Xray declaring an emergency. I am en route to Walgett flying a four-seater Cessna Skylane. ETA twenty minutes, current position forty miles southwest of Walgett. I have on board a passenger in need of urgent medical assistance. Experiencing strong winds, engine unreliable. Request emergency facilities and ambulance on landing. Over.' She listened with increasing dismay at the crackling from the earphones punctuated by intermittent bursts of very loud static.

'Walgett base, Walgett Base, this is Xray Delta Xray. I repeat this is Xray Delta Xray sending an emergency call. Emergency. Emergency.' Still only crackling and static. The engine coughed and sputtered intermittently. She had checked and rechecked everything each time she had landed and taken off. All she could do was to fly on into the gloom, hoping against hope that she would not have to make a forced landing. In her mind she kept hearing her instructor's voice: 'Aviate, navigate, communicate, and if you can't do the last, you can at least do the first two.'

Her heart gave a great leap of joy when she heard Ben's voice over the radio.

'Alice, Alice, this is Ben calling. I heard your message. I'll tell Walgett Tower you're coming.'

Alice couldn't stop the tears of relief. Over the interference she shouted, 'Ben, thank God.' A wave of emotion threatened to swamp her. 'Oh

Ben, I've got Robert in the plane and he's terribly badly hurt.' Reception was shocking. Alice's bottom lip quivered. 'Tell Walgett Base I need emergency services and an ambulance.'

On the ground Ben struggled to catch her words. The storm was causing chaos with transmission. Mercifully the rain had held off but the wind was strengthening.

'Will call Walgett Tower, Alice. You're breaking up badly. Repeat your position and ETA.' He knew the emergency transmission procedure as well as Alice, having drilled her when she was working towards her licence.

'. . . miles southwest Bundaberg station. ETA . . .'

'Repeat your position.' The radio went dead. A loud thunder crash made Ben jump. He fiddled with the radio, his heart thumping like crazy, but could get nothing at all. He had heard the bit about the engine. 'Now, think clearly; think straight.' He spoke out aloud to help himself stay calm. 'If she's talking about Bundaberg station she must be within thirty minutes of Walgett.' He tried the radio once more but it was useless. Cursing roundly, he slid across into the driver's seat and drove the car as fast as he could across the scrubland towards Billabrin. The wind was now tearing at the small scrub trees as he slipped and slid the car across the boulder-filled track swerving to miss the biggest rocks. The ground was completely flat and there was nothing to stop the rolling spinifex balls charging across the ground. As he drove past Alice's favourite windmill there was a sudden loud explosion and the ute slewed to one side. Stopping the vehicle, Ben leaped out and saw the offside front tyre had burst. He tore at his hair in frustration.

'This is all I bloody need!' Kicking the offending tyre, Ben slammed the ute door and ran at top speed down to the house. Red faced and gasping he picked up the phone. The line was completely dead. The wires must be down. It often happened with storms. If his wires were down then so were the whole of Billabrin. What the hell was he to do now? His mind turned to Alice struggling in the sky and he nearly panicked. Then he heard a frightened whinnying. Sherry! Of course! Grabbing an apple and a spare bridle he tore out of the house. Racing across to the paddock he whistled up Sherry. The wind tossed the sound away, but the horse had seen his movement. Holding out the apple to the terrified horse, Ben walked steadily towards her. Sherry tossed her head eyeing him nervously, her ears right back. She almost took off as he reached her and then changed her mind. Offering her the apple Ben spoke gently as he slipped the bridle over her head.

'We've got to help your mistress.' Leaping onto her back he dug his heels into her flanks patting her neck as he raced her towards the property beyond the levee. The owners had their own generator and were the most likely people to have some means of communication working. If only his radio hadn't packed it in. Sherry shied and skittered, her whole body quivering nervously at each clap of thunder as they flew across the ground.

Ben never heard the mighty overhead thunderclap nor felt the torrent of sheeting rain soaking through his shirt, that followed the vicious jagged flash which split the blackened sky. In that instant Sherry reared up in sheer terror and boy and horse crumpled to the ground both dead before they hit the rain-sodden dirt.

Rain lashed the cockpit windscreen and wind buffeted the plane up and down. Alice glanced anxiously at Robert who hadn't made a sound for the last ten minutes. Thank God she had got through to Ben. At least now she didn't feel so desperately alone. He would be able to contact Walgett Tower so they would be expecting her and the ambulance would be waiting. She listened anxiously to the engine's coughing and spluttering, acutely aware of the dangers of making a forced landing in these conditions. Suddenly she slapped her forehead with the palm of her hand. Of course! She wasn't thinking straight. It must be the carburettor icing up that was making it run rough. She pulled the control on the panel in front of her to apply carburettor heat. Usually the cure was instantaneous. Ten seconds later she cheered aloud when, with two more coughs, the propeller whined its way back up to full speed. Pushing the throttle forwards she checked her position. To her relief she realised she was flying out of the storm. They were going to make it to Walgett airstrip. Rain no longer lashed her windscreen and the buffeting had lessened. She had been trying the radio at regular intervals ever since talking to Ben, now on her final approach she got a response.

'Xray Delta Xray, this is Walgett Tower, we acknowledge your final approach on two seven. Emergency services will be available. Please explain your emergency.' For the final time Alice repeated her emergency message, wondering why Ben hadn't already told them. What could have gone wrong that he hadn't got through? Dropping her altitude Alice circled round lining up for the final descent, the question nagging at her. Robert started coughing beside her.

'I love you Robert. Don't die on me now.' Alice's voice was choked as she put the plane's nose down.

Before they had taxied to a stop the ambulance and fire engine were beside them. A nurse gave Robert a shot of morphine and attached an oxygen mask to his face. Stiff, cold and exhausted Alice stumbled out of the plane. Someone put a blanket around her and spoke to her as Robert was carried into the ambulance. It took her three-quarters of an hour to complete her aircraft maintenance and it was pitch dark before she finally got to the hospital and learned that Robert was in emergency surgery. She slumped down on a seat in the waiting room exhausted but too keyed up to rest. Gratefully she accepted the hot sweet tea and plain biscuits given to her by one of the nurses.

'Why don't you duck out and have a bite to eat, luv,' suggested the nurse some time later. 'It'll be quite some time before we have any news.' Alice shook her head. Until she knew Robert was out of danger she was not leaving the hospital.

When Fraser walked into the waiting room she had drifted into a half-sleep. He sat down beside her, his hat in his hand and she woke with a start.

'Any news yet, Alice?' Alice shook her head. 'If he makes it, it'll be because of you.' Together they waited in silence. Finally a doctor appeared.

'That was a very courageous thing you did, young woman,' he said. 'You know your actions saved his life. You'll be glad to know your patient is out of danger. He's lost a considerable amount of blood and made a bit of a mess of his leg and a couple of ribs, not to mention his face. He'll probably have a small scar at the corner of his left eye, but otherwise he's doing fine.' Alice relaxed visibly.

'That's really good news,' she said, all choked up.

'I thought you'd also like to know his mother just rang and so did his fiancée, your cousin Katie, isn't it? They'll both be in later this evening.' To Fraser, Alice suddenly seemed to shrink.

'But I thought you and Bluey . . .' he said when the doctor had left. Alice shook her head.

'It didn't work out.' She smiled wanly and got up. 'Looks like I'm not needed here anymore. I'll give Uncle Ray a ring to let him know where I am.' She turned at the door. 'You know it was Ben with his crazy radio set that kept me sane. Just knowing someone had heard me . . .' She stopped and blew her nose. 'I've had it.' She walked down the hospital corridor towards the phone as Aunty Bea came out of the doctor's room into reception.

'Aunty Bea!' Alice's face lit up in surprise. 'Did Ben tell you?'

'Alice, dearest child.' She seemed to have aged ten years.

'What's wrong?' The colour drained from Alice's face.

'It was an accident. Ben was riding Sherry. They were both struck by lightning and killed instantly. Darling girl, I'm so terribly sorry.' The words were hopelessly inadequate.

part two

Chapter Sixteen

ALICE PEERED AT THE TWO test tubes.

'I think we've fooled the receptor, Alice,' Professor John Dixson said excitedly. 'Would you agree there's more in the left-hand tube?' It was more a statement than a question. He sounded quite breathless. Alice examined the clear liquid. The difference was minuscule but it was there.

'Fantastic,' replied Alice mirroring his excitement. From his position as head of one of London's leading hospital units Professor Dixson was researching diabetes. His ultimate goal was twofold: to develop an oral form of insulin, and to set up clinics across Great Britain and Ireland where people could learn to manage the disease. Working mainly with mice and guineapigs in the later stages, Professor Dixson had been developing a small molecule to interact with a receptor, fooling it so that it would produce insulin-like effects.

This was the second of three major and scientifically exciting stages in the process, the third and final step being to give the molecule to animals and ultimately to humans where because it produced the same effects as insulin, the level of blood sugar could be better controlled, a situation critical to diabetes sufferers. Having been employed as a lab assistant by Professor Dixson for the past eighteen months and having watched him struggle and listened to explanations of what he was trying to achieve, Alice understood the importance of today's breakthrough and shared his jubilation.

She returned to her morning routine of cleaning up the debris of soiled test tubes and instruments listening to him contentedly humming while he checked and rechecked his findings. An untidy pile of notes, papers, torn scraps and used envelopes covered with scribble lay on his desk waiting for her to sort out, type up and file.

It was a cold English day in March 1963 and Alice could not believe how the time had flown. She had landed in London the September after Ben had been killed, emotionally shattered and unable to see any point to her life. Bea had insisted on flying over with her and had stayed on in England until Alice was set up in a small bedsitter in a four-storey building, in Earls Court, which she shared with six other Australians.

Together Bea and Alice had redecorated the place, repainting the walls and replacing the battered dusty sofa with two new chintz-covered chairs. Bea had even run to the added expense of having curtains made. The brightness of the room with its little personal touches had taken its effect and over the months some of Alice's misery had gradually retreated. She had started to look more positively on life and now found she could think about Ben without dissolving into tears. In an odd sort of way she had felt more sorry for Bea who, on top of having to tell her about Ben and Sherry, had also had to break the news about her father. On the very same day as Ben's death, Thomas' car had been crushed at a railway crossing. He had died instantly. It had almost been too much for Bea. She waited for a week to tell Alice, feeling that the girl couldn't take any more grief, but the news made little impact on Alice—by that time she had shut down almost completely. As she grew stronger, however, she felt a sad sort of emptiness that her father had finally disappeared from her life without a proper goodbye.

Bea had also insisted on seeing Alice set up in a job before she returned to Australia so when Alice had arrived at the little bedsit one cold October afternoon announcing she was to work as a lab assistant to a professor at one of London's largest hospitals doing research into diabetes, Bea hugged her with relief. Two weeks later, satisfied that Alice could cope on her own, she decided it was time to return home.

'Come back home when you're ready, sweetie,' Bea had said as she hugged her niece at Heathrow airport. She had already made her promise to write regularly and had agreed to care for Alice's two lambs. 'And if you need any money just let us know. I am sorry you won't be at Katie and Robert's wedding. I'll miss you, we'll all miss you but I want you to give yourself time to get back to enjoying your life again.' The mention of Robert had stabbed at Alice's heart. They had both fought back their tears as Bea disappeared through the departure gate.

Alice had never mentioned Robert's marriage proposal to Bea nor the way she felt towards him. There had seemed no point after Katie's revelation and it would only have soured things between the two families. So Alice had tried to put it behind her, working long punishing hours as the only way she knew to dull the aching void. And gradually, as the professor instructed her in lab techniques and gave her charge of the laboratory animals, she found herself becoming emotionally involved in his work.

In his early fifties, Professor Dixson was an extremely well-respected researcher who had earlier worked with Dr Jonas Salk, the man who developed the Salk vaccine against polio. He had fire and energy and, like a typical scatter-brained professor, was always losing things particularly his glasses, which were invariably buried in his thatch of startling white hair. As he explained to Alice, despite his work in immunology his real interest lay in finding a better way to control diabetes. Although he did not suffer from the disease himself, both his uncle and grandfather had died from it and when his wife's sister had gone into a diabetic coma from which she never recovered, he decided the time had definitely come to move away from immunology and concentrate on his real passion.

His bumbling enthusiasm and friendliness had helped soften the blow when Alice had learned of the birth of Katie and Robert's son.

'He was christened Stewart Raymond McIain last week by Father O'Reilly,' Aunty Bea had written. 'He's a dear little mite and already his father is spoiling him worse than the rest of us are.' Alice had shoved the photo of the three of them and the rest of the unread letter in her pocket, unable to see through the blur of tears. Arriving late for work and wearing sunglasses, she had then proceeded to drop almost everything in sight, including six of the professor's most recently prepared test tubes, at which point Professor Dixson had demanded an explanation.

'I'll leave now if you like,' mumbled Alice. 'I'm so sorry, Professor Dixson, I've ruined everything.' The professor bumbled around as Alice placed the guineapig she had named Greta back in her cage and started to remove her white coat. 'I'll get my things,' she said, moving to the door.

'You'll do no such thing, young lady. You will clear up this mess, put on a clean coat and take those stupid sunglasses off. Then you and I will have a cup of coffee.' He ran his hands through his wild white hair, shaking his head. 'It's all my fault for making you work these ridiculous hours. Rosie keeps warning me that I'm pushing you too hard, but I get so caught up in my work, and you're so good at working with me.' He peered at her over his heavy-rimmed glasses. Alice's sapphire eyes shone enormous out of her pale heart-shaped face. 'You look dreadful, did you have any breakfast?'

'You mean I'm not fired?' asked Alice incredulous.

'My dear girl, you are far too precious to lose. You're my right hand and the only one that knows what the left hand's doing.' After two cups of strong black coffee and two Chelsea buns Alice started to feel better. She explained away her behaviour as a sudden bout of homesickness brought on by the letter from her aunt and the news of the birth of her nephew. It was almost true and the professor was happy to accept it. In return he had insisted Alice come over to lunch with him and his wife Rosie the following weekend. It was the beginning of a warm and close relationship.

On her hands and knees, having changed into a pair of grubby overalls, her hair scraped back into an elastic band, Alice smiled to herself again at the professor's excitement over today's discovery and the luck that had landed her in a job she really loved. She sneezed as she finished cleaning out the mice cages and swept up the remnants of sawdust. Deep in thought as to how she was ever going to get all those notes for the professor's latest experiments written up before three o'clock in the morning, she jumped at the sound of a female voice. Miss Dior wafted through the air.

'Hello.'

Alice looked up in annoyance at the prospect of having to stand and chat with so much to do and caught her breath at the young woman's beauty.

'I'm Harriet Stoneham-Clarke but everyone calls me Harry,' announced the visitor holding out her hand.

It took Alice a full thirty seconds to respond. Quickly wiping her palms on her overalls she stood up and shook hands feeling utterly drab and slightly overawed. Dressed in the latest fashion, her luscious thick brown hair caught back off her face in an aliceband, 'Harry' looked as though she had stepped straight off the front cover of *Vogue*. Friendly dark brown eyes illuminated her glowing creamy skin. Alice thought her nickname singularly inappropriate.

The young woman pulled off the aliceband in a thoroughly unmodel-like way, stuffing the end in her mouth, and rearranging her hair as she talked. 'Bit confusing really when you say you're bringing Harry home to stay for the weekend,' she laughed and replaced the hair band. Her actions immediately eased the tension. Harriet was used to people's reactions to her looks.

'No, don't say it, although everyone always does. I should have been a model. I tried but I couldn't do it. Mummy wanted me to go to Lucie Clayton's Modelling School with all of the other debs after I refused to go to finishing school in Switzerland. But I got out of that too and started nursing. Poor Mummy! She and Daddy nearly dropped dead when I told them what I'd done. I'm supposed to be preparing myself for The Man after which I dutifully produce rows of grandchildren and open local fetes.' Her account was pure upperclass English boarding school.

Recovering from her initial shock, Alice found herself liking this person who had burst in on her daily routine. 'Hi, I'm Alice Ferguson,' she said warmly.

'I know. You're the Australian everyone's been talking about. Well, you look pretty normal to me.' Alice couldn't help grinning at her outspokenness and her accent.

'Were you looking for someone special?'

'Dicky.' Alice looked puzzled. 'Your boss. I fell madly in love with him two years ago and he broke my heart completely. Every so often I pop in to see if he's still as gorgeous as ever. I've got over him now, finally.' She sighed exaggeratedly and laughed again. Leaning towards Alice she said in a loud conspiratorial whisper, 'Don't try it—he's terribly married.'

'Are you leading my new lab assistant astray, Miss Stoneham-Clarke?' A white-coated Professor Dixson appeared from his workroom, his horn-rimmed spectacles halfway down his nose.

'Would I, Dicky darling?' crooned Harry ruffling his hair and kissing him quickly on the cheek. 'Can I steal her for a cup of coffee, I have to hear more of this wonderful accent?' Alice and the professor looked at their watches at the same time.

'Ten minutes!' answered Professor Dixson with mock severity, nodding at Alice. 'We work around here, you know.'

'Give me two sees to clean up,' said Alice. She disappeared laughing, reappearing moments later with a clean white lab coat thrown over a pair of jeans and a turquoise sweater that turned her eyes the colour of the sea.

Over coffee Alice learned that Harriet was twenty-three, flatted with two other girls in South Kensington, a much more salubrious and expensive area of London than Earls Court, and was in her final year of nursing at Barts, the nickname for St Bartholomew's Hospital. By the end of the ten minutes the two were chatting like old friends.

'We're looking for a fourth flatmate. Why don't you move in with us?' suggested Harriet as they walked back to Professor Dixson's laboratory.

'I'd love to but well I've kind of got attached to my little pad in Earls Court,' replied Alice.

'If you're worried about money don't, I'll help you out. We've got to get you out of Kangaroo Valley.' Alice didn't want to offend Harriet so she chose her words carefully.

'Look, it's really kind of you but we Aussies are a strange breed. It's a kind of home away from home for us. Also I don't know how long I'll be staying in England.'

'All right, I won't try and prise you away from that place but you can't leave until you've come home for the weekend so I can show you off to all my friends.'

Alice tossed back her head and laughed. 'Are we that strange?'

'Put it this way,' declared Harry, 'none of my friends'll believe you're actually real unless they meet you in the flesh. A real live species from Down Under—isn't that what you call it?' She leaned forward, her brown eyes glowing excitedly in her face. 'You've simply got to teach me some of your sayings—g'day cobber, how ya goin' blue?' Her imitation of an Australian accent was atrocious and Alice grinned broadly at her attempts. 'You don't really go around calling everyone mate and bloke and stuff like that do you?'

'Too right we do!' nodded Alice still grinning. 'And if I were a bloke I'd say you're a beaut sheila.' They were back at the lab. Suddenly Alice wanted this young woman's friendship.

'A what? That settles it, I've got to introduce you to Roody.' Harry's laughter reverberated down the corridor as she walked away. The following week Harry invited Alice round for supper.

'Alice is far too staid a name for you. I think I'll rename you Kanga,' declared Harry as she searched the back of the cupboard in the untidy well-equipped kitchen for a bottle of red wine. 'You know Kanga-Roo, that's all you have in Australia except for a few million sheep, isn't it?'

'Not quite all,' retorted Alice with mock indignation as she accepted a glass of red wine, but the name stuck.

'Chin, chin, Kanga,' said Harry and drank down half the glass. 'Actually I think we're going to have lots of fun together, you and me.'

'Bottoms up, Harry,' said Alice agreeing.

It was an early Easter this year and Harry invited Alice to stay at her home, a beautiful old sandstone house situated in a tiny village five miles outside Cirencester in the Cotswolds. Mrs Stoneham-Clarke was the epitome of everything Harry had fought not to end up as and she was enchanted by Alice. In the relaxed atmosphere of early spring sunshine, the two girls confided in one another as they walked down lanes and across meadows, seeing the primroses peep their shy heads from under the hedgerows, their legs brushing through the mist of brave bluebells that had risked the early spring frosts. Having had only the aggravation and lack of companionship with Katie, Alice rejoiced in her newfound friendship with Harry. It was the first real friendship she had known with someone near her own age and in that short weekend the two girls grew closer than ever.

Easter Sunday involved a large and social lunch that went on until late afternoon and Alice somehow felt perfectly at ease with Harry's friends as they joked and teased and admired this girl from the Colonies. In return Alice kept her end up by spinning a few yarns that definitely bordered on the improbable.

The day before their return to London as Alice and Harry strode once more along one of the windy lanes, their cheeks and fingertips pink from the brisk late March wind, Alice finally told Harry about Robert and how all her dreams had been shattered in the space of one week. Talking about Ben's death and Robert's betrayal somehow eased the burden, yet Harry hated to see the pain in her friend's face as she spoke.

'All men are bastards, let's face it,' she joked trying to dispel Alice's gloom. 'Take them seriously, Kanga, and you're doomed. You should do what I do. Enjoy them for a while and move on before they get the upper hand.'

'Like you did with Dicky?' Alice teased gently.

'That was different. I was madly in love for the first and only time in my life.' Alice suddenly went quiet. 'Sorry,' Harry said quickly, realising the tactlessness of her remark. 'I got over it in the end,' she added gently. 'It hurts less with time. You have to believe that, and now . . .' her voice returned to its usual buoyancy, 'now I'm juggling three madly handsome men, none of whom knows of the others' existence. It's terribly wicked but awfully good fun. You should try it.' Her eyes danced as she spoke.

'Is poor Roody one of them?' Alice had met Roody, an officer in the Royal Air Force, and it was quite obvious that he was head over heels in love with Harry.

Hany nodded. 'He's terribly dashing, isn't he? Actually I've known he's the one for me from the start but I'm letting him sweat a little longer before I finally relinquish myself to his undying embrace,' she finished dramatically.

'You're cruel and heartless,' accused Alice jokingly.

'You can talk! I saw you flashing those blue eyes of yours at our party yesterday. It's unfair anyone should have eyes like yours. You had men dying around you.'

The girls walked on in companionable silence for a while, their breath billowing out like steam. Alice fingered the copious Angora wool scarf wound round her neck, which she had received last Christmas from Mrs Dixson.

'One day I'm going to produce wool even finer than this,' Alice confided, pushing the soft wool away to avoid the silk-like strands escaping into her mouth.

'You really are set on this sheep thing, aren't you?' Alice nodded. 'With your determination you'll probably do it too.' Harry pulled her jacket collar up round her cheeks. 'Which reminds me, I've organised for Roody and a friend to take us out for drinks and dinner when we get back to London. His friends are all terribly eligible bachelors, personally recommended!'

'You're not matchmaking by any chance?' exclaimed Alice.

'Me? What a thing to ask!' The girls were arguing amiably once more, their cheeks rosy from the cold as they hurried back to the house for afternoon tea.

Returning to London Alice became once more immersed in her work with Professor Dixson, swinging from elation to disappointment and back again with him at each tiny step of his experiment as he struggled to monitor the levels of blood sugar in the lab animals. Time seemed to be flying by. Before long it would be June, the date Alice had given Bea for her return, and she'd be on a plane back to Australia. It would be good to be home she kept telling herself, shutting out the pain. She had lots of plans. With a reference from Professor Dixson she was confident she could get a job as a research assistant in the area she wanted to work in and she'd finally be able to get a decent tan that lasted. Yet in her heart she wondered if she would be able to cope when the time came to fly home.

Late one evening at the end of April, Alice dropped round to Harry's flat in South Kensington, exhausted but elated. She had just learned that Professor Dixson would be presenting two papers at a large medical convention in Cambridge University early next month and he had insisted she attend with him.

'I had to tell such momentous news to your face,' explained Alice. Reclining in an exhausted heap on the large flowered sofa, having just come off the late shift, Harry was suddenly revitalised.

'Cambridge did you say, Kanga? Just the excuse I have been looking for. I've been working so ruddy hard for the last month I deserve some relaxation. Now we can have some real fun.'

'Oh yes?' said Alice in a mood to agree to any madcap idea Harry suggested.

'I'll arrange to have the weekend off so if you can tear yourself away from your convention for an evening I'll round up a couple of friends in Cambridge and we'll take you on a pub crawl. We could do the King's Run: seven—or is it eight?—pubs in the one street. I did it once but I lost count after the fourth.' She laughed uproariously and flopped back onto the sofa again fishing down between the cushions, stale crumbs and old magazines for her phone book. Flipping through it she rattled off a few names and then tossed it aside grinning wickedly at Alice. 'Maybe you'll meet the man of your dreams, who knows. Cambridge. Spring. The daffodils along the river. Romance.' She sighed.

'Don't even think about it,' retorted Alice, her eyes glinting dangerously. 'I'm booked on a Qantas flight out of here at the end of June. It's set in concrete.'

'Life's a funny thing,' mused Harry dreamily.

'Not a chance, Harry,' Alice said firmly. Grinning at her friend she raised her coffee mug. 'Let's drink to a great weekend in Cambridge.'

Shortly before seven in the soft May evening, Alice and Harry were walking along one of the narrow back streets of Cambridge towards Trinity College. Suddenly three apparitions, their voluminous black gowns flying out behind them like oversize bats, came careering towards them on bicycles. Too late the three realised there was not enough room to pass safely. One cyclist rammed on the brakes and stopped abruptly; Alice and Harry shrieked in unison, not knowing which way to jump as the second apparition streaked crazily past them. The third monster, squeezing his brakes frantically but to no avail, wobbled violently in his attempts to avoid hitting the girls. Realising he had no alternative, he turned his bike to dodge a head-on collision with Alice and pitched straight into the wall. Toppling sideways he and the bike fell onto the cobblestones.

'Teddy!' shrieked Harry descending on the poor unfortunate individual and giving him a thumping kiss. The man staggered against her embrace.

'Harry! What the hell are you doing here?' he cried. Picking himself up with as much dignity as he could muster, he straightened his gown removing the hem from the bike spokes. Stroking his thick blond hair back into place across his forehead he righted his battered bicycle. Brilliant blue eyes locked with brilliant blue eyes as the shaken Alice stared back, her hands clasped to her cheeks. He had the striking good looks of a slightly eccentric English country gentleman. Small crow's-feet around his eyes added to the impact as did his flashy red suede waistcoat over an open-neck shirt, cavalry twill trousers and navy and rust cravat.

Alice put him at around twenty-eight.

'We're down for the weekend,' Harry told Teddy, grabbing Alice by the arm. 'Kanga, this is Teddy. Actually it's the Honourable Edward Turlington but we all call him Teddy. Teddy, this is Kanga my Australian friend. Bloody awful way to greet an old friend. Where were you off to in such a tearing hurry?'

Teddy felt the tenderness on the back of his head and adjusted his cravat and waistcoat. 'How do you do? Terribly sorry about running into you like that.' He shook Alice's hand with a laugh to hide his embarrassment. 'And the idiot behind you is Adrian Slade.' Alice dragged her eyes from his face and felt a blush creep up her neck to her cheeks as she greeted his friend. Teddy looked swiftly at his watch and back at Alice and Harry. 'This is all terribly embarrassing. We're supposed to be in a meeting at the master's lodge with the fellows and postgrads five minutes ago and it's definitely not good form to be late. Could we meet afterwards?'

'What time?' said Harry quickly. 'I promised Alice a pub crawl around Cambridge before she leaves England.'

'Excellent. Right. See you at the Mill at a quarter to eight. That'll give us time to do the polite bit and slip away before dinner without being too obvious. You know your way around here, don't you, Harry?' Harry nodded. 'Frightfully sorry to have given you such a scare.' Teddy brushed Alice's fingertips briefly against his lips. 'Pretty awful way to introduce myself.' Alice's blush deepened.

'Isn't he utterly divine?' sighed Harry as the three men disappeared, Teddy dragging his bike along, the front wheel now so badly buckled that it was impossible to ride. 'If my heart wasn't already lost to Roody I could fall madly in love with Teddy.'

At five minutes to eight the Honourable Edward Turlington walked through the Mill pub on the edge of the River Cam and out into the garden. As it was a mild evening the girls had escaped the crush inside and were sitting sipping shandies near the water's edge watching the punts bang together at their moorings near the Silver Street bridge.

'You can't leave England without experiencing a Cambridge pub crawl, Kanga,' Teddy announced, placing his pint of bitter on the table. He stretched languorously and checked his watch. 'Adrian had better get a move on, we've already wasted a good hour's drinking time.' The blue eyes were on Alice again. She could feel her cheeks burning as she wondered what this eccentric man would do next. Adrian joined them shortly afterwards and the four set off on the promised pub crawl. Walking from pub to pub Alice learned that Teddy was a postgraduate at Trinity College working on an ancient history thesis, that his home was near Stow on the Wold, in Gloucestershire, not too far from Harry's home, and that he was passionately interested in Turkey and the history of the ancient silk road. Alice was surprised at how easy he was to talk to. There was a gentleness about him that attracted her and she enjoyed the genuine interest he showed when she told him about her job in London.

'So you're interested in animals. Do you ride at all?' asked Teddy as they emerged from their fourth pub. It was well past nine o'clock and Alice was starting to feel slightly euphoric from too many shandies and not enough food. The mention of horses brought her thumping back to reality. Noticing Alice's sudden withdrawal Teddy quickly changed the subject. They were walking along the backs now, the wide sweeping lawns that ran down to the river at the back of the colleges, their colourful spring flowerbeds still visible in the soft evening light. 'To make amends for our terrible introduction, what d'you say we take these two beauties out to dinner at the Tickell Arms at Whittlesford, Adrian, old chum?'

'Topping idea, old chap,' replied Adrian, definitely tipsy by now.

'Wait here while I go and find us some wheels,' ordered Teddy dashing along the road.

'Is it far?' asked Alice remembering the rows of undergraduates' bicycles lining the racks outside the magnificent stone archway to King's College and wondering whether she was still sober enough to ride one. She heaved a sigh of relief when a horn sounded just behind them and Teddy drew up in a bright red two-seater Austin Healey sports car with its roof down,

Leaping out he held the passenger door open for Alice. 'Hop in, Whittlesford's only a few miles outside Cambridge. If we're quick we'll make it before closing.' Harry and Adrian squashed into the tiny seat at the back. They drove for half a mile and picked up Adrian's green MGB.

'Try the boeuf bourguignon,' shouted Adrian once Harry was safely ensconced in his car and the four set off in convoy, the girls clutching their hair that whipped across their faces as the cars sped along. The Tickell Arms more than lived up to its reputation and the two couples lingered on enjoying percolated coffee and after dinner mints until they were the last people left in the restaurant. Finally reluctantly they left and drove back to Cambridge in convoy. On the outskirts of the city Adrian honked his horn and Harry waved. Then Adrian's little green car sped up, turned right and disappeared, leaving Alice and Teddy alone.

'It's been a lovely evening,' said Alice as Teddy drove her back to the rooms where she and Harry were staying.

'I'm glad you can say that after such a disastrous beginning,' replied Teddy turning to smile at Alice. 'It has been lovely for me too.' Alice sighed as the car drew to a stop and Teddy got out and showed her to the door.

'It's funny to think that in two months this will all be a dream and I will be on the other side of the world,' she said looking up at Teddy.

'I wish we'd met two years earlier,' said Teddy. 'You're a . . . what was that phrase you used?'

'Bonza girl, but it's a bit old fashioned now.'

'Good night, bonza girl,' Teddy said with a terribly English accent and leaned forward to brush her cheek with his lips. A ripple went through Alice. Suddenly she was transported back to the old gum tree and the touch of Robert's lips. Fighting the unexpected tears she drew back quickly.

'Goodnight, Teddy,' she said shyly, grateful for the darkness. 'Thank you again for a wonderful evening.' As she walked into the house she berated herself that her love for Robert was as strong as ever. The thought that she might never love another man again filled her with sadness. Yet part of her had responded to Teddy's kiss and Alice hung on to that in hope.

Alice had barely been back in London a week when Teddy called and asked her to the Trinity May Ball. Alice, prompted by a delighted Harry, agreed. 'We'll organise a party,' she decided, and the two girls set about finding gowns.

The College May balls, held in the first two weeks of June, were an annual event at Cambridge. Following on from the tension of the university exams known as the Tripos and the madcap rowing races affectionately called the May Bumps, it was the final opportunity for everyone to let their hair down. The balls went through the night and ended at dawn. Enormous marquees with wooden dance floors were erected in Trinity Great Court and throughout the college grounds. Coloured fairy lanterns decorated the normally immaculate lawns and searchlights illuminated the impressive sixteenth century college buildings. Live bands played different styles of music, from formal to rock and roll, in each marquee. Everyone wore full evening dress; the ladies in ball gowns, the men in white tie and tails.

Traditionally guests had dinner before arriving at the ball so Alice was riding on a haze of champagne as she stepped out of Teddy's red sports car just before ten o'clock. Her shimmering turquoise gown billowed around her, her arms encased in soft cream kid gloves with pearl buttons at the wrists. Delicate seed-pearl drop earrings set in eighteen-carat gold hung from her ears—a present from Teddy—adding the final touch as arm in arm they walked into the ball under a sky sprinkled with hurrying clouds and twinkling stars. After his initial phone call Teddy had visited Alice several more times in London taking her to expensive restaurants and nightclubs and Alice had found herself opening up to this man who was a complicated mixture of gentleness and boisterous enthusiasm.

The May Ball passed in a whirl of romance, champagne and laughter. Teddy and Alice danced in every marquee and wandered leisurely through the grounds, Teddy introducing Alice proudly to his friends.

'But I really want to keep you all to myself,' he said gazing into her eyes as they stood on the replica of the Bridge of Sighs, the weeping willows on the riverbanks silver grey in the moonlight.

Alice realised that she could fall in love with this man if she tried, that she had to let go of Robert or she would wreck the rest of her life.

'Cancel your plane ticket and marry me.' Alice took a step back, shocked at the unexpectedness of his proposal. 'Kanga,' implored Teddy clutching one gloved hand and pulling her back to him, 'you must have guessed I have been falling in love with you.' Alice looked at the earnest expression in Teddy's gentle face and could not resist reaching out to stroke his cheek.

'Even if you don't love me now, I'm willing to take the risk that you might.'

'Oh Teddy.' The silence between them was intense. The feelings Teddy evoked were nothing like the wrenching all-consuming love she had felt for Robert, but still they were there. It was more a growing sense of comfort, a gentle controllable safe feeling that, given time, might develop into love.

'Promise me you'll think about it at least before you reject me utterly.' Teddy's voice was laden with emotion. Alice's eyes were filled with tenderness as she stared up at him.

'I promise, Teddy,' she whispered. Slowly Teddy leaned forwards and kissed her lightly on the lips. This time she did not draw away, instead she gently returned his caress. Finally releasing her, Teddy slipped his arm around Alice's waist and cleared his throat.

'I need a drink. Let's go and find some more champagne and do some more dancing before the sun comes up.' Already the stars were fading and the sky was lightening in the east. A photographer approached them as they stepped off the bridge, breaking the tension that had sprung up between them. They were chatting happily once again as they entered Trinity Great Hall. The edges of the hall were crowded but the polished wood dance floor was empty despite the orchestra enthusiastically playing in waltz time.

'What are they all waiting for?' cried Teddy clearing a way through the crowd for Alice as the music swelled to a Viennese waltz. 'You know you are the most beautiful woman in the room, don't you,' he said as he led her onto the floor. Ignoring the echoes of the past, Alice floated into his arms, her heart pumping with exhilaration as alone they completed one full circle around the floor before the rest of the guests joined in. By the time they emerged from the hall it was daylight.

A chill morning breeze was blowing as they met up with Harry and Adrian and went into the picturesque Green Man pub at Granchester for the traditional May Ball breakfast. Drowsy but happy Alice returned to London by train with Harry, both still wearing their evening gowns partially covered by warm jackets. As the taxi threaded its way through the London morning rush hour to South Kensington, Alice asked herself what she had to lose in marrying this man. When was she going to wake up to herself? Like it or not Robert was married to Katie and they had a son, probably a second one on the way by now. There was nothing left for her back home except misery and bitter memories. Teddy was gentle, fun and had said he was willing to wait for her to love him. Could she really ask for more? Maybe given time she could blot out the memory of Robert and be happy with this eccentric Englishman. Drifting off to sleep in her London flat she dreamed that gold stars were raining down on her and she was lying on miles of the softest wool. Two days later she rang Teddy and told him she had cancelled her ticket home.

Chapter Seventeen

ROBERT MCIAIN STRODE towards the sheds with his father George, the ram manager, Sheik Abdul Ahmed Saleem, the Sheik's entourage of four, and little Stewart who was perched happily on his father's shoulders. Sheik Abdul Ahmed had arrived by private plane that morning to inspect the one hundred merino rams and ewes he wished to purchase and Katie had pleaded with Robert to take Stewart with him. Robert had left his mother and Katie struggling to entertain the Sheik's four heavily-swathed wives, none of whom spoke a word of English.

'All these rams will give you the top quality wool you are after, sir,' explained Robert taking the Sheik round the shed where a selection of his top rams were on display.

'Breed these with our ewes and I am sure you'll be satisfied,' added George watching with pride as his son handled the deal. Robert grabbed the head of a ram that was intent on chewing his trousers, pointing out the broad clean face, alert eyes and soft muzzle that indicated the high quality of wool it was likely to produce. Satisfied he had the Sheik's full attention, he parted the wool displaying startling white beneath the grey, the even rippling lines of the crimp formation in the wool reaching to the tip of the strands which were so tightly packed that even though he pressed them wide it was almost impossible to see the skin of the sheep.

Sheik Abdul owned a vast sheep station in the Northern Tablelands, north of Tamworth as one of his many businesses. Despite the very efficient manager and stockmen he employed to run the property, the Sheik still insisted on visiting Australia once a year to personally handpick his stud rams and ewes from Wangianna. Robert was not concerned about the sale going through as the Sheik had been buying from Wangianna for the last three years. However it was the first time Robert had dealt with him in person and he wanted to make sure Sheik Abdul was given the choice of their best breeders. A lot of money was riding on this deal and it could lead to further big sales. The Sheik's purchases from Wangianna had already attracted interest from other overseas investors. Standing back to allow the Arabs to inspect the rams unhindered, Robert jiggled Stewart on his shoulders. Stewart started strumming his hands on Robert's thick chestnut hair. Robert pulled his son's tiny fingers across his eyes and for the next five minutes they played peek-a-boo. Stewart started to get restless. Catching Robert's eye George nodded to him and Robert took Stewart outside. It had been a long exhausting week and he was glad of a breathing space.

Watching the little boy running around unsteadily he could not believe that one small person could have brought him such joy. Stewart was almost eighteen months old and had been walking for the last three. In looks he was just like Katie, with startling blond hair and yellow catlike eyes that gazed out at the world in wonderment, untainted as yet by anything stronger than mischief. Their expression of innocent love was so different from the cunning, inexplicably secretive glances he sometimes caught from Katie. The little boy and Wangianna were his life. He had to face it. His marriage to Katie was a disaster.

After they were married George and Elizabeth had reorganised the house giving Robert and Katie the east wing. There they had privacy from the main part of the house and plenty of room for Stewart and his nanny. It also meant they could choose whether they joined the rest of the family for meals. Mostly they did. Robert's two other brothers Ian and Jordie also still lived in the main house. Sarah his sister was living in Sydney during term time having just started a course in design at East Sydney Technical College.

After the honeymoon there had been a short-lived period of intimacy but after the difficult birth of Stewart, Katie had shown no wish whatsoever to resume sexual relationships. When Robert had attempted to make love, suggesting they try for another child, Katie had hit the roof, screaming at him and accusing him of being totally unfeeling and lacking in any sort of understanding. Robert hadn't tried again, instead he had taken her to the theatre in Melbourne several times and bought her expensive jewellery, but he knew it would never replace what she really wanted and that was for him to love her. Robert frowned and rubbed his hand over his eyes fingering the scar at the side of his left eye. It had been more than just a bit of a scar and had taken a long time to heal, yet it had added an air of the daredevil to his face which he was far from feeling these days. How different everything would have been had it not been for Stewart. Yet how could he fail to love the little fella?

Without Stewart he would be married to Alice. Over and over he had tried to blot out that thought and her memory. But the perfume of her hair haunted him, the silky touch of her skin, the blazing happiness in her eyes when he had asked her to marry him. Every visit to the paddy paddock was exquisite torture. On bad days he would just go to that windmill to relieve the pain in his heart and stand with his eyes shut and for an instant in time she was back in his arms. Some days he even expected to see her step out from behind the gum tree where they had lain and kissed. But he could not wipe out her look of desperate misery when he had told her Katie was pregnant. Alice, she had saved his life and he loved her and had hurt her beyond forgiveness. He had lost her forever and he understood why she hated him. His love for her today was as intense as it had ever been yet he knew he had to let it go. He had never loved Katie but she was his wife and for Stewart's sake he had to keep trying to make their marriage work. Yet every time he took her in his arms he was pierced with the most terrible waves of guilt.

'Daddy, Daddy, wee wee.' Stewart clutching at himself with one hand and pulling frantically at his father's leg brought Robert out of his reverie. Stewart, his darling precious son. His hope for the future. Laughing at his son's antics he picked him up in his arms and helped him behind a nearby bush. Stewart was the only person who could bring a real light of happiness to Robert's eyes.

'Come on, son, we'd better go back and see what they're up to in that shed,' he said swinging him back on his shoulders and marching back up the ram ramp. As he had guessed, Sheik Abdul was satisfied and his father was happy with his pick of the rams. They all moved on to inspect the ewes he had rounded up for the inspection.

Lunch was back at the house and by mid-afternoon the whole deal was completed. After discussing the final details of transporting the animals to the Northern Tablelands with George and arranging a time to meet up with their lawyers, the Sheik happily flew out of Wangianna.

Over dinner everyone discussed the success of the day. Mellowed by several glasses of vintage red wine and two whiskies, and very happy with Robert's part in the whole transaction, George congratulated Katie on her behaviour as a delightful hostess.

'Not easy to entertain people when you can't make them understand a word you're saying. You'll have to come and play hostess for me one of these days, won't she dear?' said George addressing the final part of his comment to Elizabeth. Katie's eyes lit up at the unexpected praise. She had felt very important being included as one of the hostesses to such illustrious visitors. Even Elizabeth had made a curt but complimentary comment at the way she had handled herself.

Elizabeth nodded. Yawning she got up. 'I'm sure Katie would love the change from being here all the time,' she replied. 'It's been a very successful day all round but I, for one, am exhausted. Let's go to bed, dear,' she said to George. 'Goodnight everyone.' Tossing back the last of his whisky George got up and the two went to bed. As soon as his parents had left the room Ian raised his glass. 'Here's to the most beautiful woman I know, Katie McIain. I could do with you on my arm at next month's charity ball, Katie.'

Katie was obviously flattered and she and Ian started chatting flirtatiously.

Robert, extremely tired, suddenly felt profoundly irritated by his brother's antics. 'Why don't you concentrate on helping a bit more around this place instead of acting the playboy all the time,' he snapped.

Ian scowled at him. 'If you weren't so tight-fisted with money I would. Here we are selling sheep to Arab kings and the place is tumbling down around our ears. I keep offering to rebuild the jackaroos' quarters if you'd let me buy the wood.' It rankled with Ian that it was always Robert's advice Elizabeth sought over any financial transactions of Wangianna. George, who should have been the one up in charge but who recognised his own hopeless inability with money, had been happy to leave all that side of affairs to Elizabeth from the beginning of their marriage.

'He's right, Bluey,' piped up Jordie, the youngest of the three brothers. 'Don't get all shirty. Have a laugh occasionally. Ian and Katie are only having a bit of fun.'

'You know very well Mum has the final say with the finances, so cut it out,' retorted Robert lowering his voice. 'And you keep out of it,' he shot at Jordie.

'So d'you reckon your wonderful considerate thoughtful husband's going to let me build the flamin' bunkhouse, Katie?' baited Ian. Seeing the whole conversation could easily escalate into a full scale family row Robert stood up to leave.

'You're drunk, Ian, and I'm tired. I'm going to bed. Are you coming, Katie?' he asked pointedly. Katie pouted up at him patting Ian's arm.

'I'll be there in a minute. Could you check on Stewart?' Robert nodded and left the room. Ian opened another bottle of wine. An hour later Katie slid into the bedroom feeling decidedly lightheaded. Robert, needled by Ian's comments, was in bed going over the accounts for the last six months. He put down the books when she came in.

'I'm sorry I was grumpy earlier,' he said. 'It's been a long day.'

'You weren't just a teensy weensy bit jealous were you?' teased Katie crawling on top of him over the covers so her nose reached his chin and fluttering her eyelashes at him. Her breath smelt sweet and she gave out a feline odour of sex. Something stirred in Robert. He reached out and stroked her cheek.

'Do I have any need?' he said playfully, determined to make up for his earlier crustiness.

'Maybe,' Katie said, quickly slipping out of her dress and sliding under the bed sheet wearing only a low-cut bra and flimsy panties. 'I'd be flattered.' Pressing herself to Robert she whispered, 'Can we try again?' Completely taken by surprise Robert tentatively wrapped his arms around her.

'I won't break, you know,' encouraged Katie lifting her face to his.

Robert kissed her full ripe lips. Encouraged at the way she returned his advances he kissed her cheeks, the nape of her neck, her soft cleavage. Unclasping her bra Katie tossed it to the floor offering him her breasts. Now considerably aroused Robert rolled her over; cupping each luscious heavy breast in turn in his hand he suckled her nipples until she cried out with pleasure. The bed sheet slipped to the floor as he slipped off her lacy panties and slid his fingers between her legs feeling her glorious wetness. Maybe their marriage still had a chance. Maybe they could start afresh. Maybe if he stopped worrying about loving her and just enjoyed her wonderful soft pliant body it would all come right. Panting to control his excitement he very gently entered her.

'Is that all right?' he rasped. Katie shuddered at the delicious sensation of him inside her. 'I'm not hurting you?'

Katie moaned gently. She arched her back straining towards Robert as he drew himself half out of her fearful of hurting her, exalting in his arousal. 'No stay there, I want more. I want you, I want you,' cried Katie in a sudden frenzy of need, her fingernails digging into his back. Unbelieving, Robert plunged himself deep inside her once, twice, three times. How long could he hold on before he came? He was a man. She was his wife. Why had he never before allowed himself to see her deliciously voluptuously seductive body?

'Oh now, Alice, I want you now,' he cried. The words clanged like a death knell in the sudden stillness. Robert froze. Katie became as tense as steel. Letting out an unearthly shriek she pushed at him with all her force. But he was too quick. Already he was off her, backing away from her, the horror of his mistake still ringing in his ears. Dragging at the sheet to cover himself he slumped down into a nearby chair.

'Katie, oh God, I'm sorry! I didn't mean it. I lost control. I wasn't even thinking of her. I was thinking of you.' He knew his pleas were useless.

'How dare you! How could you, you cold, filthy, lying monster. How could you do it, making love to me while all the time you're thinking of her.' Her face puce with rage, Katie lunged at him tearing at him, beating him with her fists, scratching at him with her long red nails like a wild thing, screaming out all the worst foul abuse she could think of. 'You've done this since the day we were married. Oh, I've known all along. It's always been her, never me. You've never loved me. It's all been lies, lies, lies.' Her voice was choked with venom. 'Always Alice Alice Alice. How I hate her! She's wrecked our lives and she's not even here!' Great racking sobs tore at her lungs. She flopped down on the bed rocking back and forth clutching her shirt to her in a vain effort to cover her nakedness.

Robert sat numb with misery, not knowing what to do. He could never forgive himself for what he had just done. For the first time in their marriage he had managed to forget Alice just for an instant. He rubbed at a dribble of blood running down one arm where her nails had broken his flesh. Hopelessly he tried one last time.

'Katie, I was thinking of you. This time I really was. I swear it.' He raised his arms and let them fall again helpless by his side. Katie's eyes were as dull grey stones. Any hope of restoring their marriage was gone forever.

'Why don't you wake up? You can never have her. She's getting married, happily married to some idiot twelve thousand miles away. She loves someone else.' Katie spelled the last four words out very clearly as though talking to an imbecile. Bea had told her a week ago and she had been savouring her moment to break the news, at the same time dreading to see his eyes glaze over in pain. She got up from the bed and left the room.

The next few weeks were misery for Robert. Outwardly Katie and he tried to act normally but they created an atmosphere that affected the whole family. Katie fussed over Stewart, and Robert worked even harder than ever, getting back to the house late each evening and hardly speaking when the family met for meals. Even Elizabeth was unable to get more than one or two words from him. In private Katie refused to speak to Robert or even meet his eye except when absolutely necessary. At night she put a pillow down the middle of the bed and turned her back to him. The only reason she didn't move out of the bedroom was that she hadn't yet decided what she was going to do and she didn't want to burn all her bridges.

Robert struggled to focus on the two most important things in his life, Wangianna and Stewart. Out of all this mess he did not want Stewart to be hurt. Finally, after weeks of misery and silence, unable to bear the tension any longer, Robert broached the very subject he had vowed for Stewart's sake never to raise.

'Do you want a divorce?' he asked Katie from the other side of the bedroom.

Katie started to tremble. The one thing she would never ever give him was a divorce. If she couldn't have Robert's love she would have Wangianna instead. She knew she had him on the back foot and part of her wanted to laugh out loud, yet she also knew she had to be very very careful. Slowly she shook her head, her eyes dull.

'I couldn't. Stewart,' she choked. She didn't need to say more.

'I agree. Maybe we could . . .' stumbled Robert.

Katie held up her hands. 'I think I'll go and spend a few weeks in Sydney. They say you can get over almost anything if you try hard enough.' She gave a mirthless laugh. 'If you could just try to love me a little . . .' Her eyes spilled over with tears. Robert hesitated, then he held out his hand and she ran to him.

'Katie, my poor poor Katie. How can I ever make it up to you?' whispered Robert into her hair. 'I never wanted to hurt you.'

'Oh but I want to hurt you,' whispered Katie as she stared out of the window of the train that carried her down to Sydney. 'How I want to hurt you.'

Chapter Eighteen

THE RAIN WAS PELTING down on the windscreen of Teddy's tiny Austin Healey as he and Alice travelled down the narrow country lane. Dressed in his usual cavalry twills, open-necked shirt and loud cravat, Teddy was taking Alice to the Saturday market at Saffron Walden, a pretty little country town outside Cambridge. The downpour showed no sign of easing so he pulled off the road into a gateway to a cornfield. As he did so a large hay cart emerged out of the gloom and deluged them with water as it passed.

Since her decision two months ago to stay in England and marry Teddy, Alice had divided her time between research work with Professor Dixson and time with Teddy and Harry. Teddy had asked her a dozen times to marry him fearing she might change her mind and each time she had laughingly reassured him, teasing him when he grudgingly complained about the occasional day or evening she spent with Harry, although lately that had been very infrequent as Harry spent most of her weekends at the RAF base where Roody was stationed. As she and Teddy listened to the rain pounding down on the car's soft top, the heat of their bodies combined with the warmth of the steamy August day quickly misted up the windows.

'This has set in for the day. The market'll be a wash out,' said Teddy relaxing back into his seat. He reached across to Alice, idly twiddling one of her jet-black locks. Alice shrugged disappointedly.

'We could still visit some of the little antique shops,' she said.

'We could or we could amuse ourselves in other ways.' Alice blushed as Teddy leaned over and kissed her lingeringly on the lips. Slowly Alice slid her arms around his neck returning his kiss. After a long while they drew apart.

'I adore you, Alice,' Teddy sighed. 'I never want to share you with anyone. I keep wondering how I could be so lucky that you said yes.'

'And I love you too, Teddy.' It was true. Once she had made the decision to marry Teddy, each day she found she loved him more. It would never be the passionately abandoned love she had felt for Robert, but she was happy with Teddy. She loved his outlandish English eccentricity, his extravagant behaviour and his sudden unexpected bouts of gentleness. Most of all, for the first time since Ben's death, she felt happy and secure. The only niggle was Teddy's attitude towards her work with the professor but Alice had made it quite clear that for the moment that was not negotiable.

'I could take you here and now . . .' murmured Teddy, his lips tickling her ear, feeling the familiar ache in his groin when he was close to her. Goodness knows why he had not made love to her by now, perhaps it would make her more willing to bend to his will, but there was a wall of innocence surrounding Alice that he dare not penetrate for fear of losing her before they were safely married. 'I want to give you the world, to hold you close, to cherish you for the rest of—' Alice drew back sharply.

'What did I do wrong?' asked Teddy in surprise.

'Don't say that, ever,' ordered Alice. Then more gently she explained, 'Someone else promised me the world once in my life and then took it all away from me.'

'You are my world,' he said softly. Releasing his hold on Alice he reached over and pulled out a small red velvet box from the back shelf next to the picnic hamper. Alice gasped as he flicked open the lid revealing an enormous ruby and diamond ring. Speechless she allowed Teddy to slip the magnificent jewel on the third finger of her left hand.

'It's beautiful,' she gasped. 'Far too beautiful.'

'Not for you, my precious wife to be,' whispered Teddy taking her into his arms and kissing her again. A strange shiver ran down Alice's spine at his words but she steadfastly ignored it.

'It belonged to my great-grandmother,' explained Teddy shakily. 'Two of the claws had to be strengthened otherwise I would have raced up to London and given it to you the day you cancelled your plane ticket home.' He drew Alice towards him again, his expression almost desperate as he stared into her brilliant blue eyes. 'Just so that I am sure this is all real and that I'm not dreaming, tell me again you love me and that you really will marry me.'

Alice's voice was filled with tenderness as she spoke. 'Edward Charles Dominic Turlington, I love you and I will most certainly marry you.' Teddy kissed her longer and more insistently than he had dared before and Alice yielded to his caress allowing the delicious sensations he aroused to spread through her body. Flooded with happiness at her responsiveness Teddy knew that he was close to the edge of his control.

'If I kiss you any more I won't be responsible for my actions,' he said trying to sound light-hearted. He could feel he was rock hard. At that moment a part of Alice would have allowed him to do anything he wanted. Neither made a move to go further. Pulling herself together, Alice straightened up in her seat and stroked her unruly locks back off her face enjoying the strange heaviness of her magnificent ring.

'It's stopped raining,' she said looking out of the car window in surprise. Stepping out of the car she stretched luxuriantly and gazed around. Sure enough the clouds had rolled away and a watery sun shone down on the damp steamy countryside. Teddy stepped out after her. Slipping an arm around her from behind he waved a bottle of Moet & Chandon in front of her nose.

'I think, my darling Kanga, we should celebrate now.'

'What a topping idea,' Alice replied cheekily, stretching out her left hand and gazing in awe as the sunlight bounced off each diamond, sending a fire through the ruby. Maybe it was possible to be wonderfully happy after all.

ALICE AND TEDDY'S wedding was set for Saturday 21st September 1963 in the tiny Cotswold village church in Stow on the Wold. It was to be what Lord Turlington, Teddy's father, described as a quiet family wedding of two hundred people. Teddy's mother, Lady Georgina, was a friendly unfussy horsy-looking woman who had welcomed Alice loudly into the family, delighted that her son had finally found a bride, even if she was Australian. His brother and sister, both older than him and married with young children were equally welcoming. To Alice's delight, Aunty Bea, although disappointed that she would not be returning to Australia, was overjoyed the girl had found someone to make her happy and she flew over for the wedding. Despite Alice's letters, though, when she arrived Bea felt totally overawed by the grandeur of the Turlingtons' home and their glamorous lifestyle.

'Are you sure this is what you want, sweetie?' she asked Alice in a private moment.

'Why?' retorted Alice a bit too abruptly and immediately softened. 'I'm sorry Aunty Bea, I've just got pre-wedding jitters.' She twiddled her enormous engagement ring nervously. 'Harry's been wonderful and Lady Turlington's insisted on paying for everything, except the dress of course.' Her eyes filled with love as she said, 'Thank you and Uncle Ray. My dress is so beautiful and precious because it's from you.'

'We would have liked to have paid for more but Lady Turlington insisted, and I didn't want to upset her. She is a very generous lady. I just wanted to make sure you were really happy.'

'I am, Aunty Bea, truly I am. I'm just a bit tired.'

But Aunty Bea was not entirely convinced. Some of Alice's sparkle was missing. Maybe after losing Ben it was gone forever. She shrugged her shoulders and pulled on her jacket. She had to let go and allow the girl to make her own decisions in life. It was silly getting in a panic when Alice had been living overseas for the last two years and she was only here for a two-week visit. She wished she didn't feel quite so out of place.

Rousing herself she said, 'Let's go and get you a really lovely piece of furniture for a wedding present. Your Uncle Ray made me promise to get you both something really special. We want you to remember your wedding day as one of the best days in your life.'

'It's so good to have you here, Aunty Bea,' said Alice hugging her aunt. 'It will be the beginning of the best part of my life. I know Teddy seems a bit eccentric to you and everything's very different from back home, but he's very gentle and loving. I really do love him.'

'Then that's all that matters.'

'AUNTY BEA THINKS I'm just marrying Teddy for his money,' Alice confided to Harry two days before the wedding.

'Well, are you?'

'Of course not!' Alice snapped indignantly. 'It's just I keep wondering if I am being fair to Teddy the way I feel.' Harriet read her thoughts.

'Listen, cherub, you've got to leave your memories behind. Either you marry Teddy and have a wonderful life—he's got pots of money and he'll take you anywhere you want—or you can turn into a sour old spinster pining away for the rest of your days because your cousin stole the only man you could ever love.' Brutally she went on. 'That's all hogwash and ballyhoo. It takes two to get into the tangle they got into. Robert can't be entirely innocent. You need a stiff drink.' She poured her a large pink gin. 'And give Lady T a grandchild quickly. She'll be over the moon and you won't have time to worry about all this other stuff.'

'You're absolutely right,' Alice agreed taking a large gulp. 'You're such a great friend, Harry. I just got a bit panicky that I might be making a mistake marrying an Englishman.' Then in a whisper she added, 'What about my dream, Harry? Teddy'd never agree to live in Australia. He thinks it's all kangaroos and convicts.'

'God! Brides ought to be sedated until after the nuptial rites,' teased Harry throwing up her hands in mock horror. 'Give him time, Kanga. Give them all time. Tie the knot and then hit him between the eyes with your sheep thing. You'll know when. He's already eating out of your hand.' By the time Alice had finished her drink she was feeling much better.

The following Saturday, in the tiny packed country church overflowing with flowers, all concerns put aside, a radiant Alice floated up the aisle on the arm of Adrian Slade who had agreed to give her away. Alice had lost weight in the last few weeks and her shimmering white satin dress with its long flowing train clung to her body accentuating her trim figure. Outside, nature celebrated with her, dressed in its autumn splendour. After the wedding ceremony Alice felt quietly content as she walked back towards the guests, one hand tucked securely in Teddy's arm, the other carrying a long trailing spray of orange blossom and tiny bud roses. Her scalloped lace veil was tossed back over her glorious black hair, tamed for the first time in her life, revealing her dazzling smile. Teddy had chosen a loud red cravat to wear with his grey morning suit. His right hand covered Alice's fingers, his British stiff upper lip hiding the joy he felt inside. Harry and the two younger bridesmaids, all dressed in shot orange silk, followed behind. Aunty Bea surreptitiously wiped away tears of pride and Lady Turlington wept because, while she thought Alice a delightful little thing and weddings always made her cry, she would secretly have preferred Teddy to marry one of her titled friends' offspring. But it would not have been at all the done thing to admit this to anyone and she had no intention of doing so.

The Turlingtons had spared no expense for their youngest son's wedding. Lord Turlington had broken out several crates of his best champagne kept for this very occasion, and the bubbly liquid flowed continuously at the reception held at their elegant home. Close on four o'clock Alice and Teddy disappeared to change out of their wedding attire. The guests, noting the signal for the bride and groom's impending departure, spilled out onto the front lawn and cheered Alice on when she reappeared looking ravishing in a dramatic emerald green silk suit. Teddy was already waiting, dressed once more in twills, a new incredibly loud suede waistcoat and cravat, and with a monster cream dahlia in his buttonhole. Bubbling with excitement, Alice grabbed his outstretched hand, her free hand clutching her matching large-brimmed hat against a sudden gust. Bride and groom then made a dash between the two lines of guests who laughed and cheered as they showered them with confetti and rice. Stopping a moment Alice tossed her bouquet into the crowd where to her delight it was caught by Harry. Then for the benefit of the guests and photographers Alice laughingly allowed her new husband to kiss her before they finally slipped into his red Austin Healey which was plastered with shaving cream, balloons, old boots and cans, and a large placard reading 'Just married' on the back. Waving happily they sped noisily away.

As soon as they were out of sight of the wedding guests, Teddy pulled over and stopped the car. Having shaken some of the confetti from his trousers he gently removed Alice's hat, tipped out the confetti that had caught in the brim and pulled out the pins one by one allowing her hair to tumble freely around her shoulders. Drawing her to him he gazed into her eyes misty with happiness and champagne.

'Alice, my darling wife, I am the luckiest man alive today.' Then he kissed her long and hard. Alice melted into his arms. After what seemed a very long time they drew apart. Looking up at the lowering clouds Teddy said. 'Shall we risk it and leave the hood down? The place we're staying is only half an hour's drive away.' Alice nodded stroking Teddy's cheek. 'Do that again and we'll never make it before the morning.'

Alice blushed. She reached over into one of the bags and grabbed a lemon silk chiffon scarf, an engagement present from Teddy's sister, and wound it around her hair tying it at the nape of her neck so that the ends streamed out behind her as they sped noisily towards their destination.

As dusk was falling Teddy turned the car in through the gates of an impressive sixteenth century country mansion now adapted as a hotel and they banged and clattered their way up the long driveway coming to a stop in front of the magnificent carved front door. Immediately the owner and his wife, friends of Teddy's, were out to greet them and everyone was laughing and joking and kissing and congratulating and Alice and Teddy were once more showered with confetti. Dinner was served compliments of the house with more champagne and after dinner Teddy carried his bride up the wide polished stairs across the threshold into the bridal suite. Alice's eyes opened wide with delight as she saw the room where they would spend their first night together.

The bridal suite was in one of the Elizabethan wings of the manor overlooking the lush grounds and lake with an adjoining sitting room and a bathroom down the long hall. In the centre of the great bedroom was an enormous four-poster bed its heavy mulberry and gold brocade silk curtains tied back with large gold tasselled cords. Matching curtains were drawn across the windows shutting out the prying eyes of night. Bowls of flowers perfumed the room and an ice bucket holding yet another bottle of vintage champagne stood beside a table on which sat a silver tray laid with two fluted glasses and a red and white rose. The bed was turned down invitingly, its white embroidered linen covered pillows contrasting starkly against the plum satin-edged blankets. Alice's pink satin nightgown was laid out across the bed, her matching robe across the nearby chair.

'Well, Mrs Edward Turlington, have they put on a good enough spread for you?' asked Teddy setting her back on her feet and lifting the champagne out of the ice bucket. Neatly he removed the cork allowing the thin stream of white vapour to escape before he filled both glasses.

'Teddy, it's wonderful.' Alice was overcome with shyness, aware in these voluptuous surroundings of her own lack of sexual experience. Walking over to the chair she picked up the pink robe and started towards the door. Gently Teddy took the robe from her and dropped it on the floor.

'You won't be needing that, my love.'

Alice stopped, not knowing what to do next, terribly aware that if it had been Robert she would have known exactly what to do. It was all so different than she had imagined. Gently Teddy took her in his arms and started to kiss her. She could not help the tears from seeping out from under her long velvety eyelashes and sliding down her cheeks. Teddy halted a moment in surprise, her fragility inflaming his desire.

'Don't cry, my love. I promise I'll be gentle,' he whispered kissing her wet cheeks. He could feel her trembling beneath his touch like a beautiful trapped butterfly, setting his own heart pounding against his ribs in answer. He wanted to engulf her with his love.

Teddy knew he was a good lover. Yet, despite his experience, his fingers trembled as they unfastened Alice's jacket and shirt and slipped them from her shoulders exposing the creamy soft skin of her shoulders. From the first moment he had laid eyes on Alice he had longed for this moment yet now that it was upon him his usual confidence deserted him. Her looks, her vulnerability, her perfume, the voluptuous curve of her hips, the tantalising way her nipples pressed against the silk of her petticoat drove him crazy in a way that he had never experienced before. Knowing that he had only so much control, wanting her so desperately yet wanting this first time to be an exquisite experience for them both, he did the wrong thing and hurried. Turning out the lights so that only one softly shaded lamp lit the room, he picked her up in his arms and carried her to the bed.

'Oh Alice, I love you so much, I want you so badly,' he mumbled. Alice could feel his whole body shaking against hers as he laid her down and, pulling the shift over her head, tossed it aside and traced a finger along the top of her firm young breasts.

'Do you know you send a man wild with desire?' His words pierced her like a knife. Dry-eyed once more she shut her mind to the echo of another voice in another place and slid her arms quickly around him, kissing him hard on the mouth with an intensity that took Teddy by surprise.

'Hey, what happened to my shy young maiden?' he asked breathless.

'I love you, Teddy,' Alice said with grim determination, 'and we are going to have the most wonderful marriage.'

'I won't argue with that,' laughed Teddy nibbling at her bare shoulder as she helped him unclasp her bra and lay back naked on the bed but for the wisp of silk that passed for her panties. 'Oh God you're beautiful,' whispered Teddy as she pulled him to her. Struggling out of his shirt and trousers he lay beside her feeling himself become erect. 'Oh Alice, you are so glorious,' he said covering her face with kisses.

Her sudden change from timid virgin to aggressive lover helped restore his sense of confidence. Controlling himself with enormous effort, he ran his fingers down between her breasts cupping his hand around her wonderful warm roundness, feeling the joyous satisfaction of her nipples swelling and hardening under his touch. The effect was not lost on Alice. New to the barrage of sensations that swirled within her, Alice clasped her hands around his neck pulling his mouth over hers, her heart racing as she allowed herself to savour his delicious nakedness against hers. Her uncontrived open approach only served to fuel his desire. Dizzy with longing he only half felt her fingers digging into his thick hair or heard her low moan as unable to resist any longer he slid his fingers between the dark pubic hair and felt her wetness.

'Oh you sweet, wonderful girl!' he whispered hoarsely. All thought of easing her gently into the art of love gone, he lifted himself on top of her and eased himself inside her velvety folds. 'Alice, I can't wait. I promise I'll be gentle,' he rasped as he felt her tension at this first intrusion. His words banished her misgivings. For an instant he stopped as he met the expected resistance, but Alice arched to meet him urging him on, reaching out for him with her body as he plunged himself into her, feeling the exquisite pain as his passion mounted. Her moving was Teddy's undoing. His control gone, he hurtled down into a world made wholly of sensation, lost in the glorious beauty of Alice's body. Before she had a chance to become fully aroused it was over and he lay panting against her and she could feel the pounding of his heart against hers. She sensed that he had experienced something deep and fundamental but somehow she felt vaguely irritated and let down. She stroked his hair and kissed him gently.

'I'm too heavy for you,' he said rolling over.

'No, you're not,' Alice answered softly, running her finger along his chest which glistened with sweat. Teddy didn't move for a moment. Then he rolled over towards her, his elbow bent, his head propped in his hand.

'I made a mess of that for you. No other woman has ever made me lose control so quickly and so completely. But I promise next time I'll do it better.' Alice kissed him gently. He ran his fingers lingeringly over her cheek and down the soft curves of her body sending shivers of goosebumps across her flesh. Then he stood up and reached for their untouched champagne.

'To the most glorious woman in the world,' he said, handing her a drink, and downed his own in one gulp.

Alice watched him over the rim of her glass, her senses on fire as he turned out the lamp and drew back the curtains so the moonlight flooded in through the windows. Unresisting she relinquished her empty glass as he lay down beside her again and pulled her into his arms. But Alice was no longer content merely to lie still. Teddy had shown her the beginnings of love yet in her innocence she did not fully understand why she suddenly felt so restless. Sitting up she pulled the sheet off him wrapping it around her nakedness and dragging her jet black hair teasingly back and forth across his chest to hide her irritation. He laughed at her provocativeness and suddenly he was once more caught up in her enchantment.

This time Teddy was able to control himself long enough to arouse her further so that when he entered her their bodies rocked in an increasingly urgent rhythm. Then for Alice all thoughts of time and place were forgotten in a delicious blend of sensations that burst on her like nothing she had ever experienced before. When it was over they lay together quiet and relaxed, husband and wife joined in a bond that was utterly new and infinitely precious to them both.

As Alice lay in her newly-awakened state she found that Teddy had fallen asleep across her. Staring into the darkness, one hand resting lightly on his shoulder, feeling the gentle movement of his body as he breathed, she knew she could not sleep. Teddy loved her and his lovemaking had touched her, but it had not filled her being like the smell of Robert's wet hair against her mouth or the touch of his fingers as they had romped together in the dam. They had never consummated their love on that ill-fated day yet Alice felt she had given herself to him. Carefully she rolled over and stared out at the clouds scudding across the moon. She was married to Teddy. She had to lock away those other memories forever. How else would their marriage ever stand a chance. The soft rustling of the leaves against the bedroom window was the last thing she heard as she drifted off.

THE HONEYMOON LASTED two delicious weeks. As a surprise Teddy took Alice to the south of France and then in the second week to Spain where they stayed with Count Pablo and Contessa Catalina Brandini in their lavish villa in the foothills outside Barcelona. There they sipped Spanish hot chocolate and dipped churros—the long thin fried doughnuts that scoop up the chocolate as efficiently as a spoon—into their drinks and drove up into the soft clean mountain air and admired the horses from the Brandinis' stables.

Waking up one morning Alice strolled to the window and gazed down at Teddy chatting with the Contessa Catalina in the formal rose garden as she picked the best blooms. A little smile hovered around Alice's lips as she thought how contented she felt now she had found such a gentle man willing to love her but not asking too much in return. Feeling her eyes on him Teddy turned and waved to her. Alice waved back watching them idly a few moments longer before withdrawing to get dressed. She would have been far less happy could she have heard their conversation.

'You know my feelings towards you haven't changed,' Teddy said, avoiding the Contessa's eyes. 'We'll just have to leave things for a while. But when you're in London again we will find a way to renew our . . .' He hesitated. 'Our friendship.' The Contessa nodded picking another rose, a deep red heavily-perfumed bloom just bursting open. Carefully she cut the stem and slid it through the lapel in Teddy's jacket.

'You know I wish you and Alice every happiness,' she murmured in her flawless English, her hand lingering a moment warm against his chest. 'But I do not think I want to wait until London.' She sighed deeply, pouting her lips seductively, her black eyes glowing with lust out of her smooth olive-skinned face.

'Well you're going to have to my little lovebird. I'm a married man now,' replied Teddy, his eyes teasing her. He was infatuated by Alice and would not jeopardise his marriage, yet as they returned to the house he wondered just what it was that drew him so helplessly to other men's wives.

'Do not make it too long or your bird might have flown,' replied the Contessa, her black eyes caressing him. She handed him the basket of roses. 'These are for your Alice.'

Chapter Nineteen

IT WASN'T UNTIL ALICE had been married six months that she started to notice a change in Teddy. She knew that he was nervous about his first year as a teaching member of his faculty, but it was more than that. They seemed to squabble about everything.

After their honeymoon they had found a delightful half-timbered thatched cottage called Mill House a short drive from Cambridge. The cottage garden had run wild, the stream that ran beside it, which should have bubbled and sung its way along like any in a Constable painting, was choked with weeds, and the sluicegates to the weir were rusted and broken. But Alice loved it, even though it meant she had to commute to London every day.

She and Teddy had agreed she would continue working with Professor Dixson, but Alice knew Teddy disapproved. She made an extra effort to look after him, often stepping exhausted from the train to attend the functions that came with his job as a member of the university teaching staff, but the effort was wearing her out. That wasn't the problem though—Teddy's mood swings were. One moment he would be jealous and possessive, and the next he would hardly notice she existed, then he would switch to being a passionate attentive lover. Never knowing what kind of mood her husband would be in made Alice irritable and nervous. Finally everything came to a head early one Saturday morning as she was getting ready to catch the train to work.

'I don't know how you expect us to have a marriage when you're off to London six days a week and sometimes seven. What sort of a picture do you think it creates to the dons and their wives when I have to keep making excuses for your absence?' He yawned and sat up in bed scratching his head grumpily. Alice thought he looked quite gorgeous, like a crumpled puppy.

'This is only the second Saturday in three months,' protested Alice leaning over to kiss him, but he brushed her aside.

'I'm serious. Haven't you got enough to do without tearing off to your precious professor and his damned experiments? What about this house? What about helping me with my research? I can't do everything on my own you know, and how can I possibly entertain as I am expected to as a tutor at Trinity College when you are never here?'

'Hey, wait a moment, that's unfair,' said Alice taken aback by the sudden onslaught. She glanced at her watch. 'Darling, can we discuss this all when I get home tonight. I'm going to miss my train.'

'If I'm here,' said Teddy sourly. Alice didn't have time to find out exactly what he meant as the taxi was already tooting at the door. She was so angry at his unreasonableness she hardly noticed the journey to London.

For once she really missed not being able to drop in on Harry in London. Harry had finally agreed to marry Roody and, after a lovely wedding, the couple had moved up to Scotland with Roody's new posting. 'Why can't I be more like Harry?' Alice thought furiously as she clambered off the train at Liverpool Street station and joined the crush. Last time they had spoken Harry had sounded blissfully happy with no regrets at having given up her job to be with Roody. Alice found it impossible to concentrate on work all morning.

'Time for another of those cups of coffee, don't you think?' suggested Professor Dixson firmly hauling her off for a coffee break. Tearing at her Chelsea bun, Alice blurted out that she and Teddy had had their first row and that he wanted her to give up her work at the laboratory.

'I'm doing it again, expecting too much too often,' sighed Professor Dixson. 'Rosie was at me the other day about it. Trouble is, I'm a selfish old man.'

'No, you're not,' replied Alice, her anger reignited. 'And there is absolutely no reason why I should give up my work with you. It's okay for him to go dashing off to Oxford or . . . or Edinburgh or anywhere any old time of the day or night, but it's not okay for me. Oh no, the rules all change when it comes to me.' She stuffed a large piece of bun in her mouth in frustration. 'Sometimes he can be so completely unreasonable I could scream. I don't even know if he's going to be there when I get home tonight.' There was a long pause while the professor gave Alice a chance to simmer down. He noticed the deep shadows under her eyes. Slipping his hand over Alice's ringed fingers he gave them a quick, slightly embarrassed squeeze.

'You know the old saying about true love and smooth paths,' he said softly. 'Maybe the time has come, my girl, for you and me to part company. Goodness only knows how I will manage without you or if I will ever find anyone to replace you, but fighting over an old boffin's research is no way to start a marriage. You go home to your new husband, have a whole lot of babies and be happy.'

Alice's eyes filled with tears. 'But I don't want to stop working with you,' she cried, feeling as though she was right back with Uncle Ray telling her a woman's place was in the kitchen. She hadn't accepted it then and she had no intention of accepting it now.

'Do you really want to jeopardise your marriage for my work?' went on the professor noting Alice's jutting chin.

'If he loved me he wouldn't make me choose. Anyway I don't think you can manage without me,' she finished triumphantly.

'You're right, but you can manage without me,' replied the professor gruffly to hide his emotion.

After a while Alice calmed down. Teddy had not exactly given her an ultimatum but she did love him and she did want to have a family. It seemed everyone else had already agreed the best thing for her to do was to give up her work. Alice gave a big sigh and blew her nose.

'You've taught me so much and you're so understanding. I'm really going to miss you and Rosie.'

'Yes, yes dear child,' interrupted the professor patting her on the shoulder. He stood up, nodding his head. 'We'll finish this last series of tests.

Then you can get the early train home and tell your husband you'll be finishing up at the end of the week.' He ran his hand through his thick white locks. 'When and if you ever want to return you know there will always be a job here for you.' He blushed furiously as Alice jumped up and hugged him, much to the amusement of the other lab technicians having their morning break.

'I just hope Teddy has enough sense to realise what a jewel he has married,' the professor said as Alice left at the end of the afternoon. Alice stepped out of the taxi and walked slowly up the garden path deciding how to tell Teddy the news and stopped abruptly as she saw the empty space usually filled by the bright red Austin Healey. Running inside she read the note on the kitchen table.

'Gone to Adrian and Monica's for the weekend.' Crumpling the note up she hurled it across the kitchen. Then she sat down and bawled her eyes out. After three cups of tea and half a packet of chocolate biscuits she set about savagely attacking the garden. At ten that night she was lying in a tepid bath trying not to think of the empty bed she was going to have to get into, when the door opened and in walked Teddy.

'I couldn't do it,' he declared, leaning down and pulling out the plug. 'I couldn't bear the thought of wasting a night at Adrian's when I could be making passionate love to my wife.' With those words he lifted her out of the bath, carried her dripping wet into the bedroom, dumped her unceremoniously on the bed and proceeded to strip off. Alice wasn't sure whether to laugh or be furious, but their lovemaking that night was the most fulfilling she had experienced since they were married.

As soon as Alice gave up work Teddy's moodiness disappeared and the gentle side of him re-emerged as Alice juggled organising builders, painters and plumbers to finish the house. Just one small thing niggled at her happiness. One day after Teddy had returned from working late with a colleague in Oxford Alice caught the faintest whiff of perfume on his shirt. The fragrance was so faint and confused with the smell of cigarette smoke that at first she wondered whether she was imagining it, but the trace was there and it certainly wasn't one she used. In the enthusiasm of decorating the house she decided she was being obsessive and plunged the shirts into the washing machine. Some of the secretaries Teddy worked with smothered themselves in perfume. Submerging herself in wallpapering, painting, sewing cushions, curtains and bedspreads and tackling the garden, she put the incident out of her mind.

'Have you thought about children?' Alice asked thoughtfully one spring morning, stirring the remains of her tea as the two sat enjoying a late Sunday breakfast, her body still tingling from the aftermath of their lovemaking. A soft breeze blew through the open window wafting in the scent of flowers and ruffling the pretty blue gingham curtains Alice had recently made. The hum of bees outside reminded her of cool spring days in Australia.

'I have, my darling, whenever my sister threatens to come and stay. And I also think how nice it is to give them back,' replied Teddy dryly.

'But wouldn't you like to have some of our own?' pursued Alice.

'Love to. Why don't we drive over towards Swaffam Prior, Kanga my angel. It's such a lovely day and there are so many places I want to show you. We could have a pleasant pub lunch and then drop in on Adrian and Monica on the way home.' His eyes rested fondly on Alice. 'You haven't seen their new place.'

Alice hid her disappointment at Teddy's abrupt change of subject but she had learned by now that there was nothing to gain in pursuing the topic. Instead she said, 'Have you thought when we might take a trip back home?'

'Funny, I was only talking to Mother about that two days ago . . . which reminds me, have you made out your guest list for your twenty-first, it's only three months away and Mother wants it soon so she can get organised?' Alice pouted. They had been over this before.

'But I told you I wanted to celebrate my birthday in our own little cottage now that it's finished. The garden will be looking lovely in August.' But in this, too, Teddy was adamant. His mother, he insisted, would be devastated if she was not allowed to throw a huge party for Alice—she had been planning it for months.

'She'll have invited half of Gloucestershire by now.' Alice bit back the temptation to argue. 'I'd better write out that list then or I won't know anyone at my own party,' she said, distinctly irritated.

'That's my mother,' nodded Teddy. 'Now that we've sorted out the party I've got a surprise for you.' He threw down two tickets to the Trinity College May Ball. 'To celebrate one glorious year of knowing you.'

Alice's face lit up. 'Are you going to propose to me all over again on the Bridge of Sighs?'

'No, but I am going to give you this.' Fishing in his coat pocket he pulled out a long blue-velvet box, which he opened and held up a gleaming three-strand pearl choker with a big ruby at the centre. 'Thought you might like to wear it when you're gardening,' he said, grinning like a small boy.

All Alice's irritation melted. 'You're buying me off with gifts,' she laughed, her eyes twinkling mischievously.

'Yes.'

'It works brilliantly.'

'There is a price to pay, you know,' retorted Teddy.

'Oh I know, Teddy, I know,' said Alice leaping up, intent on escaping into the garden, but Teddy was too quick for her. Gathering her up into his arms he carried her back upstairs to the bedroom.

'What about Swaffam Prior?' Alice protested feebly.

'It will still be there in an hour's time,' he replied, silencing her with a kiss.

On their return from a late pub lunch Teddy and Alice found Dr Monica Slade in the garden weeding the roses. A drab young woman, dressed in oatmeal Bermuda shorts and a shabby dark blue T-shirt, she looked completely at home in gardening gloves. Her dull brown shoulder-length hair, normally twisted neatly on her head, was tied back loosely with a piece of string. Adrian had married Monica shortly after Alice met Teddy but all four had only met a couple of times since then as Monica's medical practice in Cambridge kept her very busy.

Monica greeted them both with delight. Clutching her secateurs she wiped her forehead with the back of her glove leaving a large streak of dirt behind. Alice got a whiff of stale sweat and last night's cooking.

'Adrian's round in the stables. You haven't seen our latest addition to the family, have you?' Before they could answer Monica whisked them round the side of the large house to the brand-new stables finished only days before. Piles of wood, sand and flagstones lay to one side showing there was still work to do and the smell of horse manure mixed with hay jolted Alice with their memories. Alice gasped as Adrian approached her leading a magnificent roan.

'Teddy said you wanted to try him out,' announced Adrian as Alice automatically reached up and fondled the horse.

'He said what?' she exclaimed, turning in surprise to her husband then yelping as the horse, used to being the centre of attention, gave her a sharp nip on the shoulder.

'Listen you,' she retorted, shoving the horse's mouth away from her shoulder, 'do you always get centre stage?' She ran her hand down the horse's glistening flanks revelling in its silky smooth coat. The horse shook its head and whinnied.

'Mostly,' nodded Adrian.

'Well are you going to get on it or just talk to the bally thing?' grinned Teddy. He had planned something like this ever since he had heard the way she talked about Sherry.

'I'm not dressed to ride,' protested Alice pointing to her floral sundress and pretty low-heeled sandals.

'Ride side saddle,' encouraged Adrian handing her the reins as the horse blew down the front of her sundress. 'You can borrow a pair of my riding boots.' Throwing her head back, Alice laughed. She had forgotten what it felt like to have a horse nudging at her, especially one as cheeky and egotistical as this one.

'Don't worry!' she exclaimed. Without a second thought, Alice kicked off her sandals. Hitching up her skirts she stepped onto Adrian's outstretched hand and was in the saddle.

'Take him for a walk across the field,' suggested Adrian pointing to the open gate beyond which lay a field dotted with various barrels and poles for practice jumping. 'Do you want to ride the bay?' he asked Teddy. Teddy shook his head.

'She doesn't need me. She doesn't need anyone. Look at her.'

Having coaxed the horse into the field Alice set him at a gentle walk. Quickly getting the feel of the horse she nudged him into a trot and then more confidently into a canter, her spirits rising at the thrill of a horse beneath her. She felt free. All the glorious memories of her time on Sherry came flooding back as she cantered around the field. Tears of sadness and loss and exultation tumbled down her cheeks cleansing her soul. Teddy had planned this whole day. From the moment they woke up he had known exactly what he was going to do. Now comments that had seemed out of context at the time fell into place. He had been determined to get her back on a horse and for that she loved him dearly.

'Isn't she magnificent? I don't know which is more thoroughbred, Alice or the horse,' sighed Adrian watching Alice in fascination as she cantered confidently around the field, skirt billowing around her.

'You've done a wonderful thing for Alice today, old chap,' said Teddy sincerely. 'Thank you.'

'All part of the service, old boy and worth it for a sight like that.'

Teddy was working on some papers in his college rooms in the last week of the university Tripos exams at the end of May when the door burst open and in walked Bertrand Wilbraham, a lecturer in English, two years senior to Teddy and a member of Christ's College.

'Teddles old chap, I was hoping I'd catch you.'

Teddy looked up in surprise at the sound of his schoolboy nickname.

'Bunty! What are you doing in this neck of the woods? I thought I saw your name down as supervising the second year's exams.'

Bunty and Teddy had both been educated at Harrow and Cambridge. Bunty, a brilliant member of the Harrow debating team, had slated Teddy when he had been given an honorary rowing blue after Lord Turlington donated the money for a new rowing boat shed to the school, and he had used the information against him in the Cambridge debating society. However, Teddy had gone on to prove his legitimacy by becoming a member of one of the Trinity rowing eights as an undergraduate. Nowadays their school and undergraduate rivalry had faded into a more accepting acquaintance which recognised the importance of the old boys' network.

'You did, but I've got a break and I just remembered this.' He thrust a piece of paper into Teddy's hand. Teddy glanced at it and his eye caught the words 'vacancy for research position'. The closing date for applications was March. Teddy scanned the sheet and passed the paper back to Bunty.

'Why are you showing me this now? I've missed the closing date by three months.'

'That's what I wanted to tell you. They're accepting late entries. Apparently no one really outstanding had applied and they were thinking of leaving the position vacant. Then I heard they're seriously considering offering the post to, of all people, that awful Clive what's-his-name in your department. Apparently he's created quite an impression.' He looked down his nose at Teddy. 'Can't imagine how. The man did his training at Leeds University, if you can call it a university.'

Teddy bristled at Bunty's news. Teddy was still smarting that Clive Parkin, someone who in his and many of his colleagues' view, had not gone through the right channels, had been given a position senior to him although they were both accepted as teaching staff at the same time. Not having sweated his way through the English public schools system and Oxford or Cambridge, Clive Parkin was considered by the likes of Teddy, Bunty and their compatriots, an uneducated social climber.

'Oh yes?' said Teddy cautiously.

'I thought it a bit off to have some little upstart from a redbrick university trying to take over such a prestigious position.' As Teddy said nothing Bunty continued. 'I couldn't apply. I know where my skills lie. Then I heard you were sick as a dog when you discovered you'd missed out on applying earlier this year. Look, old chap, I know we've had our moments but I couldn't just sit by and watch such a travesty be allowed to happen, old school tie and all that.'

'Bunty, I forgive you everything you said at the debating society,' said Teddy expansively. 'How long do I have if I decide to put in an application?'

'They're not making the final decision until the end of August. If you get your finger out, I'd say you've got every chance of being accepted and beating the little twerp.' Bunty sighed, noting with satisfaction Teddy's growing excitement. Teddy refrained from asking how Bunty had obtained this information. Bunty had the most extraordinary ability to squeeze information out of his colleagues. He had a persuasive skill that forced people to listen to him and to tell him things. He was a skilled political animal. Teddy could learn a lot from Bunty.

Bunty was right, he was getting excited. He had been disgusted at his own stupidity at missing out earlier in the year but now if he could put forward a good application he could be well on his way to setting up his research into the ancient silk road. There was a good possibility of an honorary doctorate going down that path. He grinned delightedly at Bunty, his mind working overtime. Bunty tapped his folder on the desk with satisfaction, correctly interpreting Teddy's silence as mounting interest.

'I think it would be better if you didn't mention this conversation to anyone else; meanwhile I might have a word in a few of the right ears. Want to keep it in the family and all that, don't you know.'

'Of course'

'Well, good luck. Ah yes, I nearly forgot,' finished Bunty casually, 'perhaps you'd be good enough to return this to your department when you have a chance. It seems to have got misplaced.' He handed Teddy the folder.

Teddy took it absently. Bunty had set him thinking. Clive had a reputation as a hard worker who came up with results. Definitely a danger. But Teddy had valid research that he could present, although he knew some of the research held weaknesses. Somehow he had to make it good enough to convince the committee to appoint him over a senior colleague.

'Oh, and I didn't give it to you either.' Bunty gave a conspiratorial nod and slipped from the room.

'I really appreciate . . .' said Teddy to the oak-panelled door. He glanced down at the file and his pulse started racing as the name on the folder registered in his brain. *Clive Parkin.* Teddy's hands shook as he opened the folder and began to read.

Cambridge seemed strangely deserted during the summer break as Alice stepped out of Monica Slade's surgery and set off towards Trinity College. The atmosphere was different. The streets, normally teeming with undergraduate life, were almost empty. The overcrowded pubs had room to spare. Instead the place was filled with foreigners either attending summer school or on vacation. Three times she had been stopped and asked to take pictures of American tourists against the backdrop of the colleges.

It was the Tuesday before Alice's twenty-first birthday and a typical sticky overcast August day, so unlike the dry heat of the Australian outback, yet Alice couldn't have cared less if she had been walking through a cyclone. It was nearly lunchtime and she was bursting to tell Teddy her news.

As she hurried down Green Street she planned how she would break the news. Teddy was still working frantically at putting together his application for the research vacancy so she would have to curb some of her usual enthusiasm when she met him for lunch. She would take him to the little pub tucked in the corner off Kings Parade and, over a ploughman's lunch and ice-cold lime and soda, calmly tell him. Her heart thumped with excitement as she raced up the worn wooden stairs to his rooms three at a time and waited until she had stopped panting before knocking gently on the door and slipping inside. Who was she trying to fool? Surely the stupid grin she could not control would give the game away. The main room was empty but Alice could hear soft voices coming from his secretary's room off to one side. She sat down trying to check her impatience. Teddy was expecting her and it was right on one o'clock. In time with her thoughts the door opened and out walked Teddy. Alice opened her mouth to speak but Teddy beat her to it.

'Darling, I'm afraid I'm going to have to skip lunch. I've still got a heap of work to do on this application and only three days left. Miss Freeman said she'd nip down and get a couple of sandwiches and we'll be working through lunch.'

As he spoke Miss Freeman, Teddy's secretary, appeared. She was a small mousy woman of nondescript appearance whose choice of clothes made her fade further into the background. She greeted Alice politely and scurried out of the door clutching her purse. Teddy was already heading back to his desk. Battling her disappointment, Alice followed him into his study.

'Can you spare your wife a kiss?' she said mentally making a quick change of plan. Her news was too important to toss at Teddy when he was only half listening. Teddy gave her a peremptory kiss and picked up the phone.

'You look radiant, my darling,' he said. Then the caller at the other end had his full attention. Alice could see it was pointless staying any longer.

'I'll see you tonight,' she whispered. Teddy waved and blew her a kiss.

'Plan B,' said Alice resolutely as she stepped out into the sticky August heat and hurried towards the shops. By six o'clock that evening the house was immaculate. The polished mahogany table shone like glass reflecting the white Wedgwood china edged with gold, the gleaming silver cutlery and sparkling Waterford crystal. Alice had bought all Teddy's favourite foods and cooked his favourite dishes. An array of cold meats and smoked salmon lay ready on the side in the tiny dining room alongside his favourite cheeses. A bottle of Teddy's favourite vintage red wine stood breathing on the kitchen bench. Dressed in a soft yellow cotton sundress that made her skin glow, Alice was stirring the gravy for the roast pheasant when she heard Teddy's car draw up. Pretending to ignore it she continued her work, her heart beating fast at the familiar sound of his key in the door and his quick strides into the kitchen. She jumped with pleasure as she felt his arms slide around her waist and he kissed her firmly on the cheek.

'Sorry about lunch, darling. I hope it didn't spoil your day.' He sniffed at the tantalising aromas and stroked her bare shoulders. 'What have you been up to?' he demanded with mock severity.

'Nothing,' she lied mischievously.

Teddy turned her to him. 'Maybe I'm soft, my darling Kanga, but it seems to me you grow more beautiful every day.'

'Pregnant women are supposed to be at their most beautiful,' laughed Alice unable to keep her secret a second longer. Still clutching the wooden spoon she threw her arms around Teddy splattering drops of gravy across the floor. 'I love you so much, Teddy.'

'What did you say?'

'I'm three months pregnant, my darling. I'm going to have a baby. Monica confirmed it this morning. Now there are two of us for you to love.' She reached up to kiss Teddy, and stopped as he disengaged himself and stepped away from her.

'Are you sure?'

'Absolutely,' nodded Alice beaming.

'I need a drink,' said Teddy abruptly. He disappeared into the dining room and reappeared carrying a glass. Striding grimly back into the kitchen he poured himself a glass of red wine without bothering to examine the label. Alice waited bewildered.

'How the hell did you let it happen?'

'Don't be silly,' Alice laughed, clinging to her rapidly fading happiness. 'Aren't you delighted for us both?'

'I thought you were on the Pill. The last thing I need in my life right now is a pregnant wife and babies.' Alice pushed back her hair, forcing away the tears that threatened to overtake her. She gave a shaky laugh.

'It must have happened after the May Ball. I forgot to get a new prescription and by the time I realised my mistake I thought I'd better wait for my next natural cycle to start again but it never happened. I thought you'd be as delighted as me. You always said you wanted babies whenever I brought up the subject.'

'I said no such thing,' snapped Teddy pacing the floor. 'I don't even remember discussing it.'

Alice's anger erupted through her hurt. 'That's the trouble. You never would,' she shouted pouring herself some wine in a cup and tossing it back. 'I've suspected it for the last month, but you'd never listen.'

Teddy's eyes blazed with anger as he turned on Alice. 'You know I've got my heart set on this research position and you do this to me now.'

Alice went to him unable to stop the tears running down her cheeks. 'But it won't make any difference, Teddy darling. You can still take the position.'

He pushed her roughly away. 'What, and traipse around Asia and Turkey with a two-week-old baby and a wife just out of hospital? And what about the entertaining we'll be required to do? What are you going to do, whip out a breast in the middle of a cocktail party for the Vice Chancellor? How could you do it? How could you be so damned careless?' He wasn't ready to be a father yet. He'd got the next three years mapped out clearly in his mind and now she'd upturned all his plans.

Alice couldn't believe his vicious attack. Dizzily she tried to block out his words as all the old arguments he had used against her when she was working for the professor were flung in her face.

'Teddy, please, don't do this to us!' she cried, sitting down and burying her face in her hands sobbing with disappointment. Teddy continued to pace.

'I never planned to have children so early on in our marriage. Of course I agreed every time you mentioned them, but you were talking five, six years away. You're so young. We have so much time together. I don't want to share you with anyone else, not even our own child. Sometimes I can't even bear for another man to be near you I get so torn apart with jealousy.'

Alice looked up, her reddened eyes filled with astonishment. Hurriedly she brushed away the tears from her cheeks and blew her nose.

'I had no idea, Teddy. I swear you have no need to feel jealous. I love you and you'll love our baby.' She twisted a fine cotton handkerchief agitatedly around her fingers.

'Look, Alice, I've had a bugger of a day,' said Teddy slumping down in one of their big chintz-covered armchairs. 'And now this.' He ran his fingers through his hair. He felt in a state of shock.

A coldness clutched at Alice. Feigning brightness she said, 'Dinner's all ready. I've cooked your favourite, smoked salmon, roast pheasant and blackberry and apple pie and cream.'

The meal tasted like sawdust in her mouth. Conversation was halting. They might have been two strangers making one another's acquaintance as they went through the routine of discussing the day's events, avoiding the one subject uppermost in both their minds. Finally Teddy pushed his chair away from the table and got up.

'I've got some more work to do tonight. We'll discuss all this when you're not so uptight.' Alice felt too miserable to react to his comment. Where was the love, the uplifting joy they were supposed to be experiencing together? She crept off to bed, a leaden lump against her heart. What was there to discuss? She didn't dare even start down that path. She shut her eyes knowing sleep was a million years away.

In his study Teddy dropped his head in his hands. Babies. That was one item he simply hadn't bargained for. He didn't want to be that grown-up, not now, not ever. It was too much responsibility. Mother would be delighted. He lifted his head and stared gloomily out into the night. Thoughts tumbled through his head—Alice, babies, his work. She couldn't do this to him. She couldn't trap him like this. Why did he always go to pieces when something hard came into his life? He was a good husband; he loved Alice. It wasn't as if he had been unfaithful to her, except that one time when she had been so difficult over working with the professor. And anyway that had been more a favour to an ex-girlfriend, a last fling for her before she tied the knot. Now Alice was doing it to him again. Stealing his youth with the threat of fatherhood. It was all right for her being so much younger. Who could he turn to? Who would understand him? The answer was blindingly obvious. It was time to rekindle his utterly lustful affair with the deliciously curvaceous, wickedly inviting, totally married Catalina. She'd be in her cosy London mews cottage at this time of year. As he dialled her number his pulse quickened in anticipation.

The next morning Alice woke up heavy-headed in an empty bed. The smell of last night's leftovers hit her like a ten-ton truck and she disappeared into the bathroom to throw up. As she wiped her mouth and sat up shakily waiting for her stomach to settle, she heard the car drive away. Staggering into the kitchen she made herself a cup of hot sweet tea. Teddy had left her a quickly scribbled note by the Aga.

'Forgot to tell you—will be in Oxford for next two days. T.'

Alice sat down and burst into tears. He didn't want their baby and he hadn't even spoken to her this morning. The hurt inside was unbearable. Gently she felt her stomach.

'I want you,' she whispered and then laying her arms on the table, sank her head in her hands.

'Anyone home?' Alice lifted her head with a start as a glamorous vision appeared in the kitchen doorway. 'Do you usually leave your front door open for all and sundry to walk in?'

'Harry!' shrieked Alice. Dishevelled and tearstained she leapt to her feet and flung her arms around her friend. 'What in heck are you doing here?'

'Visiting you, silly.' She hugged Alice, taking in the mess and Alice's state. 'You look terrible. What's going on?'

Quickly Alice smoothed back her tangled locks and straightened her dressing gown. She hoped she didn't smell of sick.

'You look fantastic as always. How about I make you a cup of tea? Would you like some cold pheasant?' Her laugh cracked in the middle.

'Are we going to make polite conversation or are you going to tell me why you look like you've just been run over by a bus?' asked Harry finding herself a clean mug and tossing the morning's papers off the chair before sitting down. Alice sat down heavily.

'I'm three months pregnant.'

'But that's wonderful!' exclaimed Harry jumping up and hugging her friend. 'So am I! Roody's over the moon.'

'I'm so happy for you both,' Alice said trying to control her bottom lip.

'And Teddy's not,' guessed Harry.

Alice nodded. 'He doesn't want our baby. Oh Harry, I'm so miserable,' she choked. Tears streaked down her cheeks. Her arms were stretched protectively around her still tiny stomach.

'I think we'd better have that cup of tea. Have you got any biscuits, I'm starving.' Alice got out the round tin and Harry helped herself to four biscuits. 'Okay, spill the beans.' Alice told her of the disastrous dinner and Teddy's reaction, Turkey, the note and the fact that he hadn't even bothered to say goodbye before charging off to Oxford.

'I'm not surprised in a way. Teddy's a darling. Trouble is he always gets far too het up about things he cares passionately about and then goes completely off the deep end. You're his main passion. He's loathed sharing you with anyone from the moment he set eyes on you. He did at least leave a note.'

'But why did he have to work last night of all nights? I heard him ringing up well after midnight.'

'His other great passion, silly. He couldn't cope with the shock so he hid behind his work. He's been harping on about this research thing ever since I've known him. He's going to change the world with his revelations.' She gesticulated grandly with her arms. Alice couldn't help laughing at her actions.

'Maybe you're right,' Alice admitted blowing her nose, Harry's logic allaying some of her fears. 'But why don't I feel any better?'

'You're pregnant, you goose. We're both pregnant. Our hormones are racing around inside us like mad things. I gave Roody hell two weeks ago, poor darling, because he refused to go and buy me a third bottle of pickles at two in the morning.' Alice giggled through her tears. 'From what you've been saying your timing couldn't be worse, old bean,' continued Harry. 'This baby is obviously the ultimate threat to his latest project.'

'No one, but no one is going to make me do anything to harm my baby, not even Teddy,' retorted Alice, glaring fiercely at Harry, her whole body tense. 'I didn't plan it this way.'

'Of course you didn't, but men can be so silly,' said Harry giving her a reassuring hug. Alice crumpled.

'What I dread is having to fight him when he finally gets round to discussing it,' she mumbled. 'Maybe this is the end of our marriage.' Her voice was barely audible. Harry helped herself to the last chocolate biscuit.

'Don't,' she said matter-of-factly through a mouthful of crumbs.

'Don't what?'

'Discuss it. Let him have his panic but don't discuss anything.'

Alice stared blankly at her friend. 'How do you mean?'

Harry shrugged happily. 'Just ignore all his nonsense. Let him rush around all over the countryside, making his plans. He'll come round. He's probably got all kinds of rubbish in his head, like you might die giving birth, or being a father means he's no longer a desirable male or this is goodbye to you-know-what in bed for the next twelve months or twelve years. Somehow I can't imagine either of his parents explaining to him about all that sort of stuff. Lady T's so wrapped up with her horsy friends she's forgotten what it's all about and poor old Lord T's far too much of a gentleman ever to discuss anything so intimate. He's probably had to ask permission each time anyway, so he'd be no help.' Her comment tipped the already overemotional Alice into helpless laughter.

'Oh Harry, you always make life seem so much simpler,' she said wiping her eyes. 'Why are you down here?'

'That's my other news. Roody's been posted to the RAF base near here and I'm house-hunting. We'll be able to grow fat together. Right now you're going to get dressed and we're going shopping for baby clothes,' ordered Harry. 'I'm buying for a girl and a boy just to be on the safe side. By the way, have you got any pickled onions?' she finished. Alice was feeling decidedly better as she climbed the stairs leaving Harry to hunt through the larder.

Alice had the best day she could remember in weeks, so when Teddy rang to say he would be returning straight to college on the Wednesday and sleeping there until the weekend so that he could finish the application, she remained remarkably calm. She explained how Harry had turned up unexpectedly and she had insisted she stay the night with them. Now determined not to get into any sort of argument, Alice also suggested she travel up to his parents' place with Harry on the Thursday to allow him to work without any other worries. Teddy sounded very happy at her plans, promising to get there by six-thirty on the Saturday night. It was almost as if he had forgotten about the existence of both the baby and the fact that it was her birthday.

That night after Harry rang Roody to tell him what she was doing she and Alice talked into the wee hours.

'Do your in-laws know about the baby?' asked Harry as they headed crosscountry towards Bedford in her sleek white Lotus Elan, a wedding present from Roody.

Alice shook her head. 'Only you and Teddy know.'

'Perfect! We'll tell everyone at once—that way Teddy can't do anything but be the adoring father.'

'Oh Harry, it seems a bit manipulative,' said Alice unsure.

'Serves him jolly well right. He's being a perfect rat. He deserves to be cornered.' She swung the car into the main highway and put her foot down.

'You're right of course. My heart is hardened. Hey, remember there are four of us in this car,' laughed Alice.

'I know and isn't it wonderful.'

'You're sure Roody doesn't mind you deserting him for two days?'

'Glad to get me out of his hair. Like the true lover he is, his parting comment last night was "Go and puke together".' She laughed heartily.

Lady Turlington greeted Alice and Harry with enthusiasm but was far too busy fussing with last-minute arrangements to ask any discerning questions. The girls amused themselves, helped with the flowers, watched as a great marquee was erected on the sweeping lawn at the back of the house and kept out of the way as Lady Turlington flew backwards and forwards instructing waiters to move boxes of wineglasses, crockery and cutlery, setting up tables and ensuring that enough champagne and food had been ordered. Her whereabouts could always be discerned by the eldritch shrieks of laughter that she let out as one or other of her horsy friends helped her with the party arrangements. The one errand she allowed them to undertake was to travel halfway across Gloucester after some particular type of cheese that had been ordered from Harrods and collected by a friend whom they eventually tracked down near Chipping Norton.

To make up for the absence of Teddy everyone made a big effort to ensure Alice's birthday was happy from the outset. Lady Turlington organised for her and Harry to have breakfast in bed, which was just as well as both girls had a bad fit of morning sickness, after which they took themselves to the hairdresser. Roody arrived at lunchtime and they told him their plan after they had sworn him to secrecy. Alice was again struck by the happiness he and Harry exuded when they were together. Then they were changing into their evening gowns and it was almost seven o'clock. As Alice and Harry walked across the wide hall towards the drawing room a frazzled Teddy burst in through the front door, his dinner suit over one arm, a small overnight bag in the other.

'Happy birthday, darling,' he said tensely and rushed upstairs, but not before his mother had swooped down on him demanding why he had not driven Alice up from Cambridge and fussing that he was so late.

'This is going to be a great party,' thought Alice dryly, deciding to let him find her when he was ready.

The house quickly filled up with guests. Lady Turlington had organised a band in the marquee and insisted that Alice sit on the right of Lord Turlington at the top table. Harry had got lost with Roody in the crush as everyone congratulated Alice and swamped her with presents. Waiters in white tie and tails plied the guests with drinks and everyone was soon extremely merry. Teddy slipped in just as they were starting the soup, smelling strongly of the aftershave she had given him for his birthday. He smiled crookedly at Alice across the table and she smiled briefly at him before he was engulfed in conversation by an extremely imposing lady on his right dripping with pearls. He had dark shadows under his eyes and one corner of his mouth twitched, a sure sign that he was overtired. Alice sighed. She felt extremely ill at ease.

After dessert was served the band struck up happy birthday and the waiters wheeled in an enormous three-tier birthday cake brilliant with twenty-one candles. Everyone cheered and Alice blew out the candles. As she dug the knife into one of the cakes wishing with all her heart that Teddy would start behaving rationally again, he suddenly leapt up and dashed out of the tent. There was a sudden commotion and then all heads turned as he led in a beautiful roan gelding, its sleek coat glistening in the candlelight. Alice's jaw dropped and the knife clattered to the ground in the silence. It was the horse she had ridden at the Slades' home.

'Ladies and gentlemen, I would like you to toast my wonderful—' He got no further as the horse tossed back his head and drowned him with his whinnying as he backed nervously against a table sending champagne bottles and glasses flying. Lady Turlington, who had by now drunk a considerable amount of champagne, shrieked with laughter.

'Teddles, you're marvellous.'

'Thank you, Mother. Alice my darling, happy birthday.'

Alice didn't know what to do. This was such a dramatic change from the last time they were together. All she could do was stutter. She caught Harry's eye and regained her composure. Walking up to Teddy she linked arms and kissed him to the delight of all the guests who cheered and clapped, their noise exciting the nervous horse even more. Handing Alice the reins Teddy slipped his arm around Alice's waist and gave her a quick squeeze.

'It's yours. I love you, darling Kanga,' he whispered and stepped back allowing Alice centre stage. Alice gave a small yelp and then laughed as the horse nipped her on the shoulder. The guests shouted 'Speech, Speech', and Alice rubbed the horse's nose soothingly waiting until they were quiet. Beckoning to Harry to join her she held her friend's hand tightly as she spoke. Her legs felt like jelly.

'This has been a night full of surprises, and I thank you for your wonderful generosity and kindness. Now I want to share another surprise with you all.' She turned to Teddy and then to Lady Turlington. 'Not only have I got my wonderful husband with me and my best friend and her husband but both Harry and I are expecting babies. I only found out a few days ago. It's the best present of all.' Amid cheers she kissed Teddy determinedly on the lips. Roody was by Harry's side and everyone was clapping and congratulating and Lady Georgina was alternately shrieking with laughter and crying, and Lord Turlington was saying, 'Jolly fine show' to no one in particular.

The excitement of the party evaporated for Alice as she stepped into the bedroom in the early hours of the morning. Wordlessly she clambered out of her evening dress and slipped into her silk nightgown while Teddy got undressed.

'I love the horse,' she said nervously. 'Did you get the application in?' Teddy brushed aside her questions presenting her with a slim red box. Alice opened it with unsteady fingers. Inside lay two gold bracelets one to fit her wrist with a message engraved on the inside and the other a tiny baby's bracelet. Alice picked it up unbelieving.

'I've been such a berk the last few days,' said Teddy his eyes resting tenderly on her tired tense face. 'Will you ever forgive me? I was so strung up about the research application, when you told me you were expecting, I just couldn't cope. Then I convinced myself you'd never ride the horse and that we'd never be able to do anything together again. Everything seemed to be falling apart. But after I'd finally handed the blooming thing in this morning I realised what a mess I was about to make of my life.' His fingers brushed hers as she held up the tiny bracelet sending an unexpected yearning rippling through her body.

'We haven't discussed names yet so I couldn't get it engraved,' he said softly.

Alice's eyes filled with tears of joy and relief. 'Oh Teddy, I thought . . . I didn't know. You're so unpredictable.'

'Shh,' whispered Teddy placing the box on the bed. 'It's part of my charm.' He covered her mouth with his.

'It's safe to make love,' sighed Alice after a long while. 'I checked with Monica.'

'Happy birthday, my beautiful Kanga,' whispered Teddy. All Alice's fears that he would not love their baby vanished as he folded her in his arms.

Chapter Twenty

KATIE LAY AGAINST the pillows listlessly watching the steam rise from the coffee Robert had just brought her, the sounds of a house awakening filtering through the closed door. She still had black days, days when her anger against Alice and now Robert swamped her. She had never forgiven him for crying out Alice's name in the middle of their lovemaking, although when she had returned home from her holiday in Sydney announcing she wanted to have another baby, she had been so buoyed up with hope that she had been willing to forget.

Both of them had believed that somehow everything would be different with a new life to care for and they had been overjoyed when she had finally fallen pregnant. But their happiness was short-lived when ten weeks into the pregnancy she miscarried. It had just been one of those strange tricks of nature, the doctor had explained. A spontaneous abortion he had called it, the foetus so deformed that her body had made the decision for her. But Katie's disappointment and anguish had known no depths. She blamed Robert for the miscarriage, accusing him of expecting her to do too much in her delicate state, completely unaware of his own distress at the loss of their child. Her resentment against Robert grew silently inside her like some great canker.

She reached for the latest *Beautiful Interiors* and flipped through it, briefly admiring the pink marble she had chosen for the bathrooms in their now almost completed luxurious new house, five minutes drive from the main Wangianna family home. Robert could pay for what he had done. In her opinion, after all he had put her through, she deserved only the very best. The magazine slipped from her fingers. Tomorrow would be better. Tomorrow she'd escape the dust and dirt of this place and go to Melbourne to act as hostess for George and then on to view the new property in Western Australia. Ian was coming with them this time too and he was always good company. She would get up after Stewart had finished his classes with nanny. She drifted back into fitful sleep.

Elizabeth McIain walked into the big airy kitchen rubbing her arms against the chill April air to find four-year-old Stewart standing on one of the sturdy old pine chairs dressed only in his pyjama top busily pouring milk over his cornflakes from an enormous pink floral ironstone jug. Robert and the others had long finished their breakfast and gone out to work on the property. The recent smell of recently cooked toast mixed with fried chops and eggs pervaded the room.

'Uncle Jordie says I can go roo shooting with him, Nan, if I eat up all my breakfast,' he announced, his attention diverted from the stream of milk.

'You can do no such thing, young man, and where are your pants?' replied Elizabeth swooping down and rescuing the jug with one hand before milk flooded the scrubbed wood table and lifting him off the chair with the other. 'Nanny, get some clothes on this child before his poor little bottom turns blue,' she called, replacing the milk jug and patting Stewart's tiny cold buttocks.

At forty-nine Elizabeth was still striking. A handsome, strong-boned woman she had thick chestnut brown hair speckled with grey, fierce brown eyes, and a presence that commanded respect and had carried her through the many rigours of dealing with the life in the outback. She also doted on her little scallywag of a grandson, so like his father at that age in all but looks, with the same mischievous gleam in his eye and, when he chose, the same charm that could melt stone. For a split second Elizabeth allowed herself to admit that of her four children, Robby had always been her favourite.

Nanny, a plump young English girl in her early twenties, came hurrying into the room clutching a pair of tiny brown shorts.

'I'm really sorry, Mrs McIain, I was only away for a moment,' she explained apologetically in her broad north country accent, blushing bright red, arms outstretched. 'He was so anxious to say goodbye to his dad before he went out.'

'Of course you were, you darling boy,' smiled Elizabeth kissing Stewart's soft cheek and handing him over to Nanny. 'There you are.' She straightened her blouse.

Stewart made rifle-shot noises pointing his finger around the room as he was wrested from his grandmother. Then he hurried out onto the verandah to join his four little Aboriginal playmates, all relatives of Melon, who were there to learn their numbers and letters with Nanny. Elizabeth liked Nanny. Her name was Jane Wiseman. She was a reliable, down-to-earth lass who had been with Katie and Robert for nearly eighteen months. Elizabeth hoped she would stay longer than the originally planned two years. She was completely unflappable and it was good for Katie to have another woman around her own age to talk to. There was Sophie, who had married Snake, but they were five hours away and ever since Sophie's second child had been born the two had hardly spoken.

Elizabeth had become quite alarmed about Katie. Although physically quite fit she seemed to have lost much of her vitality. Earlier Elizabeth had insisted on talking to the doctor herself who had then prescribed tranquillisers to help Katie get over the miscarriage. Robert had also confided to his mother that they had been advised to wait for a while before trying again for another child given Katie's raw emotional state. The only two subjects that raised a spark in Katie's eyes were the new house and travelling down to Melbourne to play hostess to George, which she had been doing regularly for a while now. It was also the reason why Elizabeth ignored Katie's extravagance with clothes and lavish presents which accompanied each trip away.

In Elizabeth's opinion much of the problem had been exacerbated by Robert's uncharacteristic thoughtlessness towards Katie. He had become obsessively absorbed with his committees after the miscarriage, and on top of that he was running the station. His commitments made so many demands on his time and energy that there was precious little left over for the two of them together. But Elizabeth could not fault him with Stewart. She poured herself a cup of tea, her pencil poised over her list of things to arrange for tomorrow's trip.

Wangianna and the City. In her mind there was no comparison. She loved the vigorous outdoor life and long hours demanded of her in running Wangianna and was happy to let George conclude the sales in town and entertain their more illustrious buyers. Yet each new trip always raised the familiar twinge of anxiety in her. George had never been her ideal man even when she married him, but it had not stopped her from loving him, faults and all, as she still did today. He was weak where she was strong, unable to resist a bet on the horses, irresponsible with money which he openly admitted, but he had the McIain charm which had won him many a sale others would have failed to secure.

After Sarah was born she and George had finally faced the fact that they were incompatible in bed. To Elizabeth, sex was for the procreation of mankind and anything more was self-indulgence. She had made it quite clear that she had no desire to enter into any of the sexual activities George seemed to want. However, she accepted that George's needs were different. There had never been any secrecy between them about George's mistress in Melbourne, in fact Elizabeth in her own way had encouraged the arrangement. She could always tell when it was time for George to visit his mistress and she was not above telling him to go to her, but she never allowed herself or George to utter her name. Somehow in refusing to give the person an identity she was able to bear the failure she felt in this area of her life.

Turning her mind back to the present, she hurriedly finished her breakfast and cleared away knowing there was a mountain of papers to see to on her desk. Today was baking day and Cook was already pounding away at the dough on the other side of the kitchen. Elizabeth hardly seemed to have started her work before it was morning tea time and Stewart came rushing in, his lessons over, clamouring for homemade biscuits and demanding to find his dad. With perfect timing Robert poked his head round the door and helped himself to a mug of tea and a large piece of fruitcake.

'Any sign of Katie?' He frowned as Elizabeth shook her head. From past experience he knew it was a waste of time going up to her.

Nanny burst into the hall looking smart as paint in a dress and jacket.

'I don't mind if I miss my day off, Mr McIain, if Mrs McIain is feeling unwell,' she offered brightly.

Robert's demeanour suddenly changed. Whirling Stewart onto his shoulders he exclaimed, 'You go on into town, Nanny. Me and Stewwy here have got work to do.' He set off with long strides towards the back of the house Stewart's chubby arms wrapped happily around his face.

'Mind the fans,' Elizabeth cried after him in alarm, but the jauntiness in Robert's step cheered her. 'You enjoy your day off, Janie dear,' she smiled deciding to pop along and check on Katie if she didn't appear soon. She disappeared back to her desk in the big airy sitting room to attend to the daily routine of running Wangianna.

Robert's spirits rose as he strode purposefully out into the sunshine. Stewart bounced up and down on his shoulders peering happily out from under his father's big brimmed hat which he had placed on his own head and which hid his curly ash blond hair and most of his face.

'Come on, son, let's go and see which rams Will's brought in for the show.' Robert whistled and Pete came bounding out of the shadows of the nearby building and trotted happily beside them. Stewart squealed with delight and continued making his roo-shooting noises through his teeth and at the same time twisted around on his father's shoulders. 'Hey, not so ferocious up there,' laughed Robert, steadying Stewart. 'You'll scare'em away before you've got'em in your sights!'

Robert breathed in the warm fresh air with its strong agricultural smell. He always felt better when he was out in the open. He felt freer. Here he no longer felt as if every nuance in his behaviour was being watched, that if his thoughts strayed to Alice, as they often did, he would not give himself away. Even the burden of guilt faded for a while. Yet as he strode across the paddocks he could not stop comparing the contrast between Katie lying sullenly in bed and the picture of Alice rejoicing in little Stewart, as he knew she would have if he had been her son. The three would have laughed and frolicked together and she would have thrown herself into the building of Wangianna with him. Time was supposed to heal. As far as he was concerned it was being bloody slow about it. He kept being reminded of his grandfather's words from when he was only a year older than Stewart.

'Remember, son, you make your bed and then you lie in it and you don't whinge.'

He was doing that all right, he thought grimly, but it was this little beggar on his shoulders that made life worth living. He patted Stewart's legs and started to jog towards the truck accompanied by more squeals of delight from Stewart. Slinging the bag Nanny had given him containing a drink and sandwich for Stewart onto the truck floor, Robert slid Stewart off his shoulders, and set him down in the passenger's seat. Ordering Pete to hop up onto the back, he jumped into the driver's seat and drove out to the ram sheds, Pete standing proud in the back, his tail wagging ferociously.

Thirty-four-year-old Will was the new manager of the rams. He was in charge of two hundred and fifty stud rams housed, when they were not grazing in the nearby paddocks, in three large corrugated iron sheds set a ten-minute drive from the house. He and Robert had got on well from the start. Robert was impressed by Will's obvious ability and enthusiasm. Will had quickly become deeply immersed in finding ways to increase ram sales and improve blood stock, with the aim of raising the already high profile of Wangianna stud rams both across Australia and internationally. Already Robert could see the improvement in the animals from those he had sold to Sheik Abdul.

Today Will was busy checking out the fifty or so rams he had brought up to the shed earlier that morning from which they would choose five to enter in the local show. Leaving Pete lying down outside, Stewart, still wearing his dad's hat, ran up the steps to the shed.

'G'day, sport,' grinned Will throwing Stewart a punch two inches from his nose. Grinning back, Stewart dodged and clambered up onto an old chair near one of the empty pens, feeling very grown up.

'How's it going, Will?' greeted Robert noting the generator that supplied the power to pump drinking water for the rams up into the shed from the nearby dam was still out of action. He pushed his way through the thick-coated merino rams with their heavy folds of grey coloured wool, peering at them as he went.

'G'day, boss,' Will replied cheerfully. 'Reckon our new feeding program's given us a head start on the other buggers.'

'My word,' agreed Robert nodding with approval. 'We'll definitely collect a few ribbons from some of this mob,' he said as he inspected the wool carefully, noting any rams with black spots on their faces that could indicate the chance of a throwback in future breeds. There was always the odd one. In fifteen minutes they had selected two top rams and put them into a separate pen. Three more and they were done. Robert straightened his back and scratched his head, surveying the rest of the mob rustling quietly in the tightly-packed pen. It was heating up in the shed. He glanced across to check Stewart who, having got bored watching from the chair, had hopped down and was busy bailing up the selected rams.

'Hey Stewwy, leave the poor buggers alone. Go and eat your sandwich under the big tree outside. Pete could do with some company.' Robert pointed to the tall grey-ghost gum near the bottom of the run-up ramp for the rams. 'And no wandering off near the dam. Melon hasn't finished teaching you to swim. I won't be long, then you and me'll go and bring the ewes down from the top paddock, that's a promise.'

'Okay Dad,' grinned Stewart trying to look grown-up.

Robert chuckled as the small boy sauntered jauntily outside his head tilted slightly back, the big hat just clear of his nose. 'Better watch out, Will. You've got some pretty mean competition in the making.' The two men laughed. Pete, who had been lying waiting patiently outside, his tongue lolling out of one side of his mouth, jumped up wagging his tail furiously and followed Stewart towards the tree. Robert, satisfied that Stewart was in full view, turned back to finish sorting the rams.

Stewart ate his sandwich and finished his drink. Then he had a game with Pete rolling in the dust. But it was hot and Pete soon got bored and went and sat in the shade, panting from his exertion. Dad was taking too long, thought Stewart. Why did grown-ups always have to take such hours? He threw a handful of dirt in the air and glanced up at the shed but all he could see was Will's head. Grown-ups always talked and talked.

'Come on, Pete, let's get you a drink.' Glancing once more at the shed entrance, Stewart slipped quietly down towards the dam edge. Pete lapped gratefully at a nearby puddle. The dam was unusually full from the recent rain. Stewart stood and thought for a while. The dam wall looked tempting. Unable to resist he clambered up the small incline, checked the shed once more and started to walk along the wall.

'What does Dad mean I can't swim? Melon says I'm a good swimmer,' he muttered to himself as he gained confidence. He tried a couple of jumps, twirling around in a circle like he'd seen his Uncle Jordie do. He had another go. This was fun. At the third attempt he overbalanced. Grabbing uselessly at the air he slid down the bank and fell into the water. Recovering from the sudden cold shock he dog-paddled fast ten or twelve times before he reached his foot down to stand up and found he couldn't touch the bottom. He turned to dog-paddle back to the bank but the water's edge seemed suddenly miles away. Panicking he speeded up his strokes and choked as he took in a great mouthful of water. Coughing and gasping for air he took in another mouthful of water. He was vaguely aware of Pete barking frantically at the edge of the pool as he sank below the surface.

'That should do us,' said Robert as he struggled to manoeuvre the fifth ram out of the pen. 'Let's get this lot tarted up for the show.'

'I wouldn't have thought you'd be bothered to expand into cotton with the standard and number of stud rams you've got,' said Will from the other side of the pen.

Robert looked up sharply. 'Who said anything about expanding?' he snapped.

'Ian mentioned something about plans in the next year or two,' continued Will, surprised at Robert's unexpected vehemence.

'Oh he bloody did, did he?' Robert shouted back scowling, still fighting with the ram. 'And did he give you the cost breakdown and the five-year plan as well?' The other rams rustled together at the unexpected loudness of his voice. Will tried to neutralise the situation.

'Hey, steady on, boss. I was just making conversation. If I'd known it would upset you that much I wouldn't have mentioned it.'

'There was more, was there?' yelled Robert, jumping to the wrong conclusion, his anger at his brother getting the better of him. He let go the ram and glared at Will. 'Well let me tell you that as long as I'm in charge of Wangianna we stick to stud rams and breeding sheep for wool.' He stopped, realising he was taking his anger out on the wrong person.

'Look, I'm a bit touchy about the subject at the moment.' His voice was back to normal. 'Ian won't let up about the success of that bloke and his cotton crop over Warren way. The man's done brilliantly I admit, but there's more to it than one lucky crop. It's not that I'm averse to change I just can't see any purpose in it for us now or even in the long-term.' He returned to his task with the ram and stopped suddenly hearing Pete barking.

'What's got into Pete?' He listened again but the dog had gone quiet. Robert glanced across at the tree and went cold. Stewart was gone. His mouth went dry. 'Have you seen Stewwy in the last ten minutes?'

'I wasn't watching I'm afraid,' replied Will looking outside the shed.

Robert's pupils dilated with fear.

'The dam!' the two men cried simultaneously. Robert moved first. Forcing his way through the rams, he slammed the pen gate shut, flew down the ramp and raced towards the dam with Will close behind. It took them less than a minute to reach the water. The first object to catch Robert's eye was his own large grey Akubra hat floating out in the middle of the dam. Terror gripped his whole being and was replaced almost immediately by overwhelming relief as he saw Pete swimming strongly on the other side of the dam. Stewart's yellow curls were bobbing along beside, his fist gripping tightly onto the dog's neck. Robert waded out to meet them, his boots sinking into the thick glue-like mud. Seeing his master, Pete swam faster.

'See Dad, I am a good swimmer. Pete's helping me,' cried Stewart, his eyes filled with pride.

Robert's relief turned to anger. 'You get over here and out of that water immediately,' he shouted unthinking and immediately dropped his voice suddenly scared he'd upset Pete before he could reach his son. Gently he called to the dog. 'Good boy Pete. Come here Pete.' Once within reach he grabbed Stewart by the scruff of his neck and lifted him to dry land. 'If I ever catch you doing anything like that again, that's it, mate, you're in deep trouble.'

'But I was all right with Pete,' pleaded Stewart, patting the dog, his little face crestfallen. 'I coughed a bit and drank a bit of water but then we swam together.'

Pete wagged his tail, licking them both and shaking water all over them, making it difficult for Robert to continue reprimanding Stewart.

'You could have drowned,' said Robert fiercely, the terror of what might have been flooding back.

'Pete's a great swimmer, Dad.' Robert could never stay angry with Stewart for long and he was obviously none the worse for his swim.

'Pete's a great dog, Stewwy, but I don't want you swimming on your own like that until you're much older. It's too dangerous. Promise me you won't do it again,' he insisted, his own fright still very real. Contrite Stewart nodded. Pulling the sodden boy to him Robert hugged him close. 'Now, what about these ewes I told you we had to bring down.' He turned to Will. 'Could you see if there's an old shirt or something in the truck I can dry Stewwy off with first?'

'Sure, boss. You listen to your dad, young fella.' He, too, was shaken.

Once Stewart had been dried off and dressed in Robert's tattered oil rag of a shirt, and Will had been dropped back at the ram sheds, father and son headed out across the bumpy track along the edge of the paddock.

'I'm hungry,' complained Stewart.

'Not half as hungry as these ewes. They've been living off fresh-air sandwiches for the last two months,' said Robert chuckling to himself at Stewart's elfin appearance, his fears receding. He leaned across and ruffled Stewart's rapidly drying blond curls. The ewes were dries that hadn't produced a lamb this season and they had been separated into one of the top paddocks while the lamb-bearing ewes were given extra feed. He hated destroying his own sheep, preferring to sell them even though the sale hardly brought in enough money to cover the cost of fuel to get them to the sale yard. As the truck bumped its way along Robert's thoughts kaleidoscoped around. Will's comments about the cotton, the likelihood of more ribbons from the show and the job ahead all jostled for space in his thoughts. But most devastating of all was the realisation that in those few seconds when Robert had seen the hat and believed that Stewart had drowned his whole world had started to fall apart. Without Stewart Wangianna was meaningless. He hadn't realised just how much hope he had pinned on his son. He stopped the truck.

'D'you want to help me drive, Stewwy?'

Eyes shining, Stewart nodded excitedly. He slid into his father's lap and proudly placed his little hands on the steering wheel next to his father's big sun-blackened knuckles.

'How about we get Cook to find Pete a big juicy bone when we get this job out of the way?' said Robert smoothly.

Stewart nodded ferociously again, grinning broadly as he stared ahead through the fly-spattered windscreen. Dad had forgiven him.

'How could you do it? How could you just let him run off into the dam like that?' screamed Katie. Stewart, still wearing his father's smelly, oil-stained old shirt, stared wide-eyed with fear as his mother railed at his father. All he had said was Pete had helped him swim. Katie had dragged the rest of the story out of Robert as he walked into the kitchen shortly after Stewart.

Robert's expression hardened.

'Not in front of the boy,' he said quietly.

'Don't you tell me when and where I can and can't speak. You're a useless husband and hopeless father. Where's that stupid girl who's supposed to be his nanny?' demanded Katie hysterically, clutching Stewart to her.

'It's her day off,' responded Robert with icy calm.

Katie glared at Robert. 'Won't anyone take any responsibility for him around here,' she shrilled. 'Now he'll have to come with me tomorrow.'

Elizabeth, hearing the commotion, hurried into the kitchen. Katie immediately sat down sobbing into Stewart's curls. Robert quickly told his mother what had occurred.

Stewart looked up sheepishly. 'I wasn't scared with Pete, really, Nan.'

Elizabeth rested her eyes lovingly on the little boy. 'I'm sure you weren't luv. Robert, go and find your son some reasonable clothes instead of that old rag, while I deal with Katie.' Elizabeth gently removed Stewart from his mother's clutches.

Having no time for histrionics Elizabeth got straight to the point. 'We all know how much you suffered losing the other baby and how precious Stewart is to you but you really cannot carry on like this. Calm down and take a hold of yourself. You know very well Robert is a good father and Stewart is perfectly safe here.' She didn't like to admit that she too had been shaken by the incident. 'What you need is something to do. Now go and wash your face and then help Cook with the baking. Tomorrow you can go and play hostess for your father-in-law in Melbourne.'

Her face softened for an instant. 'Didn't you tell me you'd found the tap fittings and door knobs you wanted?'

Katie nodded. Sniffing she wiped her eyes controlling her rage. The one person she could not afford to get on the wrong side of was Elizabeth. Elizabeth owned Wangianna. And Wangianna was the one prize Katie wouldn't lose.

*

Katie was up at the crack of dawn to prepare herself for the trip to Melbourne. Robert brought her tea and toast as always, amazed at her transformation. Yesterday she had been a sobbing vixen; today she was a dazzling beauty in a stunning pink designer dress, ready to take on Melbourne elite as she pulled on her cream kid gloves. Pretty stud earrings sparkled in her ears. Her yellow catlike eyes glittered with excitement; the dress clung to her svelte figure emphasising her long tanned legs and her slender ankles and dainty feet. Finally ready she wafted into the hall on a cloud of Madame Rochas where Elizabeth, George and Ian were waiting. Robert followed behind with her suitcase. Ian, looking decadent in his best suit and shirt, his dark hair slicked back, top button undone, tie hanging loose around his neck, wolf-whistled as she appeared.

Elizabeth glanced at her watch worrying that they would all be late getting away and wanting to forget that George, who looked quite the man about town and far too handsome for someone of his age, was going to see his mistress. Presenting her cheek to Robert and Stewart for the obligatory kiss, Katie followed George and Ian outside.

'Have a nice time dear, I hope you get all the fixtures that you want,' said Elizabeth kindly as Ian helped Katie climb into the Landrover.

Robert heaved a sigh of relief as he watched the car disappear down the long dirt road. Katie was stunningly beautiful. How could any man resist her? Yet the overpowering emotion he felt was guilt. He knew he was being irresponsible allowing her to indulge her extravagant taste yet it was the only way he could assuage his bitter inability to love the mother of his child. The house was going to end up more like a palace than a second home. His heart gave a lurch at the thought. A palace for the wrong woman. He shoved his fists further into his pockets shutting out memories that refused to leave him alone.

As soon as Katie was seated on the plane to Melbourne she started to cheer up. Her trips to 'civilisation' were her lifeline. For a short while she could escape from the dust and heat into the world she had always dreamed of: elegant coffee mornings, luncheons, dinner parties, theatre, cinema, dancing, all dust-free, not to mention those wonderful deep foaming bubble baths where she could soak away every speck of dust and grime and afterwards drench herself in perfume without Robert once reminding her not to be so wasteful with water. Last night after she had recovered from her outburst, she had made a special show of being apologetic, terrified that Elizabeth might stop her from continuing the role of hostess at the McIains' house in the elegant Melbourne suburb of Toorak. On this trip, too, there was the added excitement of conquering the social set of Perth.

Sipping on a glass of champagne she glanced sidelong at Ian who grinned at her and shifted his body in his seat so their shoulders touched. Katie blushed. Ian always had that effect on her. Casually she reached for the in-flight instruction sheet and leaned back away from him slightly, pretending to read intently. It would be too easy to encourage him, yet part of her longed desperately to do so. Ian shifted again, the pressure of his shoulder burning through her thin cotton sleeve.

'I think you're completely wasted on him,' he remarked in a low voice.

'On who?' giggled Katie fluttering her long silky eyelashes.

He leaned across her and withdrew the in-flight magazine from her seat pocket.

'You know very well,' he murmured, flicking the pages like a pack of cards under her nose. 'Pick a restaurant in Melbourne,' he said grandiosely. 'Never let me be accused of allowing my sister-in-law to be neglected while we're away.'

Katie's blush deepened and she giggled again. A pulse started throbbing between her legs. He was such a contrast to Robert. With Ian she wasn't torn apart by the knowledge that he didn't really love her. He was so boldly flirtatious. If she had met him first she could easily have fallen madly in love with him. His flattery and attention washed over her like a healing balm. No matter what Robert said she knew deep down that Alice still held his affections. Her jaw tightened at the thought. She might never win his love but she would never lose Wangianna, of that she was utterly determined.

'Penny for them,' Ian broke into her thoughts. 'They must be deep and dark and exciting to make you look like that.'

Katie laughed and shook her head.

'I always get a bit wound up when I fly.'

Ian signalled for the air hostess to refill their glasses. Katie acquiesced—she might as well enjoy herself while she was with Ian. George sat slumped in his seat across the aisle, his mouth half open gently snoring, dreaming that he was already in Maggie's arms.

'Dad's got it all worked out,' said Ian downing his champagne. Katie agreed and followed suit.

Three days later as she sat dressed in a stunning low-cut red satin evening gown, new diamond earrings dangling from her earlobes, an elegant diamond bracelet clasped around her slim wrist, she knew Ian was not the only one who had worked things out. She smiled graciously at the guests seated around the highly-polished table, revelling in her position as hostess to Melbourne's top social set. Every time she played this role it cemented her in the minds of those who mattered as the next mistress of Wangianna. The next few weeks were going to be wonderful. She would play her part to the hilt. She turned her blinding smile on the Arabic gentleman next to her who had just clinched a six-figure deal with George that afternoon. From the other side of the room Ian, placed next to an extremely dull and garrulous, overperfumed woman in her late fifties, longed to plunge his face into Katie's soft inviting cleavage.

'I've had to watch every other bloke in the room bask in your loveliness. Now it's my turn,' murmured Ian as Katie turned from ushering the last guest out of the house shortly before midnight. Katie whirled around as she felt his hand rest lightly on her hips. Ian was standing very close, his bow tie slightly crooked, one lock of hair falling over heavy-lidded blue eyes that stared provocatively into hers.

'Oh, Ian, you're such a flirt,' she giggled, her eyes glittering from the wine and euphoria of her success in playing hostess. Ian had never seen her look more seductively alive. She straightened his tie trying to look casual. They broke away as George walked up the hall stuffing a couple of cigars into his lapel pocket.

'I'm going out for a while. Don't you two young things wait up for me,' he announced. He kissed Katie on the cheek. 'You make a charming hostess, my dear. Robert is a very fortunate young man. Ian, make sure you take care of her. I'll see you both at breakfast.' Checking his pockets for the house keys he headed down the hall and into the waiting taxi.

'More like lunch judging from past experiences. Now where was I?' murmured Ian his hand grazing her cheek.

'Basking in my loveliness,' smiled Katie moving towards him with feline grace, her lips parted ever so slightly.

'That's right.' Without warning Ian pressed his lips hard against Katie's red mouth. Katie's eyes opened wide but she did not retreat. After a long while he released her.

'I've been longing to do that since the day I met you,' he said breathlessly. His eyes feasted hotly on Katie's flushed face.

Katie laughed shakily. She knew they had both drunk too much red wine but she didn't care. Ian's kiss had filled her with a sense of power and elation she had not felt since the day she told Robert she was pregnant. 'I'm cold,' she said moving toward the open fire.

Ian quickly poked at the embers and put on two more logs. Leaning against the mantelpiece he watched the flames lick around them and catch alight, his mind in turmoil. Katie kicked off her high heels and wriggled her toes in the thick lambswool rug. Putting her hand up she gently stroked his cheek. 'If you only know how good your kiss felt,' she whispered and burst into tears.

'Hey, what's all this?' asked Ian in surprise, immediately pulling her to him stroking her hair, his head spinning from the sensations her nearness aroused in him.

'Oh, Ian, I'm so lonely. Robert doesn't love me. He's never loved me. I thought he might after Stewwy was born but I was wrong. It was always Alice, Alice, Alice. We don't even make love any more. Oh Ian, I feel so, so . . . dead inside.' She buried her head in his shoulder, her whole body shuddering with uncontrollable sobs.

'The bastard,' gasped Ian, tightening Katie in his embrace. 'I knew things hadn't been perfect between the two of you for a while but how could he be such a ratbag to you.' He held her close, alternately kissing and stroking her hair. Gradually her sobs subsided. Lifting her head she wiped at the wet patch on his jacket. Her mascara had smudged into dark patches under her eyes and run in little rivulets down her cheeks.

'I'm sorry, I've messed up your jacket but I just couldn't hold it in any longer,' she said with a shudder, wiping at her cheeks with her fingers. 'I must look a fright.'

'You look as bewitching as ever,' said Ian, gently smoothing away the mascara on her damp cheeks with his handkerchief. Katie shuddered again. 'Don't take on so, Katie. He may be my brother but the bastard's not worth it. Why don't you leave him?'

'I couldn't do it to Stewwy,' she spluttered. Tilting her chin with his thumb, Ian kissed away the tears that slid once more down her cheeks. His lips grazed her full red mouth as he cupped her face in his hands.

'Love me just a little,' Katie whispered.

She felt Ian's body quiver against her own as their lips met once more in a deep lingering kiss. When finally he pulled away Katie kept her face upturned to his. 'Hold me, just hold me. That's all,' she breathed. A log crackled in the silence.

Ian held her at arm's length letting his eyes travel down the tantalising curves of her body encased in the slinky red satin. Never before had he felt so totally aroused nor so completely consumed with guilt. He dragged his gaze back to her face. Her eyes were brimming with sadness. What was he thinking of—she was married to his brother. But maybe there was no harm in just holding her. She was crying out for love and the idiot hardly knew she existed. Flicking a switch he killed all but the light from the fire. Then, heart pounding, he folded her in his arms. Katie had felt his hesitation. Revenge pulsed deliriously through her veins as she revelled in the sensation of her body next to his while the flickering flames threw shadows against the wall. She would lead him to the brink, make him want her so badly that finally he would plead with her to give in . . .

Chapter Twenty-one

DRESSED IN AN OLD PAIR of black and white dogtooth wool trousers and a red polo-neck jumper, Alice sat on the sofa in the pretty sitting room of Mill House, softly crooning 'Click go the Shears'. Dark shadows underlined eyes in a face creased with concern. Vicky lay in her arms, her long blonde lashes curling cherublike against pudgy cheeks still flushed with fever, her small chest rising and falling gently for the first time in hours. Seeing that her three-year-old daughter had finally fallen asleep, Alice cautiously allowed herself to sink back into the thick chintz cushions. A bottle of cough medicine and a spoon sat on the antique mahogany table at her elbow beside a mug of cold coffee. She pulled the flannelette nightgown away from Vicky's chin and tucked the blanket closer around them both. Vicky's eyelids fluttered and she gave a small sigh. Alice shivered slightly. In a moment she would draw the curtains and throw another log on the dying embers behind the brass fireguard across the wide open fireplace. For now she did not dare move.

She let her head fall back against the sofa, gazing a moment at the low white ceiling and black wooden beams before she closed her eyes. It was the end of a bitterly cold day which had begun with Vicky waking in the early hours with another bout of violent coughing racking her little body. Monica had promised Alice there was no cause to be overconcerned, that the medicine would clear up the infection and nature would do the rest. Vicky, she assured her, was a healthy little girl but it tore at Alice to watch her daughter so exhausted from all the coughing. This was the third infection in a row. At least this time they had been spared the terrible barking croup.

'Poor little Roo,' she whispered lovingly. Vicky had become 'Roo' from the moment of her birth as a natural follow on to Alice's nickname and her love of AA Milne's classic *The House at Pooh Corner.* Alice's own resistance was low through consistent broken sleep over the last two months and she was starting a sore throat. Added to that the Danish au pair girl had left that morning with no warning. Alice grimaced. She was the third in a row too. Everything seemed to be happening in threes. Yet Teddy insisted they have a nanny, for all the good they had done. Maybe she was just bad at choosing or she wasn't understanding enough. The truth was she had never wanted a nanny and had only tolerated them because of Teddy's insistence. Aunty Bea had alway managed and she had raised six children. Suddenly Alice felt bitterly homesick. Tears pricked the back of her closed eyes and one trickled down the corner of her cheek. She brushed it away quickly, careful not to disturb Vicky.

The grandfather clock in the hallway chimed six o'clock. Wearily Alice thought of the evening meal. For once she would have relished some home help. Carefully she bundled Vicky in her arms and carried her to her bedroom. Once tucked into her bed, Alice checked the fireguard was securely around the wall heater should Vicky wake. Teddy and she had had so much fun doing up the tiny room. Bright floral curtains covered the tiny window and on the opposite wall a large mural was painted depicting puffy white clouds against a blue sky with animals, birds and butterflies in a country setting. Alice had insisted on Australian animals so a large kangaroo standing on her hind legs had been included amongst the rabbits, fawns and mice. The head and gangly legs of a joey poked realistically out of her pouch. A koala bear stared down with the squirrels from an oak tree. Vicky adored the mural. Alice gazed briefly at it now her mind numb with tiredness. Vicky hadn't stirred. She dropped a kiss on the top of her daughter's golden curls and slipped from the room.

'Darling, I'm home,' called Teddy from the bottom of the stairs, hanging up his overcoat and scarf.

'Shh! I've just got Roo back to sleep,' said Alice creeping downstairs, shivering once out of the warmth of Vicky's room.

'Oh,' said Teddy immediately dropping his voice. He gave Alice a big hug and grabbed her hand. 'I've got some terrific news.' He led her straight to the drinks cabinet. 'How is Roo?' He poured himself a large gin and tonic.

'Better, I think, but pretty exhausted,' replied Alice, stifling a yawn and shivering again. She put out her hand as he reached for the sherry decanter. 'I think I'll make myself a cup of tea. I was on my way to getting supper.'

'You have to hear this first, my darling,' insisted Teddy, completely oblivious of Alice's exhaustion. Making an effort to revive herself Alice waited as he pulled out a letter from his pocket.

'From the Head of the History Faculty, Cambridge University,' proclaimed Teddy proudly. 'This is to inform you that after due consideration . . . blah blah blah, that your application for a grant to study and produce definitive research on the ancient silk road has been accepted and that you have been awarded a three months leave of absence in which to carry out said research to be taken . . . blah blah blah. Signed Dr Alec Baldwin.' Teddy waved the signature at her excitedly, his eyes shining. 'Isn't it wonderful, Kanga. By the middle of May I'll be in Turkey. How about that, my darling? God! I'm starving.'

'May!' squealed Alice. 'That's only two months away! How am I going to get us all organised.' Teddy looked at her strangely.

'Organised? What d'you mean? You and Vicky aren't coming. Aren't you pleased for me?' he added as Alice's excitement faded.

'It's wonderful,' she said dully and sat down heavily on the sofa.

'Now what have I said, Kanga?' asked Teddy crossly.

'You promised if this study leave did happen that we'd all go. Vicky and I'd have a holiday in Turkey while you went off along the silk road,' replied Alice trying to keep a hold on her emotions.

'Come on, Alice, be reasonable. You know it would be totally impractical.'

'That's not what we agreed before,' Alice snapped. 'It's not as if we can't afford it. Oh, sometimes you're totally impossible. If you never meant for us to come why did you suggest it in the first place?'

'Well I had hoped you'd be glad for me,' said Teddy pitifully.

'I am,' said Alice suddenly guilty. 'Of course I am. I'm thrilled. It's just that I've had a horrible day. I've been worried sick about Roo, Britta left this morning, there's nothing except leftovers in the fridge and now this.' She burst into tears. Why did all the men in her life have to keep letting her down? Teddy wrapped her in his arms and stroked her black gorse-bush mane. 'All I need is a good night's sleep,' she admitted, rubbing her eyes wearily.

'I've got some more good news,' Teddy chattered happily. 'The head of the history faculty at Oxford and his wife have been invited to stay at the master's lodge at the end of March and we've been asked to entertain them on the Saturday night.' Alice sat back into the sofa, lights from the flame of the reviving fire flickering in her tired eyes.

'That's a bit of an unexpected honour, darling. Perhaps I will have that drink,' she said making a monumental effort to sound cheerful. 'Who should we ask with them?' The man's research was recognised worldwide and he could really help Teddy. The couple also had a reputation for being extremely entertaining. Alice drank down her sherry too quickly. She reread Teddy's letter, then stood up and kissed Teddy on the nose. 'I think you're very clever. Let's go and salvage some of that cold beef.' She was starting to feel light-headed.

Three days before the dinner party Teddy roared into the house slamming the door so hard all the windows rattled.

'That bloody little creep,' he yelled, banging his briefcase down on the hall table. He stormed into the sitting room and poured himself a double gin. He had a sudden urge to ring Catalina for comfort but he knew it would be pointless—she had informed him six months ago he had been replaced as he had ignored her for too long after Vicky was born. Alarmed at the commotion Alice staggered into the house from the garden with an armful of logs, her cheeks flushed from the cold.

'I thought you were ill,' she cried wondering if she'd ever get used to Teddy's mood swings.

'Ill, that's about it. Redbrick upstart. They should never have let the little squirt near the place,' ranted Teddy.

Alice put the logs in the big copper bin beside the open fire and dusted off her jumper. 'What's he done this time?' she asked with manufactured calm knowing it was the only way to approach Teddy in one of these rages. Secretly she thought Teddy and his friends were a bit over the top about Clive's background. He was always very well mannered to her even though he did have a bit of a north country accent, but Teddy had never forgiven him for being promoted ahead of him.

'Bunty told me this morning the little weasel is threatening to put forward a case of plagiarism against me to the board. Plagiarism, absolutely absurd. Of course no one will listen.'

'The words in your last paper were awfully similar, darling, and so were the ideas. I said so at the time. Isn't that stealing?' ventured Alice.

'Don't you start,' shouted Teddy. 'I only borrowed a couple of paragraphs and you can't steal ideas. It won't make any difference to him.' He took a slug of gin. Rounding on Alice he jabbed his finger at her. 'Anyway, you swore to me it was all right.'

Alice bristled. 'I did no such thing, and don't bellow at me. I said I thought I had read somewhere there was a percentage of other people's stuff you could use with permission—but I couldn't remember how much.'

Teddy tossed back the remains of his drink and poured another. 'You're still cross with me about Turkey. Anyway, with his background the only one he'll harm is himself.'

Alice could see Teddy was revving himself up for another rage. Mercifully the phone rang. 'I'll get it!' flung Teddy. 'Probably some idiot telling me I've organised my tutorials all wrong.' He stormed out into the hall.

Alice heard his tone immediately change back to courteousness. She pulled forward the fireguard, put a large log on the fire and watched it blaze. Two minutes later he was back, rage suffusing his face. 'Bloody hell! Doesn't anything go right in this stinking hole?' He stomped across to the fireplace and kicked angrily at the fireguard.

'Please, Teddy. Vicky'll hear you,' said Alice pointing a finger towards the ceiling. Ignoring her Teddy continued to rant.

'Why am I cursed with cretinous little secretaries? The brainless halfwit mixed up the weekends. Forget intellect and wit, now instead of the head of history we've got to entertain that crashing bore from Corpus Christi with the wife who drones on about cactuses. The only reason he's been invited is because he received a knighthood in the New Year's honours list. I can't believe it.' He dug the heels of his palms against his eyes in utter frustration. 'But if we pull out now it'll only go against me and I can't afford to risk that, not after this week's little debacle.'

Suddenly Vicky rushed in tramping mud across the thick pile carpet, her pink Wellington boots on the wrong feet, her bright yellow raincoat inside out over mud-spattered pyjamas. Clear blue eyes sparkled above ruddy cheeks, her blonde hair a straggly tangled mess.

'Daddy! Daddy! I caught a frog,' she sang excitedly, waving a jam jar full of weeds and dirty water.

'Vicky! I told you to stay inside. Look at you. I thought you were upstairs. You've just had your bath,' admonished Alice.

'Show Daddy, darling.' Teddy melted at the sight of his bedraggled daughter, now fully recovered from her chest infection. Bending down he whirled Vicky up over his head her fingers still tightly clasping the jar. By a miracle most of the contents stayed inside. 'Let's ask Monica and Adrian to dinner as well,' he suggested cheerfully as if his rage and bad temper had never existed. 'You and Monica get on well and Adrian's always good for a few laughs.' Alice agreed hoping Teddy's happier mood could be sustained until after the dinner party.

Early on the Saturday morning Alice sent Teddy up to Sainsbury's, a quality grocery store in the middle of Cambridge, to buy some of their special cheeses while she prepared the food. Mrs Peters, her daily whom everyone called Mrs P, had done a marvellous job of making their little house shine but Alice still got nervous before such functions. Teddy put such incredible importance on every detail being right.

At ten past six Teddy strode back into the house and announced, 'Two more for dinner.'

'What!' exclaimed Alice up to her elbows in whipped cream. 'I can't possibly. Where's the cheese?'

'Oops. Sorry, darling, I forgot it. I ran into Judd Gimbelstein and his wife in town. They're down here visiting friends—I couldn't not ask them.'

'Oh Teddy, you're so hopeless,' Alice sighed exasperated, wondering how to make the food stretch to two extra. But she was actually curious to meet the Gimbelsteins. Judd was an assistant professor from Harvard on a three-year exchange at All Souls College Oxford. Teddy had been working with him on the silk road project and they planned to make a documentary together.

An hour later, just as the guests arrived, the skies opened, dumping the entire heavens on Cambridgeshire and showing no signs of abating. Scuttling into the house the guests shed raincoats, boots and umbrellas as the introductions were done. Judd Gimbelstein with his soft drawl and dry wit entranced Alice. Holly, his wife, in total contrast was a fast-talking energetic woman in her mid-thirties, with long red painted nails and masses of gold bracelets and chains. She immediately swept up Vicky, who was allowed to greet the guests, in a big hug and insisted on being allowed to read her a story before Alice settled her into bed.

'I adore children. We haven't had any but we're still trying,' she enthused in her clipped Boston accent as they joined the others in the dining room where, to Alice's annoyance, she found Teddy had entirely rearranged her seating plan. Judd and Monica were now directed either side of him at one end of the table, Holly and Adrian in the middle, leaving Sir Godfrey and Lady Evesham next to Alice. As the meal progressed, Alice, utterly embarrassed at having discovered neither of the Eveshams could eat much of the food that she had so carefully prepared, battled valiantly with the couple's conversation which kept leading back to long dissertations on their ailments. Alice shot envious glances at the other end of the table where everyone was enjoying themselves hugely. As Alice struggled with Sir Godfrey's gallstones and the propagation of *Aporocactus flagelliformis,* the bleak March wind howled around the house and the rain kept pelting down. Gratefully she escaped into the kitchen to organise the main course, whisking dishes on and off the dinner table, too busy to notice the black edge of water seeping under the backdoor.

Teddy struggled with a window that threatened to be torn off its hinges. 'Bit of a storm out there,' he said smoothly, returning to his seat and once more talking shop with Judd as they tucked into beef cooked with brown ale—a dish Monica had introduced Alice to—accompanied by creamed potatoes and boiled carrots.

Lady Evesham wriggled her feet in her too tight high heels, pushed most of her meal to one side of the plate and launched into another tirade about potting and mixing, having dropped a large dollop of creamed potato on her ample bosom.

'Not good weather for the old rat-tailed cactus,' said Adrian attempting a joke. He had especially read up on cacti for the evening after Alice had rung up pleading for help.

'We had the most dreadful cyclone a few years back,' started Holly from the other end of the table.

Lady Evesham smiled benignly at her, took a sip of red wine and finally giving in to her urge, kicked off her shoes. She gave a small whimper as her stockinged feet contacted water. She sloshed her feet tentatively around.

'My God! We're afloat!' she shrieked, stopping all conversation, plunging her head under the table, almost overbalancing Adrian. Everyone stared at the floor. Alice looked at Teddy aghast.

'The sluicegates!' they cried in unison, leaping to their feet. Teddy dived out of the room while Alice rushed for mops and buckets. Monica stuffed the towel from the downstairs loo fruitlessly along the bottom of the backdoor while Holly and Judd looked at one another in amazement. The entire back garden was awash and in no time the dining room was under two inches of water. Lady Evesham, a dramatically changed person, hitched up her long evening gown and grabbed a mop. Slopping and pushing the water away she chided Sir Godfrey who tentatively rolled up his dinner suit trousers and looked around helplessly. In stockinged feet Holly and Alice splashed back and forth hurriedly clearing the dining table while Judd and Adrian up-ended the dining chairs on its polished surface.

Twenty minutes later a drenched Teddy returned to a vision of white hairy toes, knobbly knees, brooms and buckets, but at least now the water was rapidly receding. The dripping Persian carpet leaned rolled up against one wall. Ornaments lay piled in heaps on the chintz chairs that had been carried out into the hall along with other easily moved pieces of antique furniture. Luckily the downstairs floor was on several levels so the hall was four inches higher than either the kitchen or the main room.

'Well you can't go without dessert and coffee,' laughed Alice with a catch in her voice, her eyes pleading for guidance from Teddy after they had managed to mop up most of the water. The room was rimmed with mud. 'The carpet's ruined anyway so we might as well dry out near the fire.'

'Good idea,' agreed Teddy avoiding Alice's eye. He squelched across the thick pile carpet and put another log on the fire. Lady Evesham, in her element, joined him, her dress still hitched up, cackling on about how it all would have been so much worse in India. Obediently the rest of the party squashed together on the sofa whose legs were stood on towels, balancing plates of *crème brûleé* on their knees around the open fire that sizzled and plopped as occasional splashes from damp hems and rolled up trouser legs reached the glowing logs. Holly examined her ruined Paris evening shoes.

'I thought you'd sacked that damned drunk,' hissed Teddy carrying in the coffee past Alice who was busy squeezing out a sodden towel into an aluminium bucket near the door. He had nipped upstairs to dry himself and was now dressed in a casual open-necked shirt and crumpled twills.

'I did, that's the problem,' hissed Alice utterly miserable, her ears alert for any cries from Vicky. Normally Teddy's domain, she had meant to remind him of the need to hire a new man to mow the fields and attend to the weir and sluicegates but it had gone clean out of her mind with Vicky's first bout of illness. Teddy returned to their guests.

'I say, terribly sorry about all this. Who would like coffee and cream?'

'I'll pour,' offered Monica taking the tray and placing it on the sodden carpet. The wind had abated slightly but the rain was keeping up a steady drone against the windowpanes.

'Look, why don't I drive Sir Godfrey and Lady Evesham home and then we can come back and give you a hand to mop up?' suggested Judd quietly in Teddy's ear.

'Wouldn't hear of it, old chap. You've done your share of mopping up. This is frightfully embarrassing,' replied Teddy. 'I'm really sorry. Blasted locals. Can't trust any of them. Take you up on the lift though.' He nodded gratefully, pushing back a lock of smooth blond hair.

'Great party. Love sloshing around in other people's houses. Really gets the old whatnot going,' beamed Lady Evesham patting the rough location of her heart as she squeezed into the Gimbelsteins' car beside Sir Godfrey. Adrian and Monica left shortly afterwards, Alice having insisted they too had done their share.

'For once in my life I wish your mother and her horde of helpers were here,' sighed Alice, tiredly dumping sodden towels into a bucket and picking it up as Teddy returned from seeing Monica and Adrian off. 'But at least we've saved most of our stuff.'

'How could you be so incompetent?' exploded Teddy. 'How could you shame me in front of the Gimbelsteins like that?'

'What the hell do you mean, me incompetent? You knew about the weir and the gates too, you know,' spat back Alice in disbelief.

'Don't be ridiculous. You're in charge of running this house and you can't even do that.' Too furious to speak Alice stomped out of the room. Her shriek was followed by a loud clatter as, forgetting the small step up, she tripped and fell spreadeagled across the floor sending the bucket flying against the far cupboard. Teddy followed her.

'Did you trip?' The obviousness of the comment was too much for Alice.

'No, I bloody flew,' she yelled clutching her shin, her face screwed up in pain. The combination of worry about Roo, Teddy's moods, homesickness and exhaustion proved too much. She burst into tears. Teddy tried to gather her in his arms but she pushed him away.

'I'm sorry I snapped at you, Kanga darling. I just felt so embarrassed. Don't push me away,' pleaded Teddy. 'It was as much your fault as mine.'

'I want to go home,' she announced baldly, tears streaming down her face. Teddy's heart missed a beat. He stepped back and cleared his throat.

'What? For good?' he asked after a long pause.

Startled, Alice dried her tears and stopped holding her shin. 'No, silly, for a holiday. Aunty Bea and Uncle Ray have never seen Vicky except in photos, and it's not the same, neither is the phone, although you never complain about the phone bill.' The words came tumbling out. 'Oh Teddy, I got so frightened when Vicky was sick. I was terrified we might lose her. It brought back memories of . . .' She took in a great gulp of air. 'I haven't been ready to go back home until now, but I am now. Couldn't we go this summer?' Alice turned her face appealingly towards Teddy. Confronted like this Teddy squirmed. She looked so utterly desirable but the truth was he had no wish whatsoever to visit Australia.

'Great timing,' he said, but then softened immediately. 'Look, we'll talk about it in the morning when we face this mess again. Right now I'm taking you to bed.'

'I will never know what to expect,' thought Alice as Teddy swept her up in his arms and carried her upstairs. The rain was still pelting down as they tumbled into bed. Mercifully Vicky had slept through the lot.

Alice brought up the subject of a holiday in Australia again the next day. Falling out of bed far earlier than she wanted at the sound of Vicky padding about in her room, Alice pulled on an old pair of jeans and a polonecked sweater she didn't mind getting ruined, dressed Vicky and went downstairs to face the mess. Looking bright as a button in an overlong turquoise jumper with a bright yellow and red rosella on the front—a present from Aunty Bea—red wool tights, and her pink Wellington boots,

Vicky tucked into a large bowl of rice bubbles while Alice munched on a piece of toast and lime marmalade as she cooked Teddy his favourite fry-up. The house smelt of damp wood, mud and wet carpet, cigars and freshly cooked toast. Bacon and eggs sizzled welcomingly in the pan on the Aga.

'Why don't we go to Australia this Christmas, darling?' Alice asked as Teddy ate his breakfast. 'I'm sure your mother would understand, and it would give us plenty of time to get organised after you've got back from Turkey.'

'Out of the question,' replied Teddy. 'Wouldn't be allowed the time off so soon.'

'But it'd be out of term, darling, and you could always come back before us,' suggested Alice wiping Vicky's face and hands and retying the big pink bow in her hair.

'Can I go out and play, now?' asked Vicky.

'Yes, darling, as long as you promise to keep these on,' said Alice pulling a colourful beanie over her hair and pair of tiny gloves over her hands. Vicky marched outside squelching her way happily through the puddles. The garden was still soggy but the paths were draining dry. A watery sun was struggling through the clouds. Teddy pulled a face in disgust.

'It's pretty awful isn't it,' agreed Alice.

'I don't want to think about it,' Teddy groaned, pushing away his empty plate and sneezing violently. 'And I don't want to talk about Australia now, not in all this.'

'You never do.'

'That's not true.'

'It could be such fun, a real Aussie Christmas,' said Alice later as they grappled with the waterlogged fitted carpet.

'What about Vicky?' Teddy was beginning to feel cornered.

'What about Vicky? She's a darned sight more likely to stay healthy in the Australian sunshine than in an English winter.' Alice stretched her aching back. 'You don't really want to go to Australia, do you?' She looked across at him through her long dark lashes, a lump in her throat.

She could hear Vicky singing in the back garden.

'Don't be silly, Kanga, of course I do,' he lied. 'If you're going to accuse me like that we'll go at Christmas.' The conversation ended abruptly as Monica and Adrian walked in the open front door dressed in old clothes.

'Hello, folks, fancy a spot of lunch out somewhere after we've helped you clean up?' asked Adrian brightly.

'What time did you finally get to bed?' asked Monica helping herself to a cup of percolated coffee and wrinkling her nose at the smell.

'About two o'clock,' replied Alice cheerfully wiping her forehead. 'Sounds like a great idea, don't you think, darling? If we keep at it, we'll have got rid of most of the mess in a couple of hours.'

'Anything to get away from the smell,' responded Teddy getting up as a small bundle of energy hurled itself at Alice screaming, 'Aunty Kanga'.

'Phoebe! Harry!' cried Alice in delight. She clasped her squirming goddaughter in her arms and kissed her roundly. Harry, carrying her three-month-old son, and Roody, armed with the carry basket, stepped carefully through the backdoor.

'My God, what on earth happened here?' shrieked Harry hugging Alice with one arm.

'What! Is this Paddington station?' demanded Adrian jokingly, as Phoebe shot past him in search of Roo.

Everyone got stuck in to scrubbing down the walls and stretching the carpets out to dry. Phoebe and Vicky swung happily on the old tyre swing while baby Roody, gurgling delightedly, pulled at the rattle strung across his carry cot. After three hours they agreed they had all had enough and, having cleaned themselves up, went in search of lunch. In a quaint little country pub with a family lounge Alice was immediately sobered when Harry informed her that Roody had been posted to Bahrain for the next three years and they were leaving in mid-June. Alice told Harry about their plans for Turkey and Australia and Adrian amused Roo and Phoebe by transforming his large purple silk hankie into a rabbit. Monica and Teddy chatted about Teddy's plans to get his research published and the likelihood of promotion within the university.

'How does the title "Civilisation without a silk shawl" sound?'

'That sounds marvellous,' murmured Monica pushing back a strand of mousy brown hair. After lunch Harry and Roody made their excuses and left having been invited to tea with one of the squadron leaders.

'I hope I stay awake,' laughed Harry giving Alice a peck on the cheek. Promising to ring soon to arrange lunch with Alice and Vicky, Harry was bundled into the car by Roody with her two children. With everyone waving furiously and blowing kisses, Roody skidded the car off the verge and down the road.

Alice felt a bit flat after they had gone. The news of Roody's posting and the events of last night were finally catching up with her so she was extremely unreceptive when Teddy and Monica made a joke about Roody being terribly RAF on the way home. A throwaway line from Teddy about starting a sheep farm in Baa-hrain as they walked back into the house sent Alice flying into a rage.

'You're being far too touchy, maybe you need a tonic,' Monica remarked adding fuel to Alice's over-stoked fires.

'I don't need any stupid tonics, Monica, I need some sleep,' retorted Alice. 'Come on, Vicky, let's go and give Skittles his evening apples.' She grabbed Vicky's hand, collected a bag of apples and apple pieces and stomped out of the house. 'If you're lucky there may be some soggy biscuits or stale cake in the tin in the bottom of the larder,' she called over her shoulder.

'Perhaps the horse needs a tonic,' yelled Monica.

'Oh don't bait her, Moni,' said Adrian feeling uncomfortable. He had grown very fond of Alice. He admired her sparkle and the vitality she brought to life in whatever she did; in fact, he thought soberly, he admired too damned much about Alice. 'Who's for a cup of tea or a Scotch?' he asked abruptly.

Alice and Vicky headed for the stable, Vicky playing a great game of splashing as many puddles as she could. The sight made Alice laugh until Vicky gave an extra large splash soaking Alice's dark green corduroy jeans to the knee. She rapidly changed the game to avoiding the puddles.

'How about I take you for a ride after we've given Skittles his apples? Would you like that?' asked Alice collecting his saddle and bridle and their two riding hats from the tack room. Delighted, Vicky let Alice clip on her hat and then pranced towards Skittles' box, pieces of apple clutched in each hand, stopping well out of reach as she had been taught. The sleek roan Teddy had given Alice on her twenty-first birthday was still skittish and inclined to shy without warning. Skittles had seemed the ideal name. Under Alice's gentle but firm hand he had settled down considerably. Alice had learned his ways and was ready for practically every trick this horse had to offer but she still didn't trust him alone with Vicky. The apples devoured and the horse saddled, Alice lifted Vicky on Skittles' back and then mounted herself. With Vicky safely astride in front with Alice clasping her tight and both holding the reins, Alice nudged Skittles forwards.

The late afternoon sun was shedding its rays across the rain soaked countryside making the whole world glisten as Alice set Skittles at a gentle trot out across the fields. The fresh damp smell made their noses tingle. Alice turned towards the beech woods. The bracing early spring air and the warmth of Vicky's body helped to calm the yearning for home that Alice knew was the underlying reason for her unhappiness. She hadn't meant to snap at Monica either but it had been an emotional day. Teddy could be so difficult; she loved him in her own way but she was bitterly disappointed that he refused to understand her need to return home. Now she was ready to go back, ready to face the memories, ready to start rebuilding her dream. Well, Teddy had sort of agreed to next Christmas in Australia and she would hold him to that. She bent and kissed Vicky on her cold rosy cheek. She could picture the three of them riding across the black soil plains as she turned Skittles for home walking him almost all the way, only breaking into a gentle canter across the final field before dropping back again to a walk along the lane and into the stable yard. Teddy was waiting, watching as the two clattered across the cobblestones.

'You two looked so beautiful and so contented together,' he said helping Vicky to the ground. He slipped his arm around Alice's waist and squeezed her fondly as they walked the horse back to its box. 'What say I get Adrian to pick out a really nice horse for Vicky to have as a late Christmas present when we get back from Australia?'

Alice gaped at him.

'Don't make bad jokes.'

'I'm not.'

'But you said . . .' Teddy silenced her with a kiss.

'I don't understand you, Teddy,' cried Alice shaking her head, her eyes shining, 'and I probably never will.'

'Didn't I tell you that's the secret of my charm,' replied Teddy and kissed her again.

Chapter Twenty-two

THE NEXT FEW months were extremely exhausting for Alice as she juggled organising Teddy's trip to Turkey with renovations after the flood and caring for Vicky. Teddy's departure date was delayed twice which turned out to be a bonus as it meant he and Judd could now travel the silk road itself as the weather started to cool. Finally Alice and Vicky waved Teddy and Judd off in the close midsummer heat of August. With a sigh of relief Alice walked back up the garden path thinking about Teddy and the previous night.

He had been as excited as a schoolboy jabbering about Marco Polo and the silk road, the Khunjerab Pass and over into Kashgar in China. When he had finally allayed her fears about the dangers of high altitude sickness, the prospect of their jeep breaking down in inaccessible mountainous terrain and attacks from nomadic tribesmen, they had made love. Teddy had been more loving and more gentle than she could remember, reviving some of the magic she had felt when she had first met him. Yet despite his unexpected tenderness, for her the chemistry simply wasn't there. If she were truthful to herself it had never been there. She longed to lose herself again in that special heady place that was all sensation and she felt she was to blame that with Teddy it never happened. With Robert it had all been so different.

Twisting the deadheads off a clump of yellow daisies, Alice admonished herself for being a fool. She was building fantasies. She had given her love to Robert and he had betrayed her. Teddy was a good husband and she was being disloyal. Yet she knew it was guilt that had made her repress her disappointment and anger at being left behind. She was also increasingly aware of how compliant she had become. Once she would have fought Teddy over an issue, now she just gave in. She watched Vicky skip back up the path, pushing away her depressing thoughts. Vicky brought her such joy. Teddy and she had a comfortable marriage. In a few months Turkey and all its frustrations would be in the past and she would be greeting Bea and Ray with laughter and showing Vicky and Teddy the magic of her own country.

Deciding it was too nice to go indoors Alice wandered idly round the garden. Trailing her fingertips across the flower heads she breathed in the perfume of the rambling roses and clambering honeysuckle, listening to the gentle drone of the bees and the skylarks overhead. Surrounded by familiar comforting sounds and smells she gradually relaxed, enjoying her sense of freedom. Space that was all she needed, space and time to dream, then her fighting spirit would return. Now she had that space why waste a minute. Diving back into the house she re-emerged carrying cool drinks, a rug and a note pad and pencil. While Vicky pottered around happily wheeling her tiny red and green wheelbarrow about under the shade of the great mulberry tree, Alice developed a plan of the stud property she planned to set up.

'What are you doing, Mummy?' asked Vicky crouching down and peering up into Alice's face after she had been working for a while.

'I'm drawing a picture of our home in Australia, possum. This year I'm going to take you there and you can see real live kangaroos and koalas; then one day we're all going to live there and have lots of sheep and you can help me look after the baby lambs.' She retied the ribbon in Vicky's hair and stroked her cheek. It could work. Even if at first she set up a manager on the property or they spent half the year in England and half in Australia. If she presented a well thought out plan to Teddy she was sure she could get him to agree. What had Harry said when Alice was getting married? Tie the knot and then hit him with this sheep thing. That seemed such a long time ago. Did she still have the passion to do what she and Ben had planned together? She looked across the garden to the lush green meadows beyond shimmering in the heat haze, yet her heart yearned for the parched dusty land dotted with dams that she once called home. Wide open spaces, the flash of green parrots, the stillness of a kangaroo watching by a dirt track, the screech of yellow-crested cockatoos. Unexpected tears sprang to her eyes as she remembered how she and Ben had laughed when the goat had eaten one of Ray's shirts. She had her answer. She stretched again. Space and time to dream. Tomorrow she'd take Vicky on an adventure. She returned to her note pad.

Her peace and privacy, however, were short-lived. Two days later, with too many bags and a plump homely young woman named Marigold Gresham-Forbes in tow, Lady Georgina Turlington swooped down unannounced on Mill House. She informed Alice she couldn't possibly manage without a decent nanny and that she had promised Teddles she would see to it Alice looked after herself properly. Having given the household a total going over, refurbished the larder, spent vast amounts of money on unwanted flowers, told Alice how the Gresham-Forbes had been family friends for generations and what a splendid help Marigold would be in bringing up Vicky, irritated Mrs P and floated around in a cloud of blue grey cashmere and heavy perfume for two days till Alice thought she would scream with frustration, Lady Georgina then whisked them all back to the Turlington country estate declaring Mill House was far too small and damp to be healthy. Infuriated by her mother-in-law's arrogance, only good manners and the fact that Alice felt suddenly incredibly tired, prevented her from fighting against her. She also surprised herself by liking Marigold immensely. Not only had the young woman given her a chance to catch up with some sleep, she was also the first nanny with whom Alice could have a sensible conversation and Vicky and she had got on like a house on fire. Marigold, she decided, was sensible and completely trustworthy. It was one of the rare occasions where she agreed with her mother-in-law.

After lying around lethargically for three weeks, not even bothering to fight the fact that her life had been taken over by Lady Turlington, Alice finally dragged herself off to see the local GP, who told her she was pregnant. Thrilled at the news, understanding her unusual tiredness and armed with some tablets to prevent morning sickness, Alice started to bounce back to her normal energetic self. With the return of her energy came a restlessness to get back into her own home. Her obstetrician was in Cambridge and Alice also wanted to get on with organising their trip to Australia. She rang Monica who was delighted to hear she was expecting another baby and informed her that if she didn't come home soon she'd need a bulldozer to shift the mail and that a long tubular parcel had arrived from Turkey. Alice could not tell Teddy the good news as in his last phone call he had informed her he would be uncontactable for the next few weeks making the documentary.

Armed with the perfect excuse Alice started packing. Lady Georgina, who had just bought two more extremely expensive hunters for her stables, while delighted with the prospect of another grandchild to brag about, showed no interest in having her life further disrupted and protested feebly when Alice announced she intended returning to Cambridge, only insisting that Marigold go with them.

'I promised Teddles I wouldn't let you behave foolishly. You can't possibly manage on your own. Look how sick you and little Roo were after Christmas,' she cried flicking a speck of dust from her cream jodhpurs and jamming her new dark blue velvet riding cap over her hair feeling she had done her motherly duty.

'Marigold and I have already agreed about that,' grinned Alice enjoying her mother-in-law's surprise.

Alice stopped the car at the front door of Mill House with a sigh of relief. The grass badly needed mowing and weeds were sprouting up amongst the flowers and the gate hinge had come loose but Alice didn't care. It was home. The leaves were starting to turn showing their autumn colours. Ripe apples hung from the trees, some recently fallen, others rotting in the grass. The sweet smell welcomed her home. Vicky insisted on immediately dragging Marigold round to Skittles' empty stable and jumped up and down until she had elicited a promise from Alice to fetch the horse from Aunty Monica who had come to the rescue after Alice had seen there was no escaping Lady T's announcement they were to stay with her. Once inside the slight mustiness of a house unlived in mingled with familiar smells. Happily she ran from room to room touching loved objects, seeing her home as though new. The faint aroma of new paint still lingered. Organised by Monica, Mrs P had been in that day and there was fresh bread on the kitchen table next to a jug filled with fresh picked flowers and milk and butter in the fridge. Never close but grateful to Monica for her thoughtfulness, after lunch having unloaded the car with Vicky and Marigold, Alice picked up the phone to thank her. Skittles was fine and they were all three invited to dinner tomorrow night. Alice then settled down to sort through the mail. She could hear Vicky's squeals of delight as she helped Marigold sort out the washing.

Most of the mail was rubbish. University information that was out of date, advertising and bills. Alice put copies of the *University Gazette* in a pile for Teddy to sort through and hungrily read a letter from Harry. The children were all wonderful. It was hellish hot in Bahrain and she missed her friend a lot. Alice then sorted through the rest of the pile. Gas, electricity, phone—she daren't open that one. Her heart missed a beat when she saw an envelope addressed in the spiky handwriting of Professor Dixson. Eagerly she slid the paper knife along the envelope and pulled out the two sheets of pale blue Basildon Bond embossed with the professor's name. Her eyes flew across the page. As she read she broke into a smile.

'No doubt you have guessed by the handwritten envelope I have given up the long battle with finding a good assistant. This is a desperate plea from a man worn down with the struggles of bad typing, inaccurate record keeping and a hopeless search for a person to wade through my muddle. I know I have no right to ask you but in short, my dear Alice, I have reached a crisis point. I cannot continue without you.'

Dear Dicky. How she had missed his steady ponderous advice, his gentle humour. She had to read the next paragraph three times before she could take it all in. Professor Dixson was inviting her to work on the third and crucial stage in his fight with diabetes, that of controlling blood sugar levels in animals using the molecule he had already created. But there was more. He wasn't inviting her back as an assistant, he was inviting her to collaborate with him, to work with him in an equal partnership. Her heart was thumping as she read the last paragraph.

'Dear Alice, I am aware that you have a life to lead and now a little person also to consider but I am pleading with you. The project has to be completed by July 1969. Please would you consider coming back knowing how desperate I am and understanding the high esteem in which I hold you and your work?'

Alice walked towards the window clutching the letter in stunned amazement. Marigold was now pushing Vicky on the rubber tyre hanging from the big chestnut tree as though she had been part of the family for years. Watching them happily playing Alice struggled to take in the full implications of the professor's offer. The letter had already been sitting around for two weeks. She reread it to check she really had understood its contents. Then she put the kettle on only to have it whistle furiously at her because she had forgotten to put in any water. Professor Dixson and her working on an equal footing! This was the most exciting thing that could have happened to her. In the space of three minutes her whole life had been turned upside down. She started towards the phone, changed her mind and instead refilled the kettle and called to Marigold and Vicky to come in for afternoon tea. Vicky crunched her way through one of Monica's homemade biscuits as Alice explained her situation to Marigold.

'Would you be happy looking after Vicky if I were away, say, two days a week?' Marigold nodded eagerly, caught up in Alice's excitement.

'You wouldn't mind if Marigold looked after you when Mummy was away sometimes, would you, darling?' asked Alice twisting one of Vicky's glorious curls. Vicky was more interested in getting Marigold to finish her daisychain.

That night Alice lay awake listening to the owls hooting to one another in the trees, tossing the details around in her head. It could all work. She had no qualms about leaving Vicky with Marigold and when the new baby arrived, well they'd cross that bridge when they came to it. Teddy would probably object at first to her returning to work but there was no need to mention it until his return and then she was sure she could win him round.

'It isn't as if pregnancy is an illness,' thought Alice switching on the light and rereading the letter. She had seen friends of Aunty Bea's working right through their pregnancy and back on the job with hardly a break after the baby was born and, besides, she'd be working in a hospital. Knowing he always went to bed late she threw caution to the wind and phoned Professor Dixson. The professor could hardly contain himself with gratitude. Alice roared with laughter as he promised to agree to anything including standing on his head if it made it possible for them to work together. Alice hung up and went to sleep. The next morning she booked their tickets to Australia. The air smelt of autumn. Even the smouldering bonfires didn't worry her like they used to, reminding her as they did of her terrible childhood ordeal. Vicky came rushing into the kitchen, her hands full of rust and orange leaves and spread them all over the table amongst her cooking. Alice felt quite absurdly happy.

The phone was ringing as she walked in the door at the end of her first exciting week with Professor Dixson. It was Teddy.

'This time it'll be a boy,' sang Teddy delighted when she told him about the baby. Alice's heart lifted at his reaction, so totally different from when Vicky was conceived. Exhilarated by her work in London, happy that Vicky and Marigold were getting on so well, she plunged in and told him about collaborating with the professor. Teddy was silent for so long Alice thought they had been cut off.

'Teddy darling, are you still there?' she asked.

Teddy exploded with rage. After listening to him rant on at her for being a selfish irresponsible mother with no thoughts other than to do what she pleased and not giving a fig for his unborn child, Alice lost her temper. Telling him she was none of those things, that it was her baby as well and it was he who was being totally unreasonable, she told him to go to hell and slammed down the phone. Guilty and miserable she immediately tried to ring back but could not get connected. Miserably she crept into the kitchen and made herself a cup of coffee. Vicky came hurtling down the stairs and threw herself into her mother's arms. Marigold walked downstairs more sedately, apologising for not answering the phone.

'That was Daddy,' Alice told Vicky trying to sound bright.

'Is he coming home?'

'Soon darling.' Having decided she had received a satisfactory amount of hugs Vicky slid off Alice's knee and went in search of a biscuit.

Seeing Alice's expression Marigold asked quietly, 'Is everything all right?' Alice bit her trembling bottom lip and laughed shakily. The unshed tears turned her eyes into liquid turquoise.

'Funny how simple things trigger memories.' She blinked several times. 'My brother and I had such great dreams for the future when we were little, just like children always do.' She gave a half-laugh. 'We used to joke about how we'd breed the best sheep in the world. With all this genetic stuff with Dicky I've been thinking of him a lot lately. I still miss him. He was a great brother. I wish Teddy understood.' She cupped her hands around her mug and stared across the darkened meadows. Teddy had no need to be so angry and unreasonable. It was not as if she was spending all her time in London and ignoring Vicky.

'Did you tell Teddy about the baby?' asked Marigold. Alice nodded.

'He was delighted,' she said dully. 'He was furious about me and Dicky. I lost my temper.' A heavy silence fell between the two women. 'Have you ever wanted something so bad it hurts just to think about it?' Alice blurted out. Marigold laughed not quite sure of how to take Alice's comment. There was an aching longing behind her words.

'I suppose I should have but not really. I just sort of muddle along,' she replied slightly sheepishly. Alice cleared her throat and stood up.

'I'm sorry, I'm just a bit upset. I shouldn't have lost my temper, not when he's so far away. I'll go and change.' But something that had long been deeply hidden was stirred up in Alice.

The following week, returning from a trip into Cambridge, Alice was met by a white-faced Marigold.

'Oh my God, Vicky!' Alice cried.

Marigold shook her head. 'It's Mr Turlington and his friend. They may have been kidnapped.' She was shaking so much she could hardly get the words out.

Alice made her sit down and tried to calm her. According to a local source Judd and Teddy's guide had been killed. There were often minor skirmishes in the foothills of the Palmir mountains but apparently this was bad enough to report. One of the Kirghiz tribes massacred another. All work had been stopped indefinitely on the road being built over the pass and the Chinese had closed their borders.

'I have to fly out and find him. I have to fly to Kashgar!' cried Alice sick to her stomach, twisting her engagement ring around her finger, her pupils dilated with fear. She knew she was talking nonsense. For starters she had no idea what she would do or where she would go when she got to Kashgar. The Palmir mountains stretched for miles. She wasn't even sure where Teddy and Judd had been staying. She didn't want to think about how the guide was killed. She didn't know what to do with herself, whether to sit down or stand up. She needed to hold Vicky but she dared not in case she transferred her own fear to her little girl. She started to place and stopped and started again, her own angry words ringing in her ears. The last words she had spoken to Teddy. Suddenly everything else seemed completely purposeless.

That week was the longest in Alice's life as she waited helpless, unable to sleep at night or concentrate on her work by day. Then on the eighth night the phone rang and to her utter relief it was Teddy. The line made conversation almost impossible but at least he and Judd were both alive and safe in Kashgar. Two days later they landed safely back at Heathrow airport. Alice, with Holly in tow, pushed her way through the crowds to the arrival barrier ready to fling her arms around Teddy and stopped, shocked at the two men's appearance. Teddy's right eye was bloodshot and half closed. The worst of the swelling had gone down from what must have been a corker of a black eye and the bruising had begun to turn all colours of the rainbow. His left arm was bandaged, his face and legs covered with scabs and bruises. Judd hobbled stiffly behind, his left leg in plaster, a large sticking plaster across one temple. His arms and right leg too were also badly bruised and scratched. Both men looked tense and haggard.

'I didn't want to tell you about it over the phone,' explained Teddy hugging Alice. 'I knew you'd worry yourself sick. We got taken to a hospital in Kashgar.'

'This man saved my life,' said Judd stiffly, hanging onto his wife's arm. 'You have every reason to be proud of him.' He blew out his cheeks. 'Christ, what a helluva time.' Before they could get into taxis they were inundated with reporters all wanting to be the first to relay their story. Flashbulbs popped everywhere and Alice and Vicky were in danger of being swept off their feet. Numbed, Alice listened with the journalists as Teddy explained how, after they had come down into the low hills below the Khunjerab Pass, they had been attacked by nomadic tribesmen and Judd had been shot in the leg. Alice shuddered as she listened. Only a few weeks ago Teddy had laughed at her idiotic fears. Now the two men had narrowly missed being killed.

Returning to Mill House the Turlingtons were greeted by more press. Marigold looked apologetic at having failed to beat them off, then relaxed as Teddy puffed up his feathers and recounted the tale again.

'Don't do anything like that to me ever again,' cried Alice through happy tears once they were alone in the bedroom. Teddy kissed her passionately. Neither mentioned their last conversation.

'I brought you a little surprise,' he said letting her go and unzipping his case with his good hand. He held out a small packet. Alice gasped with delight at the magnificent Buddha carved in glowing green jade. For Vicky he had bought a little red dopa hat embroidered with gold thread and a tiny brightly coloured donkey cart.

'And this is my greatest prize,' said Teddy dropping his voice. He shut the curtains and checked the door before pulling out a battered carved rectangular box from his haversack. 'It dates back to round about eight hundred AD,' he whispered in awe opening the box to expose several bamboo slips bound together with raw silk. With infinite care he lifted it out for Alice to see. 'I couldn't believe this was actually happening to me. This'll really make everyone sit up. I found it in an antechamber behind the cave that saved our lives.' Teddy replaced the slim bamboo booklet carefully into its container and placed it triumphantly at the back of one of his drawers. 'Don't mention this to anyone, not even Judd,' he said patting the chest of drawers. 'I'm going to pick my moment to tell him. This'll be the icing on the cake.' He pulled Alice to him. 'Now, give me a hug and let's sort out all this rubbish about you and this professor friend of yours. You know it's completely stupid.'

'I love you, Teddy,' said Alice kissing him on the cheek and slipping from his embrace. 'Don't worry about all that, darling. I'm just so glad you're home and safe.' Relieved, Teddy took that to mean that Alice was no longer working with the professor. He had to admit he did not have the strength to fight her right now.

The next day the story was spread across *The Times, Telegraph* and *Daily Sketch* proclaiming Teddy a hero. 'Only through Cambridge Don the Honourable Edward Turlington's selfless bravery was US Assistant Professor on research grant to Oxford snatched from the jaws of death,' read the article. It then went on to explain how they had spent two miserable, terrifying nights hiding in a cave with only a dribble of water and no food. Then by some miracle they had been discovered by a group of Kara-Kirghiz and taken by camel to Kashgar in China. Alice shuddered as she read the account.

Teddy flourished in his role as hero and retold their adventures as often as he was given an opportunity. Within a few days the bandage on his arm was removed and only the bruise around his eye remained as a reminder that anything had gone wrong. Alice, thoroughly relieved that he was safe and well, organised several dinner parties and accepted invitations to cocktail parties, giving Teddy a wider audience to impress. Rosie Dixson, having read *The Times* headlines, rang telling Alice to take the next week off. Wanting to avoid a confrontation with Teddy for as long as possible Alice gratefully agreed. However, she knew that she could not avoid it forever. The day she decided to tackle the problem she walked in on Teddy as he slammed the phone down on Judd. Realising her timing couldn't have been worse but that she had also run out of time, she plunged in before he could slam out of the room.

'I'll be working in London tomorrow,' she announced baldly. Teddy stopped dead in his tracks, his face changing from white to red rapidly.

'Obviously what I say doesn't matter at all around here,' he snapped. He turned on his heel and stormed out of the house leaving her standing in the middle of the room. Then, in the middle of the night, he got up starving hungry, his internal clock in a muddle, and woke Alice. While he gorged himself on a doorstep of fresh bread and locally made Stilton cheese he demanded to know whether Alice meant to take part in his life at all any more.

'Oh Teddy, that's so unfair,' retorted Alice. 'And keep your voice down or you'll wake Vicky.'

'And that's another thing,' exclaimed Teddy dropping his voice mid-sentence. 'Mother said, and rightly too, there is no way we can stay in this tiny little house any longer with Marigold a permanent fixture and another baby arriving in a few months. You should be house-hunting not wasting your time on stuff that bears no relationship to our lives.'

Alice plumped the pillow out from behind her and punched it viciously. 'I am not wasting my time, I don't want to move house and I don't care what's done and what's not done. This bloody British must-do-it-properly rubbish!' She threw the pillow on the floor and got out of bed. 'Teddy, be fair. No one is going to be neglected if I do two days work a week. My obstetrician says I'm one of the healthiest pregnant women he's seen in ages, and Vicky adores Marigold.'

'Only because she can't get near her mother.'

'That is totally untrue and you know it.' She stomped past him out to the bathroom. Teddy knew he had gone too far. On her return he put his arm around Alice.

'Oh Alice, my roaring Leo. You know how I hate to share you with anyone. Just the thought of coming home to a house without you fills me with depression.'

'It doesn't have to Teddy, really,' Alice said stroking his tired face. 'You know I love you and I thought everything out very carefully before I made my decision.' She told Teddy the agreed arrangements. 'I'll be working a lot at home. It's only in the last two months that I may have to spend more time away but two months isn't long. The whole project will be finished before Ben is four months old.' Alice patted her small round stomach.

'Oh! So now you've even chosen my son's name without consulting me,' Teddy quizzed her but there was laughter in his eyes. Grinning mischievously Alice looped her arms around his neck resting her forehead against his, wondering what kept her attracted to this unreasonable man.

'Or Beatrice Ellen if it's a girl—and I've checked that it's okay to fly when I'm five months pregnant, and I'll make sure I have time to help you if you need with finishing off your own work. After that I promise I will give you all my complete undivided attention until number two goes to school.' Teddy drew her down on the bed and kissed her gently, then reached over and turned out the bedside light.

'Will you come to the special convention when I present the bamboo slips?' he murmured kissing her. Alice giggled in the dark as his stubble tickled her tummy button.

'Of course I will, you silly.'

After a long while he said, 'If you promise to let Mother find us another house I won't make any more fuss about your working.'

'That's blackmail!'

'Yes.' Teddy buried his head in her neck. Alice grinned up into the darkness. Moving house was a small price to pay.

The two-day convention was held in Oxford which annoyed Teddy. However, he was pacified by the fact that all the people who ought to be there were there. The archaeological world hummed with excitement, waiting with bated breath to learn of the two men's experiences on the silk route, but no one, least of all Judd, expected the rabbit Teddy pulled out of the hat at the very end of two solid days of presentations. As Teddy stood up his palms were sweating, his heart beating a rhythm of triumph behind his cool British exterior. A hush fell on the auditorium. Alice watched him proudly. He looked so full of confidence.

'As you know, Professor Judd Gimbelstein and I have worked closely in collecting all our data,' began Teddy smoothly. 'But in every good relationship there has to be some element of surprise.' He smiled relaxedly over at Judd. Judd's smile became just a fraction stiffer, his shoulders more tense. 'I found this particular piece of evidence when the professor was sleeping after his terrible ordeal on the Khunjerab Pass.' A sigh of appreciation rippled through the audience. Alice noticed Judd had gone a shade pinker, his hands clenching involuntarily in his lap as Teddy talked.

'It could just as easily have been him,' continued Teddy smoothly, watching Judd out of the corner of his eye. 'I wanted to share this magical moment of revelation with you as the climax to a magnificent convention. Professor Gimbelstein has no idea of its existence.' The atmosphere was electric. Teddy waved his hand. 'Could we have the cameras a little closer please.' Ceremoniously he picked up his briefcase and placed it on the table.

'I have had to go to elaborate lengths to ensure that this secret was kept until I was able to share it with my colleague and good friend in your company,' he jested. A titter ran around the audience as he lifted the battered carved box from his briefcase and placed it on the table beside the lectern. Savouring the deliciousness of the moment, he carefully extracted the bamboo slips bound together with raw silk. Judd's jaw dropped. Alice could see something was badly wrong as he stood up gaping over Teddy's shoulder. She remembered the angry phone calls over the past weeks as her eyes darted from Teddy to Judd and back to Teddy.

'This amazing find is dated 830AD,' announced Teddy. 'We know that because the date is actually mentioned in the script. The inscription gives a fascinatingly new account of part of the journey made by the Buddhist monk Xuan Zang, the best loved of all Chinese travellers on the silk road. The account was written by one of the scribes whose ancestor was part of the Xi'an court of Xuan Zang's day. The exciting part is that it reveals a whole new side to the man Xuan Zang and the Tang Dynasty.' The whole place erupted in applause. The translator, whom Teddy had rewarded handsomely for keeping quiet, could hardly contain himself in the front seat.

Once all was quiet again Teddy continued. 'Professor Gimbelstein in his generosity has agreed that the artefact will return with me to Cambridge although our other research will remain on show in Oxford for the next two months before a decision is made as to where the collection will ultimately reside. Professor . . .' Triumphantly, Teddy held out his hand for Judd to step forward, staring his associate full in the face as flashlights popped and the hall once more echoed with thunderous applause. Judd's palms were sweating as he shook hands with Teddy in front of twelve hundred people; Teddy could see the rivulets of sweat running down the sides of his face and onto his collar. There was nothing left for him to say. Teddy had walked off with all the glory. His opponent had been checkmated.

After the success of the convention Teddy was at his best. With the accolades that followed he showered Alice with expensive gifts and promises, listening to her plans to buy a property in Australia. Delighted he showed her his face plastered across the front of the *National Geographic* and told her of subsequent follow-up articles promised. He even kept his promise allowing her to continue her work with Professor Dixson. The only subject he would not discuss at all was Judd's reaction to his disclosure of the bamboo booklet.

Happy to be allowed to get on with her work in peace, Alice left the subject alone, enjoying Teddy's good humour while it lasted. In between her trips to London she sorted out all the details for their visit to Australia. She and Vicky studiously crossed off the days on the big calendar each morning and counted those left with mounting excitement. Teddy was the only one who showed little interest in all the preparation.

'You and Marigold seem to have got everything under control,' he said over dinner in the first week of December after Vicky had been tucked up in bed. He still didn't approve of Alice working.

Alice shivered as a blast of cold air whistled around her feet and pulled her red wool cardigan closer round her swelling figure. She knew he was very tired having just returned from a lecture trip around Northern England and had set himself tight deadlines with his work before they left for Australia, but she couldn't help wishing he'd be a little bit more enthusiastic. He had had a tiring week giving lectures he was ill-prepared for having spent most of his spare time discussing the sale of the bamboo booklet with Bunty.

Alice passed him a helping of plum pudding made from plums bottled from their garden by Mrs P.

'You know, I think you'd make a great gentleman farmer,' she laughed across at him in the candlelight. 'Don't you, Marigold? You'd never need to wear yourself out over lectures like you do now. I'm so longing to show you both my country.' She sighed happily. 'Seriously though, would you consider moving to Australia permanently if you could get a university post? It's a fantastic place to bring up kids.'

Teddy stopped the spoon halfway to his mouth about to reply when the phone rang. 'I'll get it,' he said quickly, patting Marigold's shoulder.

Teddy came back into the room, his face grey.

'Whatever's wrong?' cried Alice.

'It's my brother Hugo. He's had a heart attack and been rushed to Cheltenham hospital. No warning. He just collapsed.' Teddy slumped down in his chair pushing his unfinished pudding away. 'They don't know whether he'll make it through the night.' Suddenly no one was hungry any longer. Marigold busied herself clearing away the dishes.

'What did you say to your mother?'

Teddy looked bewildered. 'I didn't know what to say. I . . . she . . . It was such a shock.'

Alice took charge. 'We'd better drive over there tonight.' Teddy looked thankfully across at Alice. 'Vicky will be fine with Marigold. I'll go and sort out a few things.'

Within half an hour they were on the road to Cheltenham and at three in the morning they arrived at the hospital. Rugged up in their winter coats they shivered in the subzero temperatures stamping their feet as they entered the sterile warmth of the hospital. Lord and Lady Turlington were both at Hugo's bedside. A drip was running from his right arm and he was breathing shallowly but unaided. His complexion was yellowy-grey. A nurse was monitoring him every fifteen minutes. Having kissed everyone Teddy and Alice sat down. Lady Turlington seemed to have aged ten years. Lord Turlington looked lost. Eventually the matron came in.

'There has been no deterioration for the last two hours and he does seem to be stabilising. I suggest you go home and get some sleep. We'll call you immediately there is any change.'

'I'll stay,' said Lady Georgina firmly. The other three stumbled tiredly out.

Hugo recovered but it put a whole new complexion on life. Teddy spoke to Alice before a family luncheon the weekend after his brother was discharged from hospital.

'The doctor warned Mum this could happen again at any time. This may be the last Christmas we'll all have together,' he said brokenly. 'If you still want to take the kids to Australia without me I won't try to stop you.'

Numbly Alice fingered her soft green wool maternity dress. Of course they couldn't go to Australia at Christmas with Teddy's brother's health so uncertain and no, she wasn't prepared to go without him. There was no question of choice. Poor Teddy. He was so helpless in a crisis.

'I'll have to explain to Vicky so she isn't too disappointed,' she said smiling bravely, a tremor in her voice.

'Don't mention any of that stuff about buying a property in Australia to Mother either, will you Alice?' Teddy added anxiously.

Alice stared unbelieving at him. Suddenly she felt terribly alone. Had he ever meant for them to go? She chided herself for being so untrusting. Her pregnancy was making her overemotional. Teddy, she rationalised, distraught at seeing his brother so sick and his mother in such a state, was fearful of making her worse at the mention of money. Their latest bank statement had shown an overdraft which had trebled in one month, despite Alice's protests, which Teddy had dismissed with the comment that Mother would help them out if they got stuck.

The hardest bit was ringing Bea and hearing the resignation in her voice when she explained what had happened. She chose an evening when Teddy was out at a meeting and Marigold was busy. That was another thing that worried at the back of her mind. There was a real likelihood she would lose Marigold before long. To take her mind off her disappointment, Alice decided to do something practical. The air tickets would need to be returned promptly to get the rebate. She couldn't remember if the insurance covered the full price. She scrummaged about in her purse for the piece of paper and pulled out everything except the one piece she needed. How did purses get this messy? In despair she pulled everything out of every compartment and shook the purse upside down. A small scrap of well thumbed paper fell out on the top of the pile. Alice opened it and stared at the writing. It was Ben's poem. She knew it by heart.

Roses are red
Violets are blue
Don't grow up too quick, sis, 'cos
I want to be part of your palace dream too.

The poem blurred as her eyes filled with tears. What had happened to her dream? What had happened to her life? All the disappointments of the past year—Teddy's rage and insensitivity, his unwillingness to hear her needs and her longing to go home—flooded over Alice. Angrily she brushed away the tears. To cry would be utterly self-centred. Hugo had hardly planned his heart attack. She was the one who had refused to take Vicky on her own to Australia. Damn her loyalty.

Clasping Ben's poem to her she stared out at the North Star in the clear moonless sky. She had made her choice. Her life was fine. No one had forced her to marry Teddy. She was happy with him, mostly, and she could live with the disappointment that he did not love her country as she did. Why, then, did this thing, this unidentified feeling, keep tugging at her heart? Why couldn't she let go of the need for those great wide open spaces in the harsh unrelenting land of her childhood? Why did she sometimes feel she might burst with longing for a real Aussie yarn or an understated joke? She looked back at Ben's words smudged by long ago tears.

'It didn't work out like that, Ben,' she whispered. 'I'm sorry.'

Chapter Twenty-three

ROBERT HEAVED THE last stubborn ewe around and shoved it down the race, a corridor he had erected between the holding yards and the sorting pens. It was just wide enough for one animal but sometimes the animals took fright and managed to turn round pointing the wrong way. He, Melon and five other stockmen had been sorting the lamb-bearing ewes from the dries. There were thirty thousand ewes to sort over the next few weeks. Today they had brought a mob of six thousand down to the stockyards. It was hard, tedious, dusty work and they had been at it since dawn. Robert's back ached, his eyes and skin were dry and itchy, and his throat felt like sandpaper.

'That's the last of the silly old tarts,' he said lifting his Akubra to scratch his forehead, nodding to the wiry young stockmen. 'Time to knock off, what d'you reckon, boys?' Replacing his hat he called his dogs and clapped an arm around Melon. 'I need to talk to you. Come up to the new house and we'll get a drink.'

'Sounds good to me, boss,' replied Melon his teeth white against his dark skin.

The dogs jumped into the back and the two men stepped into the truck and drove over to Robert and Katie's house. They had moved in several weeks before and the house still smelt of fresh paint. Katie and Stewart were nowhere to be seen. Grabbing a couple of cold beers, Robert handed one to Melon and the two men quenched their thirst on the verandah. In the still heat of the evening, as the sun slipped behind the horizon in a blaze of oranges and reds, they discussed aspects of running the property. As orange turned to liquid gold and the paddocks darkened, Melon stood up.

'Better be off back home afore I gets in too much trouble from the missus,' he chuckled.

Robert nodded watching affectionately as the Aborigine strode off. He was lucky to have Melon. He was more like an uncle than an employee. Melon had been a part of his life ever since Robert could remember. He had taught him almost all he knew about the land and caring for it and he ran the other stockmen with an ease and discipline that both Robert and his father now took wholly for granted.

Robert's thoughts drifted around as he opened another beer. It had been backbreaking work but satisfying. He was lucky about a lot of things. The property was doing well. The men worked hard. Stewart, his pride and joy, was always asking questions and wanting to learn more about working the mob. Robert smiled in the dark. He was growing into a fine boy. Maybe one day he'd have a little brother or sister to add to the McIain dynasty. Even Katie had cheered up ever since she had learned that Alice wasn't coming back home. He frowned and took another sip of beer. Jesus but he was weary. He settled back into his chair.

He had been shocked by the excitement he had felt at learning of Alice's impending visit. Excited yet fearful. He dreaded the blank casual courtesy he guessed he would see in her eyes as she greeted him as Mrs Alice Turlington. Yet part of him ached to feast his eyes on her once more, if only to finally destroy any lingering hope that somehow magically their love had lasted. His relationship with Katie was now stilted and cold. When they made love, which was almost never, it was perfunctory and confusing. Encouraged by Katie's apparent initial interest, afterwards he was left feeling emptier and more lonely than before, as if he was an inconvenience to be endured. If it weren't for Stewart, he thought as he drifted into sleep, he would have left her years ago.

Robert woke with a start, dry-mouthed and hot. He looked at his watch and swore. Dinner would have been over hours ago and he had promised his mother they would all be together as Ian was home from Karri Karri, the Western Australian property. Staggering into the house he hurriedly showered, changed and drove over to the main house. Sneaking in through the kitchen he found Stewart picking at the remains of the trifle.

'Nan's mad at you and they've all been talking about growing cotton. Would we have to get rid of all the sheep to grow cotton, Dad?' asked Stewart licking his fingers.

'We're not growing anything except sheep, Stewwy, and get your fingers out of your Nan's pudding or you'll be in trouble too,' replied Robert. He walked in to the dining room where Elizabeth and George were still talking quietly over cups of tea. Seeing the concern in his mother's face Robert quickly apologised.

'I fell asleep. It's been a long day. No,' he added, 'Katie and I haven't been arguing again.'

'Well that's nice to know. You might like to go and say hello to your brother. He's out on the verandah with Katie.' Robert kissed his mother on the cheek and nodded to his father.

'G'day, Dad.'

'Son,' George acknowledged. Deciding not to ruin the evening by raising the contentious issue of Ian and cotton, Robert headed for the front door.

For a moment Robert stood on the verandah, staring up at the brilliant, shimmering Milky Way, soaking up the healing silence. Then he turned and walked its long flower-edged length in search of Katie and Ian. Turning the corner he stopped in shock. Ian was holding Katie in an obvious embrace, his arm draped casually around her waist, one finger tilting her chin up to his face. Katie's hands rested idly on his chest. Robert quickened his pace.

'Hello, little brother. Overdoing the concerned brother-in-law a bit, aren't you?' Instantly the pair jumped guiltily away from one another.

'Oh Robby, I didn't hear you coming,' said Katie a little breathlessly. Tan was just telling me about the new property. It sounds so hard to manage.'

'Hello, Bluey. Katie and I were just talking about the new property.'

'So why are you spinning this yarn about growing cotton again, little brother?' snapped Robert, his irritation at Stewart's earlier comments fuelled by seeing Ian and Katie together. Ian shoved his hands in his pockets and stuck out his chin.

'Now wait a minute. Before you bloody go off your head. It's a dust-bowl out there and cotton at Wangianna's a darned good idea.'

'Why do you have to start having a go at him as soon as he gets home?' interjected Katie moving back to Ian. T think cotton's a good idea.'

'You don't know what you're talking about, Katie,' snapped back Robert. 'I thought you wanted to be mistress of Wangianna. If we start growing flamin' cotton there won't be any Wangianna.'

'Bulldust!' exclaimed Ian. 'And don't "little brother" me. The trouble with you is you go around wearing blinkers.'

'Do I?' said Robert his anger mounting. 'Is that why I saw you kissing Katie?'

'Don't be absurd,' retorted Katie.

'She's my sister-in-law. What's wrong with brotherly affection?'

'That wasn't brotherly affection and you bloody know it!'

'I don't know what's got into you tonight,' Katie hissed. 'First you can't be bothered even to make it to dinner and now you attack me. I'm not standing around to listen to all this.' Throwing him a deadly glance she flounced back inside.

'If I catch you pawing Katie again I'll knock your teeth into the back of your head, little brother,' warned Robert through clenched teeth. 'We may not have the perfect marriage but that doesn't make my wife any man's game.'

'You're off your flamin' block!' yelled Ian. Storming past Robert he strode off the verandah and into the night. Robert shook his head. What was happening to him? He sat down and put his head in his hands. Katie was a flirt but his own brother?

'Has Ian been acting improperly before?' demanded Robert as he and Katie undressed for bed.

'What do you think?' replied Katie coldly, slipping her cotton nightgown over her head.

Robert shuddered. Had Ian watched her do that too?

'I don't *think* anything. I want to know the truth.'

'He might have. Would you mind?' Katie's eyes teased him. She moved seductively towards him, attempting to slide her arms round his neck.

'For Christ's sake, Katie. Do you know what you're saying? He's my brother,' Robert replied, angrily pushing her away.

'Would it make any difference? At least he knows I'm alive.'

'You're my wife. We're married.'

'We don't have a marriage and you know it. We've never had a marriage,' she spat. 'Ian loves me and we're having an affair.'

Robert stepped back at the venom in her voice. There was no regret, no shame, just triumph in her eyes. Rage bubbled up inside Robert with such intensity he had to turn his back to avoid striking her. His mind went blank.

'How do you think it feels knowing that every time we make love you're thinking of Alice?' screamed Katie. She grabbed Robert so he was forced to look at her, a coiled serpent ready to strike. 'Did you think giving me a pretty house and pretty clothes and letting me play hostess with your dad was going to make up for it all? Did you? Did you?' she goaded. 'Well, Ian is better in bed than you could ever be.'

Robert flinched as though she had struck him. He stared back, seeing her as a stranger. She was right. He had tried and failed. He had never wanted her. He had wanted Alice. The guilt had been unbearable. At least now he no longer need pretend. Yet there was no Alice, only a memory of what might have been, which had slowly but surely eaten away at his marriage, destroying whatever could have been. He could almost forgive her for having an affair but not with Ian, not with his own flesh and blood. Robert sat down on the bed the world lurching dizzily around him. How could all this be happening?

'When?' he asked dully.

'In Melbourne. And don't look at me like that. How long was I supposed to wait? The whole family knows our marriage is a sham.' She moved to the window staring out at the thousand brilliant stars.

'I'll start divorce proceedings in the morning,' said Robert his emotions once more in check. He picked up his pyjamas. He got as far as the door before Katie's words hit him.

'If you try to divorce me I swear you will never see Stewart again.' An icy hand squeezed at Robert's heart. Slowly he turned to meet the hatred pouring from Katie's eyes. 'How could you, how could you treat me like this? Why couldn't you just love me?' she cried.

'How much do you want, Katie?' Robert asked with chilling calm.

'I want to be mistress of Wangianna. If you agree to sign over your share of Wangianna to me I will divorce you. Otherwise I want to continue my affair with Ian without anyone else knowing and I want you to leave Ian alone. And I want you to promise never to mention this conversation to anyone, ever.'

'You must be crazy. I'm not agreeing to anything so utterly ludicrous,' fumed Robert. As the words left his lips he knew he was fooling himself. Katie's eyes gleamed with malice.

'Then go and kiss your son goodnight for the last time while I start packing.' Katie was between him and the door. She could see she had him cornered. White-lipped Robert replied, 'There will be no divorce. Now please move out of the way, I'm going to sleep in the spare room.' Katie stood aside.

'If I hear even a sniff of suspicion from anyone anywhere, you can forget your son,' she shot triumphantly.

Robert knew he was beaten. Weighed down with misery he closed the door behind him.

Chapter Twenty-four

TEDDY WAS RATTLING around in the large kitchen of their new house trying to remember where Alice kept the saucepans. He banged the cupboard doors in frustration, loudly cursing his wife for working late on Marigold's day off. Not that that was unusual, Alice was always working late these days and when she did get home she just fell into bed exhausted.

Teddy wasn't happy at all. He was furious with himself for ever having agreed to Alice returning to work and he was coping very badly with her success. Already there had been a write-up about her work in the *Lancet* and another in an American medical journal. Meanwhile everything to do with the bamboo booklet had been put on hold while his brother was ill and while interest grew in Alice's research, no one was taking any notice of him at all. To top it all the British translator examining the inscription was being incredibly slow hampering Teddy's negotiations to sell the bamboo slips. Both the British Museum and Cambridge's Fitzwilliam museum had expressed enormous interest in buying the booklet from the outset. Teddy, seeing an opportunity, had refused to put the booklet up for auction at Sotheby's, instead bumping up the price by purposely playing one Museum off against the other, having secretly decided to sell to the Fitzwilliam knowing he would gain more respect from his colleagues by this grand gesture of keeping it within Cambridge University. While he had acknowledged the sum of money they were talking about would come in very handy in clearing their disastrous overdraft and adding to the mounts in his stables, it was the glory not the money that was of paramount importance to him.

On reflection Teddy wasn't merely coping badly with Alice's success, he wasn't coping at all, besides which she was breaking all the rules. Praise from some of his more envious colleagues at Alice's independence and her ability to juggle married life with a career only served to upset him further. Teddy didn't want an independent wife, he wanted a decoration to assist his progress up his own career ladder, one who listened to his woes and administered large dollops of admiration, praise and sympathy when required. Alice was not at present doing any of this.

Suddenly Vicky ran full pelt into the kitchen almost knocking Teddy off his feet. Just as he was about to give her a good smack, Ben, now six months old, started crying.

'Here, have a biscuit and stop that bloody row,' yelled Teddy. Pushing away the proffered rusk, Ben only cried harder and Vicky, frightened by her father's anger, joined in too. Then Alice walked in. 'Why the bloody hell can't you be a proper mother? I'm going demented trying to cope with all this,' shouted Teddy.

Taking in the chaos Alice dropped her briefcase and ran and picked up Ben from his playpen. Jiggling him up and down she soothed his frantic cries. His bottom was soaking.

'It's all right, darling, Mummy's here.'

'For more than five minutes I hope,' snapped Teddy sarcastically. Alice continued to soothe Ben, refusing to rise to the bait. 'How am I supposed to manage?' continued Teddy. 'I've got the men coming to tear out the old stables tomorrow and I promised Adrian I'd go over and check out the two hunters he's picked out for me. I can't think straight with two screaming kids.' Alice frowned and opened her mouth to speak. Teddy glared back at her. 'Now don't you go on at me. One of them's for Vicky.'

'That's lovely of you, Teddy, but we can't afford—' attempted Alice.

Teddy cut in over her. 'And next week I've organised for us to whiz over to France for a couple of weeks. I've managed to sneak a bit of extra research leave and, God, I could do with the break.' This was too much for Alice. Her face black as thunder she disappeared to change Ben.

Returning she picked up the offending rusk and gave it to Ben who chewed on it tearfully. Muscling up some calm she then shooed Vicky upstairs to get undressed for her bath and turned to Teddy.

'Darling, we've got to slow down a bit. Our overdraft's been climbing since December, despite your mother helping us out yet again. We can't just keep spending and spending and expecting her to fish us out of trouble every time the bank complains.' Teddy pouted. 'Honestly, all this can wait. Vicky is perfectly happy learning on Phillip's pony and as I'm not riding at the moment you can ride Skittles.'

'Why do you always have to be such a wet blanket? If you spent less on train travel and taxis and all this other stuff . . .' he started.

Alice walked away in disgust, Ben still in her arms. She was too tired for all this and had too much work to catch up on.

'Okay,' Teddy called from the end of the hall. 'I'll cancel the workmen and finance and tell Adrian to hold everything until I've spoken to Mother.' Alice shrugged her shoulders. He hadn't heard a word she'd said. She loathed being rescued by Lady Georgina although it obviously didn't worry Teddy and she had no idea how to make Teddy stop spending money like water. Right now she didn't have the energy to argue. She had a problem to solve and a deadline to meet. She disappeared upstairs to put the children to bed.

Teddy rang his mother who said she would send him a cheque at the end of the month. He then strode over to the stereo system and put on the latest recording of the *Verdi Requiem*. The music boomed through the house.

At the beginning of August with their overdraft still skyrocketing, Teddy received the report from the translator. Swearing at the slow cogs of bureaucracy he was nevertheless delighted that at last he could do something. He drove into Cambridge to visit the senior curator of the Fitzwilliam who rarely took a holiday from his beloved museum.

Mr Henry Scudds was in his early sixties. A stanchion of the museum and a stickler for detail, he had over the years procured some of their greatest exhibits. Old manuscripts were his forte. Teddy found his pedantic need to, as he put it, 'explore every avenue and dislodge every stone' before making a decision incredibly irritating. Every time he dropped his H's and stuck them back in the wrong place it grated against Teddy but he had enough wit to try to keep the man on side.

'Good news, Scudds,' he pronounced confidently, leaning on the back of a brown leather upholstered chair in the senior curator's well-appointed office. 'Here is the report from the British translator.' His eyes glinted excitedly as he shoved the report in Mr Scudds' hands. 'Read it! It's all there. It may not be quite as old but I told you this find was on a par with the Rosetta Stone.'

The booklet contained exciting revelations about the Tang Dynasty although, to Teddy's disappointment, so far, with typical reserve the reaction amongst the British archaeological scene had been very subdued. Mr Scudds' gnarled fingers trembled slightly as he glanced at the papers. Teddy sighed. To still his impatience he started reading titles from the fascinating array of reference books that lined the room. After what seemed ages Henry Scudds removed his gold-rimmed half-glasses and placed them neatly on the desk. He then rang for some tea and biscuits.

'You will partake won't you, sir?' he asked as a dumpy woman in her mid-forties brought in a tea tray with bone china cups and a plate of chocolate wheaten biscuits. Teddy nodded impatiently. With studious lack of haste Scudds picked up a biscuit. 'My favourite,' he explained as he examined it as though it were a precious china shard before crunching his false teeth into it.

'Well, are you satisfied?' demanded Teddy running out of patience. Scudds cleared his throat. When he spoke he displayed not one ounce of emotion.

'This is very exciting, sir. Indeed, I am most gratified we now have these reports. However, I have to inform you that at the last meeting of our governors it was agreed that before we can proceed further we must insist on a third independent assessment.'

Teddy burned his throat on his tea. 'What? But that's totally unnecessary. You have now received conclusive evidence from two world-renowned experts, one in America and the other in London, of the authenticity of the booklet. How can you possibly query these people's judgement?'

'I'm sorry to disappoint you, sir, but for us to hand over such a substantial amount of money, and it is a substantial amount of money—' He replaced his half-glasses and peered over them at Teddy. Deep furrows crinkled his pale forehead and his red-rimmed lower lids hung down reminding Teddy of a bulldog. '—the governors have insisted there be another assessment under our conditions.'

Pompous little ass, thought Teddy, his temper rising.

'This is utter balderdash,' he replied glaring at Scudds who, completely unperturbed was sipping his tea, little finger crooked.

Slowly replacing his cup he said, 'Balderdash it may be to you sir, but these are the conditions. The governors have asked Mr Clive Parkin to do the assessment. They regard him firstly as exceptionally highly qualified in this subject and secondly as a completely uninterested third party.'

Teddy nearly choked. His cup rattled in the saucer as he replaced it on the desk. 'Not him, anyone else but him,' he pleaded. 'He of all people is bound to come up with adverse findings.'

'I'm afraid it is out of our hands, sir,' explained Scudds as though talking to a small child. 'Of course, if you do not feel this is appropriate we would naturally understand the need to withdraw your offer. Although it would indeed be a sad day for the Fitz if it came to that.'

Teddy panicked. 'Now come on, Scudds. In fact, I came here especially to say I am happy to accept your last offer. I realise it is quite a drop from the British Museum but I want to ensure that the booklet stays in Cambridge.' His palms were sweating, his smile shaky.

'I am sure the proposal would go down very well with the governors, sir,' Scudds concluded smoothly. 'Pending, of course, the outcome of the independent assessment.'

'Of course—pending the outcome of the assessment.' Teddy left the museum almost foaming at the mouth. To calm himself he went to the Anchor for a pint of bitter where he ran into a group of rowing friends down for some out-of-term coaching. After his third beer he proclaimed loudly that he was giving the booklet away to the Fitz even though the British Museum had offered much more. His admission made him feel very generous and was greeted with raucous hurrahs and clapping and prompted another round of drinks.

After the drink wore off, however, Teddy started feeling sick with nerves. He dropped into Monica's surgery to get some sleeping pills and left feeling much better. His spirits were further boosted when on his arrival back home Alice told him that one of the editors of the *British Geographic* had rung wanting an interview with photos.

Halfway into the second week of the Michaelmas term Teddy got the call he had been waiting for from Henry Scudds. To his intense relief, the results of Clive's report agreed with the other two reports.

'The governors are quite satisfied with Mr Parkin's findings, Mr Turlington sir, and are now happy to accept your offer for the purchase of the bamboo booklet.'

Overjoyed, Teddy dialled home and then remembered with distaste that Alice was in London yet again. Replacing the phone as Marigold answered he hurried across to tell the Master of Trinity, who had been following the whole affair with great interest.

The very first Master of Trinity, dressed in a black gown with an ermine-lined hood, stared hawk-eyed down at Teddy from above the big marble fireplace in the drawing room of the Master's Lodge. The current master, a living replica, swayed back and forth in front of the neatly set unlit fire, his thin shoulders slightly hunched in his dark grey suit, his piercing eyes fixed on Teddy. The room smelt of cigars and furniture polish.

'Magnificent stuff, Turlington. My heartiest congratulations. Mr Scudds informs me the presentation date has been set for the Tuesday after next.' He shook Teddy warmly by the hand. 'While we all acknowledge this is a private sale we would like to make it a very special occasion, with your agreement of course. I know I speak for the other fellows of our college as well as myself when I say your generosity and the honour you are bringing not only to this college but to the entire university in ensuring that this magnificent piece remains in Cambridge has not gone unnoticed.' He looked out of the window at the fluttering autumn leaves, his hands clasped behind his back. 'Mr Scudds told me of your generous decision to make it possible for the Fitz to buy it. As you are aware, the Fitz houses some of the finest ancient manuscripts in the world. Your contribution will sit very well alongside. Congratulations again, my dear chap.' The master then went on to suggest some of the high profile academics of Cambridge and Oxford that Teddy might like to consider inviting to the presentation. 'And of course the Prince of Wales, naturally, as a student of the college,' he ended.

'Naturally,' agreed Teddy. He came away walking on air. Unable to concentrate on his tutorials he dismissed the first year undergraduates early and rushed home. Bursting into the house his jubilation turned to anger as Marigold told him Alice had rung to say she would be staying in London for an extra day. Swearing about wives who didn't know their place he drove off to the local pub leaving Marigold to feed Vicky and Ben.

The morning of the presentation Teddy woke feeling as nervous and excited as the day he had bought his first Austin Healey. Alice was once more in London so, after another argument, they had agreed to meet in town. As Teddy changed into a clean shirt in his college rooms in the early evening, only his shaking fingers gave him away as he struggled with his tie. He was going over his speech, the butterflies mounting in his stomach, as Alice walked in looking stunning in a black silk cocktail dress, his three-strand pearls around her neck emphasising the glow of her creamy skin. Alice gave him a peck on the cheek and squeezed his hand. No-one would have guessed the panic she had been in thirty minutes before as she scrambled into her gown having missed her usual train.

'I'm so proud of you, darling,' she said relaxing finally as they swept up the wide steps of the museum and across the cavernous marble foyer, the precious box containing the bamboo slips clutched in Teddy's hands.

'I'm glad you could find the time to come,' Teddy said curtly. Putting his comment down to nerves Alice merely squeezed his arm.

The drawing room of the museum was packed, the air filled with expectation. Magnificent paintings by Leonardo da Vinci, Michelangelo, Monet and Durer graced the walls around them. Scudds had asked the dress be formal college attire and had raked up every dignitary he could think of from the Vice Chancellor of Cambridge to the Dean of Somerville College Oxford. All the dignitaries of the university were present and some from Oxford too. Also present were the heads of the British Museum and the Victoria and Albert, the President of the British Archaeological Society and of course the entire staff of the Fitzwilliam Museum. The press, too, had been invited. The room was awash with academics in black and red gowns, men in suits and elegantly dressed women. Champagne flowed and waiters moved through the crowd balancing silver trays of smoked salmon and cucumber and asparagus rolls, caviar and melt-in-the-mouth chicken vol au vents. Still very tense, Teddy left Alice chatting with the Prince of Wales and went to check the final details of the formal part of the evening with Scudds. He nearly collided with Clive Parkin coming out of his office. Riding high on the tidal wave of his success for once Teddy acted magnanimously towards the man.

'Evening, Parkin, good to see you here. Did a great job on the report.' Before Parkin had a chance to speak a white-faced Scudds practically fell out of the door into Teddy's arms. Collecting himself almost immediately, he put his hand to his mouth to stifle a nervous cough.

'Good evening, sir, a word please.' His eyes glistened like a madman and his gait was jerky as he led the way back into his office. 'I am afraid I am going to have to cancel tonight's proceedings,' he said almost inaudibly. It was the only way he could keep the husky tremor out of his voice.

Teddy, thinking he had heard wrong, ignored him. 'Scudds, you have excelled yourself.'

He stopped as Scudds, standing too close to him, said this time quite clearly, 'We have to cancel tonight's proceedings.' Teddy stopped, the colour draining from his face. 'I am not prepared to accept the booklet until we have organised a further examination.' Teddy suddenly felt sick.

'Further examination? What are you babbling about, man?'

'Mr Parkin has just informed me that the booklet is almost certainly a fake.' Teddy turned puce. 'Please stay calm, sir. Let me explain.' Scudds took a deep breath; his voice, when he spoke, held only the slightest tremor. 'I have every confidence in Mr Parkin. Having done a thorough examination of the inscription and unable to come up with any definite evidence against the findings he presented his report to us agreeing with the other two testimonies. However, in his own words he did not like the furore surrounding the discovery of the artefact. Everyone wanted to believe it was genuine and in his view no one would look at the possibility of it not being so. It was a close Chinese friend of his who picked the error immediately. A tiny clue all the others in their excitement had missed. Part of one minor character used by the Chinese scribe convinced him it was a forgery. This particular way of expressing the character had not evolved until two hundred years later. Mr Parkin then cross-checked with a known Chinese forgery exposed in the 1930s and found a similar error had occurred, equally difficult to detect, which had ultimately led to its exposure. In his estimation the booklet is only fifty years old.' Teddy looked as though he was going to have an apoplectic fit.

'You're not going to believe any of this gibberish, are you?' gasped Teddy. 'You have written reports from two recognised authorities and you let one man's hysterical jabberings terrify you into believing him.' Waves of panic swept over him.

'We cannot possibly proceed until these doubts have been ironed out.'

Teddy's back was to the door so he didn't see Parkin push the door open a crack and listen, neither was he aware of the gathering press as his rage overtook him.

'You can't be serious. The trumped-up little redbrick nothing! Didn't I tell you?' Scudds backed away as Teddy advanced on him, the box containing the cause of his rage raised menacingly in his face. 'Didn't I tell you he'd come up with adverse findings?' he shrieked, his voice crescendoing close to hysteria. He was drowning in panic. 'Didn't I tell you? He's out to get me, the bloody little creep. He couldn't stand that I'd done something he never had a hope of bettering.'

'I must inform our guests, Mr Turlington,' said Scudds, now shaking with rage himself, his face quite grey, the sweat standing out on his forehead. He tried to pass Teddy but he blocked his way.

'I insist you let me past.' Teddy didn't budge. Clutching the box to his breast he ranted on.

'You don't know what you're doing, you decrepit old man. I should have sold it to the British Museum in the first place instead of wasting my time trying to placate a lot of half-dead dotty old windbags.' Only the flashing of camera bulbs as the press pushed past Parkin and swarmed in thrusting microphones in Teddy's face stopped him. Shutting up abruptly, Teddy fought his way to the door. Shoving Parkin against the bookshelves he stormed back into the drawing room. Grabbing Alice by the wrist he dragged her protesting out into the October chill and roared home leaving everyone gasping.

That night he got solemnly roaring drunk. The next morning, with a colossal hangover, he stared in utter dejection at a picture of himself on the front page of *The Times* shaking the box in Scudds' face under the headline FAKE ARTEFACT REVEALED AT FINAL HOUR. The *Daily Telegraph* shouted CAMBRIDGE DON CAUGHT IN ART FRAUD! The *Daily Sketch* screamed TEARFUL TEDDY THROWS TEMPER TANTRUM.

Alice put her arm out to Teddy across the breakfast table. 'Oh, Teddy darling, I'm so sorry.'

'My reputation is in tatters, Kanga,' croaked Teddy struggling to hold back the tears. 'Why did it have to be that little worm Parkin? I'm the laughing stock of the whole academic world. The master's already been on the phone calling me every name under the sun accusing me of ruining his reputation and the college's reputation and the faculty's reputation. Oh God.' He swallowed some more Alka Seltzer. 'Don't leave me today, Kanga, I can't bear to be alone.'

A knife turned in Alice's breast. She was fighting deadlines herself and if they didn't complete their research within the next two weeks the money would run out. Yesterday they had come so close. The taxi was already honking outside the gate.

'Teddy, I love you. Be strong. I promise I'll ring you as soon as I get to Barts and I'll ring you at lunch and all through the day and every day for the rest of the week. It's crucial I go today, please understand.' Teddy managed a feeble smile as she kissed him and ran out to the waiting taxi.

Once in the lab it was all Alice could do to keep her mind on her work.

'Go and ring him or I won't get a bit of sense out of you for the rest of the week,' ordered Professor Dixson.

Alice rushed off to the phone but their number was engaged. She tried again at the midmorning break but there was no answer. Finally she got through at lunchtime and Marigold told her Teddy had gone out and would not be back until late.

'I think he said it was to do with the Rowing Club but Ben was playing up at the time.'

Alice was relieved that at least Teddy was feeling good enough to face some of his friends. She left a message suggesting he meet her in London for dinner the next night. He rang the Dixsons' house where she was staying at fifteen minutes past midnight saying that he was much better and not to worry, Adrian and Monica had invited him to dinner on Wednesday. 'You and Monica are loyal friends,' she said quietly to Adrian the next time she saw him. 'I don't know that I can help Teddy on my own right now.'

Once over the initial shock of the revelations Alice helped Teddy pick up the threads of his life. In the wake of the calamity she suggested he renegotiate the price with Scudds, which he did, agreeing to less than a tenth of the original offer, and she calmed the Master of Trinity by telling him they had probably got the best example of a forgery in the world. The general public, greedy for more scandal, soon moved on to new headlines once Teddy's fall from grace had run its course.

Alice was now working all week in London only returning at weekends to collapse or bury herself in her studies. Exhausted she walked into the sitting room one Saturday night as Teddy turned on the television to watch his favourite current affairs show and froze as the cameras homed in on Judd Gimbelstein. With increasing horror they both stood mesmerised as his words shattered any remnants of Teddy's reputation.

'Not only is the man a liar, a cheat and a complete idiot as a researcher, he is a coward too.' Alice's eyes were glued unbelieving to the television as Judd Gimbelstein, friend and collaborator, went on to explain how, when he and Teddy were attacked in the Khunjerab Pass, Teddy had left him to die while he saved his own skin. Teddy cringed as Judd described in detail how he had dragged himself, suffering from altitude sickness and dehydration, a bullet wound in his leg, across the stony path through a blistering sandstorm into the cave where Teddy was hiding and how Teddy had made him swear to tell the world that he rescued him or else he would wreck his career.

'This can't be true,' whispered Alice. Teddy's face was ashen.

'I knew with his contacts it was quite possible for him to carry out his threat,' continued Gimbelstein. 'Under pressure sometimes you make bad decisions.'

'You show here a picture of Edward Turlington sporting two black eyes,' said the interviewer. A close-up of the photo followed. 'You say these were your handiwork. How did you find the strength?'

'I don't know, I was just blazing mad. I passed out straight after that. That was when he must have found the booklet.'

'Why did you continue to work together?' asked the interviewer.

'Once I realised what a despicable person I was dealing with I had no desire to be part of his activities. However, making the documentary was a firm agreement that I was not prepared to break. Once that was complete we broke off relations. I had no idea the booklet was a forgery. I am very disappointed for archaeological study.' Judd laughed at the camera. 'Personally, however, it does seem a nice piece of rough justice.'

'So it turns out that you haven't lost very much after all,' concluded the interviewer. Teddy turned off the television. Neither said a word.

'Why did you do it, Teddy?' whispered Alice finally. Teddy couldn't meet Alice's gaze.

'I felt so ashamed. I couldn't think of anything else at the time. I knew if the truth got out that would be the end of me,' said Teddy miserably.

'No, I don't mean that, I mean why did you lock me out? Why did you lie to me? Surely as your wife I could have helped. You could have prepared me for this.' Her voice was barely audible. Teddy ran his hands through his hair.

'It all got so complicated so quickly and you, you're so competent and organised in everything you do.' His haunted eyes searched Alice's face. 'If I could change it all I would, believe me. I was terrified on that pass.' Alice could see how hard it was for him to make this last admission. Her emotions were in turmoil as she watched his torment. 'After Judd passed out I made him comfortable and then started checking out the cave for intruders. I dislodged some stones and fell backwards down into an antechamber. It was obviously part of a rabbit warren of crypts of a ruined Buddhist temple. The booklet was in a half-closed sarcophagus. Now that I think about it, it was too bloody easy to find the damned thing, but I just closed my mind to logic. I wanted to believe it was ancient. I'm no different from all those other so-called experts who got so excited.' He turned away, his shoulders shaking, and wiped his eyes with his hand.

Alice stood stiffly staring at him. So this was the man she had married. The suave handsome outer shell hid a weak, cowardly liar. Now she understood the withdrawal of Judd and Holly from their lives, the angry phone calls, Teddy's refusal to discuss Judd's reaction to the discovery of the booklet. It all came into focus with frightening clarity. How much more of their marriage had been lies? She remembered the perfume on Teddy's shirt she had dismissed as her own insecurity, her concern when she couldn't reach him when he was supposed to be working in Oxford, his selfishness she had refused to acknowledge, his unpredictability.

Teddy shoved his handkerchief in his trouser pocket and turned around.

'I love you, Alice,' he mumbled, crushing her to him. 'I promise you as long as I live I will never lie to you again.'

By early November Alice and the professor were under pressure to come up with results. Already they were four months behind schedule. At ten past six on Wednesday evening, two days before their funding dried up, Alice measured the blood sugar in a control group of mice. Her hands trembled with excitement as she read the results. They were successfully controlling the level of glucose. Bursting into the professor she showed him the results.

'I knew it was possible!' he cried, beside himself with excitement. Together they retested and Alice spent the next five hours writing a draft report. Exhausted but elated Alice leapt onto the late train out of Kings Cross not wanting to waste a moment in telling Teddy. It was after midnight when she reached home. Rushing up the stairs two at a time, uncaring if tonight she woke up the whole household, she flung open the bedroom door, words of excitement bubbling on her lips, and stopped dead in disbelief.

The blankets discarded in a rumpled heap, Monica Slade was writhing naked on top of Teddy.

'Oh Christ!' exclaimed Teddy grabbing for the sheet.

'Bloody hell!' exclaimed Monica leaping off Teddy's naked sweating body and frantically climbing into her knickers.

Alice's blush spread down her neck as she backed away feeling like some peeping Tom. Fearful she might vomit, she clasped her hand to her mouth as she fled downstairs.

Trying to make sense of what she had seen Alice stood twisting her rings, staring blankly at the sitting room's undrawn curtains as Monica, now dressed, rushed past and out of the house. Her stomach churning, Alice vaguely heard Monica's car speed away down the lane as Teddy came slowly into the room. Why? Why? She had tried so hard to be a good wife.

'I thought you weren't coming home until Friday night,' said Teddy accusingly. He poured them both a large brandy.

'We made the breakthrough,' Alice replied flatly. 'I wanted you to be the first to know.' She stared blankly at Teddy as he handed her the smooth tawny liquid as though nothing was wrong. Automatically, her fingers wrapped round the large bulbous glass, the fumes tickling her nose. The glass got as far as her lips and then something inside her snapped. Flinging its contents in Teddy's face she screamed at him, her anger finally unleashed.

'How do I manage it? How do I manage to attract every filthy rotten cheating man? I didn't ask for it. I don't want it and do you know what? This is the last time I'll ever let it happen to me.' Dragging in great gulps of air she continued, no longer caring how much her words hurt. 'How could I have been so blind? That's it, Teddy, I'm leaving you, leaving your tears and your lies and your deceit and your temper tantrums. I'm going home and I'm taking the children with me.' Teddy blanched.

'I say, old girl, that's going a bit over the top, isn't it? Moni and I aren't serious, you know.'

'Over the top! Over the top! This is real life, Teddy. I find you in bed with Monica and I'm over the top.' Her voice had risen to a shriek. How could he hurt her like this and then pretend it was all so trivial? 'What about the perfume on the shirts that wasn't mine or all those weekends away? Who were you with then? When did it start? On our wedding night with Catalina? How many more of them were there? Did you do it with your secretary all those nights you were working in college?'

Defensively Teddy backed away. 'Don't be disgusting. Where were you when I nearly died in China?'

'Disgusting, that's a joke!' scoffed Alice. 'If I had been there, would you have saved me like you did Judd?' Now there was no going back.

'If you leave me I'll kill myself,' said Teddy sitting down suddenly deflated. 'I can't bear to think of life without you.' Alice was too hurt and too angry to heed the warning bells.

'That would be one way to solve my problems,' she flung. 'That sort of rubbish won't rub with me, Teddy, not after this. You don't even have a gun.' Slamming out of the room Alice stumbled upstairs and started searching the attic cupboard for her suitcases, tears blurring her sight. Squeezing past a muddle of dusty boxes she froze as she heard a muffled shot. Quaking with terror she blundered back past the piles of junk.

'Oh God, Teddy I didn't mean it, I didn't mean it,' she whispered hoarsely over and over, almost falling in her panic to get down the stairs. 'Please let him be alive.' The sitting room door was shut. Her hands were trembling so much she couldn't turn the doorknob. When she finally managed to open it she found the room empty. Her chest constricted so she could hardly breathe. Her limbs wouldn't move fast enough as she raced towards his study door. Hurling it open she stared at Teddy standing ashen-faced in the middle of the room, trembling like a leaf, a gun in his hand. Her legs nearly buckled under her with relief. A shattered Dresden figurine lay on the floor beside a priceless picture given to them as a wedding gift by Lord Turlington, now with a gaping tear. In the silence that followed she heard Marigold padding about upstairs.

'Christ, the bloody thing went off in my hand,' stuttered Teddy. 'I wasn't really going to do it, Alice. I just wanted to frighten you so you'd see how much I love you. You can't leave me, Alice darling, Alice I beg you. You don't understand. I was lonely. Everything got too much. I love you, I want you, Alice, I need you.'

'Just like you needed Monica,' replied Alice in disgust. Turning on her heel she walked out of the room.

part three

Chapter Twenty-five

ALICE DROVE THE BATTERED old Falcon stationwagon she had bought for a song in Sydney along the long straight road towards the black soil plains, chatting excitedly to the children and Marigold. Her heart sang as she pointed out familiar landmarks and remarked on changes that had happened in the eight years she had been away from Australia. The vast rolling countryside was scorched as brown and dry as she could remember. Memories flooded back, good memories full of familiar sounds and sights. The brilliant blue cloudless sky lifted her spirits. She welcomed the heat, the strong smell of the countryside that filtered through the windows, the dust, the midge-spattered windscreen they repeatedly had to stop and wipe clean, the sudden uprush of pink-bellied galahs. Even the flies made her feel good. She was home, she was back where she belonged. In a few hours she would be hugging Bea with her magical warming smile and Bea would be hugging the children and they would all be hugging and laughing and crying and telling their stories. Joy welled up inside her. She wanted to shout it to the world. Her roots were here and here she would rebuild her life, nurture her children and teach them to love this vast untameable land as much as she.

'We'll start again, Marigold,' she bubbled. 'This is a whole new life. I'll build my palace here, just like I always dreamed. And you'll love Aunty Bea,' she added for the umpteenth time. 'Oh Marigold, I haven't been this excited for so long. There are so many things I want to show you all, people I want you to meet.' She felt as though a part of her locked away so long she had almost forgotten its existence had suddenly come alive, as though a great weight had rolled off her shoulders.

Poor Teddy. Poor silly, glamorous, weak Teddy. Part of her had loved him at first. It was not his fault he had never captured her heart. He had hurt her with his actions, hurt and angered her, but that anger had turned to resolve. Resolve that she would never again allow a man to distract her from her goals. Firmly she shut her mind to further thoughts of Teddy. That part of her life was over. What lay ahead was what was important. An emu raised its head in a nearby paddock and she pointed it out gleefully to Vicky who squealed with excitement, her nose glued to the window.

Alice sighed, remembering the deep sense of inner peace she had experienced along with her excitement as she stepped off the plane at Mascot Airport clutching Ben in her arms. With each mile closer to Billabrin that sensation deepened. Even the thought of meeting Robert no longer produced the gut-wrenching reaction it once had. She was over him, she convinced herself as they sped through the progressively flattening countryside. She was a wife and mother with two wonderful children and a purpose in life. Theirs had been puppy love, filled with ideals and not much reality.

The road changed from bitumen to dirt and gravel and for the next two hours they bumped and laughed their way along as the light changed and the plains took on a warm glow from the afternoon sunshine. As the shadows lengthened Alice swung left over Harris' Bridge and into the wide streets of Billabrin, drawing up at the familiar hardware store, its freshly painted sign 'R K Downing and Sons 1892' clear above the door. Even before Alice had stopped Aunty Bea was rushing down the garden path and through the tiny wrought iron gate, her arms wide open, her big welcoming smile lighting up the dusk.

'Aunty Bea!' shrieked Alice tumbling out of the car followed by Vicky. Just as she had imagined the two were swallowed up in an enormous hug. Alice promptly burst into tears.

'Alice, darling, it's so good to have you home.' Bea was crying too. 'I would have come to the airport if you'd let me. Vicky darling, let me look at you. You're so pretty!' Happily Alice wiped her eyes, proudly watching her aunt hug her daughter. She felt safe again. Marigold got out with Ben, his reddening face curled up ready to bellow at having been disturbed.

'And this is little Ben,' beamed Bea breaking away and taking the howling child in her arms.

Everyone hugged everyone else all over again and Alice introduced Marigold. Uncle Ray joined them more slowly, his gruff features wrinkling with pleasure at the sight of Alice and her little family. Alice was shocked at how much older he looked and at how stiffly he walked. His watery blue eyes still scanned her critically but the old ferocity was gone. She threw her arms around him and kissed his lined, weather-beaten face. Aunty Bea too looked older than Alice expected and there were worry lines around her eyes and a slight edge to her voice, but her eyes had not lost their glitter nor her smile its brilliance. Alice caught the joy that passed from Bea to Ray as she kissed Ben's chubby cheek.

'Come in and we'll have something to eat. Tea's been ready for hours and this poor darling needs a change,' said Bea brightly, jiggling Ben up and down. Ben stopped bellowing, big eyes watching this stranger with suspicion. 'My golly, he's like his Uncle Ben,' Bea exclaimed.

Buddy, now a burly twenty-eight-year-old and the only one still living at home, appeared from the back of the house. He gave Alice a punch on the arm and proudly showed her a healing scar from a shearing accident. Alice gave him a hug.

'He's doing very well,' said Bea proudly nodding at her son. 'He was gun shearer last year. Beat the lot of them, even the experts. His father couldn't believe it. Sheared two hundred and three sheep in one day.'

Tea was filled with light chatter and news about what had been happening with the family and around the district. Paddy was working up in Queensland and Billy had gone overseas. Dan had got married and Don had a steady girlfriend. Katie popped in when she could but life at Wangianna was very hectic. Bea carefully kept to all the cheerful news. After they had finished and cleared away and Ray had disappeared with Vicky to see the tame possum, Bea turned to Alice.

'Are you coping all right, sweetie? Have you got enough money?'

'Oh Bea, you're always so thoughtful,' smiled Alice. She shifted Ben who was getting fractious again. It had been a long journey and the change from freezing temperatures to thirty-five degree heat, although welcome, was debilitating. Suddenly Alice felt terribly tired. She could hear Vicky starting to get overexcited. Any minute now there would be tears. Marigold, knowing the strain Alice had been under over the past few weeks and excited to be in Australia, offered to put the children to bed.

'I'll be all right,' said Alice shaking her head.

'You sit tight, sweetie. Marigold and I can manage,' said Bea firmly.

Alice smiled gratefully. 'I'll come and give them a goodnight kiss, Aunty Bea.'

'Come on, little one,' said Bea scooping up Ben and heading for the bathroom. She worried at the black smudges under Alice's eyes. The girl was so thin. The sudden unexplained end of her marriage was as much a shock to Bea as it had been to Alice.

Goodnight kisses over and the children settled, Bea and Alice returned to the verandah. Marigold had decided to go to bed and Ray had moved to another part of the verandah. The pungent smell of his tobacco wafted across the hot evening air nudging at Alice's memories as she listened to the sounds of the bush and noisy singing of the cicadas. It felt so good just to be.

After a while Bea asked quietly, 'Do you want to tell me about it?'

Alice stood up and walked to the verandah edge. Running her fingers along the newly painted rail, she stared out across the countryside she had missed so desperately, her stiffened back showing the tension she had tried to hide. She stood still for so long that Bea thought she had forgotten the question. When she turned around her eyes were glistening with tears.

'I tried to make it work,' she whispered. Her shoulders sagged and she poured out the whole ghastly series of events that had led to the breakdown of her marriage.

When she had finished Bea hugged Alice tight wishing she could do more to alleviate her misery. 'There is no shame in what you did and you've got two beautiful children.'

Angrily Alice dashed away unwanted tears. 'It won't ever happen again, Bea. I'll make sure of that,' she said grimly, showing a glimmering of the fighting spirit Bea remembered so well.

Bea smiled. 'I think I'll go and put the jug on and we'll have a nice fresh cuppa.'

Alice's smile lit up her tired face. 'I haven't heard those words for so long. I've missed you so much, Aunty Bea. I've missed you all so much.'

'What amazes me is that amongst all of this you managed to come home with the children,' said Bea returning with more tea and fruitcake. 'How on earth did you manage it? Forgetting Teddy for a moment, how did you get round Lady Turlington? I know I would never have allowed my grandchildren to disappear across the other side of the world without a fight.'

Alice gave a sharp laugh. 'She tried at first, but you've met her, you know what she's like. She's more interested in her horses than her grandchildren. Once she saw that she would very likely end up bringing them up as well as paying for their education, she backed away.'

'And Teddy?' asked Bea holding Alice's hand tight. Alice looked away determined not to cry again.

'He never really wanted kids. He loved them because they were there.'

'But this Monica woman, she's got a child hasn't she?'

Alice nodded. 'Phillip spends most of his time with his dad and the racehorses,' she explained. 'And when he turns eight he'll be packed off to boarding school. At least I don't have to fight Teddy over that for Ben.' She picked at the crumbs on her plate. 'We agreed that either Teddy would fly out once every six months or the children could go back to England to see their dad once they're older.'

'So he could be out here in July?' Bea bristled.

'Actually, I don't think he'll do anything about it—it's all too hard—and anyway at present he's flat broke.'

'How can someone with his background be broke?' asked Aunty Bea amazed.

'Very easily. He's hopeless with money because he's never had to learn. Whenever we ran into trouble Lady T fished us out. It made me feel so inadequate.' Alice pleated the table cloth. 'I loved him but I think I always knew deep down that he'd never grow up.' Aunty Bea sighed and patted Alice's arm.

'What are you going to do now you are home?' asked Bea biting into a piece of fruitcake.

'I'm going to build my palace,' said Alice grinning.

'Still my determined Alice, aren't you?' said Bea relieved to see a glimmer of her old sparkle. 'How are you going to do that and with what?'

Alice moved closer to her aunt. Clasping her roughened hands in her own, she explained her plans to build her own sheep stud farm, her enthusiasm mounting as she spoke.

'And you'll do it too, if I know you,' said Bea. 'Mind you, there'll be a few disapproving diehards you'll have to work around, but you can be sure you'll have my support and Ray's.'

The time just slipped away as the two talked on. Finally Bea got stiffly out of her chair stifling a yawn. 'It's so good to have you back. I could sit here talking all night but you'd better get some shut-eye if you want to be fresh for all these people you plan to see.' Alice kissed her aunt fondly and went to bed.

The next day Bea organised for her and Alice to visit her bank manager and a real estate agent.

When Alice and Teddy had formally agreed to separate he had insisted that she keep all the jewellery he had ever given her which, over the years they had been married, had amounted to quite a pile. Although she was still smarting from Teddy's betrayal she had not been able completely to crush him so she had agreed, even to keeping the engagement ring she had tried to hand back, although she had informed him she would sell it to pay for their fares to Australia. It had fetched a fair price, leaving her with a little bit of cash on her arrival in Australia which paid for the stationwagon. The wedding ring she had decided to wear for the moment as a protective measure. The rest, while not a vast fortune, she knew would help when she needed a loan.

The bank manager, Albert Munro, having heard Alice's story and listened to her plans, shook his head at Bea. After Bea assured him she and Ray would stand as guarantors and Alice explained she had a little capital of her own, he agreed to give Alice a small loan but only because she was Bea's niece.

The real estate agent had two properties he reckoned were the sort of thing that would suit Alice and were within her price range. Alice made a time to go and see them later in the week, then she rang Fraser Bowen.

Fraser, surprised and delighted to hear Alice's voice, immediately suggested she come out to the property, offering to fly in to collect her. Bea insisted on being allowed to take charge of the children. Firmly she shoved both Alice and Marigold out of the door. Feeling much more optimistic, Alice jumped into the ute with Marigold and they headed out towards the airstrip, the two young women chatting nineteen to the dozen as Alice pointed out places and told her tales.

'You'll love Fraser, he's like a great cuddly bear except he's all muscles,' explained Alice. 'I don't think there's a girl in Billabrin didn't fancy him at some stage.'

Fraser was waiting next to the four-seater they used as regular transport, his big bushy hat pushed back from his forehead, canvas protectors covering his socks and boots at the end of strong brown legs. Alice introduced Marigold explaining that she definitely wasn't a whingeing Pom; in fact she was here to stay if they didn't all scare her off. Fraser flashed brilliant white teeth in a sunburned face and helped them into the plane. The years Alice had been away evaporated as they climbed into the sky and headed northwest. Two and a half hours later they landed on the Bowen property. Alice's heart turned over as she saw the old petrol pump still the same as she remembered. The terrible journey to save Robert's life might have been yesterday.

When Fraser had agreed to keep Alice's two sheep all those years ago he hadn't thought it right that he keep everything he made from breeding from them and selling, so without telling anyone he kept ploughing half the money from sales back into breeding with top quality rams to keep the strain going, just in case Alice came home. He had never forgotten the way Alice had saved Robert's life, nor understood how two people so unmistakably in love could have parted so abruptly. It pained him to watch his friend Bluey struggling in a marriage that was obviously not working. Now Alice had returned he was really glad of his decision.

'You've done well with your two little'uns. Your cousin's young fellah comes over and gives me a hand now and then,' said Fraser cheerfully as they strode towards the holding pens behind the homestead. 'He's a great little lad Stewwy. Just like his dad. I wouldn't mind a son like that.'

'Are you getting broody by any chance?' joked Alice not wanting to talk about Robert and Katie.

'I might be, then again I might not,' he grinned in reply. 'What'd you make of Australia, miss?' he touched his hand to his hat.

'Marigold, silly,' giggled Alice. 'Give her a chance. She's only been here five minutes.'

'What I've seen I love,' replied Marigold shyly, blushing to the roots of her hair.

Fraser shifted the gate and led them into a pen containing twenty young ewes. In the next pen were three big merino rams.

'These are some of the best ewes I've bred from your original two lambs,' he said proudly. 'Strong healthy beasts. Carry some of the best merino wool I've seen around in years.' He grabbed one of the ewes and pulled back the wool showing Alice the quality. 'Mind you, I think you're mad getting into wool growing right now the way prices are plummeting and folks being forced to buy in feed.'

'So you're happy for me to buy them back off you?' asked Alice confidently ignoring his last comment.

'Well no, Alice, to tell the truth, I'm not,' Fraser replied straight-faced. Alice looked stunned at his comment and then exploded with rage in her disappointment.

'Okay, so why the bloody hell did you drag me all the way out here just to tell me that?' Fraser put his hand on her shoulder, his brown eyes boring into hers. Alice tried to shrug him off but his grip tightened.

'Listen, fiery lady, there's no way I'm bloody taking money off any sheila.

I'm giving them back. Me blood wouldn't be worth bottling if any of me mates found out I'd made you pay, and that's something I'm real proud of—the quality of me blood, that is.' He stepped back, his face splitting in a broad grin. Alice was ready to punch him.

'You're impossible!' she exclaimed calming down. 'But I can't just take them.'

'You can and you will. You've got far more problems ahead of you than worrying about accepting sheep from me if you're serious in setting up this stud farm you keep talking about. The way things are now d'you realise how hard it's going to be?' Alice went to hug him but he pushed her away. 'Now, none of that soppy stuff. This is a man to man business deal we're talking here, d'you understand?' Then he crushed her in his big arms and kissed her on both cheeks. 'I owe you one, little Alice, remember?'

Alice finally decided on a small property northeast of Billabrin with a tumbledown shack of a house on the edge of the black soil plains. Although the house was large it was in a pretty disastrous state but it was all Alice could afford. With her usual optimism she believed it could be turned into something good over time. Of greater importance was the quality of the land. Given a good rainfall, at least half of it was excellent sheep grazing pasture. The other half was fair. The rainfall had been well below the expected average for the past three years and the place was dry and dusty. The previous owners, having arrived in a boom year and inexperienced in survival farming techniques in the Australian outback, had walked off the property in despair.

Coming out of the real estate agency in Coonamble with Vicky and Marigold in tow, happily clutching the signed papers, Alice bumped into Katie struggling with nine-year-old Stewart over a new jacket.

'You'll wear it because I say so,' screamed Katie.

'Hello Katie,' said Alice in surprise. Katie's blonde hair, now cut in a flattering shoulder-length style, had been freshly done and she was wearing a fetching cotton dress. Alice was amazed at how pretty she looked, only the expression on her face marred the effect.

Katie looked up, stopped, turned dead white and then bright pink.

'Alice,' she stuttered, nervously glancing back up the street.

'How are you?' asked Alice turning to introduce Vicky and Marigold.

'I'm fine. I'd heard you were back. We've been terribly busy. How's Mum?' replied a flustered Katie grabbing Stewart by the arm and ignoring Vicky and Marigold. Alice's heart sank at Katie's animosity.

'Aunty Bea's fine,' she replied smiling at the young boy. 'Hello, you must be Stewart.' Stewart continued to stuff the new jacket into the smart department store plastic bag.

'Say hello to your Aunty Alice,' demanded Katie shaking his arm.

Stewart looked up sullenly.

'Hello.'

'We've got to go,' said Katie quickly. Gripping her new leather handbag so tight her knuckles glowed white, she turned to Alice. 'And don't think you can come flaunting your nannies and ramming your children down my and Robbo's throat. The three of us are fine as we are, thank you.' Turning on her heel she dragged the unhappy Stewart down the street leaving Alice and Marigold stunned at her attack.

At the end of the street Katie grabbed a tall man and hurried him across the street. Alice's heart started pounding against her ribs. She would have known that back from a thousand miles. He half-turned to greet Katie and Alice's knees turned to water. As she caught sight of his handsome face the ache in her heart intensified. Shocked at her own reaction she turned quickly and walked in the opposite direction. Gone were any illusions that her feelings were under control. She could not fool herself. Disgusted she realised she was still in love with Robert McIain.

'She's a very grumpy lady,' said a small voice. Alice squeezed Vicky's hand and slowed down.

'Your aunty's a busy lady, sweetie. Let's go home and tell Aunty Bea about our new home.' Still trembling from the impact of seeing Robert, Alice was trying to gather her thoughts. She waved the title deeds at Marigold with determined cheerfulness. 'Then we'll start working on Uncle Ray. If he won't wield a hammer I'm sure he'll lend us one.'

Uncle Ray was only too happy to get stuck into fixing up Alice's new home. Nearly sixty-five he had reduced his own workload and now used contractors for many of his jobs. His back gave him periods of considerable pain but working on Alice's house in his own time gave him immense satisfaction, soothing some of the disappointment of being unable to contribute to his own daughter's life. Katie had shut them out as much as she could without actually severing ties altogether.

Within six months Alice's place looked entirely different. The roof and verandah were mended and repainted, the dry wilderness of a garden dug over and replanted with a few hardy species that struggled against the drought. The property fences still needed attention but the inside of the house sparkled with simple polished pine furniture from second-hand shops and castoffs from friends of the Downings. Uncle Ray had bought a bright new green and red play gym for Vicky and Ben which sat in the backyard and glaringly refused to melt into the Australian landscape. Because the property was quite a distance from Billabrin he had also checked that the old pedal radio in the back room was in good working order.

'Looks more like a palace every day,' joked Ray with satisfaction as Alice defiantly banged the last nail into the wooden plank bearing the name 'MerryMaid Stud'. 'Never was sure about names and you. That'll start tongues wagging,' he added nodding at her handiwork.

'No point having some wishywashy name no one remembers,' retorted Alice, laughter in her brilliant blue eyes. Ray gave her an unexpected squeeze.

As the months passed, Alice slipped into the yearly program demanded of a sheep breeder. Because of money restrictions Alice had decided initially she would invest in a mixture of breeds. Taking advantage of the drought-depressed prices, she stretched herself financially as tight as she dared, taking out two further loans from the bank, with Bea and Ray once more standing guarantor, and bought as much stock as she could afford. Ignoring the jeers and prognosis of other property owners who, also struggling against the effects of the drought, predicted she would shortly go under, Alice built her stock up to two hundred.

Gratefully she accepted Fraser's advice at the sheep sales and listened to his suggestion that she look at a method of hoarding feed as a safety measure against the drought persisting longer than anticipated. While she got much of the stock at rock-bottom prices many were in poor condition needing time and quality feed to build them up to good wool producers and not all of them were suitable to breed from. It was a start but sometimes she wondered if she were merely digging a hole to bury herself. The work was long, arduous and never-ending. Each day brought with it the reminder that she had minimum equipment, vehicles and manpower, problems with water and feed and constant pressing bills. Without Bea and Ray's support and Fraser's knowledge she wondered if she would have had the courage to keep going.

The first lamb drop was due towards the end of June and Alice was waiting to see what range of quality it would produce before she decided whether to build up a variety of well-known strains or create her own special line. Some days, having spent all day working on fences or struggling with sheep or tending to all the small jobs she knew must be done to ensure the property's survival, she fell into bed so exhausted that she doubted she would have the energy to rise the next day. At other times she read into the small hours poring over her books on sheep husbandry, knowing the next day would be harder because of her lack of sleep.

The outlook was bleak. Wool prices continued to fall. Money drained away faster than she expected on the ever-rising cost of feed. But Alice refused to let go of her optimism. Out back, she had long ago learned, there were the good times and the bad times. Failure, in her book of rules, was not a consideration. The only thing that niggled constantly at her was Robert. So far she had been so busy running the property that their paths hadn't crossed. However, sooner or later if she was really going to build her top class stud farm she was bound to run into him at a sale or a show. He too was always looking for top quality animals.

'The sheep aren't the only tarts that are stubborn around here, begging your pardon, Alice,' announced Fraser on one of his regular visits. He admired Alice's guts and used the pretext of seeing how 'his' ewes were progressing to check how she was coping. He had also fallen in love with Marigold although as yet had made no move towards doing anything about it. 'It's about time you got rid of some of that pride and got some more help.'

Alice was rounding up the ewes for crutching. 'With what, Fraser? My friendship with Mr Munro is stretched to the limit and the price of feed has just gone up again.' She rubbed the back of her arm across her sweaty forehead brushing away wisps of jet black hair made wilder and more unruly by the dust and wind.

'You're not seriously considering doing the crutching yourself, are you?'

'Well they aren't exactly lining up outside the door and I can't afford to pay anyone.'

'I'll have a word with a couple of mates,' promised Fraser.

Two days later a young thick-set Aborigine rolled up onto the property drinking from a beer bottle. Alice's eyes narrowed as he sauntered across the paddock towards her.

'The boss said to come here,' announced the young man taking another swig and rolling his eyes in her direction.

'If this is Fraser's idea of a joke I'm not laughing,' said Alice fingering her car keys and judging the distance to the stationwagon.

'The boss said you'd need help fixing up them fellas,' he waved his bottle at the mob in the pen. Alice had been up since before dawn and was in no mood to deal with some stranger drunk on her property. She took a risk.

'If it was Fraser who sent you and you're serious about wanting to work here get rid of that for a start.' She pointed to the beer bottle. Her eyes flashed dangerously. The black fella took another swig watching her out of the corner of his eye.

'You must be Miss Alice. Me dad said if I got you a little bit mad I could make your eyes flash real bright just like they did when I was little.' His black mouth split in a toothy white grin and he held out his hand. Alice's jaw dropped.

'Jimmy? Melon's Jimmy?'

'That's me. Mr Bowen told him you needed some help, so Dad sent me.' He held the beer bottle upside down. 'Orange juice, miss.'

'Well, I'll be blowed.' Alice burst out laughing. 'The crafty old so and so. I didn't recognise you. Last time I saw you you only came up to my knees.'

Jimmy started working for Alice straightaway and with extra help from a jillaroo happy to work for board and experience only, plus Buddy and a couple of mates as shearers and Fraser chipping in with advice, Alice scraped her way through to the end of her first year on MerryMaid Stud. However, while she rejoiced at her success, many muttered at two young women living on their own with two small children miles from anywhere. Bea tried to dismiss her unease at this criticism of Alice's endeavours to break into this man's world as idle prattle of mischief makers but it worried her. Alice simply ignored the gossipmongers refusing to allow them to divert her from her goal. She had a five-year plan mapped out, and while it might take time and energy, she was building her dream.

Chapter Twenty-six

GEORGE LEFT KATIE at the Toorak residence after the last guest had departed and sauntered down the steps in the cool August air to the waiting car. The chauffeur needed no instructions. He turned the car towards Maggie's apartment. The evening had gone well. Katie as usual had been the glittering hostess dazzling all the guests with her easy chatter and stunning Paris outfit. It was easy to see how bewitched the men became in her company. For him, though, he preferred riper fruit. There was a tartness about Katie that had never really appealed, he thought as he stepped from the car and turned the key in Maggie's front door.

Maggie was waiting for him with open arms. At fifty she still exuded warmth and excitement. Tonight she looked particularly ravishing and smelt utterly enticing. After a single brandy each they retired into the bedroom. Carefully laying his consummation cigar, as Maggie jokingly called it, on the bedside table, they tumbled into the big double bed. Their lovemaking was as warm and satisfying as it had ever been. Afterwards Maggie lay dreamily gazing out at the darkened world thinking about the strange life she led with this man. Cosily she nudged him.

'Don't tell me it was that good,' she said waiting for George to reach for his cigar. He didn't stir. She reached over and turned out the light then and was asleep within seconds. At ten past four she woke up wondering why she was so cold. She cuddled up against George and then drew away quickly. He was freezing. Unable to find his pyjama top in the dark and knowing his proneness to chills she turned on the light to look for it. Then she saw the ghastly grey of his skin. Anxiously she felt his cheek. It was icy cold. Gently she shook him.

'George darling, are you all right?' There was no reaction. Maggie shook him again, this time more ferociously. Her hand shook as she felt for a pulse in his neck watching for the natural rise and fall of his chest. Neither was there. 'Oh God, no, please no,' she whispered unbelieving. Jumping out of bed Maggie paced up and down the room rubbing her arms and trying to think what to do first. Grabbing the phone with shaking fingers she dialled her friend's number, biting her long red thumbnail as she waited for the answer at the other end. It came.

'Fay, it's me Maggie. Oh God . . . George is dead.' Maggie was frantic. 'I just woke up and found him like that. What am I supposed to do?'

Her friend, who only lived two blocks away, was over within five minutes. After one look at George, Fay rang her doctor and then made the shaking Maggie a warm sweet drink. She was trembling almost as much herself. The doctor arrived half an hour later.

'He's had a massive heart attack,' the doctor informed Maggie as she stood in her dressing gown, arms crossed, unable to stop shivering despite the warmth of the room.

'But there was no warning. He was so healthy. He never once mentioned chest pains or anything.' She slumped down in the chair clasping her quivering hands to her haggard face, unable to think of anything except that her darling George had gone.

The doctor gave her a mild sedative and said, 'Given who he is, although there are no suspicious circumstances, I am going to have to inform the police. They will then inform his next of kin.' Maggie nodded like a zombie.

'What are you going to do now?' asked Fay.

Maggie shook her head. 'I don't know, Fay,' she whispered, 'he was my life.'

Neither of them had ever considered their passionate affair could end. They had been like two children constantly on holidays. Irresponsible maybe, but oh how happy. For years Maggie had blocked out that other part of George's life. George had rarely mentioned it and they rarely disagreed about anything. She was his love in Melbourne. Only for short bearable bursts had she been excluded from his life. Now suddenly she was having to face life alone. She felt utterly terrified. Maybe if she shut her eyes it would all go away.

Elizabeth was in one of the sheds with the vet examining three of their top ewes when Robert brought the news. Numb with shock she went to the bedroom, locked the door and stared at the wall. When she had finally realised that she could not cry she combed her hair, went into the office and rang up the family solicitor Stanley Fenton in Melbourne. Replacing the phone she went back out to recheck the ewes. Anything to take her mind away from the thought that George had died in his mistress' bed. George's body was flown out of Melbourne later that day and laid out in the local mortuary.

Shortly before ten on Saturday morning Stanley Fenton drove up the long dusty road to the Wangianna homestead. Robert was on the verandah to greet him. He was surprised to see not one but three people step out of the car. Accompanying the solicitor was a woman elegantly dressed in black, a velvet dotted veil on her fashionable wide-brimmed hat concealing her face. A fair-haired young man in a suit and tie walked beside the woman, his hand solicitously placed under her elbow. Robert guessed the woman to be a few years younger than his mother and the man to be about the same age as he was.

'G'day Mr Fenton,' said Robert soberly as the three stepped onto the verandah.

'G'day, Robert. I'm sorry we meet again under such sad circumstances,' nodded Stanley Fenton. He turned to his companions. 'I don't know if you have met Mrs Holt and—' Robert nodded to the pair quickly, interrupting the solicitor, annoyed. 'I thought it was just family members.'

'Your father instructed they be present,' replied Fenton dismissively. 'Why don't we just get on with things.'

Robert led them into the big dining room where the whole family was assembled around the red cedar dining table. Elizabeth stepped forward from her place at the head of the table to greet the solicitor. Beside her was an empty seat for Robert with Katie on his right. The two younger sons Ian and Jordie sat opposite with their sister Sarah. Stewart sat next to his mother, glaring at the world, sweltering in the formal suit and tie she had insisted he wear.

'Stanley! So good of you to come all this way at such short notice,' greeted Elizabeth, her eyes flicking quickly over the two visitors.

'Elizabeth my dear, not at all. I only wish I was here on a less painful duty. It was, as you know, your husband's wish that his will be read within forty-eight hours of his death,' began Fenton placing his large briefcase on the table as Robert showed the two visitors to their seats and then sat down stiffly next to Katie.

'We were all shocked at the suddenness of his passing. George was a very fine man.' Elizabeth accepted Stanley's peck on the cheek, studiedly ignoring his companions. 'I suggest we get this over and done with as quickly as we can,' he said slightly nervously. The veiled woman had not sat down. Clutching her black suede purse tightly to her breast she spoke directly to Elizabeth.

'If I could have avoided causing you this extra pain, I would have,' she said huskily, stumbling over her words. 'I only came because they insisted I had to be here. I assure you that after today you need never bother about me ever again.' Refusing to acknowledge the woman, Elizabeth returned to the head of the table. Trembling, Mrs Holt sat down. The young man leaned across and whispered something in her ear.

'What are they doing here? They're not family.' Katie asked Robert in a loud voice. Robert gave her knee a sharp nudge.

'Shut up. I'm not sure but I think she was Dad's mistress,' he whispered.

'Yes, why are they here?' asked Ian belligerently. Robert stole a glance at his mother, cursing Katie's tactlessness under his breath. Elizabeth's controlled expression gave nothing away.

'Everyone who has to be present before this will can be read is now present. Would you allow me to proceed according to George's wishes,' said the solicitor sternly. Ian and Jordie started objecting. Firmly the solicitor interrupted. 'I do not wish to get into any arguments at this point. The late Mr McIain requested that no statement be made by any person present until completion of the reading of the will, at which time it will be clear to all what is to happen. Do you wish me to proceed, Elizabeth?' There was a sudden hush.

'I don't really know what's going on but I certainly don't want us all to start quarrelling,' replied Elizabeth. 'If those were my husband's instructions then I think you had best get on with it.'

'Are you sure this is all proper, Robert?' hissed Katie.

'You heard what the man said,' whispered Robert testily. 'Let's get this over and done with so we can all get on with our lives again.' Katie scowled at Robert. Pouring himself a glass of water with great deliberation, Stanley Fenton took a sip and started to read.

'I am hereby charged to read the last will and testament of Mr George Albert Robert McIain on this day Saturday twenty-eighth of August 1971.' The tension in the room increased.

George had described exactly how he wanted all his possessions to be divided, right up to the last detail. To Katie he had left the sum of four thousand dollars and an antique chaise longue. To Elizabeth he had given her life-long entitlement to live at Wangianna, the town house in Toorak, the town house in Perth and a number of paintings and other investments as listed, all of which ensured she was financially secure for the rest of her days. To his sons Robert and Ian he had apportioned twenty-five per cent each of Wangianna as detailed on an enclosed map and twenty per cent to his youngest son Jordie. Sarah was left another house in Melbourne and a sum of four hundred thousand dollars. The property in Perth was divided up in the same way between the boys. Fenton took another sip of water, took off his glasses and mopped his brow. Replacing his glasses he continued.

'"To my eldest son Andrew—"'

'What!' exclaimed the family members as one.

Stanley Fenton looked across at the astounded faces. Katie went grey. 'May I remind you of the deceased's wishes. There will be plenty of time for discussion,' he said formally. 'Please bear with me, Mrs Holt,' he added, gently restraining Maggie as she attempted to leave. He repeated, '"To my eldest son Andrew I leave thirty per cent of the property Wangianna, financial investments as listed and my ivory paper knife. Unless formally agreed by all parties and legally documented, the said property Wangianna will continue to operate as one entity. I also request that at this point Appendix B be read."' Fenton looked apologetically at Elizabeth. Only the tight set of her jaw gave away her tension as she nodded. Appendix B was dated May 16, 1970.

'"My darling Maggie, I am so sorry to have to put you through all this emotional distress but I wanted you to know that I have finally faced up to my duty as a father. By your presence when my will is read I am assured our son will finally receive the recognition I was too cowardly to give him while I was alive."' As one the McIain clan stared at Mrs Holt, then her son and finally at Elizabeth. Shrinking back in her seat, Maggie fought back the tears. Elizabeth, ramrod straight in her chair, did not flicker an eyelid.

'"Andrew Holt is the only son of my union with Margaret and as my eldest son by two years is entitled to his rightful inheritance. I feel that in not acknowledging him as my son I have done both him and Margaret a great wrong which I now wish to put right. His mother has never once uttered one word of complaint at my refusal to recognise our son in public although I did ensure that he received a proper education. What I would never give him was the respectability I know she craved for him as my son and heir. To rectify this I have bequeathed Andrew the greatest portion of Wangianna which he will inherit on my death.

'"To you, Maggie my darling, I leave the apartment that we have shared for so long with so much love, and a stipend that will see you financially secure for the rest of your days on this earth. Elizabeth, I have always admired you and respected you and I have loved all our children. I have seen to it you will not suffer. I know you will see that my wishes are carried out to the final detail. I love you Maggie. God take care of you all. George."'

There followed a stunned silence. Elizabeth had turned deathly white. Robert went to her and laid his hands on her shoulder.

Katie was the first to speak. Confused by all the figures and missing the crucial point she cried, 'Robert still gets Wangianna, doesn't he? He has to, he's the eldest son.' Her voice was strangely high-pitched. Catching Elizabeth's disapproving glance, she turned on the solicitor to cover her own indiscretion. 'I really don't think it suitable that we have some unknown clerk taking notes about our family affairs.' Startled, Fen ton opened his mouth to reply but Elizabeth beat him to it.

'Be quiet, Katie dear, I believe our unknown clerk, as you put it, might have something to say or maybe his mother does.' All eyes focused once more on Maggie. Under their hostile gaze Maggie flushed bright red. With trembling fingers she pushed back her veil appealing to Elizabeth.

'I had no idea.' Her voice was almost inaudible. The electric silence that followed was shattered by the scraping of wood on polished wood as Maggie's son stood up. He exuded an arrogant confidence. Maggie gave a stifled sob.

'It's time for the whole truth, Mum,' he said, shifting his gaze back to the sea of shocked faces. Robert was still standing behind his mother and she reached up and clasped his hand as Andrew continued. 'Yes, I am George Mclain's eldest son. Our father fell in love with my mother when she was eighteen but our grandfathers, because of their own perverse snobbery, forbade the marriage. I was the result of that love.' His voice reverberated around the room. Maggie was now crying openly. 'Two years after my birth my father married your mother Elizabeth Mclain and for seven years no one spoke of my father and he never had any contact of any kind with my mother. She bore her pain alone.' He stared directly at Elizabeth. Her clasp tightened around Robert's hand, but her eyes met his gaze unflinching.

'It was only after he was thrown out of his wife's bed that he started seeing my mother again.' For a moment Andrew had to pause. 'My mother told me who my father was when I was seventeen, when she thought she could trust me not to do something impetuous and foolish. It is only through respect for her wishes that I have kept silent, but many times I wanted to shout the truth. I loved him. I wish I had never been told he was my father. I learned I was the bastard of a bastard who thought lavish apartments and expensive schooling could make up for the cowardly refusal to marry the woman he claimed he loved and to acknowledge his own son. For that I will never forgive him, nor will I forgive the pain he caused my mother. For too long she has worried more about the damage the disclosure of my existence would do to this family than about her own happiness.'

No one uttered a word for thirty seconds then Maggie stood up, a handkerchief pressed to her trembling mouth, tears streaming down her face.

'The bastard's finally paid his dues, Mum,' finished Andrew. But Maggie didn't hear—she had already stumbled blindly from the room.

The following Monday, dead tired after having been up again the previous night taking shifts with Jimmy and the jillaroo at trying to catch a wild dog that had been terrorising the district, Alice sat down to cheer herself up by listening in on the morning galah session on the radio while Ben pottered unsteadily about under her feet. Marigold was working on basic reading skills with Vicky, a job the two women took turns in. The bush telegraph had been working overtime and everyone was talking about George McIain's sudden heart attack and the repercussions at Wangianna. Alice helped herself to a piece of stale cake and listened.

'Terrible business. Took him with no warning. They're talking of splitting up the property. It's a real tragedy. That Bluey, he's a good boy and he knows a thing or two on how to run the place, but it's Elizabeth I feel sorry for. She's been the backbone of that place since she and George were newlyweds. We all knew about his little escapades in Melbourne but she was never one to grumble. Just got on and coped like the rest of us. Now some blow-in turns up with his grand city talk, flaunting university degrees as long as your arm, for all the good it'll do him, threatening to turn the whole place upside down. Wangianna is her life. She must be devastated, poor woman. Fancy finding out your husband's got a child that's older than your first. I dunno as I'd cope.'

Alice got onto the line to Aunty Bea.

'Is it true?'

'Yes, luv, Katie's in a terrible state. She stayed with us last night. She's talking about them maybe having to move out of Wangianna altogether. I'm sure she must be exaggerating but she's terribly upset. Could you come over? I know you two don't always get on but I thought maybe as her cousin you can knock some sense into her. It'll only be her. Stewart's at home with his dad. She made me promise not to tell anyone but can you imagine keeping something like that quiet around here? What a mess.'

Alice's heart went out to Robert. He had once told her that if he lost Wangianna it would be like cutting off an arm. For Bea's sake she promised to come over for tea, although she had no doubt as to the reception she would receive from Katie.

'You know what you oughta do?' said Jimmy later as he drove another fence post into the ground.

'What's that Jimmy?'

'You oughta buy that city fella out. You've got more up here about sheep than he'll ever have,' he said tapping his head.

'They won't split up Wangianna, Jimmy. That's just all talk. Anyway, what would I use for money, bits of bark?' laughed Alice more brightly than she felt. If only she could. Her overdraft was increasing at an alarming rate and there was no sign of the drought breaking. If the rains didn't come soon, she might be the one selling MerryMaid to Wangianna.

Chapter Twenty-seven

NOT EVEN ROBERT knew how devastated Elizabeth was. She had spent the whole of her married life building up and managing the property, coping where George failed, even mentally preparing herself to take over when he died. Her security had been the knowledge that Robert would eventually take over. In a matter of minutes the very foundations of her life had been destroyed. Struggling to cope with the fact that she no longer had any control over the running of a place she had loved for so many years, she also had to accept the ultimate insult—that the majority share holding of Wangianna had been snatched away from her eldest son and handed over to her husband's bastard. But Elizabeth was a proud woman. Refusing to allow any of this to crush her, she buried her pain and did her best to welcome Andrew into the bosom of the family.

Once Ian had got over the shock of having a half-brother he quickly worked out that if he, Andrew and Jordie clubbed together Robert would have no hope of being able to control what went on. He pointed this out to Jordie who had also reached the same conclusion.

'Cotton!' they said simultaneously, slapping right hands together in the air.

Robert had no intention of ganging up with anyone. He was deeply wounded by his father's actions and could barely bring himself to speak to Ian. He was also furious at the way his father had treated his mother and said so to her face.

'What good will anger do us? I loved him, Robby, and what he has done cannot take that away from me. But I knew the man I married.' She looked pale and drawn from sleepless nights.

'But this bloody blow-in doesn't have a rat's tail of an idea how to run a place like this.'

'Andrew is your half-brother, Robby. You will show him some respect and you and I will have to teach him,' Elizabeth replied meeting Robert's dark eyes steadily. Robert saw the pain in their depths and was the first to look away.

'I have had a good life so far and I intend to live to see my grandchildren run this place,' sighed Elizabeth. 'What we all have to do is stay level-headed and continue to make our home work as it has for the generations before us.'

While these were eminently admirable sentiments they were easier said than done. Every mealtime managed to erupt into a major argument largely led by Ian and always revolving around the same subject: whether to stay as they were, a stud and wool producing property with a long history of success while wool prices plummeted and the drought worsened, or to diversify into cotton and fat lambs. Robert was dead against the idea of change.

'Wangianna has survived far worse conditions than this because of its reputation,' he pointed out at dinner after an exhausting day rounding up ewes for joining. 'What's more, if we can sit out the bad times we'll be able to buy up the better rams at low prices like we've done before.' Ian immediately started arguing hotly with Robert.

Andrew wasn't sure which was the best option but he was heavily swayed by the idea of new ventures and modern technology. Like his father, he loved to take risks but like his mother, Maggie, he was bad at making decisions. What he was sure of was that he didn't want all three half-brothers against him. He had already got both Ian and Jordie's ear by listening to their plans to diversify into fat lambs and cotton so he sided with them. The whole meal once more escalated into a full scale argument.

Suddenly Elizabeth had had enough.

'Stop this! Stop this at once!' she ordered. 'Your father has been gone less than a year and you are squabbling like a bunch of three-year-olds.'

The room went very quiet. 'Wangianna is your home. Your history. It is a place you should be proud of, not continually fighting over. I will not listen to any more of your childish bickering.' She got up and left the room. Her greatest fear was that she would not be able to stop them from splitting up Wangianna.

Katie was not only devastated by the outcome of George's will, she was also terrified. Her marriage was dead in all but name and now her dreams of becoming the mistress of Wangianna were in danger, her vision of Stewart as the son and heir trampled underfoot. Her only lever left was her knowledge of how much Wangianna meant to Robert. Christmas had been awful and she hadn't been to Melbourne for months, but at least Andrew had cleared off to his mother for those few days. Katie knew she had to do something drastic. Breaking the silence between them she tackled Robert one April morning while Stewart was listening to School of the Air.

'You aren't really just going to stand there and let this nobody do what he likes with what is rightfully ours?' she started. 'Your mother is being quite horrible. She never cared about your father. Now she doesn't even seem to care about you any longer. How can she side with that thief?'

Andrew had moved over into one of the small cottages on the property but Elizabeth insisted he be included in all meals hoping in doing so she would promote more union within the family. His presence, welcomed by Ian and Jordie, continued to infuriate Robert as did his arrogance, smart quips and use of fancy technical terms gleaned from his university days. Robert's own pride and pain at his father's treatment of the family that had loved him went too deep to voice so he was in no mood to listen to Katie's whining. Slowly he raised his eyes from the accounts his mother had given him to examine the night before and stared coldly at his wife.

'We had an agreement, Katie. I would not interfere in your life and you would not interfere in mine. Right now I have got more important things to worry about than hurling insults.'

'But can't you see, if you don't do something we'll lose Wangianna. *You'll* lose Wangianna,' she cried desperately.

Robert sighed. The books showed that Ian had got Karri Karri, the property in Western Australia, into a hopeless mess taking funds from Wangianna and showing tremendous losses. With this to sort out, the last thing he wanted was to waste the morning fighting Katie.

'The will is law, Katie, and much as you would like me to, neither I nor my mother can change the law.'

'Well if you won't say something I will. You can't just give up.'

'No one's giving up. My father left Andrew the largest share of Wangianna and as his eldest son he has much of the responsibility of running the place. If we antagonise him totally, heaven knows what might happen. For once in your life I am asking you to keep quiet.' It had taken all Robert's bargaining skills to get the others to agree to him buying more rams at today's sale. Their talk about cutting back and even selling some of the land terrified him. If Katie blundered about insulting everyone now, it could prove disastrous to the future of Wangianna.

Katie burst into tears. 'Can't you do anything?' she sobbed.

'I am. I'm going to buy some more rams if you'd let me get out of this room.'

'Don't be like that.' Katie's sobs redoubled.

'Cheer up. It could be a lot worse. Who says he's going to stick it out? After a year or two he might decide the bright city lights are far more attractive than struggling with the land. The best I can do now is to make sure he doesn't completely wreck Wangianna in the meantime.'

Slipping his wallet into the back pocket of his moleskins, Robert quickly ran a comb through his thick chestnut hair, picked up the keys to the ute and departed, leaving Katie sitting forlornly in his chair.

Alice bounced out of bed, dashed some water across her face and dressed quickly. She had put on weight again and, with the demanding outdoor work and her own sense of purpose back in her life, was looking terrific. Everything had at last started going well. Because of Fraser's advice about presenting a meticulously clean wool clip she had received a reasonable price for her wool, and Ernie O'Keefe, one of the top wool classers, had remarked on its cleanness. Earlier that month she had bought a ute for a song from a friend of a friend. It already had a wire cage fitted on the back and was more reliable and much more useful than the stationwagon. It also meant she and Marigold had two vehicles on the property.

Fraser had taken them all to the movies one Friday in Dubbo and she had even had the energy to add a few feminine touches to the kitchen. Weaving straw had always fascinated her and she had made a straw doll for each of the children which sat proudly on the sideboard in the kitchen next to the tea caddy. Today she was off at Fraser's invitation to a private ram sale. She could hug him for his support. So far she had been forced to buy only at open sales which, while increasing her flock, would never get her access to the top breeding lines almost invariably sold at private auctions. With the little bit of money she had saved and a further small cash advance obtained from the bank after much persuasion, she planned to buy three more good rams today, bringing her budding stud up to ten. Having acquired the good stud stock she would then sell four of her present rams and buy more top ewes for her breeding program.

The sale was at a property over two hours' drive away and she wanted to get her routine jobs out of the way early to give her plenty of time to get there and look over the rams. Gobbling through her breakfast and leaving Marigold to see to the children, she ran out of the house and bumped into Jimmy carrying his shotgun.

'What's up, Jimmy?' Alice asked. Then she saw his expression and her heart missed a beat.

'That wild dog got the rams, Miss Alice,' replied Jimmy grimly. Alice's stomach gave a sickening lurch.

'I'll get the ute?'

Jimmy nodded.

Calling her two cattle dogs Alice roared the ute into gear and the two sped out towards the paddock where she had shifted the rams two days before. The sight that met them was horrific. Of the seven only three had not been mauled. Terrified, the survivors stood huddled together at one corner of the paddock. Three lay gruesomely gouged to death, the flies buzzing around their ripped flesh. As they approached another gave a pitiful bleat, staggered and toppled on its side. Alice grabbed the gun. Doing the only humane thing possible, she shot it through the head. Dark-eyed with misery, she stared at the carnage, her mind refusing to work.

'I thought the mongrel'd been shot,' said Jimmy shaking his head. Alice felt quite numb. She, too, had been convinced the wild dog that had done all the damage last year on other properties had been destroyed, otherwise she would never have moved the sheep so far from the home paddock.

'At least let's see if we can save these last three,' said Alice, pushing away the hopelessness that threatened to swamp her.

The vicious brute had got her best rams. Two of the three survivors she had planned to sell anyway to upgrade her stock. She whistled up the dogs while Jimmy pulled out the short removable ramp on the back of the ute. Carefully Alice got the dogs to ease the terrified rams up into the ute and slammed the metal cage shut. There were no obvious tears in the merinos' big folds but she wasn't taking any chances. She got on the car radio to the vet who said he'd be right over but that he'd have to stop on a couple of urgent calls on the way.

Alice, unable to bear the sight of her decimated rams, left Jimmy to dispose of them and drove back to the house, cursing herself for having moved them to the far paddock. If they had been closer to the house maybe she or Jimmy might have heard the dog and got to them before it did. But she really had no choice. There was nothing to graze on in the home paddocks. Now she had not only lost four good rams, it looked like she would miss the sale as well, but she dare not leave without checking first with the vet. From past experience she knew he could take anything up to three hours to get to MerryMaid. Alice called up Fraser but he had already left. His mother, however, informed her that the sale time had been changed from twelve to two as the property owners were expecting some interstate buyers.

Willing the vet to hurry Alice wiped a fly from her mouth and went to check the jillaroo had fed and watered the ewes in lamb.

The vet arrived quicker than Alice had expected. Having to retell the story almost reduced Alice to tears. The vet, who admired Alice's tenacity, offered her what comfort he could. Dealing with such a situation was never easy, either for the owner or the vet.

'Righto. That's them fixed up,' said the vet carefully packing away his instruments after checking out the surviving rams.

'To be honest, I'm not really sure where I go from here,' admitted Alice. She told him how she had planned to use some of the money from the sale of the now dead rams to pay for a ram shed. The money from her jewellery was long gone and she simply didn't have the money to replace the rams and buy the shed. Yet this whole ghastly scenario could happen again. She started to wonder at the sense of it all.

'You know what my advice is? My real advice, fair dinkum, not just polite noise?' offered the vet.

'I'm listening,' said Alice.

'Forget the shed for now and put all this behind you. Go buy yourself some more rams—the best and as many as you can afford as quickly as you can. Hock yourself up to the eyeballs. Let the bank own you for a few more years and set up your artificial insemination scheme as fast as you can.' The vet snapped shut his bag preparing to leave. 'It's the chicken and the egg. I've mentioned your ideas to a number of farmers and they were sceptical but definitely interested. If what you've told me works—and you've convinced me it could—with a lot of damned hard work you'll be laughing in ten years. Personally I really admire your guts. I don't know of many women who'd still be hanging around after something like this.'

It was just the boost Alice needed. Waving him off she sent up a prayer of thanks for having him as a friend. Recently she had become disheartened when she had learned that a number of people apparently heartily disapproved of her audacious attempts to move into a man's world—Fraser had already warned her some of the people attending today's sale were of that ilk—and there were others who simply treated the whole idea of MerryMaid Stud as a joke.

'Unless they tell it to my face I'm not interested,' she had retorted bravely, but her outward show of courage hid her disquiet. She knew also it was Fraser's standing in the community that had got her invited to the auction, not her own; but one day, she vowed, that too would change. Today's savage attack on her rams had left her feeling vulnerable and by the time she arrived at the property where the sale was being held she was feeling distinctly nervous. She parked the ute alongside the latest model Landrover and hurried towards the dust and noise.

The auction, although private, was a joint effort of several property owners. Seventy rams exhibiting different traits were on sale, separated out in a long line of holding pens containing between one and five rams. All were expected to fetch high prices. It was hot and dusty and the air was filled with the sounds of bleating sheep and the smell of wool and sheep dung. Men in different-shaped hats, sweating in their shirtsleeves and trousers, gathered in groups pointing and talking in excited undertones. Some were in holding pens examining rams, studying the thickness of the wool or checking out the sheep's stance. Everyone seemed to Alice to be extraordinarily experienced. She felt a complete novice. Two small children sat up in one of the few trees near the pens giggling and pelting tiny hard gold fruits onto the hats below. The auctioneer was well into his stride, barking out bids around one of the middle pens containing two magnificent looking rams. Following his every move was a talker who repeated everything he said in a semibark, two spotters who scoured the crowd for bids and a clerk frantically scribbling down bids and names. Pushing past the groups of men huddled together, Alice's stomach tightened part in nervousness part excited anticipation at moving into this inner circle as she searched for Fraser wondering if she was too late.

'Alice,' greeted a red-faced Fraser. 'I was beginning to wonder if you'd make it.'

'I thought I wouldn't three hours ago,' said Alice breathlessly, jamming the Akubra she'd been clutching back on her head. 'I'm terribly sorry.

I've had a disaster at home—I'll tell you about it later. How long have they been at it?'

'They're down to the last few pens. I've picked out three good 'uns I think you should make a bid for. Come, I'll show you.' He started striding down an aisle between the sheep pens. 'By the way,' he said as Alice half ran to keep up with him, 'remember that conversation we had last week about owners occasionally putting ringers in to push up the sales. I've been watching the last few bids pretty carefully and I'm certain we've got one of those here. See that bloke?' He pointed out a stocky man wearing a battered cream hat and short-sleeved blue shirt shovelling sheep across into a different pen. Alice nodded. 'I reckon he's the one so just watch your bidding.' He kept striding towards the pen. Alice dodged past people and nearly ran straight into someone.

'Sorry,' she said without looking up.

'Hello, Alice.'

Alice's heart missed a beat as she looked up at the big strapping man blocking her way. It was Robert McIain.

'Robert, what are you doing here?' she babbled, taken by surprise, and blushed hotly at how silly she must have sounded. Of course he could be expected to attend a sale of this quality.

'You look great,' said Robert shyly.

Alice was suddenly lost for words. Her emotions in turmoil, she stared up at the man she had struggled for so long to put out of her mind. There was a sadness at the back of his eyes that tugged at her heart and his crooked smile twisted down more than she remembered, yet he was still deliriously handsome. For one brief mad moment she wanted to rush into his arms and sob out the terrible events of the morning and to feel herself safely enfolded in his embrace, to tell him how often she had fought to rid herself of the bittersweet memory of their love. Then she returned to reality. He had sworn undying love then betrayed her by sleeping with her cousin. For that she could never forgive him.

'I've come to buy some rams with Fraser,' she said stiffly.

Stewart stepped out from behind his father.

'Hello, Aunty Alice.' She hardly recognised the beaming boy from the miserable sour-faced child she had seen with her cousin.

'Hello, Stewart,' she smiled back, relieved to have an excuse to avoid Robert's eyes.

Robert's chest tightened as she bent to acknowledge his son. He had caught that first unbidden rush of emotion in her eyes and had felt the pain as the shutters came down. He had seen the casually comfortable way she chatted with Fraser, how her arm had brushed his shirtsleeve, how Fraser had leaned towards her so she could catch what he was saying, and his whole being was engulfed by envy. The contrast between Alice and Fraser and the scene he had so recently played out with Katie made the meeting all the more painful, yet when he had seen her from the further aisle he had been unable to stop himself from coming over to meet her.

'I'm helping Dad pick the rams,' said Stewart proudly. Robert ruffled his son's hair, drinking in Alice's proximity and her soft warm perfume evocative of another sweeter time.

'He's a very lucky dad,' replied Alice, Robert's gaze making her go hot. Stewart's boyish enthusiasm helped loosen her tongue. 'Mr Bowen's picked out some rams for me to inspect. I'd better go and see what I'm supposed to be buying. I've only just got here.' Robert stood back to let her pass. At the last minute he lightly touched Alice's shoulder. The heat from his hand set every nerve tingling.

'Just take it easy with the bidding. Don't get fooled into going too high. See that bloke there?' He pointed to the ringer Fraser had already identified. 'He's a cousin of the fella that owns this property and he's purposely been pushing up the prices.' Alice looked sharply at Robert her body still reacting to his touch. There had been no need for him to go out of his way to warn her.

'Aren't you buying too?' she asked, squinting against the sunlight.

Robert nodded. 'It doesn't mean you have to cheat on your mates.'

'Fraser said the same thing about that bloke when we were coming across but thanks for the tip.' She smiled gratefully at Robert and quickly fled through the crush after Fraser.

To Robert it was as though the blazing sun had suddenly disappeared behind a thick black cloud leaving him in a feeble half-light. At that moment he would have given anything to change places with Fraser Bowen.

'You want to go for these ones,' said Fraser pointing at a pen containing two heavy looking, bright-faced merinos. Alice made a note of the lot number. 'You can strengthen your strain with those and I reckon you'd get quite a bit of interest when it came to selling lambs. Should get the two for a reasonable price.' Fraser moved on to the broad shouldered merino with massive curling horns alone in its pen. 'Personally I'd go as high as you dare with that one, but don't let them rob you. I'd stop at five hundred and fifty dollars max.' Alice nodded trying to steady her racing thoughts as she ran her eye over the rams he had picked out.

The auctioneer was still rapping out his bids, his talker encouraging the play, his two spotters scanning the crowd for nods and hand signals, the clerk scribbling frantically. Rams were going rapidly and fetching between three hundred and fifty and four hundred dollars each. The atmosphere grew tense as the bidding moved to the final pens and the prices crept up but Alice was confident she could still compete. A hot wind sent sharp swirls of dust in the air and her eyes and mouth felt full of grit as it came to her turn. Despite herself she kept glancing across the pens to see where Robert had gone. Once she caught his eye and quickly looked away. She fanned herself with her auction sheet while the auctioneer and spotters positioned themselves for the next bid.

'Good luck,' said Fraser in her ear. 'Take it easy.' Her throat was dry. The bidding moved fast. Alice's pulse quickened as she tried to understand the price excitedly barked out by the auctioneer, and the talker and the spotters, joining in like the rattle of a machine gun with the bids. The rams rustled uneasily in their pens.

After she had settled down Alice found the bidding less terrifying than she had at first thought. She got the first ram quickly for three hundred and fifty dollars. Several bidders went after the second ram she had picked out. Halfway through the bidding her tension increased as she realised Robert had joined in. The price quickly leaped up and to Alice's disappointment she had to drop out. The final ram was the one Fraser had said go for. The bidding started at three hundred dollars. Crossing her fingers Alice prayed she could afford it.

'Magnificent beast this, ladies and gentlemen,' sang the auctioneer. 'Magnificent strong wool ram, three times New South Wales and Easter Show champion, best ram you'll see this side of the black stump. We have three hundred and fifty dollars, thank you Bert, yes we have three hundred and fifty. We have four hundred dollars. This is a ram you cannot pass up. Do we have four hundred and fifty?' Alice put up her hand. 'Yes we have four hundred and fifty thank you ma'am.' He raised his hat. 'Four hundred and fifty dollars, ladies and gentlemen. You won't see rams like this again in a hurry. This is a once-only offer. Do we have five hundred dollars? We have five hundred dollars from Wangianna.' Alice's eyes flew to Robert. Damn. He was bidding against her again. 'Five hundred dollars, the bidding stands at five hundred dollars.' Alice felt Robert's eyes on her. Quickly glancing across she saw him imperceptibly shake his head. Interpreting it as a threat defiantly she shouted, 'Five hundred and twenty-five.' 'Five hundred and fifty,' called the auctioneer. 'We have five hundred and fifty dollars from the gentleman in the blue shirt, thank you sir.'

It was the ringer Fraser and Robert had warned her about. For a moment Alice panicked. What did she do now? She had reached her limit but after today's tragedy she needed that ram more than ever. With it she could still establish a breeding line that farmers would buy. Why had Robert warned her not to let the bloke rob her? Perhaps it was his way of trying to frighten her off. Perhaps his warning was ever meant to be altruistic. She could feel the sweat trickling between her breasts and under her arms. Her hands were sweating as she felt the roll of notes in the pocket of her jeans.

'Six hundred dollars,' she cried and was immediately outbid by the ringer. Last year she would have been laughed at with such a bid. Now she knew the ram was blatantly overpriced. She glared at the man in the blue shirt. Then Robert jumped in with a bid of seven hundred and fifty dollars. The ringer glanced surreptitiously in Alice's direction and waited.

'Seven hundred and fifty dollars thank you Mr McIain,' called the auctioneer.

Robert was shaking his head at her again.

'D'you have two hundred and fifty in cash to cover me right now?' whispered Alice to Fraser.

'Sure,' replied Fraser quickly. Alice's hand shot up. Furious that he dared to tell her what to do knowing she was way beyond her limit and sure she had lost the ram she made her final bid. 'Eight hundred dollars.' Her voice rang clear in the tense silence.

The spotters' eyes dashed from person to person. The auctioneer waited. 'I am bid eight hundred dollars for this magnificent ram. Eight hundred dollars. Any advance on eight hundred dollars? Going once, going twice; this magnificent merino ram sold for eight hundred dollars to MerryMaid. Thank you ma'am.' He raised his hat again. The tension dissolved. The auctioneer and his mates moved on. The ram was hers for eight hundred dollars. Three hundred above what it was expected to fetch but she had got a ram to give MerryMaid the kickstart it needed. Alice turned round and hugged Fraser.

'We got it! We got it! What a brilliant brilliant ram. You're a darling. He looks so regal with those massive shoulders and haughty head. I'm going to call him The Emperor.' It was far more than she had wanted to pay but it was a magnificent beast and one known across New South Wales. Stepping back she said sheepishly, 'I'll give you the money back straight-away, I just don't have the cash on me.'

'Not a problem,' Fraser said cheerfully as Robert came up behind them.

'Congratulations, Alice, that's a top stud ram you've got there. Sorry you had to pay such a wicked price though.' She could hear the regret in his voice. 'They've got sandwiches and drinks laid on over at the house for the buyers. You two feel like wandering across?' Alice was too overjoyed at her purchases to refuse.

'You know that mongrel was feeding the price, don't you, Fraser? I tried to warn Alice to stop bidding,' Robert said handing out a plate of sandwiches.

'What d'you mean, stop me bidding?' exclaimed Alice incensed. 'So that you could have my ram? What is it about you blokes that you're so scared when a woman manages to succeed on her own?' Angrily she gulped down a glass of orange juice.

'Fraid you missed out this time, Bluey lad,' grinned Fraser distracted by a large man bearing down on the group.

'Fraser Bowen, you young rascal, where have you been hiding all these months?'

Fraser nodded at Robert and Alice. 'Scuse me a sec,' he said as he was whisked away.

Now they were alone there was an awkwardness between them. Alice's legs started to tremble. She daren't look him in the face because she knew her anger was prompted by her longing to hurl herself into his arms.

'I was trying to buy the ram for you, Alice,' explained Robert stiffly. 'I thought if I could scare the mongrel off we could keep the price down and you could have given me a reasonable price. Four hundred and fifty dollars would have been fair.'

Suddenly Alice felt very small. The sandwich in her mouth tasted like sand. She blushed ferociously not knowing where to begin. Stewart streaked past his hands full of sandwiches.

'Greedy young beggar,' grinned Robert breaking the tension. 'Don't get lost! How's MerryMaid Stud going?' he inquired politely.

'Were you really trying to buy that ram for me?' asked Alice.

Robert's mouth tightened. 'Like I said, I don't like cheating on my mates.'

Alice blushed fiery red. She had been so sure he was against her it had never occurred to her he could have been trying to help. Now listening to his offer she was reminded of the lover before the betrayer and could not deny the longing she felt towards him.

Robert had to stop himself from reaching out and running his fingers through her wild black mane. She looked so defenceless in her embarrassment.

'I'm sorry you got caught like that,' he said fishing in his pocket. Pulling out a couple of boiled sweets he handed one to Alice. 'I wish there was some way to control mongrels like him but it's hard to prove anything was crooked. No doubt he'll get a nice fat cut for the day's work.' He unwrapped his sweet and popped it in his mouth, wondering why he was talking about such mundane stuff when really what he wanted was to cover Alice's exquisite heart-shaped face with kisses.

'Haven't seen him for five years. And he hasn't changed one bit either,' announced Fraser joining them again, relieving Alice of having to reply to Robert. She was having trouble thinking straight. Robert felt a stab of jealousy as Fraser casually linked arms with Alice. 'We'd better go and pay for your spoils. By the way what was the disaster you were talking about earlier?'

'That wild dog they said had been shot got four of my rams,' she replied, plunged back into the misery of the morning. 'But I'm not letting that beat me. I'm not letting anything beat me,' she said squaring her chin, her eyes brilliant sapphire.

Robert could hardly bear the pain of being so close yet so impossibly far from the only woman he had ever truly loved.

Robert found Katie hot and tired, brushing flies off the steaks for tea. Stewart beat his father to the fridge for a cool drink. 'Wash your hands first,' ordered Katie. Patting his son's head, Robert walked to the fridge and poured himself some iced water.

'I need to talk to you, Katie,' he said.

Wiping her hands on her apron Katie placed a tea towel over the meat and started washing a limp lettuce.

'I've just been discussing it with Mother and we've agreed that the only thing is for me to go and live at Karri Karri for six months to sort out the mess Ian's made out there.' He paused for a fraction of a second before adding, 'Ian will come back to work at Wangianna.' Avoiding Katie's eye he fiddled with his glass.

'I want Stewart to come with me. It is part of his inheritance and I feel it would be a good idea if you came, too, to stop people talking.' He waited for the stream of abuse but none came, instead Katie sat down heavily in one of their big wooden chairs.

Robert walked to the open window determined to do what he had decided after he had left the sale yard. Today had highlighted for him that his love for Alice had not diminished one iota. It had also made him realise he had to put it behind him forever if he were ever to gain peace of mind. 'There's something else,' he continued, struggling to find the right words. Finally finishing his drink he placed it on the table.

'Is there any hope for you and me?' he stumbled. 'Could we start afresh for Stewart's sake?' Katie looked startled. 'I mean, I know things have been bad between us but it hasn't all been you. I love Stewwy so much and I want to try to make things better between us. If only for his sake, would you be willing to try again?' Katie's amazement grew as she listened. 'I know I began this marriage loving Alice and not you, but couldn't we put all this behind us and make a fresh start? Going to Western Australia for a couple of years as a family could give us that chance.'

Katie's eyes narrowed and she rubbed her forehead where a headache thumped.

'You would be willing to try again knowing I had been having an affair with your brother?' she asked amazed.

'I'd do it for Stewart.'

'You don't hate me?' Katie's bottom lip trembled.

'I don't know what I feel, Katie. All I know is that you and I are married, that we have a son we both love and that maybe if things had started differently we wouldn't be in this mess.'

'This isn't some kind of trick is it?' asked Katie suspiciously.

Robert shook his head. 'On my honour, Katie, I want to try again.'

'I have to tell you something then.' Katie's voice cracked. Eyes lowered twisting the apron viciously around her fingers, she whispered huskily, 'There never was any affair. Ian kissed me twice when we were drunk and that was all.' Tears filled her eyes and spilled over her cheeks as she met his gaze. 'I was so mad with jealousy I said anything I could to hurt you.'

Letting the apron go, she rushed into Robert's arms and buried her face in his shirt. 'I was so afraid when Alice came home that you'd leave me. I was desperate, Robbo, I was so desperate.' Her voice was barely audible.

Stunned by this latest revelation Robert didn't move. But what he didn't know was that in the end Ian had been too much of a gentleman to allow his brother's wife to seduce him.

'Hold me, Robbo. Oh hold me. I love you so much,' pleaded Katie. Uncertain, Robert gathered her in his arms.

'Let's go and tell Stewart,' he said after a while, kissing her lightly on the top of her head.

Chapter Twenty-eight

ALICE RUBBED HER EYES and stared blankly at the papers in front of her. For the past two hours she had been going over and over her five-year plan, searching for better ways to manage the property. Her purchases at the last ram sale had pushed her to the financial limit and she was three months behind on her mortgage repayments. What should have been rich grazing ground was parched and brown and there was no sign of rain. Alice was bone weary and, if she admitted it, frightened. The bank had recently foreclosed on several neighbouring properties and each day she woke wondering whether it would be her turn next.

Alice knew she had to begin her artificial insemination program soon, that was to be the mainstay of MerryMaid Stud. From her research with the professor into genetic manipulation, Alice was confident she could develop a strain which would produce precisely the wool type she wanted. What she desperately needed was more stock, but more stock meant more feed, and Alice's meagre store was perilously low, despite the fact she had taken Fraser's advice before the drought reached crisis point and hoarded what she had managed to grow. The only way she could afford feed for more rams and ewes was to buy it in, and money was the one thing she didn't have.

Alice put her head in her hands and sighed. She had given it everything she had but it was beginning to look as though that wasn't enough.

Distracted, she wandered into the kitchen for a cup of tea.

'Mr Munro just phoned for you, Alice,' said Marigold as she buttered the scones for morning tea.

'It's finally come,' she said grim-faced.

Squaring her shoulders she dialled the bank in Coonabarabran and was politely asked to make an appointment to see Mr Munro as soon as possible. Plunged into gloom yet seeing no point in postponing the inevitable, she made an appointment to see him that afternoon. It was Friday and afterwards she could go straight on to pick up Vicky from Bea's. Vicky, now seven, had been attending the local primary school in Billabrin for the last six months, staying at Aunty Bea's during the week. The decision had been a hard one for Alice but MerryMaid was just too far out and even with school of the air and Marigold's help, Alice felt Vicky would do better at Billabrin.

As she travelled to Coonabarabran she choked back the tears at the thought of losing MerryMaid. In the short time she had owned the property she had re-established her roots. It was her home. She knew every inch of every paddock and every one of her mob. Questions raced unhappily through her mind. Had she just been a blind fool to believe she could take on the outback with so little experience? How could she ever repay Bea and Ray for having faith in her? How could she now face them knowing she had failed them? Her dream was slowly falling apart.

'Don't be a damned fool, girl,' she chided herself. 'You're overdramatising again. Stop jumping to conclusions.' But the sinking feeling stayed with her as she walked into the bank. Smiling bravely she allowed Mr Munro to usher her into his office shutting the door carefully behind him.

'How long before I have to get out?' she blurted out, sitting down quickly to hide her nervousness and crossing one long leg over the other.

'I beg your pardon?' replied Mr Munro arranging Alice's fat file on his empty desk and sitting down opposite her. Alice's heart hammered too loudly in her ears.

'You want to foreclose, that's why I am here, isn't it?' Alice stated unable to bear the suspense. Mr Munro looked across his wide desk a kindly smile on his face.

'On the contrary. I wanted to discuss this telegraphic advice that arrived two days ago.' He pushed a sheet of paper across the desk. 'It's from a Mr Dixson instructing us to make available to you funds to the value of twenty-five thousand pounds sterling. Is that right? It is addressed to you but it's an awful lot of money for a young lady like yourself to handle.'

Alice's jaw dropped. For a full minute she stared uncomprehending at the paper. 'There must be some mistake,' she said finally. She had kept in touch with the Dixsons on her return to Australia but this was completely unexpected.

'You don't know this person?'

'Don't know him? I worked with him. He's almost family.'

'A letter was telegraphed with the advice in case there was any confusion about the money,' explained Mr Munro. 'The gentleman certainly seems to know you.' He pushed a second sheet of paper across the desk. Alice read Professor Dixson's letter with increasing amazement.

'For our work together, dear girl,' she read. The professor went on to explain how he had received the Sir Arthur Cavendish Award for Excellence in Research for his work with diabetes. Furious that the board of judges had refused to include Alice's name in the award he had sent her half the prize money. 'I can be stubborn and difficult when I choose and I sincerely believe I would never have made the breakthrough without you. This money is rightfully yours. Keep in touch, dear child. Love to you all. Dicky.'

Alice put down the letter overwhelmed. She swallowed hard fighting back tears of gratitude. In his generosity Professor Dixson had given her far more than money. He had given her back MerryMaid.

'Does this mean you would like to clear your debt with the bank?'

Alice cleared her throat. 'Yes I suppose it does,' she replied struggling to grasp the reality of the situation. Coming out of her trance she leaned forward excitedly. 'I'd like to discuss taking out another loan.' After she had signed all the necessary forms she handed him a copy of the MerryMaid accounts for the last financial year and a breakdown of projected costs she had brought with her as a last bastion against foreclosure.

'There are a couple of private auctions coming up in the next few weeks that I would like to buy stock from,' she explained excitedly. 'And with the drought and drop in the wool market there are bound to be more.

I need money to buy while the prices are low. I need top quality feed and lots of it, because I just don't have the feed in my paddocks, and I need people to help run MerryMaid. In the next three years I aim to have trebled the size of MerryMaid Stud and have got my artificial insemination scheme up and running. Then when prices pick up I can sell off some of my good ewes and rams, keep only the cream, and buy better again,' Alice said hardly stopping to breathe between sentences. At the end she took a deep breath and sat back in her chair.

'Oh yes,' replied the bank manager looking at her slowly. He wasn't sure if he approved of this energetic young woman with her wild black hair and startling blue eyes, but he certainly admired her spirit. He examined the MerryMaid accounts carefully and then her current bank statement. With this unexpected injection of cash her present financial position was greatly improved; however, life on the land could be fickle. 'You know there's a pretty lot of competition out there?' he said working out figures on his calculator.

'I've thought of that,' interrupted Alice excitedly. 'With more help around the place I'll be able to spend more time developing my AI process.'

'Oh yes?' said the bank manager again, a little uncomfortable with Alice's frank talk about breeding.

'What the process will do,' rushed on Alice ignoring the scepticism in his voice, 'is decrease the loss of semen between the freezing, transporting and thawing processes so that sheep-breeding by this method becomes as good if not better than with cattle.'

A slightly flushed Mr Munro leaned back in his chair patting the tips of his fingers together, his eyes fixed on Alice.

'You really are out to show us blokes a thing or two, aren't you, Alice. Well, all I can say is good luck to you, MerryMaid.'

'Does that mean I get the loan?' asked Alice unsure whether to laugh or be offended.

Mr Munro drew his eyebrows together and returned to his calculations. For the next few minutes the only sound in the room was the soft click of his fingers on the calculator and his slow breathing. Alice crossed her fingers and toes under the desk and held her breath. Street sounds floated through the window, a dog barking, the chatter of people walking by, a car. Finally he looked up.

'If you think you can come up with the repayments I think we can organise a further loan for you, Mrs Turlington,' he declared formally. 'Mind you, I don't know as though I'd want to be in your shoes right now.'

Alice let out a long sigh. Thank goodness she'd made the effort to work everything out before her visit. She wanted to hug him. Instead she stood up, her eyes shining, and shook him warmly by the hand.

'Keep me posted, Alice, and good luck again,' he added, admiration seeping through his polite veneer as he showed her to the door. Only just managing to contain her elation until she had crossed the wide street to her car, Alice then let out a great whoop of joy making passers-by turn their heads in astonishment. From his window the bank manager smiled in amusement. The blokes in the bush were going to have a hard time slowing that one down.

'You'll never guess what!' screamed Alice down the phone to Aunty Bea, too excited to wait until she got to Billabrin. Bea was as amazed and excited as Alice. Having told Bea, she drove on to her aunt's place, her mind in a whirl.

Vicky greeted her carrying a week-old kitten. Brown as a nut, her face sparkled with health, she was wearing a pretty new eggshell blue blouse and new denim jeans and had shot up in the last few months. Alice always got a shock at how like her own mother Vicky was. 'Mum'd be proud of me,' she thought with a lump in her throat. 'I reckon even she'd agree this was thinking big enough.' Then Bea appeared smiling behind her. How I love them both, she thought happily.

'Can I take her home?' asked Vicky stroking the tiny little creature.

Alice smiled at her daughter. 'If Aunty Bea says yes.' She couldn't say no to anything today. 'But don't forget you live here during the week.' Alice went inside and told Aunty Bea all over again about the money, her success in securing a further loan and her plans for MerryMaid.

'I'm thinking of buying some more land too,' Alice said resting her elbows on the old pine kitchen table. 'I can afford to now and the place that backs onto mine with the creek running down the side's up for sale. It'd be great to have that creek actually inside my property. It usually has a trickle in it even in the really dry times like now. Come decent rain those paddocks'll be lush.'

'D'you mean old Charlie Weston's place?' Ray asked slowly. His eyesight was failing and he was going slightly deaf. 'I heard he was planning to put the place on the market. Done so already, has he? I was up his way a couple of weeks back and he told me he was having shocking problems with the drought. Thoroughly depressed about it too, he was.' Ray shook his head, peering fondly at Alice.

'You've been lucky, my girl, Charlie told me he's lost nearly a third of his stock. Got nothing to feed em on. Shocking. Then there's the McCreedies walked off their place last week. Just left everything where it was and went. Bea and I were worried it would be your turn next.' He shook his head again and pulled out his pipe. Many of the dams were almost empty and there was no sign of the drought breaking.

'So was I until a few hours ago, Uncle Ray,' Alice said cheerfully, kissing him on the cheek. 'Come on, Roo, we'd better be getting back or Marigold'll be wondering what's happened to us.'

'Bring Marigold over again next time you come. She's such a nice girl and we haven't seen Ben for a while,' suggested Aunty Bea kissing her niece on the cheek. 'You're lucky she's stayed with you so long.'

'I'm lucky about a lot of things,' said Alice quietly, slipping a wad of notes into Aunty Bea's pocket and holding out her hand to Vicky. 'That's a belated birthday present from us. I wanted to get you something special but with all the recent work I haven't had a chance.' Bea pulled out the wad and counted it. Her jaw dropped. Alice had given her three hundred dollars. Quickly she folded it up and gave it back to Alice.

'Don't be ridiculous, Alice. Here you are borrowing from the bank and then handing the stuff around as if it grew on trees,' said Bea crossly.

'Okay, it's not a birthday present,' said Alice undaunted. 'It's because

I love you and Ray and you do so much for me and my little family and it's my way of saying thank you for believing I can make something of MerryMaid.' Her eyes glittered dangerously. 'And if you want to insult me completely you'll force me to take it back but I know Vicky's dresses didn't come from St Vincent de Paul, not to mention Ben's new shoes.' Bea's expression softened a fraction. 'Please, Aunty Bea, let me help just a little?'

Aunty Bea melted completely. 'I don't know about your mother,' she said to Vicky and hugged them both tight.

Alice and Vicky got back to the property to find Ben fast asleep and Marigold sterilising bottles in the outside laundry. Creeping into the cheerfully painted room she kissed her three-year-old sleeping son and returned to tell Marigold the joyful news.

'How did the boys get on fixing the windmill?' she asked, referring to Fraser and Jimmy, after Marigold had digested her news. Vicky had disappeared with the little kitten to make up a bed for it in the hay barn.

'Fine!' Marigold plunged the last bottle into the sterilising solution. 'I've had the most wonderful day too!' she bubbled glowing with happiness. 'Come and I'll show you.' She grabbed Alice by the hand and led her at a run slowing at the entrance to one of the sheds. Putting her finger to her lips she signalled Alice to stay quiet. Alice looked into the temporarily erected pen just inside the shed, the floor area covered with straw. Fast asleep in the gloom snuggled next to a warm blanket lay a startling white lamb, its black umbilical cord still dangling from its belly.

'Fraser found her when he and Jimmy were fixing the windmill. She's an orphan. He heard this pitiful bleating from the scrub and brought her back down to the house. Then he showed me how to feed her.'

The glow about Marigold was almost tangible. Alice felt a sudden sharp envy as memories came flooding back of Robert's present of the two orphaned lambs. She wanted to cry.

Marigold, surprised at her unaccustomed lack of enthusiasm, asked with alarm, 'Are you okay?'

Alice blinked and nodded, forcing herself to smile back at her happy companion.

'It's been a long day. I must have got more wound up about the thought of losing this place than I thought and I get really sentimental about orphaned lambs.'

'The poor little thing was starving,' explained Marigold still excited about the lamb. It was obvious she was overjoyed at the thought of looking after another little creature. Alice gave Marigold a friendly pat chasing away her own unwanted memories.

Fraser accompanied Alice again to the next private auction in late August. It was much bigger than the last auction Alice had attended in April. There were hundreds of ewes and a good turnout of rams. Alice's heart started to race as she and Fraser strode towards the vast pens of restless sheep stirring up the yellow dust. There was something about the shouts of the auctioneers and talkers, the gesticulating of the spotters, the familiar smells and the dry comments of the buyers that never ceased to send the blood pumping through Alice's veins. This time she realised with mixed feelings there would be no chance of running into Robert. He, with Katie and Stewart, had now been in Western Australia since mid-April and Bea had said they were not due back to Wangianna until Christmas, much to Katie's disgust. Katie loathed living there, so Bea informed Alice. As far as she was concerned the house was a dump and she never got to go anywhere. Ray's comment that it was character building had brought a smile to Bea's lips followed by a quick rebuke.

The animals Alice was interested in today were three merino rams, who had won championships in local shows, and a batch of top ewes. This time she had allowed plenty of time to inspect them. Jostling through the crowd she stepped into the pen indicating to the ringer which ram she was interested in. The ringer doffed his cap to Alice then, amidst loud swearing, shoved and pushed the other rams out of the way and grabbed the chosen ram by its curling horns, forcing its head towards Alice. It had a magnificent soft white face and broad well-set shoulders. Thanking the ringer Alice moved on to inspect the ewes who rushed stupidly around the pen climbing on one another's back and leering nervously out of the sides of their eyes. In no time Alice was sweating under the sun's ugly glare, her throat as dry as the dust that swirled around her.

Today the mood was sombre and bidding started surprisingly low. Alice scanned the faces of the bidders searching for the ringer who had hiked up the prices at the previous auction but there was no sign of him. The sheep, though still in reasonable shape, would need to be hand-fed to keep up the wool quality, the paddocks being so dry and dusty. When Alice's turn came she found she had little challenge except from an extremely grumpy individual who kept pulling his hat down over his ears. Alice walked away from the auction with one hundred top medium wool fleece ewes and the three champion rams.

'Does she think we're in for floods or summat?' said the bloke who had just lost the bidding. Sourly he nodded his head towards Alice and spat out his chewed tobacco. 'Them lot'll be dead in a week with a sheila in charge.' He pulled his hat further down over his ears and walked away in disgust. Alice blushed to the roots of her hair at the laughter from his mates that followed.

'Don't take any notice,' said Fraser in her ear. 'Think it a compliment he sees you as a threat, which he obviously does, else why bother with the wisecracks?'

Alice relaxed. She was glad Fraser was here. This time she had felt more comfortable than at the last auction and had even been greeted by some of the other farmers, but the taunt still stung.

A week later she made an offer for Charlie Weston's property on the other side of the creek from MerryMaid. On the edge of the black soil, with more water in the creek, the yellow paddocks would quickly turn into prime grazing land. She then hired several more hands to run MerryMaid giving her the freedom to concentrate on her research. The property agent, Ross Gleeson, got back to her within the week and she put down a deposit. She then took a trip to Sydney to buy some equipment and check a few aspects of breeding with an acquaintance working in the CSIRO. Two weeks later, having heard nothing from the property agent and anxious to finalise the deal, Alice dropped into his office. Slightly startled at her unannounced arrival, Ross Gleeson quickly recovered and indicated a seat.

'How you going MerryMaid Alice? Still as merry as ever?' Alice was often teased about the name of her property but from the outset she had mistrusted this man with his slicked-back hair and close-set eyes. Now not only was she annoyed at the use of her first name, she found the way his eyes flitted intrusively over her body profoundly offensive.

'Fine thanks,' she said remaining standing. 'I want to fix up about buying Mr Weston's land.' She rummaged in her bag for her chequebook. The agent's stare got bolder.

'Oh that,' he said smugly. 'Sorry, MerryMaid, I'm afraid you missed out.' Alice's hand froze inside her bag. Her eyes flew to his face.

'What d'you mean I've missed out. I made a fair offer and I put down a deposit. All I had to do was exchange contracts and organise the rest of the money.' She was unaware she was waving her chequebook in the air.

'No need to wave that at me, it won't make any difference. The land's been sold,' said Ross Gleeson with smug finality.

'What d'you mean, the land's been sold?' Alice was livid. She shoved her chequebook back in her bag. 'What the heck's going on? Why didn't you get back to me and ask if I'd reconsider? You knew how keen I was to buy.' The man looked more and more smug.

'Business is business, lady. I got a better offer.'

'But that's illegal. You had my deposit. You should have rung me.' Alice was dumbfounded.

The man opened his hands and shrugged his shoulders. 'Sorry, lady, that's the way the cookie crumbles. Mr McIain cabled us from Western Australia. Knew straightaway you couldn't have bettered his offer.' Ross Gleeson thoroughly disapproved of women invading what he considered men's territory.

Alice's eyes blazed with rage at his condescension. How dare he tell her what she could or couldn't do and how dare he think he could pass his nasty unethical little tactics off on her. The taunts from the man at the auction rang anew in her ears as did all the other little digs about her as a woman running a stud property. Leaning across his desk she grabbed a handful of Ross Gleeson's shirt pushing her face close to his, the waves of his cheap aftershave nearly asphyxiating her.

'Is that a fact?' she hissed taking him completely by surprise. Ross went bright red and tried to back away, but Alice still had a firm hold of his shirt.

'I can have you up for assault you know,' he said trying to brush away her hands.

Alice's eyes flashed like slate caught in the sun. 'And I can have you up on a breach of property regulations,' she snapped, letting go of his shirt.

The man straightened his clothes with trembling hands. That could mean a hefty fine and possibly relocating.

'No need to get so excited. With things as they are what's a man supposed to do? I knew Mr McIain's money was good.'

'And mine isn't?' Alice was ready to explode.

'Mr McIain is a long-standing client of ours. He flew all the way back from Western Australia specially to buy this property.' Gleeson had retreated from Alice and was starting to regain his confidence. The top button of Alice's blouse had come undone reminding him he was dealing with a female. 'I also know you've upset a lot of the folks round here by what you're doing. Two women working all alone out in the bush is asking for trouble. What you should be doing is running a nice little craft shop in town. Let me show you an excellent bargain.' He attempted to move towards his books. Quivering with fury Alice stormed round the desk blocking his path, her voice crescendoing in outrage.

'I come here with good money to complete what I understood was a genuine deal and you tell me to run a craft shop.' Poking him in the chest with one finger she forced him back until he was trapped between the window and the filing cabinet. 'If you'd been honest and had half a brain you'd have worked out you could have pushed up the price by getting back to me.' The man tried to speak but Alice drowned him out. 'It's people like you this district doesn't need, not ones trying to make a go of things.' They were eyeball to eyeball. The door opened and Ross's receptionist put her head round the door.

'Everything all right in here, Mr Gleeson?' she asked and gasped at the sight of her employer bailed up in the corner like one of Alice's sheep.

'Quite all right thank you,' snapped Alice stepping away from him as though he carried some vile contagious disease. 'Your employer has an interesting way of doing deals and I want my cheque back.' The woman sprang to his defence but he held up his hand.

'Could you find Mrs Turlington's deposit on the Weston property,' he said red-faced and sweating.

'I'm sure the other property agents would agree what you've done here today is very bad for business.' Alice stepped backwards satisfied he was finally looking decidedly unhappy.

'Don't you threaten me again, young woman,' Gleeson growled, relieved she wasn't going to pursue things further.

'I'm not threatening anyone, Mr Gleeson. I'm letting you know you will never, ever do anything like this to me again.' Grabbing the cheque and her bag, Alice stormed outside slamming the door so the windows rattled. Striding down the main street of Coonabarabran still boiling with rage she wondered why it was necessary for some people to be so loathsome. 'I'll show them I'm not just some tall poppy to be cut down,' she raged. Disappointed though she was at the loss of the land it was the unfair way she had been treated that stung the most. And to cap it all it had been Robert who had gazumped her.

'What got up her nose? Heard she's terrible to work with,' offered the receptionist. 'Are you sure you're all right?'

'I think I might grab a bite to eat,' replied Ross Gleeson once more the slick operator. He strode off down to the pub. Puffing himself up he went over to a couple of his mates who were propping up the bar. They were builders, swarthy men in sweaty shirts, baggy shorts and battered dusty boots.

'You look a bit rugged, mate. Had a bad morning?' asked one of the men.

'Had a bit of a run-in with the young lass from MerryMaid. Tricky customer,' he said and started to explain.

The builder knocked back the rest of his beer. 'Set 'em up again, Shirl, and one here for Ross,' he called to the hard-faced woman who ran the pub. She had pricked up her ears at the mention of MerryMaid. The woman produced three ice-cold schooners, wiping the bar as they were lifted. 'Put a couple of these under yer belt, mate, and you'll be right,' said the builder to Gleeson.

The story was all over town by nightfall, only Alice was portrayed as the hysterical female, Ross Gleeson as the hero.

Ten days later, still smouldering at being gazumped, Alice was staring down at a broken pump that when operating lifted water from the nearby creek into her sheep troughs. The creek divided her land from the Weston property, now owned by Robert. Raising her head she caught sight of a haze of dust approaching in the distance. Straightening up she watched the dustball became a Landrover. Driving across the paddock it stopped a few metres away from her. The door opened and out stepped Robert McIain. Disgusted, Alice stared at the heap of rusty metal at her feet.

'G'day, Alice,' Robert called out.

Alice ignored him, determinedly pulling at a piece of rusty pipe. It broke off in her hand. Frustrated she tried to fix it. It was hopeless—she could see at a glance the whole pump would have to be replaced. A flock of white cockatoos flew screeching from the trees nearby. Lucky them, she thought, watching them circling above her, her back firmly towards Robert. They could fly around without worrying about people lying and swindling.

'These darned things don't last more than five minutes,' Robert said in her ear.

Alice nearly leapt out of her skin. Whirling round she stared into Robert's brown eyes and her heart missed a beat. Furious with her reaction she grabbed the pipe.

'Get off my property!' she shouted, swinging it furiously in his direction.

'Hey wait a sec,' exclaimed Robert backing away. 'What's got you so fired up?' Her angry beauty stirred up all the old emotions.

'You're trespassing! Get off. Get off my land,' raged Alice. Robert held up his hands.

'Okay, okay. I'm going. You just looked like you needed some help with that pump.' He backed away, unable to take his eyes off her.

His helpful offer twisted at Alice's heart inflaming her anger further as she watched him wade back through the muddy creek bed and climb across the broken fence onto his own property.

'Don't pretend you don't know what went on. I could have trebled my offer and still not felt the pinch,' she yelled racing after him. 'Is the only way you can get land, by cheating on women?'

'What the heck are you on about?' yelled back Robert. 'I haven't cheated anyone.'

'Gazumping, that's what I'm on about. You gazumped me, Robert McIain. That should have been my land.' The two glared at one another across the creek. Robert opened his mouth to yell again and the light dawned.

'You wanted to buy Charlie Weston's place? I had no idea. Ross said no one else was interested.'

'That'd be right,' she fumed. 'I'd like to scratch that man's eyes out.'

'From what I heard you nearly did.'

'Oh yes?' Alice raised her eyebrows inquiringly. Her anger subsiding, her interest piqued she moved closer. Robert looked so damned handsome, his hat tilted back off his face, chestnut curls tickling his ears, bewilderment mixed with annoyance in his face.

'He's got the marks to prove it, so the story goes.'

'Yarns certainly flourish in the bush,' Alice said tartly after Robert had told the version of the story that was going around the district and had apologised for accidentally gazumping her. 'I suppose there's no chance you'd reconsider?'

Robert looked at her for a long time and finally shook his head. It was tempting and in another life he would have given Alice the world but he needed this land to save the top paddocks Andrew and his two brothers were threatening to sell off. Anyway, as far as he and Katie were concerned it would be disastrous. As it was he had been forced to buy Gillgully Downs, as he had renamed Weston's place, in his own name. Actually he felt rather good about the deal. It was the first piece of land that was entirely his.

'I wouldn't have either,' admitted Alice. 'But it was worth a try.'

'You're becoming quite a legend around here, you know,' said Robert in admiration, breaking the silence that had fallen between them.

'About time too,' Alice sparked back. 'I'm sick of being told women can't do what I'm doing.'

'Well you're doing it that's for sure. I hear you just bought three local champions for your stud.' He stuck his hands in his pockets fighting his longing to gather Alice in his arms. 'The reason I came up here was to check out the best way to set up a new irrigation system. Then I was going to drive over and discuss how we could share the water in this creek.' He pushed back his hat and scratched one ear. 'Would you let me look at the pump?'

Alice nodded. Perversely she could not drag herself from this man in whose presence she felt such an agony of longing.

'It's a pretty good rust bucket,' she said peeping at him out of the corner of her eye as they stood over the pump. Her stomach twisted. They could almost be husband and wife standing so close, discussing the management of their properties so casually.

'I'm sure we can manage to share what water there is without coming to blows, don't you?' she said brusquely, feeling safer on the defensive.

'My word. In fact I'm pretty sure I've got an old pump you can have back at Wangianna.' He bent down to pick up the broken pipe accidentally brushing her arm as he stood up. Together they stopped, each profoundly affected by the accidental contact. Brilliant blue eyes stared into velvet brown. Involuntarily Robert reached out to touch her, hesitated and instead jiggled the pipe embarrassed. 'I'd better get going. I'll ask one of the men to drop this down in the next day or so,' he stumbled.

'Would you?' said Alice dizzily.

'I'd drop it in myself only we're flying back to Western Australia tomorrow.'

His words brought Alice back to reality with a thump. Immediately she was all politeness and efficiency.

'I'll return it to you as soon as I get a new one sent up from Sydney. How are Katie and Stewart?'

'Oh, they're good. Katie hates Karri Karri and isn't looking forward to returning, but Stewwy loves it.' His eyes lit up as he mentioned his son. 'What about your kids?'

'Good, really good.' The atmosphere had become tense again.

'I'll see you get that pump,' said Robert frowning. To stay in her company any longer would be disastrous. His body ached to hold her and with each passing second his resistance weakened. Quickly he strode back onto his property, his emotions a maelstrom. Alice was merely his neighbour. He could not afford to think of her in any other way.

Alice watched the Landrover disappear in a haze of dust, twiddling her wedding ring. Why did it have to be Robert who had bought the adjacent property? It was like some endless torture not being able to escape the one man she wanted to forget.

Just before Christmas Alice got a letter from Teddy's solicitor. The temperature had been 42 degrees for two weeks solid with hot winds blowing across the plains sapping energy and bringing dust storms that got into everything. The London address jerked her back to the realisation that since 1970 there had miraculously been no demands from Teddy to send the children back to the UK, although he had regularly sent birthday and Christmas presents, usually outlandishly expensive but remarkably appropriate. Alice suspected Lady Turlington had a hand in picking them. Alice's hands started to shake as she slit open the letter. Everything had been going so brilliantly well she prayed that he wasn't going to upset her life all over again. Scanning her eyes down the typewritten page she read with relief that their divorce papers had come through and once she returned the enclosed document she was a free woman. Alice's immediate reaction was elation which turned almost immediately to emptiness. What was the point of being single if the one person you loved was married to someone else? She signed the paper with a flourish and stuck it on the dresser with the other letters.

Then she went outside in search of Fraser. She found him fixing up the fencing that divided her property from Robert's. Slumping down in the shade of the ute she chewed on a piece of grass. The last two months had been one problem on top of another. First she'd had arguments over the price of feed, then complications with delivery of the feed. Just as she needed him Jimmy had gone walkabout and then the high tensile wiring on her property had been purposely cut so some of her sheep had got mixed up with some from Wangianna and the new chum Andrew Holt had come charging over, arrogant and abusive, so that in the end she had given up trying to explain what had happened. It had taken her three days to sort out her mob from theirs.

'Is it me or is the rest of the world intent on stopping me from getting on with my job?' asked Alice spitting out the blade of grass. Fraser straightened up, his job finished.

'You're a real barrel of laughs today, Alice. It's not like you to let things get you down.' Alice was about to tell him about the divorce and the hopeless irony of the situation but paused realising the stupidity of such an admission. Fraser, interpreting her silence as despondency, continued. 'This is the outback, Alice. You know that, just as you know we men guard our territory furiously. It's not that we mean to half the time, or that we don't recognise we need you women.'

'I know all that but why can't people see I'm simply trying to do the best I can like everyone else?'

'Not everyone can handle what you're about. It's bad enough having to sell off all your stock, but when a woman goes and buys it all up like you just did well, let's just say some folk find that difficult to swallow. If you'd wanted an easier life maybe you should have taken up Gleeson's offer to run a craft shop,' he finished straight-faced.

'Now don't you start,' growled Alice standing up and shaking her legs, but his comment had brought a smile back to her lips. 'What I really want is more winners. Tell me where to look.' Fraser grinned at her.

'You're timing's uncanny,' he admitted. 'I heard today the ram that won Sydney Champion two years running is up for private auction next week along with some other beauties. Owner got in too deep and now with the drought and wool still down, plus a run of bad luck, he's putting the lot up for auction before Christmas and getting out of wool. Anyone who gets their hands on that lot will be a force to be reckoned with. They're not cheap mind.'

The sheep Fraser had told her about were superb. With money from ealier sales Alice bought the lot. Her purchase was soon being talked of across the state. By Christmas 1972 the name MerryMaid had started to mean a whole lot more in the sheep breeding and wool industry.

Chapter Twenty-nine

STEWART RAN FROM BEHIND the Karri Karri tractor shed towards Robert, waving a dead rat by the tail. Chris, the young stockman Robert had hired three months ago, followed more slowly.

'Shall I bury it or cook it for dinner, Dad?' Stewart chortled grinning cheekily. 'Got to be better than the muck we had last night.'

'Cheeky beggar. Don't you dare let your mother hear you.' Stewart's eyes lit up with devilment and he rushed off gleefully in search of Katie.

'Did you put him up to this?' demanded Robert.

'What me?' replied Chris, all innocence. The screams from the kitchen quickly proved Stewart had found his mother. His re-emergence dragged by the ear demonstrated that she had not appreciated the joke.

'Did you tell him to bring that filthy thing in here?' she shrieked, searching around for Robert who with Chris had hurriedly vanished into the tractor shed like two naughty schoolboys.

'Aw, Mum, it was only a joke. Ouch! Ouch!' cried Stewart as she dragged harder on his ear. Wriggling free he dropped the dead rat and charged towards the shed.

'Not to me it wasn't!' shouted Katie, her pretty mouth distorted in anger. 'Your father'll hear more of this.' She was left to drop the vile thing in the bin herself.

'She didn't think it was funny, Dad,' cried Stewart grinning wickedly.

'I warned you, lad,' choked Robert. The three of them doubled over with mirth. Wiping the tears from his eyes Robert clapped Stewart on the shoulder. 'Now you can go and hunt out any more and burn them in case the dogs get at them, and then go and finish your school work.'

'I did,' said Stewart scampering off.

Proudly Robert watched him go. At ten he was growing into a responsible young stockman. For this year he was doing school by correspondence but next year he would need to go to boarding school to give him more opportunities. That was another thing preying on Robert's mind. He was scared of how he would cope without Stewart about to remind him why he kept trying with Katie.

'I'm going to miss you, you little blighter,' Robert thought, suddenly sober.

'You two'll be in deep trouble later on, boss,' laughed Chris his shoulders still shaking.

Robert nodded his agreement. Maybe he'd just have to find the money to send Katie to Perth again.

Except for the recent short trip home the three of them had been living on the Western Australian station since their agreement in April. Katie hated the place. Vast and isolated it had none of the glamour of Wangianna, but once working again it would be a solid income earner. At the moment it was hot and dusty, the parched cracked earth hardly capable of sustaining the sparse clumps of spinifex that dotted the landscape. Their nearest neighbour was thirty kilometres away and they took turns to call each other up at around six each night on the pedal radio to check there had been no accidents. Robert got around the property on an ancient motorbike and in the two-seater Cessna 150 for the weekly inspection of the fifty-two windmills that pumped the water up from the bores and wells.

Concerned at the way Wangianna was going with Andrew at the helm, Robert had ploughed all his own money into building up Karri Karri and maintaining the stock, which meant no spare cash and no shopping sprees. He had suggested Katie join the Country Women's Association, which she had tried but quickly managed to get almost everyone off side. The locals, while trying to include her in their projects, found her continual whingeing and complaining, coupled with tales of her extravagant life when George was alive, hard to stomach. They neither admired her flirtatious behaviour with their men nor her unwillingness to muck in and help. Local feeling was you supported your man and you got on with the job of helping him and everyone else whether you liked it or not. Katie failed on all counts. So after the brief September respite at Wangianna Katie felt doubly alone on their return, frequently crying herself to sleep at the state of her cracked reddened hands and broken nails and the endless backbreaking work demanded of her. Her cooking was abysmal and her housekeeping worse. Her unwillingness to try and make things work totally frustrated Robert, but they had agreed to give themselves and Karri Karri a year before returning to Wangianna for good. And as Katie had no money of her own except what Robert gave her there was nothing much left for her to do except get on with things, which she did mostly with extreme bad grace.

Always at the back of his mind Robert worried about Wangianna. Wangianna should be doing what MerryMaid was doing, buying in good stock while prices were dropping and planning survival tactics for the next few years. They had the capital but when he had mentioned this to his brothers he had been shouted down.

When his mother informed him Andrew had sold off some of their good ewes for ridiculously low prices to avoid having to buy extra feed he felt like weeping with helpless frustration.

It was at these low moments that his thoughts invariably turned to what life might have been like with Alice, and his heart filled with misery. Chris's attitude helped. Robert was astounded at how hard he worked.

'What made you pick Karri Karri to work?' he asked Chris as they worked together in the sweltering heat fixing the pump on a windmill to the far northeast corner of the property.

'Dunno really. I like the isolation. Too many people fuss me. I was raised in this part of the world. This place is a challenge and I like challenges. As soon as I've saved enough money me and me girlfriend plan to get hitched.'

'Then you'll be moving on soon?' He had hoped to train Chris as the manager of Karri Karri.

'Not unless you sack me first. Me girlfriend keeps asking when she can come out and join me. She's not one for the bright lights either. She's just happy as long as we're together. I reckon I'm a real lucky bloke.'

'I'll say,' remarked Robert suddenly ashamed of Katie. His spirits, already low from being unable to stop the potential ruin of Wangianna through the stupidity of his half-brother, swung around to his own predicament. Perhaps he should stop struggling with a marriage that didn't work, accept the loss of Stewart and try to win back Alice. But as he struggled with an obstinate bolt, he knew perfectly well it could never work. There was no way he would ever compromise his son's happiness.

'Well that's her going again,' he said finally, patting the steel pipe with his spanner and listening with satisfaction to the sound of the pump working again. Chris picked up the tools and they walked back to the plane.

In the first week in December an exhausted Katie jerked the truck to a halt outside the house in forty-two degree heat. She had just driven the four-hour round-trip to their nearest town Meekatharra to collect the monthly groceries and pick up the mail. Rattling and shaking along dirt roads she had alternately fried with the windows up or choked from the dust with them down. Her thin cotton dress was drenched with sweat, her blonde hair a tangled strawlike mass; she was dying of thirst and she had a splitting headache. Having decided to ignore the doctor's warning of further miscarriages and fall pregnant again, she had just discovered she was not, and her disappointment, coupled with exhaustion and the inevitable cramps, spiralled into rage.

Staggering into the kitchen under a mound of groceries she was confronted by the disaster she had left behind that morning. A large blowfly buzzed over the remnants of last night's tea and today's breakfast. Dirty dishes and glasses overflowed the sink. Limp vegetables she had forgotten to pack away in the ancient refrigerator lay alongside bits of garden hose she had been trying to mend. A wine-soaked packet of tea sagged next to a mangled dried-out loaf of bread she had baked the day before and was sure she had put away before setting out to Meekatharra. Baking bread was the one talent she had in the kitchen. An ever growing pile of mending glared at her from one corner. Without even looking she knew the laundry was bulging with dirty, stinking clothes. Tears of exhaustion sprang to her eyes at the enormity of the task of clearing up, not to mention packing away. Timing it badly Stewart scampered in chewing on a large hunk of bread.

'Hi Mum! What's for tea?' he asked.

Katie rapidly took in Stewart, the bread in his hand and the mangled loaf on the side. At the same time she tripped over a pile of magazines she had left strewn on the kitchen floor so the case of eggs balanced precariously on the top of her parcels slid] to the floor with a sickening thud. Egg yolks leaked out all over the floor opening the floodgates of her bitterness against the world.

'That's it!' she screamed. 'Go straight to bed, now! You mangle my bread. You don't deserve to eat anything else.'

Robert chose that precise moment to walk in.

'Come on, Katie, that's a bit steep,' he said seeing Stewart's hollow-eyed expression. 'It's only a loaf of bread.'

Katie rounded on her husband. 'You would say that. You always side with him. It doesn't matter what I do or how I feel. No one cares that my hair is like straw, that my hands are wrecked, that I am so exhausted I can hardly stand—' Her tirade was cut short by the piercing shrill of the telephone. Grabbing the receiver before anyone else she shouted angrily into the mouthpiece.

'Hello.' Immediately her whole personality changed as she waited for the operator to connect the call. Her shoulders relaxed while her expression changed to one of cunning.

'No, Elizabeth, everything's fine, really. You just caught me at a bad moment.' Her voice was slightly too high. 'Well, things get a little bit tough now and then but we're fine. I'll pass you over to Robbo. Here he is.' She handed the phone to Robert and went in search of some tablets for her headache.

'Katie just got back from collecting the groceries. It's bloody hot and she's feeling a bit rough, Mum,' he explained. 'Stewwy's fine.' He told her about the dead rat which brought a small smile to Stewart's lips.

'Remember I did the same to you when I was about his age. Katie wasn't amused either. I don't know what it is about you mums and rats.'

He listened for a moment then asked, 'What did you ring up for, Mum? I know you only call when you're worried.' Robert's face became grimmer and grimmer as he listened. Finally he put the phone down and scratched his head.

Returning, Katie stepped over the mess of broken eggs to get a drink of water. Swallowing the tablets she sank into a chair and opened the month-old *Warren Advocate* from the mail she had collected, only to toss it on the floor in disgust.

'Cow! No doubt if Alice were running this place everything would be perfect and you'd all be happy and the mending'd be done and there'd be soup bubbling on the stove.'

'Whatever made you say a stupid thing like that?' asked Robert irritably, mopping up the spreading yolks, riddled with guilt as he had earlier been thinking those very thoughts. He picked up the *Advocate* that had narrowly missed the broken eggs and his heart lurched as he stared into the happy smiling face of Alice flanked on one side by her latest champion ram and on the other by 'The Emperor'. Surrounded by smiling stockmen, two bonny children and Marigold, she was the romantic ideal of the successful wool breeder. The caption read MERRYMAID'S SUCCESS.

Katie buried her head in her hands and burst into tears. 'I can't do this any more. I'm so miserable. I want to go home,' she gulped between sobs.

Stewart, still standing in the doorway, crept forward and peered at the picture. He liked his Aunty Alice. Robert stared down at his wife's sobbing frame. Maybe he had asked too much of her, living and working on this isolated place month after month with him away most of the day and no other female company, catering for the irregular stockmen and only occasional radio contact for days on end. But it was all he had been able to think of to try and rebuild their marriage. He had succeeded to some degree.

'Make your mum a cup of tea,' he ordered Stewart. He picked up one of Katie's rough chapped hands and ran his fingers along the chipped nails that had been so perfect eight months ago, surveying the chaos around. 'Don't take it too hard, Katie, we've only got a few months to go, but

I really need you to be here. If we can keep this place going there's a chance we can save Wangianna. Stewwy and I'll give you a hand to clear all this up and I'll make tea.' Katie continued to sob. 'Mum suggested you meet her in Melbourne and go Christmas shopping.'

Katie's reaction was instantaneous. The sobs stopped and she sat up. 'But your mother hates Melbourne.'

'Things are rather tense at home at the moment and she wants a bit of a break.' Katie's wan expression changed to jubilation. Cashing in on her positive reaction Robert went on. 'I've never made a big deal of this because I didn't want to raise your hopes, but quite frankly, and after what Mum's just told me, I don't think Andy's going to last the course. I think he'll pack in running the place before the new year.'

'And we'll get Wangianna back?' asked Katie hopefully. Life suddenly looked brighter.

'Well, it'll still belong to us three brothers. D'you want to ring her back when you're feeling better and tell her you'll go shopping with her?'

'I'm better right now,' exclaimed Katie excitedly and leaped up to call Elizabeth. Just the thought of escaping this hellhole was enough for her. 'What about money?' she asked suddenly cautious as Robert poured the dripping egg carton into the bin.

'I expect we'll be able to find the odd bob or two for Christmas,' replied Robert, relieved to see how she'd rallied. He attacked the mess anew and Stewart started to pack away the groceries. 'Let's have a barbie tonight. It's too hot to cook inside.' Katie didn't answer—she was already talking to the operator.

After dinner Robert poured himself another glass of beer and watched the sunset blaze red turning the trees to black silhouettes. Katie had fallen into bed almost immediately after tea. Robert thought about his conversation with his mother. Andy, according to Elizabeth, was spending money they didn't have and on all the wrong things, and Ian and Jordie were just following suit. He kept upgrading vehicles and machinery that could easily be made to last another five to ten years and buying unnecessary high-tech gimmicky gadgets, stubbornly ignoring the need to spend money on the basics like feed and irrigation. Having recently harvested a couple of paddocks, ignoring Elizabeth's advice to keep it for their own needs, Andy had sold almost the entire harvest to the highest bidder. It had sold for a hefty price but if Robert had learned anything it was that the price of feed they desperately needed to preserve stock would rise dramatically in the next few months, as would interest rates, making a mockery of the sale. They were moving into the driest part of the season in the worst drought for years and this idiot was making matters worse daily.

Watching the sun creep down over the horizon, listening to the sounds of the outback, Robert put aside his cares for a few moments. It was so beautiful at this time of day. In the fading light kangaroos crept cautiously out of the scrub where they had sheltered from the searing heat. Gradually more appeared, moving swiftly in great lolloping bounds, until thirty or more had congregated to drink from a lone puddle by a leaky water trough. Only the soft sup-sup as they drank thirstily disturbed the hot stillness. He'd have to fix that trough tomorrow. All the troughs needed replacing. He'd have to cull some more roos soon too. They were beautiful regal animals standing so completely still, their tall ears pricked for danger, but they were a farmer's curse. If you didn't keep the numbers down they downgraded your land and threatened your sheep. He'd talk to Chris tomorrow and see if his neighbour was interested in helping.

A flock of noisy galahs shrieked across the darkening sky and were gone, so that soon the land was dotted with tiny bent figures foraging for food in the sparse dryness. Robert took a sip of beer. Katie'd fly out on the fourteenth of December. With Chris willing to trial as manager over Christmas he'd feel secure heading home with Stewwy on the twenty-second. A big tree goanna slunk along the ground in search of food as Robert drifted off to sleep.

Robert was shocked at how drawn his mother looked when he arrived back at Wangianna. He wondered whether shopping with Katie had been such a good idea, but Elizabeth assured him she had enjoyed the break. Katie had gone over to see Sophie and Snake and show off some of her spoils. Determined to prove how nice she was she had bought Sophie's children presents as well as the family and even bought one each for Vicky and Ben. Later that evening Elizabeth sat and talked to Robert on his own.

'I miss running Wangianna with you, Robby. It's like a part of me has been cut out.' Her voice was filled with sadness. 'The boys and I had a bit of a falling out over the sale of the lucerne hay and now I don't get to see the figures any more,' she told him, rubbing at the top of her chest. There was a resignation in her voice Robert had never heard before. 'But I can see what's happening, Robby. I can see what's happening and it terrifies me.' She frowned, fearing the tight rein on her emotions might suddenly break. 'I don't think any of them have an idea of what they are doing.'

Robert hugged her close, feeling his anger against his father growing.

Elizabeth clasped both her hands around his and gazed intently into eyes identical to her own. 'Don't do anything foolhardy, Robby, but I have to say this: Wangianna needs your strength.' She recovered her poise. 'Be honest with me, where do you think we should be taking the place?'

'The same way it's always been going, Mum,' said Robert flatly. 'Breeding sheep for wool and keeping up the quality of the stud. I admit we're going through a bit of a slump but I can't see any reason to change.'

'Then call a family meeting and try and make the others see sense,' she pleaded.

'Some hope with that idiot Andy.' His tone was suddenly unexpectedly harsh. Elizabeth's agitation increased.

'You're still mad at what your father did, aren't you?'

Robert stood up swiftly. 'Mad? You bet I'm bloody mad. Madder than a Mallee bull. If it hadn't been for Dad's bloody stupid behaviour none of this would have happened. To satisfy his own guilty conscience, not content with shaming you by stuffing his mistress' son up your nose, he has to indulge in petty heroics and wreck all our lives as well. Why couldn't the bastard have just left him some money? That would have been quite sufficient.' He paced up and down the large sitting room. Elizabeth started tidying the cushions. Quickly he went to his mother. 'I'm sorry, Mum, that was unpardonable of me.'

'I understand, dear, I understand,' said Elizabeth blowing her nose. 'Let's get through Christmas and then see if there's any hope of sorting out this mess. All I ask is we keep the property together.' It was all she had thought of for nights on end. 'I don't want to be disloyal to your brothers but Ian and Jordie think we're swimming along and won't listen to any advice, but of the three it's Andrew who terrifies me the most. Robby, we could end up bankrupt.' She was rubbing her chest again.

'Are you sick, Mum?'

'It's nothing. I'm just overtired.'

But Robert didn't like the way she looked. Christmas Day burned hot and dry with the temperature well into the forties, fraying tempers and making a traditional hot Christmas dinner an unbearable task to prepare and harder to eat. By the end of the day Elizabeth, who was a stickler for tradition, was looking exhausted. One bonus was that Andrew spent Christmas Day with his mother's family in Melbourne but anxious that Robert might work on his other two half-brothers in his absence he was back at Wangianna on Boxing Day. The day after Boxing Day despite the continuing high temperature, Robert organised a family meeting, insisting that Elizabeth and Katie be included. Katie sat filing her nails and flapping her dress under the fan in an effort to cool down. Remembering Robert's forecast of doom for Andrew she decided to keep quiet.

Robert started by asking Andrew to put them in the financial picture with some basic profit and loss figures. After carrying on in his usual arrogant way for twenty minutes Andrew produced the figures to the end of October. He could show nothing for November and December. His projected outcome for the next six months sounded decidedly shaky to Robert's ears. Swallowing his frustration, Robert started outlining what he thought were the trouble spots and where they should be moving. However, Ian immediately leapt to Andrew's defence.

'It's all very well your coming roaring in here like this telling us what to do. You haven't even been bloody working on the property for nearly a year. I'm buggered if I'm going to put up with you dictating rules and criticising our management.' He took a swig of beer.

'I'm not telling anyone what to do,' said Robert trying to stay calm. 'I'm just trying to understand why all of a sudden things aren't looking so rosy around here.'

'We've decided to diversify into cotton and fat lambs. We agreed that before Christmas, subject to Andrew getting approval on the bank loan,' retorted Ian. 'I've already ordered a whole new irrigation system and a cotton harvester and we're cutting our wool stock by three-quarters over the next two months.' Having dropped his bombshell he sat back watching Robert's face with delight.

'Is this true, Jordie, Andrew?' Robert searched their faces, the colour draining from his cheeks. 'Did you know, Mum?' Elizabeth's mouth was a thin tight line. She shook her head in despair. Robert's jaw tightened. 'Do I have a say in any of this or is that it?'

'There didn't seem much point hanging about,' continued Ian gleefully. For once in his life he was leading his big brother by the nose. 'Between the three of us we own seventy-five per cent of Wangianna so your vote's fairly irrelevant.'

Robert was stunned. He had known he would have a battle on his hands but he never thought it would all be so completely out of his control.

'This is crazy,' he stood up angrily. 'Mum's been running this place on her own since before we were born. If you won't listen to me, listen to her. I guarantee in three to five years wool prices will rocket and we'll be laughing again if we get it right now.'

'The market's changing, Bluey,' said Andrew. Robert loathed him calling him Bluey.

'Oh it is, is it Andy? How much did the bank lend you?' The two men glared at one another. Andrew cleared his throat.

'That was the next point I was going to bring up.' He reddened under Robert's frosty stare. He looked at the others. 'I might as well get this over with.' He got up and moved slightly away from the group. Suddenly everyone was listening. 'There's no easy way to say this. The bank manager refused the loan.'

'What?' chorused Ian and Jordie.

'He can't have!' cried Ian.

'That's ridiculous!' said Jordie.

'He's supported us since you were babies. Did he give his reasons?' asked a white-lipped Elizabeth her voice cutting through the silence.

Andrew tried to brazen it out. 'Seems if you've lived here for most of your life they hand out loans like lamingtons, but if you've got a college education to prove your ability you're forever the "new chum" and you don't get offered the same service.'

Ian, frightened at losing out on his cotton plans, leaped up. 'I'll ring him straightaway and ask him what the hell he's thinking.'

'It won't make any difference,' explained Andrew sheepishly. 'I approached him in early September and he told me my potential was unknown. He gave me three months under observation to prove myself, and that took us to the beginning of December. From the way he was talking at the time I didn't see the need to worry anyone about it. By the time my so-called probation period was over we'd had an unexpected run on the dollar, interest rates had risen and we'd sold off some of our mob cheap.' Andrew rattled the coins in his pockets looking more and more uncomfortable. 'Seems he took exception to some of my decisions so he turned down the second application.' Ian and Jordie were staring at him in stunned amazement. Elizabeth sat her face immobile. Andrew hated having to ask his next question. 'What do you suggest we do, fellas?'

Robert, still reeling from having been excluded from any discussions, jumped in first. 'The best thing you can do, Andy, is piss off back to the city before you destroy everything we've ever worked for.'

Andrew glared across at his half-brother. 'The name as you well know is Andrew and I have no intention of doing anything of the sort,' he replied coolly. He focused on Ian and Jordie. 'We can work this out together, I'm sure.' But he could see as soon as he spoke that he had already lost the confidence of his other two half-brothers.

'We do as we'd planned and diversify into cotton and fat lambs,' said Ian sounding less certain.

'But we don't have any money to cover initial outlay without the loan, Ian,' cried Jordie. 'If he's stuffed up our bank credit we've had it.'

'Don't be so panicky,' snapped Ian. He swallowed his pride. 'Robert, you go and talk to him. He'll always listen to you.'

Robert gave a short laugh. 'You must be bloody joking.' No one spoke. Robert caught the pleading in Elizabeth's eyes. 'Only if Andy agrees to shift over and let me and Mum run the finances of Wangianna with Mum again,' he replied decisively.

Katie looked up in anticipation. Her nails were looking much better already. Maybe they would get Wangianna back yet.

'Over my dead body!' shouted Andrew fighting like a trapped animal. 'My father left me Wangianna to run and that's what I'm doing. All I need is a little support.'

'That's another bloody joke. You've had your chance, mate, and you've blown it,' retorted Robert. 'If we don't make some major changes around here the only people running this place'll be the bank.' Ian and Jordie were looking decidedly chastened. Robert turned to his mother. 'I know you don't want to hear this, Mum, but the only solution I can see is we split the property and take our share while it's still worth something.'

As much as the thought of splitting the property tore at his heart at least this way he could save his share of Wangianna and also his mother's. 'I'll vouch to take on extra stock you don't want to look after and you can run whatever you choose on your land. We share equipment when we can and buy our own when we can afford it.'

For a long time no one spoke. Andrew's face was a mixture of surprise and relief. Ian was giving the idea serious thought.

'Better still,' said Robert, 'for your share of Karri Karri, Ian, I'll buy you your cotton harvester.'

Ian leaped at the offer. 'You're on.' He, like Katie, loathed Karri Karri. Inappropriately named after the eucalyptus tree, in his view it was a lonely dustbowl that the flies and kangaroos could keep. Elizabeth had gone quite still. Katie stood up about to open her mouth but Robert silenced her with a glance. Everyone started arguing again.

'What do you think, Mum?' asked Ian suddenly.

Elizabeth stared at her three sons, fighting the choking sensation that threatened to overwhelm her. It broke her heart to see everyone at each other's throats. Why, oh why had George done this to her? She stood up.

'As you were so quick to point out before, Ian, I no longer have any legal say,' she said breathlessly, her fingers working at her chest again. 'You must do whatever you think's best. I think I'll go for a walk.' A kookaburra cackled in the sudden silence. Slowly, head held high, Elizabeth walked down the verandah steps. Everyone watched the lone figure stride across the parched earth. Robert wanted to cry. What a bloody awful Christmas. How the heck had they ended up in a mess like this?

'We'll put it to the vote,' he said.

The splitting up of Wangianna was the first time all four brothers had managed to agree on anything.

Alice spent Christmas with Bea and Ray. It was as stifling at Billabrin as it was at Wangianna. Halfway through the day Ray disappeared to fight grass fires at the back of a mate's property and Ben got extremely fractious and clingy in the heat. But nothing could destroy Alice's happiness. Her artificial insemination program was underway and The Emperor was magnificent. Starting small, the program was steadily growing with The Emperor's progeny set to spread worldwide as interest grew from overseas buyers. She had also invested heavily in new irrigation systems across her land. Her last two loads of feed had arrived without problems and she had just stocked up two big barns of reserve hay. The kids were thriving, although Ben was becoming rather clingy and she missed Marigold who had gone back home to England for Christmas, but she was managing surprisingly well on her own. Everyone except Katie and Billy, who was still working overseas, managed to get home for Christmas Day. Paddy had finally got a girlfriend and they were planning to get married in four months' time.

Alice's other happiness was a Christmas card from Rosie and John Dixson congratulating her on her work and a long letter from Harry and

Roody talking of a possible two-day stop-over in Australia on their way to their next posting. Confident she could risk leaving MerryMaid under the astute eye of Jimmy for another couple of days, Alice decided to stay on at her aunt's.

Halfway through lunch on twenty-seventh of December there was a knock on the front door. Alice, who was collecting dessert, opened the door and was greeted by a young man in his mid-thirties whom she did not recognise.

'Hello, Alice, long time no see.' The young man held out his hand.

'Do I know you?' Alice asked curiously.

'Jo Perry, remember, back in the days when you were learning to fly with Joker? I was the one with the oily rag.' Alice stared blankly and then recognition dawned.

'Jo!' she squealed. 'What an amazing surprise. How lovely. What are you doing in Billabrin?' Dark haired and confident, Jo was far from the callow youth Alice remembered from her early flying days.

'I'm working for the Royal Flying Doctor Service and when Joker found out I'd be coming over this way he made me promise to drop your present in. He said to tell you he'll be back from America in the New Year with his latest purchase and you can be first in the air with it. So here I am.'

Jo was equally surprised. If anything Alice had grown more beautiful. Instead of the usual jeans, shirt and Akubra Alice was for once wearing a soft flowing dress. Her wild hair was caught loosely back with a large cream ribbon to keep her neck cool. He had forgotten the amazing colour of her eyes. Jo gave a low whistle and Alice blushed.

'He gave me this to give to you. Happy Christmas.' He held out a small wrapped gift. Delighted Alice opened it. It was a bottle of L'air du Temps.

'Dear Joker I need something to make me smell a bit better around here. Thank you,' she smiled warmly. 'We're just finishing a very late lunch. Come and join us for dessert.'

'I can't stay long. I'm picking up a doctor mate of mine who's been staying with his wife's folks for Christmas out on the Lochlans' property,' explained Jo. 'Actually, I was wondering if you'd like to come for a flight.'

'In the new machine? I'd love to.' Alice's face lit up with excitement. Everyone had heard about the new Royal Flying Doctors' plane recently bought from America.

'Not so new now. She's covered a fair stretch of country since I brought her back home.'

'You collected her? You lucky duck,' exclaimed Alice, envy in her eyes. 'Come and meet everyone and let me change into something more appropriate.'

After Alice had done all the introductions, Bea said, 'The Lochlans' place is over beyond Wangianna. Perhaps you could drop in Stewart's Christmas present as they didn't make it down here.' There was an underlying disappointment behind her smile.

'My word,' replied Jo.

'And I can drop in Robert's new pump,' added Alice. 'I've had it sitting in the truck for over a fortnight.' She dashed out to get changed. Ten minutes later Jo and she were heading towards the local airstrip.

'She's a pretty classy machine,' said Alice into the boom mike once they were airborne, shifting her earphones and readjusting the mike to suit her face. The plane had been fitted out with all the latest gear, including emergency equipment for severely injured passengers, so the inside of the plane was more like an intensive-care unit.

'She flies like a bird,' replied Jo into his mouth-piece. 'Try her.'

Alice's pulse raced as she took over the controls at three thousand feet. It seemed all she had done since she could remember was slog away on the ground. Planning, bidding, adding up figures, puzzling late into the night over research problems she had only half believed she could beat, but all that seemed a million miles away as they soared through the sky. The sense of freedom she felt was an exhilaration she had forgotten existed. She was amazed at how easily she fell back into the flying routine. If only she could share this moment with someone she loved, she thought wistfully as she glanced briefly at the profile of the man beside her. It had been four long years since her divorce from Teddy and there had been a loneliness she could not always ignore.

As if he had read her mind Jo said, 'I was sorry to hear about your divorce. Mind you, I don't know why some lucky beggar hasn't snatched you up again by now.' Alice laughed. 'I've been too busy building up MerryMaid to think about marriage,' she replied quickly.

'Head a bit further over to the west.' Alice veered to the left. 'I heard about your place. Not bad, eh, in four years. Bush telegraph still works as well as ever.'

'I'm pretty pleased how it's all gone,' Alice said loving every nuance of the great bird.

'And there's no one else on the scene?'

'Nope.'

'Amazing! D'you reckon I'd be in with a chance?' joked Jo.

'If you promised to let me fly this thing every day for the rest of my life I'd consider anything,' bantered Alice.

They chatted on until they could see the Lochlans' property and Jo called them up to land. As they had to be careful with daylight they stopped only briefly to pick up the doctor and were quickly airborne again heading off towards Wangianna, this time with Jo at the controls. Half an hour later Alice called up Wangianna and spoke to the cook.

'They're all in a family meeting at the moment, Miss Alice, but Mr Holt used the strip only on Boxing Day so you should be right to land.'

'Thanks,' said Alice and pointed out the strip.

'Coming in to land,' crowed Jo as he touched down gently and rolled onto the hard-packed dirt, bouncing along the strip lifting a stream of dirt behind them. 'You little beauty,' he chortled as he brought the plane to a stop.

'Nice landing, mate,' said the doctor from the cabin.

'Don't you worry walking in this heat. It's not far to the house. I'll just drop off this pump and be back straightaway,' said Alice jamming on her Akubra, knowing the other two didn't want to hang around.

The heat blasted at her as she stepped out onto the ground. Leaving Jo and the doctor in the relative cool of the cabin, she hurried towards the house. Her heart quailed as she saw a tall figure walking in her direction.

She would know that proud stride anywhere. Elizabeth McIain. She had never forgotten the scorn with which Elizabeth had regarded her all those long years ago. Alice kept walking, bracing herself to meet the woman. Elizabeth was passing a big grey ghost gum in the paddock beyond the house. Suddenly Elizabeth grabbed at the tree, missed and crumpled in a heap. Before she reached the ground Alice was running. Quickly crossing the ground between them Alice put down the pump and Stewart's present and shook Elizabeth gently by the shoulders.

'Mrs McIain, it's Alice, Alice Ferguson, can you hear me?' she cried. Her maiden name sounded strange on her lips.

Elizabeth's eyelids fluttered and her eyes half opened. 'They split it,' she said weakly. Her eyes fluttered closed again. Quickly weighing whether it was better to rush to the house or back to the plane; Alice decided the latter.

'You'll be all right, Mrs McIain,' she comforted. 'I'm going to get help.' Elizabeth groaned. Leaving Elizabeth in what shade there was she ran back to the plane. Jo met her halfway across the paddock.

'It's Mrs McIain, she's passed out,' she panted, red-faced and sweating. 'I don't know what's wrong. She looked grey. You got any water?'

Jo handed her a cup of water which she gulped down while Jo called up the house again. The doctor grabbed his bag and together they hurried back to Elizabeth. By the time they had got back to the tree Elizabeth had come round and was lying moaning and clutching her stomach, her breath coming in shallow rapid pants. As the doctor checked her out Robert drove up in the Landrover with Ian. Jo arrived shortly after.

'She's suffering from heat exhaustion and dehydration,' explained the doctor. 'We need to get her to the house immediately.'

Carefully Robert and Jo lifted her into the Landrover. Alice slipped in beside her, cushioning her against the bumps as best she could as Robert drove them carefully back to the house. Once laid out under one of the big fans in the sitting room the doctor gave her a further thorough examination. Satisfied that his diagnosis was correct, he got her to take small sips of water sweetened with sugar while Alice sponged her clammy forehead and arms and Cook grabbed a packet of frozen peas wrapped in a tea towel as a temporary ice pack for her stomach. The others waited anxiously outside.

Katie, hating anything to do with sickness, fussed around getting cool drinks for everyone. She set a large jug of water near Elizabeth and retreated rapidly from the room. As Elizabeth gradually cooled and the cramps subsided, her face lost its ghastly pallor.

'I think you'll be all right, Mrs Mclain,' said the doctor finally. 'Lots of rest and keep up the drinking.

'I have to go too,' explained Alice apologetically.

Elizabeth's eyes fluttered open and she reached for her hand. 'Thank you, my dear,' she whispered. Alice smiled and returned the squeeze. Then she followed the doctor out of the room.

'Mrs Mclain is suffering from acute stress, exhaustion and dehydration,' explained the doctor to the rest of the family standing around silently. 'Has she had any undue shocks lately?' Robert explained briefly that there had been some concerns over finances and then clammed up. Everyone else avoided his eye. 'We must not overlook the passing on of her late husband,' said the doctor. 'That could also be causing delayed reaction. I understand his death was completely unexpected. These things often take time to be accepted by close relatives. I don't think she needs hospitalisation but she must be given complete rest with plenty of fluids and no stress.' He gave Robert a prescription and a small bottle of tablets. 'Get her to take one twice a day for two weeks and contact her own doctor again.'

'Come on, old girl, let's get you another drink,' said Jo slipping an arm casually around Alice's waist. She was looking dishevelled and hot herself.

'She won't take the pills,' said Robert as, after cool drinks all round, he drove Alice, Jo and the doctor back to the plane.

'Stop! Your pump and Stewart's present!' shouted Alice suddenly as they passed the gum tree. Robert nearly jumped out of his skin. He stopped the car with a sudden jerk, throwing them all forward. 'Sorry!' cried Alice stepping quickly out of the vehicle into the heat and hurrying over to where she had left the parcels. Robert followed her more slowly.

'What's going on?' she asked as she handed the pump to Robert. It had been impossible not to notice the tension in the house. 'Elizabeth's the last person in the world to get stressed and you could have cut the atmosphere with a knife, and it wasn't only because of your mother.' Robert shrugged but Alice sensed his misery.

Seeing the two standing together immersed in conversation, Jo called out from the Landrover, 'We'll walk back to the plane, it's not far. Don't be long.'

'I won't,' called Alice. She turned back to Robert, swatting away a fly. 'Well?' He held himself like an old man.

'You always could winkle the truth out of me and you'll hear it soon enough anyway, so why not.' His next words seemed as though they were being dragged out of him. 'We're splitting up Wangianna. We'll be fixing it up with the solicitors next week.' He looked so desolate Alice couldn't bear it. Impulsively she dropped the pump and threw her arms around him.

'Oh Robert, I'm so sorry.' Her lips brushed his cheek. Somehow, somewhere in amongst her embrace, everything got mixed up and she felt his arms slip around her back pulling her into his powerful hug. He smelt so welcoming, like the heat of a summer's night.

'Alice,' he rasped.

Her head spun and her legs turned to jelly as he kissed her full on the mouth. Dizzily she started to pull back but as he kept kissing her she realised she wanted him to go on and on. Letting the waves of ecstasy course through her body she revelled in the warm softness of his lips, returning the pressure of his mouth, her passion increasing as he reawakened the love she could no longer deny. Her lips pressed to his, she faced what she had always known, that from the moment she had stared into his adorable velvet brown eyes all those years ago she had loved him. She had never stopped loving him. Her love for Teddy had been like weak tea compared to the full-bodied intoxication she felt for this man. She could never escape this love. She never wanted to escape this love. She gave herself wholly to his embrace.

Robert pressed her closer losing himself in the glorious remembered perfume of her skin, reviving all the tender yearning he had tried so hard to forget. His fingers entwined in her wild tresses, his mouth against her soft sensual lips, he finally accepted the love he felt for her. For so long he had been only half alive. No longer could he hide behind the belief that he could block out this love. Since the day he had set eyes on her it had consumed him. It would consume him to the grave and beyond. He kept on kissing her, all sense of time or place lost, no longer able to tell where his body ended and hers began. All that mattered was that he loved her and she was in his arms.

'Robbo!' Katie's voice jarred against their ears.

Alice broke away, horrified at what she had allowed to happen.

Katie slammed the door of the car and stormed across to them, clutching two small parcels, her eyes smouldering with hate.

'I forgot to give you your kids' presents but it seems you wanted more,' she spat.

'It wasn't what you think,' rushed Alice.

'Alice was being sympathetic over the breakup of Wangianna,' explained Robert still reeling from the impact of their kiss. It sounded limp even to his ears.

'Good try, Alice, but you're not fooling anyone,' sneered Katie. 'We both know you've never let up since you came back, prying and sneaking around behind my back. Well now I can say it to your face. Leave my husband alone, you dirty little tramp. I'd have thought your long-running affair with Fraser, poor stupid sod, would have satisfied your greedy animal appetite not to mention this pilot bloke who's all over you like a rash.'

Alice cowered with embarrassment, furious at herself for her impulsiveness, wishing she could deny the joy of Robert's kiss, fled towards the plane, speechless with misery. Jo had the engine running.

'So this is how Andy quits and we win out, is it?' shrieked Katie, beside herself with rage. Tossing Vicky and Ben's presents in the dust she ground her heel into them one after the other.

Robert heard the cracking of the doll's face and the plastic bus as if from a long way off.

Kicking the mangled remains towards him Katie shrilled 'Why don't you run after the bitch and give them to her?' Then she turned and stormed back to the car.

Robert didn't know where to look. He should never have let it happen. The joy he had felt with Alice in his arms had left him trembling from head to foot. Slowly he bent down and picked up the crushed toys with shaking fingers. How could he have been such a fool? He had won only to lose. But how much had he lost? Only once before had he seen such malice in Katie's eyes. Had he finally won back the woman he loved only to lose his son and maybe even his inheritance?

Chapter Thirty

FOR THE NEXT FEW days Katie and Robert prowled cautiously round one another, neither sure what the other's move would be. Expecting a tirade of abuse that never came and wishing to avoid exacerbating the situation, Robert apologised for his behaviour with Alice and then proceeded to act as though nothing had happened. Inwardly his nerves were like taut wire as he waited for Katie to make her move. Terrified she might try to wall out with Stewart when his back was turned he kept the boy near his side or under Melon's eagle eye as much as he could. His other fear was that she might start legal proceedings culminating in the loss of both his son and his portion of Wangianna. Under the terms of George's will Wangianna was not yet officially split so high legal costs could catapult them all over the edge into bankruptcy. Torn between Alice and Stewart, knowing his marriage to Katie was dead, the same question kept spinning in his head. What should he do next?

Katie, however, was terrified Robert might raise the subject of divorce again. With the image of Alice in Robert's arms still vivid Katie nevertheless forced herself to stay outwardly calm. Her greatest fear was that she would be forced to carry out her threat and leave with Stewart thus losing Wangianna which was so nearly within her grasp. Her only hold over Robert was Stewart.

And Robert, she realised, was the only one of the brothers who really knew what he was doing. He had built up Karri Karri when the others had been disinterested. He'd understood its potential to make money and he was well respected when it came to wool, wool management and breeding. She had been stunned and flattered when before Christmas, for the first time in their marriage, he had confided in her, revealing his plans to buy out Andrew and Ian by selling Karri Karri. His offer to provide the cotton harvester for Ian in return for his share of Karri Karri had shocked all except Katie who understood his motives. Not wanting to rock the boat Katie went out of her way to be as sweet and malleable as possible. She enthused at the thought of returning to Karri Karri, repeatedly expressing her willingness to support Robert, kept her temper with Stewart and even attempted to keep the house tidy. Robert was utterly confused by her uncharacteristic behaviour and doubly suspicious. Neither did she show any signs of packing her bags and leaving. There had been hardly any tears and no screaming matches. When she then told him she had arranged to have lunch with Alice to make sure there were no hard feelings, he agreed on the spot to her plea to spend a few days with friends in Sydney before they returned to Western Australia. Happy Chris was coping, Robert extended their stay at Wangianna using the extra time to sort out some of the legalities of formally dividing Wangianna.

Alice was punishing herself with work, trying to escape from her confusion, anger and misery. Filled with self-doubt she constantly questioned her behaviour, torturing herself that she could have allowed Robert to kiss her like that, wondering if she had some deep-seated need to take revenge on her cousin she hadn't faced up to.

Then came incessant questioning of Robert's motives. How could he have kissed her with so much passion knowing Katie was only a few paces away? As far as Alice knew their marriage was a happy one. Could she really be conceited enough to believe that after all these years one kiss could prompt him to leave Katie and rush into her arms? Round and round her mind went and the more it circled the harder she pushed herself, knowing her only escape was exhaustion. Finally, much to Alice's relief, Marigold arrived back from England full of Christmas cheer and bursting with energy. The children were overjoyed at her reappearance and Alice started to relax.

Then Katie rang. Alice was thoroughly distrustful of her cousin's sudden about-face, but she agreed to her suggestion that they meet for lunch in Coonamble, insisting, however, that Marigold and the children accompany them. Happy to bide her time, Katie cooed over the children and asked Marigold about her trip home. Ignoring her reply she switched the topic back to herself, picking at her salad as the children ate their way through fish and chips followed by ice-cream cake. She got her opportunity when Marigold took the children to the toilet.

'I know you're bound to have got all fussed about kissing Robbo, Alice, but you really don't need to,' Katie said softly.

Alice blushed fiery red. 'He looked so wretched I just wanted to give him a reassuring hug. That was all it was, Katie.' Alice felt acutely uncomfortable. This was the very conversation she had been determined to avoid. She wished Marigold would hurry up.

Katie entwined her fingers with their long red polished nails watching her cousin carefully.

'Robbo adores me, you know,' she said smoothly. 'He quite understood that with the sudden shock of Elizabeth being unwell, I wasn't myself.' She gave Alice a sickly sweet smile that didn't get near her eyes. 'I admit I overreacted. Let's just put it all in the past, especially now we're neighbours.'

Alice shivered involuntarily. 'What's going on Katie? What's wrong with Elizabeth? Why is Wangianna being split up?'

Katie looked guarded. 'Things have got a bit tense. Mind you, it sounds terribly dramatic but Robbo's so clever he'll sort everything out.' She leaned forwards. 'Actually he's already started. Robbo reckons Andy'll be gone in six months. He'll never survive the split. Then Robbo'll buy his portion and I'll be mistress of Wangianna.' She sat back, stretching luxuriously, admiring her reflection in the window, twisting her silver locket.

'Darling Robbo. I love him so much. He was wonderful last night. You'd better watch out or he'll buy you out too.' She watched Alice from under her lashes thick with mascara then leaned forward, her mouth twisted. 'You laugh now but surely you don't think it's just a coincidence that of all the land he could have bought he chose to buy next to your place?' she hissed.

'It's good fertile land and he wanted access to the creek,' protested Alice.

There is other fertile land around with creeks,' Katie replied, innocently examining her nails.

Marigold and the children reappeared and Katie was once more purring sickeningly over the children. Suddenly Alice had had enough.

'Come on. Time to go,' she said sharply, hurrying the children outside.

Alice's first reaction was to treat Katie's comments as lies, Katie trying to make trouble as she had so often done in the past. Yet seeds of suspicion once cast have a habit of growing. As Alice returned to MerryMaid she couldn't entirely rid herself of the notion that maybe it wasn't purely coincidence that Robert had bought Charlie Weston's place after all. Maybe she had imagined far more in that kiss. Maybe it had all been hope on her part and design on his. Whatever else, there was no getting away from the fact that Katie's words had disturbed Alice greatly.

Katie stepped out of the Landrover at the tiny outback airport, for once oblivious of the dust and heat. In a couple of hours she would be on her connecting flight from Dubbo to Sydney. Still racked with worry over losing Stewart, Robert had given her a wad of cash to spend and a decent credit limit on their account at David Jones. Confident that she had sown enough seeds of discontent in Alice to keep her well clear of Robert while she was away, and deliriously happy that she was about to be spending ten blissful days shopping, wining and dining in civilisation, she pressed her cheek against Robert's to avoid smudging her lipstick.

'The first thing I'm doing is getting my hair back to looking like hair instead of straw. Then I'm buying a whole new wardrobe and a dress for the Perth charity ball,' she announced presenting a cheek for Stewart to kiss. 'Now you be a good boy for your dad.' Stewart squirmed and dutifully kissed his mother.

'He'll be right. You enjoy yourself,' said Robert hoping his expression didn't betray his relief at her departure. He and Stewart watched Katie onto the plane, waving as it climbed into the cobalt sky. When it was a mere speck in the heavens Robert let out a deep sigh and turned to

Stewart. 'Looks like it's just you and me, son,' he grinned conspiratorially. Stewart grinned back.

Returning to the Landrover Robert pointed it towards Gillgully Downs. There was work needed to be done on the property and he wanted to go somewhere where he could forget Katie. He felt as light as air.

'Can I drive, Dad?' asked Stewart as they were speeding down the bitumen.

'As soon as we hit the dirt road, son.' For a while they laughed and joked together, then both fell silent. Stewart's thoughts turned to the fun of being alone with his dad, Robert's to the plan that had been evolving in his mind since the division of the property. Ian had agreed to hand over his share of Karri Karri. If he worked hard at it he might get Jordie to part with his share too. Jordie had never shown the slightest inclination to visit the place. In fact, he wondered if Jordie, given half a choice, wouldn't rather scarper off to the city. He had recently been muttering about becoming an architect or landscape gardener. Until now it had been his mother's iron will that had kept all three boys on the property. Andy. Well, Andy would very soon no longer be a problem. He might be singing about being at the helm now but Robert would stake his share of Wangianna that once the property was finally split he'd get himself in such hopeless financial straits he'd be pleading for Robert to take the property off him. He turned onto the dirt road and stopped the Landrover.

'Righto, son, here we are.' Stepping out he walked round to the passenger's seat and got in again while Stewart, eyes shining, slid over into the driver's seat. 'Go easy, now. Watch out for rocks and potholes and keep the speed down.'

'It's okay, Dad. I know.'

'Oh you do, do you? Well let me remind you—you're still a minor and I still have the last say,' teased Robert. He had every confidence in Stewart. For all his youth and exuberance the boy was learning to be a careful driver. 'Bit of a luxury having my own chauffeur,' he chuckled and settled back to enjoy the drive.

Stewart grinned broadly as he drove along. He felt ten feet tall. He loved his dad and he loved the opportunity to show off his growing skills. The hot breeze fanned his face from the open window as they rattled over the bumpy surface. From time to time they both sipped at their water-bottles. The heat and dust made driving thirsty work. There had been talk of electric storms building up later in the afternoon but now the sky was clear with only a few wispy clouds gathering above the heat haze. Flocks of galahs rose from either side of the road as they covered the miles home. In the distance a shy emu grazed near the scrub.

'Stupid birds, they always wait until the last minute to get out the way,' exclaimed Stewart slowing down as five or six pink-bellied birds flashed across their path. The dirt road went on uninterrupted in a dead straight line to the horizon beyond and behind. 'D'you think the drought's gonna break soon, Dad?' asked Stewart.

'Got to sometime. They've been having floods up in Queensland, which means the water'll have to come down here eventually,' responded his father glancing out through the fly-spotted windscreen. The white puffy clouds were slowly building. Stewart sped up as he drove off the pothole-filled dirt and onto a recently gravelled surface, the loose bleached chips gleaming in the sun. Half an hour and they'd be at Gillgully Downs.

'Take it easy, son, and keep your eyes open for those flamin' birds,' warned Robert.

'Sure, Dad,' replied Stewart cheerfully. 'When can I come on your next roo shoot with Melon?' As he spoke a large flock of galahs rose out of the dry grass almost on top of them.

'Watch out!' yelled Robert.

Too late Stewart stamped on the brakes and swerved as the birds slammed into the windscreen with a sickening thud. Ducking automatically Stewart sent the car into an uncontrolled skid. Slewing across the loose gravel it pitched into the ditch, jarring to a halt as the front wheels hit a large rock. The impact sent Stewart's slender body thumping against the steering wheel, his forehead bouncing against the dashboard. At the same time Robert was flung against the windscreen crazing the glass before being tossed back against the car door, the blow knocking him unconscious. Blood seeped out of a gash just above Stewart's right eyebrow. A thin trickle of blood oozed down Robert's cheek from the tiny fragments of glass in his reddening forehead. The sun beat mercilessly down on a suddenly still world.

Jimmy whistled as he bumped across the paddocks on his new motorbike with Alice's smallest kelpie Bitsa crouched behind. He had been across the back paddocks. Now he needed to check the fences along this road.

'Let's see how she goes on a real road eh, Bitsa,' he spoke over his shoulder to the dog, his black face splitting into a toothy grin. Bitsa thumped her tail panting hard. She wasn't sure about this new mode of travel. Jimmy turned up the throttle and the bike roared away across the hard dirt road. The kelpie crouched lower into his back. Jimmy's grin grew as he dodged potholes and bounced over ruts until his teeth rattled, his pulse pounding at this new exhilaration, his stomach occasionally turning inside out as he lurched over an unexpectedly large rut or skidded rather more than he had intended. After twenty minutes he reached the junction that took him towards the newly gravelled road that led to Gillgully Downs.

'Time for a smoko. Then we'd better head back and earn our keep else there'll be no tucker for you and me tonight,' said Jimmy bringing the bike to a stop. Bitsa sat tight. Out of habit Jimmy searched the countryside for signs of life, watching as a car sped out of the shimmering mirage. Waving as it passed he searched for his cigarette packet. His hand froze on his pocket as he heard a horrible crunching thud.

'Don't sound good, Bitsa,' he muttered. Stamping on the starter pedal Jimmy roared off in the direction of the crash. The back wheels were still turning as he reached the Landrover. Leaping off his bike he ran towards the vehicle, his heart pounding.

'Geez, don't look good neither.' Jimmy started to shake as he took in the state of the occupants. One glance and Jimmy recognised Robert, head fallen backward against the passenger's door. Stewart lay slumped across the steering wheel. For a moment Jimmy just stared, wondering what to do. Then he opened the car door and checked to see if Stewart was still breathing. He was. Carefully he lifted the boy backwards, cradling his head as best he could and laid him in the shade of the car. Stewart's forehead was bleeding badly. Jimmy's pulse raced as he found the first-aid kit, slapped a wad of dressing on Stewart's cut and tore off a strip of sticking plaster with his teeth sticking it across the dressing to hold it in place. Then he rushed round to Robert. It was early afternoon and the sun was beating down on the Landrover. Heaving Robert out he dragged him round and laid him next to Stewart. Leaving the car doors open to make what shade he could for them he leaped back on his bike and tore off back to MerryMaid. Fifteen minutes later he burst onto MerryMaids verandah hollering for Alice. Alice came rushing out.

'There's been an accident, Miss Alice. You've got to get the ambulance quick,' gasped Jimmy. He was panting so hard he could hardly speak.

'Who is it? What's happened?'

'It's Mr Robert and Stewwy—they're both hurt. Stewwy's cut bad and I don't know what's wrong with Mr Robert. He didn't wake. I bandaged them up as best I could but they look mighty poorly.'

Alice grabbed Jimmy by both arms. 'Righto, Jimmy, slow down. Tell me exactly where they are.'

Jimmy gulped in a few deep mouthfuls of air. 'On the new gravel road just past our turnoff.'

'Towards town or towards Gillgully?'

'Towards Gillgully.'

'Come with me,' ordered Alice diving back inside, adrenalin charging through her veins.

Within seconds the two emerged armed with the MerryMaid first-aid box, blankets and a full water bottle. 'Take the stationwagon and get back to them as quickly as you can,' she panted running towards the stationwagon. Shoving the blankets in the car she turned to Jimmy. 'Now listen carefully. Check your bandages are still controlling the bleeding and use one of the blankets as a shade for them. If either comes round keep them calm. I'll be there as soon as I've called the ambulance.'

Wide-eyed, Jimmy hurtled back down the road while Alice dashed inside and radioed the ambulance coordination centre in Coonabarabran. Satisfied the ambulance was on its way she leaped into the ute and set off after Jimmy.

Alice's heart turned over when she saw the two bodies lying so still at the side of the road, Jimmy holding the blanket to shade them. Kneeling down she quickly checked they were both still breathing, then she rechecked the bandages. Jimmy had done a good job of staunching the blood flow from their wounds. Seeing there was nothing more she could do for either of them except wait for the ambulance she carefully reached into the Landrover and tried the radio. It worked. She called up Wangianna Station repeating the call several times. Just as she was about to give up Elizabeth came on the air.

'MerryMaid, this is Mrs McIain. Is that you, Alice?'

'Yes it's Alice, Mrs McIain. There's been an accident. Robert and Stewwy have gone off the road on the new gravel just past the MerryMaid turnoff on the Gillgully side.' She heard Elizabeth's intake of breath. 'The ambulance is on its way. They'll probably take them in to Walgett Hospital. We're with them now. Could you please tell Katie so she knows what's going on.'

'Katie's gone to Sydney, Alice. They were on their way over there after dropping her off.' Elizabeth's briskness covered her shock. 'Don't you worry about that. I'll get straight over to Walgett Hospital. Is there any sign of the ambulance?' Alice told her there wasn't and signed off. She took a sip of water and then sat down beside Robert, her eyes glued to the road. She felt utterly helpless as she waited in the heat fanning the flies away, watching the seconds tick by.

A small cloud of dust on the horizon signalled the arrival of the ambulance. Agonisingly slowly it crept along the straight dusty road until it reached them. Immediately the stillness turned to action as the ambulance ground to a halt and two men leapt out. Quickly one ambulance officer placed an oxygen mask over Stewart's face, and a cervical collar to protect his neck.

It made his thin frame appear all the more fragile. Then the officer and Jimmy were lifting Stewart onto the stretcher.

'Can I do anything to help?' Alice asked feeling useless.

'You could stay by the boy while we fix up the other bloke. Watch to see he keeps breathing,' replied the senior officer as they lifted the stretcher into the ambulance. The ambulance officer knew the boy needed to get to hospital urgently. He had all the classic signs of internal bleeding. He was in profound shock, which alone could kill him, and from the way he had been hit, his spleen had almost certainly been ruptured.

Alice nodded and stepped into the ambulance next to Stewart, her palms sweating as she watched the shallow rise and fall of his chest. Robert groaned as he was lifted onto a second stretcher and into the ambulance beside his son. There was dried blood across his cheek and he had a bandage over the bruise in his forehead but he had escaped major injury mainly due to the sturdiness of the Landrover and the fact that they had been travelling at a reasonable speed.

'Take it easy, mate. We'll soon have you in hospital,' the officer told Robert, shutting the ambulance doors and getting in the driver seat. 'We'll take them straight to Walgett Hospital,' he told Alice. 'Have you informed their next of kin?' Alice nodded.

Suddenly empty she watched as they sped off towards Walgett. There really was no place for her with them. Elizabeth would be at Walgett with the family by the time they arrived at the hospital and Katie was no doubt already on a plane heading back to Walgett. Shock was beginning to set in as she drove slowly home behind Jimmy.

Katie was not on a plane back to Walgett. When the message for her came over the loudhailer at Dubbo airport she was in a very bad temper having learned half an hour ago that her flight to Sydney would be delayed two hours. When Elizabeth told her what had happened her first reaction was to burst into tears as much through frustration at the interruption of her trip as through concern for Robert and Stewart. Once she realised the seriousness of Stewart's condition she panicked and Elizabeth had to spend another ten minutes calming her down. Having finally succeeded she told Katie to hire a plane to fly her back to Walgett where she would arrange for the town taxi to collect her and bring her down to the hospital. In total panic Katie slammed down the phone and rushed off to one of the airport officials demanding a plane immediately. The official explained quietly and kindly that he couldn't, as though there were plenty of planes available there were no pilots. Throwing up her hands in frustration she wasted precious moments screaming at the man and then sobbing her eyes out. When she had been calmed yet again she was finally reduced to renting a car and driving the four-hour journey back.

Having been informed of the condition of the patients, the matron immediately alerted the doctor in charge of the small country hospital. From the description of his condition they both agreed the boy would almost certainly need an immediate blood transfusion and probable surgery. This would require speedy cross matching of his blood type and for the emergency theatre to be made ready. By the time the ambulance arrived at the hospital the nursing staff had everything well under control. Rushing Stewart in, one nurse took some blood while another prepared him for theatre and the doctor scrubbed up.

Robert, who had come round by the time they arrived but was still dazed and nauseous, was put in a bed in the emergency ward. The splinters of glass were removed from his forehead and he was examined for any undetected head or chest injuries, then placed under observation in case of complications.

Elizabeth arrived to learn that Stewart was about to go into theatre so they were unable to see him and that Robert was resting. Elizabeth marched into the ward. Still mildly concussed and with a large bandage covering the bad contusions on his forehead, Robert looked grey. Going over to her son, Elizabeth brushed his cheek with her lips and gently squeezed his hand.

'They're having to operate on Stewwy,' said Robert brokenly. Elizabeth patted his hand fighting back the tears.

'The doctor has it all under control. Now you rest and don't fret,' she ordered.

A decidedly sober Ian and Jordie shuffled from one foot to the other making conciliatory noises and telling Robert that everything'd be right. Andrew paced uncomfortably out in the waiting room. After staring embarrassed at a spot above Robert's head for two minutes Ian cleared his throat.

'I'll go and organise for the Landrover to be collected,' he said and retreated with Jordie.

Elizabeth pulled up a chair and sat down. 'You look exhausted, love. Try and rest. Matron said it would be at least two hours before Stewwy's out of theatre. You won't help your boy by making yourself worse, you know.'

Robert shook his head. 'I can't sleep till I know he's out of danger.'

Elizabeth shrugged and sat down. To her relief, in spite of his words Robert eventually dozed off, and she crept out to get a cup of tea.

Robert woke with a start. Seeing Elizabeth was no longer beside him and thinking he had only dozed off for a few seconds, he pressed the bell. A nurse bustled in through the curtains around his bed.

'How are we feeling now, Mr McIain. That's a nice long sleep you had. Would you like a cup of tea?' she said reading the eating instructions under his name above his bed.

'Is my son out of surgery?' asked Robert fearing the answer.

The nurse smiled encouragingly. 'Twenty minutes ago and doing very nicely, thank you. We've got him in one of the single wards.' Robert got out of bed and staggered slightly. 'Now, Mr McIain, I think it's a little early for you to be walking about,' insisted the nurse catching him under the elbow.

Robert steadied himself. 'I'm going to sit with my son.' Ignoring the nurse's indignation he walked into Stewart's room and stared down at his son's fragile face, his long fair lashes curled on his pale cheeks. A tube filled with blood ran from a bag on a stand to his left hand. The bedclothes were supported over a frame so no weight lay on his abdomen. The rush of emotion that swept over him just seeing Stewart sleeping peacefully made Robert feel weak. He reached for a chair and sat down, rubbing the tears from his eyes.

The nurse had rushed off to find the doctor, but after rechecking the results of the various tests done on Robert, all of which had come out negative, and rechecking Robert, who showed no signs of further problems other than slight concussion, he decided it might be less stressful for Robert to sit quietly near his son.

Stewart was breathing evenly and quietly. Robert's gaze shifted. Staring at the bag that contained the lifesaving blood, the words swirled unfocused before his eyes. If Stewart died he'd never forgive himself. Why had he let him drive on that damned gravel? He knew the dangers of driving off the bitumen. He'd seen the flocks of birds and still let him drive. The accident was his fault. How could he have been such an irresponsible fool? The bag seemed to be the only thing in the room above Stewart's parchment face. RH positive. The words were blurred. Thank God people gave blood. Thank God they had the right sort. He had been giving blood for years because RH negative was less easily available. Now perhaps he could persuade Katie to do so too. In fact, why didn't he give blood now? In his confused state the decision became all the more urgent. What if another boy like Stewart needed some of his type today? What if they ran out of blood and didn't have enough for Stewart? His eyes focused on the bag. RH positive. Suddenly the words sunk in. RH positive! It couldn't be. Both he and Katie were RH negative. They must have made a mistake. My God! They were giving him the wrong blood! They weren't saving him, they were killing him. He was on his feet, the world swimming around him. Grabbing the bell at the top of the bed he pressed the button several times. Frantic with fear he blundered to the door shouting for the nurse. He practically fell into her arms. She was young and pretty and had just come on duty.

'Sit down, Mr McIain.'

He brushed aside her attempts to calm him. 'I have to see the doctor. He's giving my son the wrong blood.'

The nurse went pale. Quickly checking the sheet at the foot of Stewart's bed she rechecked the bag and let out a sigh of relief. The instructions matched the blood grouping.

'He's fine. He's getting the right type.'

Robert refused to believe her. Staggering down the corridor, he charged towards the matron, shouting at her in his panic as she tried to deliver instructions to a couple of other nurses.

'Why is this patient out of bed?' demanded the matron giving him a withering glance, unaware of the doctor's decision. Robert ignored her questions.

'You've given my son the wrong blood,' he raved. 'He's RH negative and you're giving him RH positive, you pack of bloody idiots. You'll kill him.' Robert was nearing hysteria.

'Mr McIain, I am sure there is no mistake,' replied the matron trying to remain calm, but he had rattled her. She called up the doctor and Robert subsided into a chair only to leap up when the doctor appeared and explained all over again.

The doctor clapped him on the shoulder. 'Listen, mate, you've had a nasty time and you're still in shock. Matron's quite right in insisting you return to bed. Hop back in like a good fella.' Firmly he started walking Robert towards the ward. 'I've got a good team here, you know, not like some country hospitals. The nurse checked your son a short while ago. He's doing very well considering he's just had his spleen restitched and lost a pint and a half of blood. He's got age on his side but even so he's doing well, remarkably well.' He patted Robert on the shoulder. Robert was practically weeping. The room was swirling round again.

'But he's RH negative, you don't understand. He can't be RH positive. It's not possible.' The doctor caught him as he passed out.

Robert woke up in the hospital bed and vomited. Lying back against the pillows one face emerged from the blur in front of him. It was Alice. Unable to bear the agony of sitting at MerryMaid not knowing what was happening, she had driven to the hospital.

'It's okay, Robert,' she said gently. 'Katie will be with you in a few minutes.

She's just arrived and she's in seeing Stewart. He's doing fine. Elizabeth's sitting with him as well. How are you feeling?'

Robert smiled wanly and reached out his hand. 'We keep meeting in hospitals.'

Alice squeezed his hand and quickly withdrew it as Katie rushed in, tears streaming down her face.

'How could you do it? How could you let him drive like that?' Exhausted from the drive she had worked herself up into a hopeless state of anxiety. Relief opened the floodgates of her wrath. Alice slipped out of the room. Robert vomited again, had a sip of water and leant back on the pillows.

Clutching a handkerchief to her mouth, Katie quickly removed herself to the other side of the room.

'Did they clear up about the blood?' asked Robert, too exhausted to bother with her rantings. His head throbbed.

'Didn't you hear a word I said?' she snapped angrily.

'Are they giving him the right blood?' persisted Robert.

Katie looked puzzled. 'What are you talking about?'

'They gave him RH positive. I saw it for myself.' He was heaving himself up on his pillows.

'So?'

'You're RH negative. We're both RH negative. You know that, Katie.'

'The doctors know what they are doing. Try and get some rest,' Katie replied immediately, all supplication. 'I'm sorry I went off at you, darling. The car journey was hell. I was frantic with worry and you know how hopeless I am when anyone's ill. I love you. I'll be back to see you later.' As she spoke a lightning flash streaked across the sky followed by a loud clap of thunder. 'You're in the best place. They're predicting bad electric storms tonight.' She blew him a kiss and left the room.

Robert lay back against the pillows rubbing his eyes wondering if he was going crazy. A nurse changed his sick bowl and asked if he felt like anything to eat or drink.

'No, but could you do me a favour, straightaway?' He looked up at the nurse imploringly.

'With a look like that Mr McIain, who could refuse?' she flirted, raising her eyebrows questioningly.

'Check what blood they're giving my son and what blood group he belongs to.'

The nurse disappeared, returning almost immediately. 'AO RH positive and he's AO RH positive. Satisfied?' she replied straightening his sheets.

'You're sure, you're absolutely sure?' Robert grabbed her by the arm.

The nurse nodded, bemused. 'Is it a problem?'

Robert was on his feet. 'My wife, I have to find my wife,' he rasped brushing past the nurse. Tearing down the corridor he spied Katie heading across the hospital garden, almost at the street. Letting the flyscreen door slam behind him he stumbled down the step, light-headed from the effort, and charged towards her, shouting out, stopping only to throw up again in the flowerbed. Katie, hearing the commotion, turned to see her husband, ashen-faced and barefooted, his hospital gown billowing around him.

'Robbo, what on earth . . .?'

'How could you do it, Katie? How could you swear you loved me and do this to me?' he gasped, grabbing her by the arm, the world spinning madly.

'What are you raving on about?' she cried trying to pull away, but Robert was too strong.

'It never happened did it? Nothing happened. Our whole marriage has been a lie from the very first moment.' Katie went grey. 'AO positive! Stewart's AO positive.' He tightened his grip, his eyes never left her face. 'Stewart is not my son. It's not possible. Katie, tell me it's not true,' he choked. They glared at one another.

'Have you lost your wits? Robbo, of course he's our son. You're not well. The accident is making you confused. You have to get back to bed.' She started to tremble, the wildness in his eyes striking fear into her heart. Robert gripped her by both arms and started to shake her.

'You have to tell me the truth. I have to know the truth.'

'They're lying. The doctors are lying about the blood,' she whispered in panic. 'You got so hysterical they said anything to shut you up. Look at you, you're behaving like a madman. Let me go.' Robert's fingers dug into her flesh, his knuckles white.

'He can't be my son. I saw for myself. RH negative would have killed him. I want to hear the truth from your lips. I want to hear the one piece of truth in the whole of our marriage.' His fingers were hurting her. She turned on him with all the fury of a trapped animal.

'What do you want me to say? Shall I scream it out to the whole district that your son was fathered by another man? Is that what you want? That your precious dynasty is a joke.' Her eyes were narrow slits, her breath coming in rasping gasps. 'Shall I, shall I? Or shall I tell them the real truth that you're cruel, scheming and this is one more way for you to cut off your wife and son from what pitiful inheritance we have left. You're mad. You're completely insane. Let me go!' she screamed. The doctor and nurses were running down the path.

'The truth, Katie, so we can end this farce.' Katie was sobbing with rage. 'What really happened on that night?'

'The truth, you want the truth. You can have the truth. Nothing happened, you useless, pathetic . . .'She was spitting like the wild feline creature she was, shaking with uncontrollable rage. 'You were drunk, rotten, stupid, whining drunk. All you could do was slobber over me and drool on about Alice. You kissed me a couple of times and fell asleep. I hid the trousers under the carpet. When you left the next day I couldn't bear it. I was so miserable.' She was openly sobbing now. Robert's eyes were like a madman's, his face pressed close to hers.

'We're finished, Katie. I'm starting divorce proceedings as soon as I get out of here but first you'll tell me who the father was.' He was clutching onto Katie as much to keep him upright as to stay her.

'No, Robbo, no. You don't understand. I love you, Robbo,' she pleaded wildly. 'I was desperate. It was the only way I could get you. All you saw was Alice and she didn't care. You didn't even know I existed. Oh Robbo, I'll make it up to you. I promise. Please! I'm sorry! I'm sorry! It was working, you and me, it was working. Don't leave me. Stay with me. Stay with me for Stewwy's sake. Don't leave me.' Tears streamed down her face. She was clawing at him hysterically, refusing to let him go, searching for some way to win him back.

'The father, tell me his name.'

'Russell Heaton. You met him at the debs' ball. You can't leave me, Robbo, you can't, you can't,' she sobbed. 'Nurse, nurse, help me. He's gone crazy!' she shrieked. The doctor and two nurses rushed up grabbing at Robert as he let go of Katie.

'Come on now, sir, you're going to be okay. You've been through a rough time. We'll give you something to calm you down.'

Robert wrenched himself free. Ignoring the heaving in his stomach he staggered back into the hospital past the gaping outpatients, along the corridor and burst into Stewart's room. He had to see once more for himself. To be absolutely sure. Stewart was lying peacefully asleep, his forehead bandaged, a faint pink tingeing his delicate cheeks, his chest rising and falling evenly under the raised blue hospital blanket. Above him the blood bag bore the words Robert dreaded to see. AO RH Positive. His mind was so focused on reading that he didn't notice his mother move towards him from her seat in the corner.

'Give him a moment. We'll be right,' she said quietly stepping between Robert and the frantic medical staff. Robert stared down at the sweet precious face. How he adored the boy. His whole world was bound up with this child. He had built his hopes and dreams around him. He was the next generation of the proud Wangianna dynasty. Yet there was no way on earth that he could be his son. Elizabeth laid her hand on Robert's shoulder.

'I know,' she said very gently. Robert's shoulders slumped. Like an old man he sank into the chair beside the bed. Slipping his hand over Stewart's slender fingers very carefully, he laid his head on the bed and wept silently into the sheets.

Chapter Thirty-one

ROBERT STARED ACROSS at the burly sawmill owner seeing the resemblance between Stewart and this stranger in the set of his jaw, the shape of his nose. There could be no doubt this man was Stewart's father. After Robert had been discharged from the hospital it had taken him three weeks to hunt Russell Heaton down. When he had finally located him Robert had insisted on coming to visit him alone. That way he could be sure that he was in control.

'I was as flabbergasted as you when you told me,' said Russell drawing his dark eyebrows together in a frown and fiddling with his glass of beer. 'The wife and I have talked about it at length and we've both come to the same decision.' He hesitated. Robert waited conscious of a terrible sense of emptiness. 'Look. The boy's grown up with you and as far as he's concerned you're his dad. You love him, so why mess up your life further? What's done is done. We have our own family; leave Stewart where he's happiest.' A great weight rolled off Robert. He stared at Russell, relief spilling openly from his face. He talked a bit more of Stewart, the pride obvious in his voice.

'I love the boy more than I could ever say,' he finished thickly. 'And knowing his father has his wellbeing at heart makes me feel a heck of a lot better. I can only thank you from the bottom of my heart.' He smiled crookedly. The two men stood up.

'I'd say it'd be best for everyone if we just forgot all about this meeting. If it's okay with you I'll just be Uncle Russ like I am to most of the kids round here if you ever feel like bringing the boy over to meet me and the wife. Warn me first, though. Otherwise it really isn't anyone else's business is it?'

'Not really,' said Robert gratefully. 'Not really.' The two shook hands and Robert left. As he drove back to Wangianna he thought how fortunate he had been. If he had chosen he could not have picked a more solidly decent bloke to have been Stewy's father. Meeting him had removed some of his own aching sense of loss, so it was with a slightly lighter heart that Robert walked through his own front door braced for the last unavoidable scene with Katie before their marriage was finally finished. It started after Stewart had gone to bed. Having exhausted all her pleas to make him drop the idea of divorce, Katie rounded on him.

'If you go through with it I'll make sure you never see Stewwy again,' she screeched, clutching at straws. 'I'll tell everyone who his real father is. You'll be the laughing stock of the whole district. I'll drag your name through the mud.'

A muscle tightened in Robert's cheek. 'The boot's on the other foot, Katie,' he replied quietly. His terrible calm sent icy shivers through her veins. 'Tell who you like. Tell your friends. Tell the whole world whatever you want. They are far more likely to see me as the hero who rescued you than the villain who forced you to stay.' Katie gaped. Robert continued coldly. 'I will see you are well looked after. I have discussed it with Mum and you may have the Perth house. Live in it or sell it and do what you want with the money. I will also arrange for you to get a thousand dollars a month to live on until you remarry. As for Stewart, he must choose which of us he wishes to stay with and I will abide by his wishes. I cannot stop you poisoning him against me. I just hope as his mother you have enough compassion to see that telling him now about his father as well as asking him to cope with our divorce is too much for him to take all at once.' Katie slumped down on the sofa.

'I've lost everything,' she sobbed, her eyes dull. 'How could you be such a beast? You've twisted everything so now no one will believe the truth.' Robert stared unmoved at his wife's drooping shoulders.

'I have twisted nothing, Katie. I simply will not allow you to use Stewart's natural father as a weapon. We will tell Stewwy together that we are getting divorced and when we do so we will make quite sure he understands none of this is his fault.' He poured himself a large whisky.

'It's over, Katie, our sham of a marriage is over.'

The following week, armed with three suitcases and a few personal belongings, Katie drove back to Billabrin alone.

Bea opened the door in surprise as Katie walked in, dumped her suitcases on the floor and ran sobbing into her mother's arms.

'My marriage is over,' wept Katie. 'We're getting divorced.'

'Oh darling,' said Bea, bewildered. She patted Katie again and picked up two of the bags. 'Come on, we'll put these in your room and you can tell me what happened.'

Katie followed her mother to the room and flopped down on the bed. Her tears started afresh as she gulped out her version of the story.

'How did it all get this far?' asked Bea aghast.

'It's Alice, Mum. It's always been Alice. Alice has done this to me all my life.'

'Done what, sweetie?'

'Stolen everything I ever loved. As soon as she got here she shovelled me aside and you all thought she was so cute with her grand talk about her palace. I thought she might finally leave me and Robbo alone once she'd grabbed MerryMaid for herself but, no, she has to have everything. The way she's going now the palace she'll get is Wangianna. Oh Mum, it's all so dreadful.' Katie buried her face in the pillow, her whole body shuddering. Bea bristled.

'Calm down, Katie, and explain. I can't believe Alice is to blame because things have gone wrong between you and Robert.'

Katie sat up rubbing her swollen, reddened eyes. 'Don't take her side this time, please, Mum. She started going after him as soon as she set foot back in Australia. They meet at sheep sales but I pretended it wasn't happening. Then, then . . .' In a choking voice she told Bea about the kissing incident at Wangianna the day Elizabeth collapsed.

'I'm sure she was just trying to be comforting. You know how impetuous she can be,' excused Bea remembering grimly that Alice had returned in such a strange mood that day and rushed back to MerryMaid with hardly a word.

'She just kept going after Robbo, promising him MerryMaid when Wangianna was about to split up, promising him everything. He says he wants a divorce and I can't stop him.' Her cheeks were blotchy from crying, her hair dishevelled. 'Oh,Mum, I couldn't bear to stay a second longer in that place knowing how he felt.'

'Is it absolutely final or are the two of you still talking?' asked Bea heavy-hearted.

Katie sniffled and searched for a handkerchief. Using the end of her blouse she wiped her nose. 'He says I can have the Perth house and a measly monthly allowance. The Perth house, Mum. It's the other side of the world. All my friends are in Sydney and Melbourne. He rang the solicitor yesterday. It's all over between us and I love him so much.' She covered her face with her hands, her body heaving. Bea put her arm protectively around her shoulder and held her tight, wiping away a strand of blonde hair from her forehead.

'You've got to stop. You'll make yourself ill if you keep crying like this, Katie,' she said firmly. 'At least you've got something to live on.' She didn't know what to believe about Alice.

Katie raised her ravaged face to her mother. Her voice was husky with misery. 'And he's stolen Stewwy from me.' Her words echoed around the room. Bea went cold.

'How about you wash your face and we talk about all this over a cup of tea?' Katie nodded through her tears.

'What do you mean he's stolen Stewwy?' asked Bea, her hands shaking as she poured the tea. 'What's going on, Katie. What are you hiding from me?'

Katie took a deep breath. 'I think Robbo's gone a bit strange, Mum. It all started after they agreed to split up Wangianna. He started threatening me, just about little things at first, but then after the accident it suddenly got much worse.' Katie tried to speak but her lips were shaking so much the words wouldn't form. Finally she whispered, 'He said he'd kill me if I tried to take Stewwy away. Oh Mum, I'm so frightened.'

Bea pulled Katie to her. Clasping her to her plump bosom she rocked

Katie back and forth like a baby, trying to protect them both from the enormity of her admission.

'Oh my darling, darling girl. How dreadful. How wickedly dreadful.' Mother and daughter rocked together until they had both stopped shaking. Then Bea said, 'I think you and I'd better pay a visit to Billabrin police station. It's not right that he can threaten you like that.' Katie's face contorted with fear.

'No, no!' she said pulling away and twisting her hands. 'It'll tip him over the edge. I'll just give him a bit of time. All he needs is a bit of time.' Her eyes were wild, the pupils dilated. She started pacing. 'If it comes to a divorce I'll fight him over Stewwy in the courts. No, I'll rent a cheap place in Melbourne and then I'll decide what to do. I have to get away from here but I don't want to do anything that might upset him. At least at the moment we are all alive and I have a little bit of money till I get a job. We'll leave it at that for now, Mum, please.'

Bea had never seen Katie so agitated. 'Well, if that's what you want, darling,' she said uncertainly.

Katie nodded. 'It is. Don't tell Dad about Robbo's threats, it'll only scare him. Promise me, Mum.'

'I'll make my own mind up about that,' Bea replied decisively. 'What I will do is have a quiet word in Alice's ear and find out if she has any idea of the damage her impulsive generosity has caused.'

Bea waited until Katie had flown down to Melbourne and then rang Alice. Refusing to divulge anything over the party line she insisted Alice come over to Billabrin immediately. Alarmed at the urgency in her aunt's voice, Alice complied.

'It's a pack of lies, Aunty Bea,' said Alice after hearing Bea's story. 'You don't seriously believe it, do you? Katie's still up to her old tricks.'

'Well, my girl, Robert's divorcing Katie, she's beside herself, and from all accounts he needs money that MerryMaid could very nicely provide him with. Katie's fear certainly seemed genuine. She was so terrified she flatly refused to go near the police.'

Alice bristled. 'When have I ever lied to you, Aunty Bea? You know I've never tried to come between him and Katie. I gave him one kiss because he looked so devastated,' she protested. 'And I certainly never offered him MerryMaid. Do you really think I'd sell my dream to the man who'd betrayed me? She has to be making it up.' She wished she didn't feel so guilty about that damned kiss.

Bea sat down heavily, rubbing her hands up and down her thighs over her dress. 'I don't know what to believe, Alice. Of course I want to believe you but I'm nearly demented with worry. It sounds like the man's become completely unhinged since that car crash.'

'I just can't believe Robert would threaten Katie like that,' said Alice soberly. 'It's so against his nature. Robert'd never hurt a flea. I've seen him at work, Aunty Bea. You couldn't find anyone more gentle or more loving.'

'That was over ten years ago. You're living in a pipedream, my girl, and it's time you woke up to yourself. Get yourself a man to live with you over at MerryMaid and just watch out when Robert is around. Thank goodness he's flying off to Western Australia in ten days. But just you take care and please don't mention any of this to a soul. I don't want to place Katie's life in further danger.' Alice stared across at her aunt. She saw real fear in Bea's eyes.

Alice drove back to MerryMaid considerably shaken. Had Robert really changed so much that he could threaten to kill Katie? People did go strange under too much stress and she had seen Robert's face in hospital when Stewart was in theatre. Katie's comments about him buying her out resurfaced, and her reference to his mental state ate away at Alice. For the first time in Alice's life Bea had made no effort to hide her fear. Alice felt extremely troubled by the whole situation.

'It's so good to have you back,' said Alice for the umpteenth time since Marigold's return as she helped her fold the washed clothes. 'We did wonder if you'd ever come back. It's so different living out here than on a farm in England.'

'That's why I'm back,' said Marigold happily. 'I really missed the space and the heat, would you believe? Mummy and Daddy have got Woodcot End looking really lovely. They'd just had it all redecorated inside when I got back and we had a big family reunion at Christmas with heaps of old relatives I hadn't seen for years. When we were all sitting around the great open wood fire after Christmas lunch, having eaten far too much, I kept thinking of you and Vicky and Ben sweltering in the heat. Then on Boxing Day when I was dishing out soup to my brother and some of his friends before they joined the hunt, my fingers so numb I thought they'd fall off, I realised I was homesick for the wrong place.' She laughed, adding a pair of tiny socks to Ben's pile.

'Really?' said Alice looking pleased. 'Well you've just given me the excuse I've been looking for.' She had been feeling decidedly gloomy after Bea's revelations about Katie and Robert. Marigold looked across expectantly. 'How about we throw a special "Marigold's back and we're really glad" party for you and ask all our friends?'

Marigold's face lit up with pleasure. 'What a super idea! But I'd be just as happy with a nice quiet dinner party with Fraser and the children.' She tossed a dress of Vicky's onto the ironing pile. 'Actually, why don't we invite Jo Perry and make it even numbers?' she said with a provocative twinkle. Alice had mentioned Jo and flying several times in the conversation recently and Marigold thought it wouldn't do her any harm to have an admirer around.

'Is he about?' asked Alice sounding mildly interested. She stared down at her ringless fingers—she had decided it was time to stop wearing her wedding ring.

'I'm sure if he knew he was invited to dinner with you he'd make himself available,' laughed Marigold.

'Don't be a dope. He's just a friend I fly with sometimes, that's all,' said Alice but she agreed to include him on the list of guests. After much discussion and laughter they invited twenty and ended up with fourteen including themselves and the two children.

A gentle wind was blowing the dust across the plains as Alice and

Marigold put the finishing touches to their meal on the evening of the party. Delicious aromas filled the house. Bea, who had arrived early with extra salad and fresh fruit, was bustling around in the kitchen while Ray and some of the other guests sat in the sitting room under the whirring ceiling fan. Neither Alice nor Bea mentioned their previous discussion, both wishing to avoid anything that might put a dampener on the evening.

Fraser, who had been working all day on the property overseeing the joining of the rams and collection of semen at MerryMaid, walked into the kitchen having showered and shaved in the shearers' quarters and smelling quite uncharacteristically of Old Spice aftershave. After greeting Bea he then deluged both girls with flowers which he had hidden in one of the cool rooms kept for the AI project. Alice and Marigold's shrieks of delight as they searched for vases to put the huge bouquets in drowned out the arrival of Jo.

'Anyone home?' he called, tapping politely on the fly-screen wire and patting Alice's two kelpies who had leaped up from their spot on the verandah and were now frantically wagging their tails and rubbing themselves against him. The door burst open and Vicky and Ben fell out followed by Alice and Marigold almost hidden by the bouquets.

'He said he digged them up,' explained Ben dressed in a smart shirt and shorts, his innocent brown eyes enormous in his cheeky little face framed by freshly shampooed brown hair.

'Dug,' corrected Vicky frolicking around in a new apple-green party dress frilled with white cotton lace, two long ribbons flowing down her silky blonde hair. 'And he hid them in the fridge. You must be Jo.'

'Jo, come in,' welcomed Alice. 'You remember Vicky and Ben.'

'Hi Vicky, Ben,' grinned Jo. He handed both girls a present. 'I didn't know what to bring so I thought you could share them.'

Alice gave Jo a melting smile and turned round in a full circle trying to work out how to manage to accept the present with her arms full of flowers. Then she and Marigold both burst out laughing again.

'Vicky, you take the presents, darling,' said Alice. Vicky obliged and led the way inside. Plunging the flowers into water Alice rescued the rest from Marigold and excitedly they opened their presents from Jo. One was a large box of Cadbury's chocolates, the other a bottle of Tia Maria. Then, with introductions over, everyone was soon chatting happily.

Dinner was a lovely affair. The interior of MerryMaid house was surprisingly cool despite continuing scorching daytime temperatures. Between them Alice and Marigold had prepared a simple but splendid menu of cold thinly-sliced roast lamb with some of Bea's homemade pickles, cold roast potatoes, salad and fresh homemade bread rolls and butter. Bea had added fresh green salad sprinkled with pungent herbs from her own garden. Marigold, after hunting everywhere, had cooked pasta tossed in curry powder and butter and scattered with black olives, tiny pieces of fried bread and bits of bacon. The table looked spectacular. While Alice showed the guests to their seats and organised Fraser to pour the wine, Marigold quickly arranged some of the sweet smelling flowers into a small low bowl and placed it in the middle of the table.

Everyone ate hungrily although Jo and Fraser made a few joking comments about foreign food on seeing Marigold's pasta dish. Dessert was a chocolate mud cake which had broken when Alice had turned it out. Rescuing the potential disaster, the two young women had swamped it with chocolate icing, decorated it with wobbly white icing reading 'Welcome home Marigold', and stored it in the fridge so it would not melt before the evening. The main course over, Alice placed the cake in front of Marigold. Everyone egged Alice on when she insisted Marigold make a speech and cheered her after she stood and said how happy she was to be back. The cake was deliciously cold and disappeared in no time. As offers for seconds came round Fraser refilled everyone's glasses.

'I have an announcement to make,' he said, his ears very pink.

Everyone stopped talking and downed their forks in eager anticipation. All evening there had been a feeling in the air that something special was brewing.

'I'm not very good at this sort of thing but there is someone here I have . . . well I have loved for a very long time.' Alice glanced over at Marigold who, blushing furiously, was suddenly very preoccupied wiping the chocolate off Ben's fingers. 'To be truthful, from the moment I set eyes on her. Someone I think is a most courageous, wonderful and open-minded person and who I have not until now had the courage to ask that special question.' He took a sip of wine. He knew his sentences were getting tortuous but he feared losing his momentum. Someone clinked a glass. 'Tonight I have decided to take that final step before it's too late.'

'Well get on with it,' encouraged Alice.

Fraser raised his glass. 'We men from the bush take our time but I am asking you, Marigold, will you do me the honour of becoming my wife?'

Letting out a squeal of joy, Marigold leapt from her chair, rushed round the table and threw herself into Fraser's arms.

'Oh Fraser, I thought you'd never ask. That's why I came back, silly, but then all you did was keep hinting.' Everyone laughed and clapped.

'As I said, we bushies take our time,' repeated Fraser enveloping Marigold in his great bear hug. In front of everyone he then fished a little box out of his pocket. Opening it he took out a milky opal ring flashing with red and green lights surrounded by tiny sparkling diamonds and slipped it on the third finger of Marigold's left hand. It was too big but Marigold didn't care. The women let out a sigh of admiration.

'It's wonderful!' she cried and shyly kissed him while everyone clapped and cheered again. Someone proposed a toast and they all drank to the happy couple.

Relaxing back into her chair Alice felt extraordinarily happy for Marigold, glad that finally Fraser had taken the plunge. After all the hubbub and congratulations had died down Alice gave Marigold a hug.

'I don't know how you didn't guess ages ago that I was nuts over him, especially with the young lambs,' glowed Marigold. 'I knew if I started talking about my feelings for Fraser I'd never stop, and he never said anything. I didn't want you to think I wasn't doing my job properly.'

'I think it's great,' said Alice.

Ben presented a chocolate-covered face to Marigold. 'Does that mean you'll have babies too?'

'Not just yet,' laughed Marigold, her cheeks burning from all the sudden attention. 'Goodness, it's way past your bedtime.'

'Don't you worry, I'll put these two monsters to bed,' said Alice. 'You enjoy the limelight.' She ushered the tired mildly-protesting children upstairs.

By eleven-thirty everyone except Fraser and Jo had left. They stayed on, sitting in the comfortable darkness of the verandah with Alice and Marigold, drinking Tia Maria and getting very merry. Finally Fraser stood up a little unsteadily.

'Time to make tracks,' he slurred happily.

'If I'm to be your wife for the next hundred years the only tracks you're making are into bed.'

'Yes please,' grinned Fraser. Gathering her up in his arms amongst squeals of delight he disappeared inside with his bride to be.

'Feel like a bit of a wander?' asked Alice stepping off the verandah staring up at the big silvery moon that had risen and was now lighting up the mackerel sky. She felt restless and too wide awake for sleep. Jo followed her, slipping his arm casually around her as they walked. Alice didn't resist. She felt comfortable around Jo.

'Nights like this always smell so good,' she murmured as they sauntered along. A frog croaked and an owl hooted.

'Have you given any more thought to remarrying?' asked Jo taking Alice completely by surprise.

She glanced at him quizzically. 'I haven't had time,' she said quickly.

Jo stopped, his arm still around her slim waist. The moonlight gave an elfin quality to her face, a gossamer sheen to her hair.

'You have grown very beautiful Alice. Do you mind if I kiss you?'

Alice laughed at his serious old-fashioned courtesy but she didn't resist as he bent and kissed her gently on the mouth. It was such a long time since anyone had kissed her without tearing her apart. She found she liked it. She slid her arms around Jo's neck. He was a nice man. Easy, uncomplicated, unattached. She could be comfortable with him. She had missed the warmth and companionship of a partner. Maybe it was time for her to find another father for her children and someone to share her dreams.

'Will you give it some serious thought?' asked Jo when they finally broke away.

'Don't rush me Jo, but yes, I'll give it some thought.'

Chapter Thirty-two

ROBERT WATCHED THE feed dribble out of the heavy hessian bag slung from his shoulder as he trudged across the pale yellow dirt at Karri Karri. It was mid-March. Not even a weed had survived. Sheep rustled around following his food trail, eating the grain as soon as it hit the ground. Every so often he stopped to stretch his aching back and examine his mob with satisfaction. There were still good things in his life. Chris was off the other side of the property fixing a windmill pump. There was always one giving them trouble. Chris was turning out to be as competent as Robert had hoped and they were holding their own against the drought, not brilliantly, but they were surviving. Feed costs were astronomical and their wool this year would be down in quality but they hadn't lost a sheep. There were signs the drought might finally break soon too. The weather bureau was predicting storms and fierce winds over the next two to three months. Despite the day-to-day worries, Robert was confident they'd make it.

'I'd say I'm better at farming than I am at managing my private life,' Robert thought grimly as he dropped the empty bag in the truck and heaved another full one out.

Yet without Katie's constant demands and safe in the knowledge that Stewart had chosen to live with him, his life had improved dramatically in a remarkably short time.

Somehow the revelation that Stewart was not his natural son had intensified his love for him and while the boy had patches of moodiness, they were becoming closer and closer as they shared cooking and washing as well as the outside work when Stewart was not at the local school.

Before returning to Karri Karri he and Stewart had visited the cottage on Gillgully Downs. Robert intended to refurbish and renovate the building, and then move in thus removing all traces of Katie from his life.

Robert had made the decision to wait to tell Stewart the truth about his father until he was sure the boy could cope. He had also ceased to worry that Katie might decide to tell him. Doing one of her usual double backward somersaults Katie had made it clear she didn't want to take on the responsibility of raising Stewart, making the excuses that the allowance Robert had given her was inadequate and there simply wasn't the room in the elegant Melbourne apartment she was renting. The message Robert received loud and clear was that if she couldn't have Wangianna then she wasn't interested in the rest. No longer able to be hurt by her, Robert's only emotion was relief.

There had been moments of tenderness in their marriage, thought Robert as he continued to lay out the feed, but he realised now they had all been conditional. Once the divorce came through he would be a free man again. He relived the dizzy sensation of Alice in his arms, the warmth of her body close to his, the heady smell she exuded, his lips pressed to hers. He could still feel the unbearable yearning that filled him as her lips returned his kiss in her passionate admission of love. With a rush of fervour he made his decision. He wouldn't muck about. He'd ask Alice to marry him on his next trip back home which, judging by the weather forecasts, might be sooner than he had anticipated. Well what more did he have to lose?

His step was light as he returned to the truck and moved off to the next mob thinking of the future with Alice. Opening a new feed bag he frowned as doubts quickly replaced his sudden burst of euphoria. Would Alice believe him? Would she forgive him? What if he had simply imagined her love for him was still alive because now he so desperately wanted it to be so? Did he dare risk telling her the truth only to have her reject him and jeopardise Stewwy's future for nothing? Yet to win her back he had to tell her the truth. These thoughts worried away at him as he went through his feeding program and checked the silos. Two were almost completely empty. He'd have to go into town to get more feed.

The weather report that night worried Robert. The Queensland coast had already been hit by another cyclone. Having wiped out the little town of Yameena, it was now wreaking havoc across the countryside with vicious winds and heavy floods near Rockhampton. The rains were spreading southwards into New South Wales. Just as everyone was cheering that it looked like the drought had finally broken, the Australian weather, with typical harshness, turned drought into flood. Over the next three weeks heavy rain and storms lashed the countryside making Robert very nervous for Wangianna Stud. Although the split-up of Wangianna was still going ahead, Stanley Fenton was taking his time and the property was still as one. With Andy at the helm and with Ian's lack of interest anything could happen in a crisis. He gave Elizabeth a call.

'Listen, Mum, I don't like the weather forecast over there. I've decided to hand over to Chris early and Stewwy and I are heading home next week. I would just feel happier being on Wangianna if we're going to have the bad floods they're predicting,' he said expecting resistance.

'It's dry as a bone here still but to be honest I would feel much happier too, with you here to guide things.' He could hear the relief in her voice. It was the only time she had spoken out against Andrew since the reading of the will and it signalled to Robert her deep concern over his half-brother's management of Wangianna. He wished the lawyers'd stop wrangling and wrap up the split of the property.

The next day Robert went into Meekatharra to stock up on feed, supplies and collect the mail. Returning after a long hot day he dropped his Akubra on a chair and pulled an icy cold beer out of the fridge. Taking a long drink he placed the bottle on the table, wiped the back of his mouth with a sigh and started sorting the mail. Bills, bills and more bills. He tossed them in a pile to the side along with the bank statements and local paper. His heart gave a nasty jerk as he recognised Katie's handwriting on a smart white envelope. What the hell was she bothering to write to him for? This month's allowance had already been transferred to her account and he had organised to have the Perth house signed over into her name wanting to reduce contact with her to a minimum. He slit open the envelope and pulled out the single sheet of extravagantly elegant paper.

'Dear Robbo,' Robert read, 'I hope you are well. I just wanted you to know I never meant to hurt you in any way.' He nearly tossed the letter in the bin then and there. However, curiosity got the better of him—Katie never did anything without a motive. He kept reading. 'I am managing okay and I've found a buyer for the Perth house. I also think I've found a nice little place in Melbourne.'

'Great news about Marigold and Alice. Mum told me when I rang. Fancy Fraser finally popping the question and to Marigold of all people. Are they planning a double wedding? You've heard of course that Alice is planning to marry Jo Perry. She'd make an ideal RFDS pilot's wife, don't you think? She was telling me the other day she was thinking of selling up and training to be a field nurse so she would be able to spend more time with Jo. I was stunned. How is Stewwy? I'm sure you are looking after him well. Tell him I love him and I miss you both. Big kisses. Your loving Katie. PS I bumped into Andrew the other day and he took me out to dinner. He's not so bad.'

Robert put down the letter and stared across at the cobwebs that hung over the Aga. Alice getting married to Jo Perry. He couldn't believe it. He reread the letter, his heart heavy at this cynical twist of fate. Once more Katie had succeeded in plunging the dagger in and twisting it. Suddenly terribly tired he called Stewart in for tea and told him they were returning to Gillgully Downs.

One Sunday at the end of March Alice was woken by a soft drumming on the roof. The night had been unusually hot and the room was stuffy. It was still dark despite the earliness of the day. Believing she was still dreaming she rolled over and pulled up the covers. As the drumming increased she realised what it was. Leaping out of bed she rushed to the window. It had started to rain. Before her eyes the droplets turned to streams and the streams to sheets blotting out the countryside. In no time the hammering on the tin roof was deafening. Charging into Marigold's room Alice shook her by the shoulders shouting in her ear.

'It's raining, Marigold! It's bloody raining cats and dogs!' Marigold sat bolt upright and then jumped out of bed peering bleary-eyed through the windowpane. She had never seen rain like this, it was so heavy she couldn't see the trees near the house. Alice grabbed her in a hug and danced her around the room.

'D'you know what this means?' she cried as she dragged Marigold out of the bedroom and down the hall. Letting go of Marigold's hand she flung wide the front door and tore out into the rain. In seconds she was drenched, her thin nightdress turning transparent, clinging to her slim body, her wild hair flattened into obedience. Holding her hands up to the sky she laughed and laughed. Marigold stood on the threshold watching in amazement.

'You're quite barmy, Alice!' she exclaimed and then she too stepped out into the rain. Within seconds her baby doll pajamas were also sodden. Vicky and Ben, woken by the commotion, came tumbling downstairs rubbing the sleep out of their eyes and stared wide-eyed at their mother and nanny sopping wet, dancing in the rain. Reassuring the children they had not both gone completely mad Alice and Marigold went inside to dry off and get dressed.

For the next two weeks the rain kept on and on. Stopping for the occasional glimpse of blue sky the heavy black clouds rolled across the countryside emptying their contents on the land, turning the paddocks green and filling the dams. Then the farmers' delight turned to concern as riverbanks rose and people were forced to move their stock to higher ground. Water poured down creeks that had been dry for months. Each day Alice checked the creek that ran between her place and Gillgully Downs and listened in on the radio to reports of river heights.

When the weather bureau reported further rises in river levels Alice decided to leave Vicky with Bea. The levee bank that surrounded the town, broken in the early 1960s, had been reinforced and the townsfolk, though concerned, were confident it would hold this time. Even so they reinforced it with sandbags and watched it around the clock. Ben fretted when he was parted from Alice and he was developing a head cold so she decided to keep him with her until the situation became really desperate. She guessed she had another two weeks before the water level at Merry-Maid became serious.

The day Alice decided to drop Ben over at Aunty Bea's the Macquarie River burst its banks.

'You'll never get through, darling,' said Bea over the phone. 'The bridge over Harris' Creek collapsed last night and all the roads on your side are already two feet underwater. With the water still rising it's simply not safe.' Her anxiety increased with the realisation that the nearest person to Alice was Robert. So far there had been no sign of the violence Katie had warned her about, but Bea was still very worried about his state of mind.

Alice listened to her aunt and agreed it would be stupid to try and get through. She also tried to calm her aunt's fears about her safety. Right now she was more worried about the stock than herself and Ben. Yet as she and Ben rattled around the empty house her aunt's words made her feel jittery. The rivers were still below the level of earlier floods and for the moment all she could do was to sit tight, listen and wait. She called up Jimmy who was out with the other men moving the stock onto higher ground for the fifth day in a row. Marigold was over with Fraser helping at the Bowens' place. Alice kicked herself for letting her jillaroo have her day off last Thursday. Now the girl was stranded in Dubbo.

All day the water level rose spilling over the banks of rivers and creeks. The colour of milky tea, it spread rapidly across the paddocks. Although the district was basically flat to the horizon, there were undulations in the ground. The house had been built on one of the small hillocks which extended behind the house and to the hay barn. The ram shed had also purposely been built on higher ground and a fair distance from the creek. Alone at the house with Ben, Alice listened on the radio as water levels crept steadily higher. As she stared at the pelting rain she decided that for tonight at least they were safe, unless the water rose beyond all predictions. Leaving Ben snug in the sitting room she squelched her way across the bog to check the rams. Then she cooked tea and went to bed. With Ben snuffling beside her she slept fitfully, waking every hour to listen to the weather report and check the height of the water outside with a torch. Alice woke at dawn to find the paddocks beyond the house underwater but there was still land around the house.

From then on the water rose more rapidly. By mid-morning it was lapping around the base of the ram shed. The helplessness Alice felt was overwhelming as she watched the water creep across to her precious garden. It broke her heart to see the devastation as the plants she had battled to keep alive during the drought slowly drowned in the waterlogged mud. She had no word from Jimmy or the other stockmen. At four in the afternoon Alice got a call over the radio.

'Alice, it's Robert. I've just been down the creek that divides my land from yours and it has broken its banks. Did you hear that Karina Downs has just recorded a peak flood three feet higher than what we have here right now?' Alice drew in her breath. Karina Downs was fifty miles upstream of MerryMaid. That meant they could expect another three to five feet to come through within the next twenty-four hours. 'It's still raining up there so we don't know how much it'll rise but it's certainly not going to be dropping for another two or three days. I recommend you evacuate now.'

Aunty Bea rang almost immediately. 'I heard all that. Be careful, sweetie.' Alice only just caught the last three words.

'We're fine, Aunty Bea. We're getting out. It's two feet all round the house and still rising,' said Alice glad of the familiar comfort of her aunt's voice. 'I was just about to get the boat ready when I got Robert's call.'

Leaving the radio she glanced quickly over at Ben dozing fitfully on the sofa, his breathing snuffly from his cold, and hurried into the laundry where she pulled out the small outboard motor she kept for just such emergencies and sat it by the front door. Confident that it worked because Fraser had done the routine maintenance just before the rain started, Alice strode round the verandah to fetch the small rowing boat from where it was tied up at the back of the house. She reckoned she had one more hour before the water reached the verandah. The other worry was the encroaching darkness. For the moment it had stopped raining but the sky was dark and overcast, speeding the approaching dusk. As she rounded the end of the verandah her heart stopped. The rope securing the boat dangled empty from the railing. There was no sign of the boat. Unable to believe her eyes she examined the rope end. It wasn't even broken. The knot had simply come untied. Alice looked again at the space then at the rising water and knew she had only one choice. Praying her instincts were right, Alice raced back inside and called Robert back on the radio.

'Robert, the boat's floated off. I'm going to need help to get us out of here,' she said squirming at her own incompetence, wishing the whole district didn't need to hear.

'We're halfway to Wangianna,' replied Robert. 'Sit tight and I'll be right back to get you. Get whatever you need ready. If necessary get up into the roof. I'll be there as soon as I can.' His voice sounded so calming, so like the old Robert she had known, that all her fears about his mental state evaporated.

'Thanks. What about my rams? Isn't there any way we can save them? I can't just leave them to drown.'

'You're going to have to leave them. There's no way we can move them now. I'm really sorry. Open the shed doors.' After Alice had signed off she stepped off the verandah towards the ram shed, now completely surrounded by water, with a growing sense of helplessness. The wind was getting up. In a few short hours everything that she had worked for could be lost; her palace and all she had built gone and she powerless to do a thing about it. Flooding was almost worse than fire. She didn't even want to think of the grim losses Jimmy must have discovered as the waters rose or of the terrified animals bogged down in the clawing mud unable to free themselves. Shaking away the horrible visions she waded through the water, now up to her waist, to the ram shed. Climbing out she ran up the steps. The rams shuffled closer to one another, eyeing her in the gloom as she threw wide the doors at both ends, tying them back so they would stay open, and checked the ram chute was secure. Then she filled up the food and water troughs and, with one last look, left them and waded back to the house.

'Now at least they can swim for it if they have to,' she thought as she packed two boxes of food, two waterbags, extra clothes and her important documents. Next she dragged the kitchen dresser near the trapdoor in the ceiling that led to the roof. Ray had set up an escape platform made from floorboards across the rafters. Secure that she could get herself, Ben and the two dogs up there if it came to that, she then turned her attention to the rest of the house. For the next ninety minutes she sweated away, rolling up carpets, stacking boxes and emptying cupboards so that if the water did flood into the house, as much as possible would be saved. While she worked, the two dogs milled around whining fretfully. In no time the place looked like a junk shop. Ben woke up halfway through and started crying. Talking to him while she worked Alice kept going. Finally when she had moved as much as she could, she picked him up and cuddled him.

'Your Uncle Robert will be here to take us in his boat soon. That'll be a bit different, going out in the dark.' She kissed his forehead.

The last strands of light had faded from the sky and the water was lapping over the edge of the verandah as Robert drew alongside in his boat. It had started raining again. The only emotion she could feel towards him was gratitude.

'Gillgully's almost afloat too,' said Robert. 'Let's get you out of here before it gets too dark to see where we're going. It'll take a good while to get back to Wangianna with this wind.' Alice passed Robert the boxes and waterbottles. Then she handed over Ben, looking like a little elf wrapped up in his raincoat, wide-eyed with wonder, the hood pulled well down over his face, and ordered the dogs to hop in. The older dog obeyed immediately but Bitsa whined anxiously, padding back and forth in front of the boat, crouching down until her belly touched the ground. Exasperated, Robert grabbed her by the scruff of the neck and, finally, protesting, she jumped in. Alice hopped in after her. Her heart was too full to worry about Robert as they chugged away from MerryMaid Stud across the paddocks in the pelting rain leaving her home to the ravages of the water. Clutching Ben to her, shading his face from the strengthening wind, she choked back the tears as she watched the ram shed disappear into the night.

The wind was increasing in strength. Looking out for landmarks looming out of the dark, Robert had regularly to lift the motor half out of the water where he guessed the fences would be to save the propeller from getting caught on the wire. The whole exercise kept slowing their progress down. By the time they were halfway between MerryMaid and Wangianna vicious squalls scudded across the darkness knocking the boat about and chopping the water into tiny waves. Forked lightning suddenly rent the clouds lighting up the three travellers' white faces, followed immediately by great thunderclaps. Terrified, Ben started to cry. The dogs cowered in the bottom of the boat against Alice's knees. Trees bent against the ferocity of the wind, their great branches bowing against its force. By now they were all three soaked to the skin as gale-force winds lashed around them repeatedly forcing the boat off course so Robert had to struggle to steer in the right direction. At one point they were blown backwards and Robert had to zigzag to get them back on course. Leaves and bark flew at them in the dark and the rain, driven horizontal by the wind, lashed onto their bent heads. Her arms wrapped tightly around Ben, Alice started to pray. As they approached the lights of Wangianna a spectacular fork of lightning lit up the sky for an instant as it struck one of the majestic old gum trees, splitting it clean down the middle. As though revelling in its own strength the wind tore one side of the tree away, tossing it like a toy into the frothing water. Robert had the motor turned to full throttle as they struggled across the final stretch of water to the house. Then suddenly the fury had passed and the rains eased as the boat bumped against Wangianna's verandah.

Elizabeth was anxiously waiting for them, wrapped in a raincoat and hood. Shivering, Alice and Ben squelched up the steps while Stewart helped Robert make the boat fast. The dogs, without prompting, leapt to the safety of the verandah.

'Thank heavens you're all safe,' said Elizabeth.

There was a slight fracas as Alice's dogs met Robert's, but a couple of sharp commands from Elizabeth sent them slinking back to their beds while Alice tied her two up at the other end of the verandah. Then she and

Ben were ushered into the warmth of Wangianna homestead and given hot drinks and hot baths.

With Ben safely asleep, exhausted by the day, Alice hugged her hot chocolate as she listened to the radio forecasts with the rest of the McIain clan. After it was over Andrew started issuing instructions to everyone and was immediately told to shut up by Elizabeth.

'I think it might be sensible to let Robert take charge just until the worst is past as this is your first experience with floods like this,' said Elizabeth firmly. Ian and Jordie said nothing. Andrew reddened and subsided into silence.

To everyone's immense relief by ten that night no further rise in water level had been reported. Alice fell into the bed next to Ben and lay wondering if any of her rams had survived the storm.

'If they have to go please let The Emperor survive,' she prayed and drifted into a light sleep.

She woke to a wet misty world. As the day heated up the sun brought out the cruellest part of floods, tiny midges and sandflies. Neither by day nor night could anyone escape the pitiful cries of the animals tormented by these merciless tiny predators. The sounds wrung their hearts.

'It's what I hate most about floods. I feel so helpless,' admitted Elizabeth to Alice, shaking her head in misery as the two women worked together getting meals ready while the men were away in the boat attempting to feed and rescue stock. Stewart, whom Alice thought looked remarkably healthy and happy, had gone too.

'Loss of stock is something you have to learn to accept. Houses can be scrubbed clean or built again but the suffering of the animals is almost more than I can bear,' Alice agreed, worried about her own stock, not totally at ease with this woman who in the past had shown such strong disapproval of her. Looking across the flat milky brown sea dotted with the tops of short scrub trees she could see a few spots of higher ground still showing through where some of the animals huddled.

Elizabeth suddenly put down her knife and leaned on the table. 'Now is as good as any time,' she announced.

Alice looked up from her chopping, wondering what to expect. 'I want to thank you, Alice, for what you did for me at Christmas. For the first time in my life I had let things get on top of me. I will always be grateful for the way you helped me when needed it. I thought I was a good judge of character but with you I have to admit I got it all wrong. I learned that day that you are a person who doesn't bear grudges. I want you to know that you and your family are welcome at Wangianna at any time.' Alice could not have been more surprised if the sky had fallen in.

The next two days dragged by. At the end of the third day, the water still showed no signs of receding. Jimmy, thank heavens, had radioed in. He had spent two nights in a tree on the far side of the property after getting most of her ewes up onto one of the roads. The other stockmen were also safe so no lives had been lost, but no one had been back to the house.

Finally, by the fourth day, the water started to drop but boat was still the only means of transport. Alice was up at sunrise staring out at a world hidden in a thick white blanket. Grey blobs of trees were just visible in the gloom. A faint glow in the east indicated the sun. In a few hours its rays would burn off the cloud bringing back the sticky heat and black clouds of midges.

'I've got to get to my rams,' said Alice urgently to Robert who had joined her on the verandah. 'Some of them may still be alive. If they haven't drowned they'll die of starvation if I don't get over there.'

Robert nodded. She had told him how she had left the doors open in the vain hope of saving the rams. He hadn't had time to think about Alice or his own emotions in the crisis. Now he stared at her in admiration. She looked exhausted yet her whole being was focused on saving her animals. God, he loved her! Why was life so unfair?

'We'll go straight after breakfast. Mum'll look after Ben for you,' he said levelly.

After breakfast, having explained to Ben what was happening, Alice jumped into the boat with Robert. Weaving their way through the gradually clearing mist searching for familiar landmarks that rose up at them out of the whiteness and with the wind still blowing strongly behind them, it took far less time than Alice expected to reach MerryMaid.

They headed for the ram shed first. It had been built at the start of the higher ground and the water had dropped around it to a few inches but it was the shed itself that struck terror into her heart. A thick gum tree had fallen across it crushing the tin roof and tilting the whole building to an extraordinary angle. All Alice's grim fears came to the fore. Leaping out of the boat she sloshed through the water towards the shed. Running up the steps two at a time she peered into the dark interior. The tree had made a hopeless mess of one end of the shed and it was empty. So were the feed troughs. When she had left she had filled them up to overflowing. Maybe there was hope of finding some animals alive yet. Her heart leapt as she heard the familiar rattle of rams blundering up the chute.

'They were round the back of the shed paddling about up to their knees in water,' grinned Robert. 'Come outside and see if there are any more nearer the house.' In the next hour they found most of the rams and herded them back up into the ram shed. The rams would be safer here despite the damaged roof than left to wander around with the risk of getting bogged down in the mud. Robert refilled the food troughs while Alice re-counted the rams and checked them for injuries. Her discussion with Elizabeth had strengthened her acceptance against loss. She had been fortunate so few had gone missing. Her main concern now was The Emperor. With a sinking sensation in the pit of her stomach she searched through the mob.

'The Emperor's not here,' she called. Robert looked up immediately.

'Are you sure?'

'I'd recognise him a mile away. He's my best ram. If I lost all the others I could still survive with The Emperor.' She ran down the steps. 'I'm going to have another look over by the house.' For the first time since she had seen the tree through the shed she felt utterly disheartened. Robert followed her out. Alice set off at a run back across the high ground. After twenty minutes they had found nothing.

'He can't be far.' She hit her forehead. 'Why didn't I think of it before? He's probably up by the hay sheds looking for feed. It's one of his favourite spots.' The wind caught her hair tossing it around her face. 'We'll find him I'm sure,' she said bravely, catching the strands away from out of her eyes and mouth. She took off towards the sheds, wading through water up to her calves, the thick gluey mud sticking like great platforms to her boots.

'I'll try the other side by the shearers' quarters,' called Robert setting off in the opposite direction.

'He has to be here. Please let him be here,' repeated Alice chewing her lip and scanning the sodden paddock. As she rounded the shed she caught sight of The Emperor standing in three inches of water, a look of disgust on his proud regal face.

'Emperor!' she cried as a large branch caught in the storm cracked above her head and smashed down knocking her face-down into the water.

Robert was having no luck at all near the shearers' quarters. All he had managed to do was fill one boot with water and slip and fall on his backside in the mud. There were dead branches and leaves strewn all over the ground. Heaving himself up he hobbled to the steps of the shearers' cabin and emptied his boot. As he replaced it he heard a loud crack. Like a man in slow motion he raced round towards the hay shed, mud slowing him down as it sucked at his boots.

'Alice!' he shouted. 'Alice' Then he saw her lying face-down in the water. It took an eternity to cross those last few yards. 'Alice my darling, don't die on me now.' As he knelt down and grabbed her shoulders she rolled over. Her face was covered in mud.

Coughing, she sat up, momentarily bemused. Supporting her with one arm, Robert gently wiped away the mud on her lips and face with his handkerchief. Alice lay back against Robert's arm, rubbing her throbbing head, tears from the blow smarting in her closed eyes.

'Open your eyes, Alice,' Robert said urgently. 'Can you see me?' Alice opened her eyes and looked at Robert in surprise. Seeing the anguish in his eyes she smiled.

'Don't be a dope, Robert. Of course I can see you. That bloody hurt. What happened?'

'You were hit by a branch.'

Alice took in the branch a few feet away. 'Lucky I wasn't clobbered harder. People have drowned in three inches of water. What a sight I must look,' she added wiping her hands on her jeans. 'Where's The Emperor?'

'Thank God!' Robert, so utterly relieved that she was not hurt, crushed her to him, kissing her hard on the lips. Startled she started to resist then relaxed letting him kiss her. 'Alice, I love you. I have never stopped loving you. I was so scared I'd lost you,' mumbled Robert between kisses. 'Are you sure you're okay?' Without giving her a chance to reply he kissed her again.

Drawing back he clasped her lovely face in his hands and stared into her brilliant sapphire eyes. 'You can't marry Jo,' he said fiercely. 'I won't let you. You're going to marry me.' He felt her stiffen. Immediately he dropped his hands. 'God, now I've made a complete fool of myself but I can't bear the thought of losing you again.' He was plunged into misery.

'Did you just ask me to marry you?' cried Alice, her eyes brimming over with love, her throbbing head forgotten.

'You don't have to reply. I know you're engaged to that blighter Jo Perry,' Robert said hopelessly.

Alice looked at him sharply as he helped her to her feet. 'If I am it's news to me. Who told you?' she asked hitting at the mud that was already caking on her clothes.

'Katie.'

'Katie!' exclaimed Alice. 'Doesn't she ever stop her dirty little tricks?'

'Well, aren't you? The rest of the district thinks you are too.'

'The rest of the district can mind its own bloody business.' The tension of the last few days had finally caught up. The relief of finding The Emperor coupled with the longing Robert's kisses had stirred in her proved too much. The blow from the branch was the last straw. She burst into tears. Thinking her tears were for Jo not him, Robert was filled with a sudden emptiness.

'Well, are you engaged to Jo?'

Alice shook her head. Slowly Robert tilted her face to his and stared into her deep sapphire eyes. Waves of hope washed over him as he wiped away the tears that glistened on her cheeks. Neither knew who moved first but as their lips touched their pressure ignited a fire that spread through their veins. After a long time they moved apart.

'Will you marry me, my precious beautiful Alice?'

Alice took a deep breath. Bea's warning rang in her ears. 'I have to ask you something, Robert.' She stepped back reluctantly, her heart pounding against her ribs.

'Anything, just say yes,' said Robert his hopes rallying.

'Did you really threaten to kill my cousin if she took Stewwy away with her?'

Robert's jaw dropped. 'What?'

'Katie told Aunty Bea you threatened her. She also said you had been mentally unhinged by the accident,' she rushed on.

'The lying . . .' He took a deep breath. 'Katie said that and you believed her?'

'No,' said Alice firmly. 'But I want to know what made her say such a thing.' Her heart was still racing. Robert looked at his hands and then back at Alice for so long she wondered whether he intended to reply.

'Even in the worst moments of my life I could never have threatened to do what she said,' he replied. Alice's sigh was audible. Robert paused. 'She was cornered. She could see the hold she had over me for so long was gone. You see, Alice, Stewart is not my son.'

Alice's eyes opened wide in shock. 'What?'

'After the accident I nearly went mad convinced they were killing him with the wrong blood. The only person who was wrong was me.' He explained how he had asked a nurse to confirm the blood and then it had all fallen into place.

'I don't believe it,' whispered Alice. 'You mean that night all those years ago . . .?' Robert nodded.

'No, no it can't be true.' Alice turned from him and stormed across the paddock, an anger so intense welling up in her she hardly knew what she was doing. Katie's callous manipulation knew no bounds. She had won. Oh how she had won. For so many long, years she had laughed in Alice's and Robert's faces.

Robert stood by the fallen branch, his face empty of expression. He had told her and now she thought he was a liar.

Suddenly Alice realised what she had said. Rushing back to Robert she threw her arms around him.

'Oh you poor, poor darling,' she cried kissing him passionately on the lips. 'Of course I believe you. I was so shocked that Katie could do such a vile unspeakable thing . . . What can I say that will help?'

Robert wrapped her in his arms his heart pounding against his ribs. Looking deep into her eyes he whispered, 'You can say yes.'

'Poor Jo, I'll have to explain,' she murmured feebly.

'You can still say yes,' Robert insisted.

'I don't believe I'm saying this,' Alice cried breathlessly, her eyes shining. 'Yes, Robert, yes yes, a million times yes.' Her laughter carried across the dripping paddocks as Robert smothered her with kisses. Drawing back at last, he gazed down tenderly at the woman he had loved for so many years, hardly able to believe that at last they would be together.

'Do you remember how I promised to build you your palace?'

'Could I forget?' murmured Alice snuggling against him.

'This time nothing will stop me.'

Alice put one finger against his lips. 'We'll build it together. We have our land, we have our children, and we have each other.' A rustling made her turn her head. 'And we have The Emperor too.' She giggled as The Emperor tossed his regal head, wiggled his bottom in their direction and trotted down the shallow slope towards the shed in disgust. Tossing her long black mane back over her shoulders Alice gazed into Robert's eyes.

'I didn't think it was possible to be this happy,' she laughed exulting in his kisses as he buried his face in her neck.

Sweeping her up in his arms he carried her towards the house, across soggy paddocks glinting in the sunshine. As he set her down on the verandah of MerryMaid, the grey dirt drying on her sunburned face, her clothes caked with mud, Robert thought she had never looked more beautiful.

'How I love this place. And how I love you,' she murmured as Robert pulled her to him and she surrendered unconditionally to his embrace.

As they stood locked in one another's arms, the sun burning down on the vast waterlogged plains, above a single crow struggled against the breeze. Alice could have sworn it was flying backwards.

Acknowledgements

I HAVE BEEN amazed and delighted at the willingness with which both friends and complete strangers have helped me research the background to *Reach for the Dream*. To all of them I am indebted. In my travels I have met many fascinating people whose enthusiasm stayed with me as I wrote. In particular I would like to thank Diana and David Brennan who invited me to their property 'Webegong' and spent many hours explaining the running of an Australian sheep property and who arranged for me to visit Haddon Rig, the ladies at Warren Library and Bernadette from the Diabetes Association NSW. Many people skilled in many different fields have helped me and they have my heartfelt thanks for their generosity with their time and expertise. They include:

Janet Boakes, Dan Cleary—Camden Aviation, Camden Animal Health Department, Andrew Davidson—Farm Safe Australia Agricultural Health Unit Moree, Tony Damond, Roz Dawson—Bathurst library, Yvonne Gregory, Bronwyn Grierson, Edith Irwin, Nance Irvine, Dennis McGrath—Elders Stock and Station Agents Dubbo, Massey Ferguson Tractors, Rob Marshall—Carlingford Animal Hospital, John Martin, Tony McCullagh, Chris Montgomery, Rod Palmisano, Dr Porges—University of Sydney Veterinary Teaching Hospital Camperdown, Nola Rennie, Wal Rennie, St John's Ambulance, Hornsby branch, Department of Agriculture Warren Walgett Area, and Zoe from the Australian Museum.

My sincere thanks go to my agent Selwa Anthony for believing in me as a writer, for her wisdom, energy and continual encouragement and support; to Jane Palfreyman for accepting the manuscript and to my editor

Julia Stiles for her gentle approach and excellent advice and for loving *Reach far the Dream* with me; to my family and to all my friends who have taken such an interest in the progress of this tale. With these people beside me there has been little time to be a lonely writer.